No Cause For Shame

No Cause For Shame

Richard Stein

Library of Congress Control Number: 2011962539
ISBN: Hardcover   978-1-4691-3661-5
                   Softcover   978-1-4691-3660-8
                   Ebook   978-1-4691-3662-2

This is a work of fiction. Names, characters, places and incidents either are the product of the author's imagination or are used fictitiously, and any resemblance to any actual persons, living or dead, events, or locales is entirely coincidental.

This book was printed in the United States of America.

To order additional copies of this book, contact:
Xlibris Corporation
1-888-795-4274
www.Xlibris.com
Orders@Xlibris.com
109196

To Adele, Neeta, Kristin, and Stacey

PART ONE

Chapter One

Sunday, June 6, 2004, 11:44 PM

All appeared quiet at the end of Woodland Hills Lane in Highland Heights, a wealthy suburb of Chicago. Large homes, some would consider them mansions, graced both sides of the windy road as it ended in a cul-de-sac, where the largest and most expensive of the homes was located on a two acre lot. It was the home of United States Congressman James Miller of the 10th Illinois Congressional District.

The front lawn was well-manicured. It was soon to be trampled by local police, the FBI, and reporters attending a series of press conferences. In exactly eighteen minutes, a woman standing on that lawn would take an iconic photograph. As a symbol of female empowerment, a symbol of rising above the worst that life can throw at you, the photograph is on a poster that hangs in the dormitory rooms of over two hundred thousand American college women. At the top of the poster are the words "No Cause for Shame," the name of a charity that was founded to aid victims of physical, emotional, and sexual abuse. On the poster, running from the lower left corner to the upper right corner is the signature of one of the most famous young women in America, Amibeth. Of course at 11:44, there was no Amibeth, her name was still Amy Elizabeth. A lot can happen in eighteen minutes. A great deal can happen in 61 seconds. Fame and fortune sometimes come at a very high price.

Behind the home was a swimming pool, in use only three months of the year. For most of the year it served as a water feature for the lovely gardens of Mary Nell Golden Miller, the Congressman's second wife. The gardens had been selected to be on two charity garden tours in 2004 alone. The Japanese garden at the northwest end of the property was especially serene and was Mrs. Miller's favorite place to meditate. It was through a glass door leading from the Japanese garden to the living room that the two men had broken in.

Amy Elizabeth Golden was twenty two at the time and the older of the two girls. She was tall and blond. Her face was a little too thin to be called beautiful, but she was certainly attractive. Of course, if you have seen her on television you know that, but some people only know her from her syndicated radio show. Two weeks earlier, Amy Elizabeth had graduated from Colby College in Waterville, Maine, with a major in Psychology and a minor in Marketing. She had been a Dean's List Student whose major extracurricular activities had been dating and theatre.

"Marry well," Mary Nell was fond of saying. "That's what life is about." Amy Elizabeth did not believe that her mother had married well the first time when she married Amy Elizabeth's biological father. As for the Congressman, Mary Nell had indeed married very well. Amy Elizabeth liked the Congressman, though she had minimal contact with him. Amy Elizabeth had been away at college when her mother remarried three years earlier.

Amy Elizabeth's biological father, Nathaniel Golden, had been a Baptist preacher in Kenton, Tennessee—Middle of Nowhere Tennessee she called it. He came from one of the wealthiest families in Gibson County, and was very well respected. As far as Amy Elizabeth was concerned, he was despicable. Fortunately, from Amy Elizabeth's point of view, he had died of stomach cancer before he had done anything to her.

Amy Elizabeth had been in nearly every undergraduate production at Colby's Strider Theatre. She always auditioned for the lead role, ended up with a small speaking part, and acquitted herself reasonably. As her drama teacher would explain when everyone connected to the Golden Girls was being interviewed, it was not that Amy Elizabeth lacked talent, it was just that there was no role for which she was sufficiently motivated. Amy Elizabeth was very unmotivated. Her plan for the summer was to hang out at her stepfather's swimming pool and the pool at the Highland Heights Yacht Club.

Before the carnage on Woodland Hills Lane, she was the kind of girl of whom it is said in their eulogies that she was a sweet young woman with a great deal of potential. At 11:44 it would have appeared that the eulogy would be coming soon, for Amy Elizabeth was being raped by one of two Hispanic men that the FBI profilers had dubbed The Roofers. Over the course of twenty three months they had raped and murdered twelve women. That Amy Elizabeth was on the verge of the role of a lifetime would seem inconceivable. While 'potential' is a way of saying that one has accomplished little, it is also a way of saying that amazing things might happen.

The Roofers were itinerant laborers who worked for various roofing companies as they moved across the upper Midwest. They were in the country legally, as was revealed when, after the fact, some right-wing politicos tried to use them as an argument for better enforcement of the immigration laws. As in their other attacks, The Roofers cased houses and found potential victims by offering free estimates for roof repairs as they were completing work on other houses in the neighborhood. They had been working on the roof of Dr. Steven Federoff next door, but sixty yards away from the Miller mansion. Estates are large on Woodland Hills Lane.

It was bad luck that Amy Elizabeth had opened the door two days earlier and accepted the offer of a free estimate for roofing repairs. Amy Elizabeth had been away at school when the reports of the rapes had been in the papers. AJ, the younger of the two sisters, was twenty-one and had completed her junior year at Northwestern University, thirty minutes from the Miller home. She was an English major but planned to be a physician or an attorney. She hoped to transfer to Vanderbilt in Nashville; she had applied and been accepted. She knew she was perfectly capable of handling the independence. The issue was convincing her mother of that fact. Mary Nell was convinced that AJ would do something to embarrass the family if she went to school far from home.

AJ read the internet version of the newspapers. If she had been the one offered a free estimate for roof repairs, she would have let the men get on the roof, would have called 911, would have taken her stepfather's shotgun from the gun safe upstairs and—worst case scenario—would have been holding two scared men who were not The Roofers at gunpoint when the police arrived. One did not mess with AJ, and if you feel I am overstating what AJ would have done, you obviously missed the news coverage.

Two days before the attack on Woodland Hills Lane, during the fifteen minutes that The Roofers spent examining the Miller's roof, they overheard Amy Elizabeth on the phone telling a friend that Congressman and Mrs. Miller would not return from a Baltic Cruise for days. Of course, it was not all Amy Elizabeth's fault. AJ was supposed to have set the alarm before the girls went to bed that night. She had forgotten.

That the rape of Amy Elizabeth was occurring on the marble floor in the front hall of the Miller mansion rather than in a bedroom was the modus operandi of The Roofers. They wanted family or friends to discover the carnage immediately upon arriving home, when they had little reason to suspect what awaited them inside.

The only thing standing between Amy Elizabeth and death at a young age was not standing. AJ Golden was lying naked, gagged, and partly bound on the marble hall of the front foyer. At five feet six inches tall, AJ was four inches shorter than her sister. She was the prettier of the two girls, probably the smarter of the two, and possessed a wicked sense of humor. She was also blonde, but that was not a natural phenomenon. During high school, AJ had experimented with a number of colors including black, blond, and eggplant. It seemed extremely unlikely she would live long enough to experience grey, let alone revert to her natural shade of red.

AJ had experimented with pot—didn't like it, and alcohol—did like it, sort of. It was her arrest for driving with a blood alcohol level of .086 that had prevented AJ from going on a trip to Curacao with her best friends. Mary Nell was trying to lay down the law. Six thousandth of a milligram per deciliter lower and AJ would not have been on Woodland Hills Lane. While it is really no one's business, her experience with sex was limited and had been pleasant—no more, no less.

At this point, AJ had been minimally bruised and had not yet been raped. That AJ was relatively unharmed would not have surprised the FBI team that had profiled The Roofers. From forensic evidence, the FBI knew that one of The Roofers would repeatedly rape one woman while the other woman watched in terror. Only then would they start on the second woman. The second rape and murder were very quick, for while the first woman was always Rodrigo Diaz's prize, the second woman went to Roberto Diaz who did not like sex, at least not sex with women, as much as he liked killing. The Roofers had a sick but effective style.

Forensic evidence is useless when there is nothing to which it can be matched. The Diaz brothers had never been arrested, had never been fingerprinted, and had never even received a moving traffic violation. Ironically, the only person in the front foyer who had ever been fingerprinted was the once impaired driver, AJ. The FBI had DNA and fingerprints from The Roofers but did not know their names.

Amy Elizabeth knew she was going to die and was beyond caring. A shallow scar ran from her left shoulder between her breasts, to her right hip. It wasn't a deep cut. It was designed to breed fear and it had done exactly that. She had seen enough television to know that the autopsy incisions would make the cuts irrelevant. She just wanted the ordeal to be over. As a child she had learned to dissociate herself from horrible events around her, and her mind was taking a vacation. It seemed to be her destiny that her soul would soon leave her body and join it. The woman who would become famous for advocating a never give up attitude had given up.

AJ had tried closing her eyes but every time she did, Roberto, the younger one, the one who was not raping Amy Elizabeth would say, "Watch them sweetie or I'll kill you now." AJ considered the offer. In addition to being naked and gagged, she was wet from mid-thigh to her ankles. She had urinated on the cold marble floor. In accordance with the total randomness of the universe, that simple fact would extend her life and change the expected course of events on Woodland Hills Lane.

At Northwestern, AJ's only extracurricular activity was running track, specifically the 400 meter dash. Her best time was 52 seconds, four tenths of a second off the school record. Unlike her sister, AJ had not given up. The thought keeping AJ alive was the thought of getting to a better place. AJ was not a believer and heaven was not the better place of which she was thinking. AJ was intending to go upstairs where Congressman Miller, a Republican defender of the second amendment, kept a shotgun and a handgun. The handgun, a Walther P22, was in the Congressman's desk drawer, it was unloaded. The bullets were in the gun safe along with the shotgun. The gun safe had a combination lock. AJ had gone hunting with her stepfather, once. She knew gun safety. She knew how to load and fire a handgun. She was pretty sure that she knew the combination to the safe.

She had a plan, and considering the alternatives, she figured she couldn't end up more dead and more raped than she was about to become.

The problem of course was getting to the guns. However, since Roberto was paying her less and less attention as the minutes passed, he had no idea that she had loosened the rope that tied her wrists together. Roberto was very efficient at slitting throats. He was not good at tying knots. It was a fatal flaw in a serial killer. The two men hadn't bothered to tie AJ's ankles. They didn't need to. AJ had seen what happened to Amy Elizabeth when she tried to run after the men had told her not to move. Plus the men had knives. Roberto kept pointing to himself and saying "hombre peligroso." He was indeed a dangerous man. He had no idea that he was dealing with a "mujer peligroso," a dangerous woman. I suspect AJ had never considered herself in that light either.

AJ tried to be as still as she could be. She had realized that by keeping her legs untied it would be all that quicker to rape and kill her when they were finished with Amy Elizabeth. She just had to determine when to make her move up the stairs. The man was going to be finished with Amy Elizabeth soon. It was now or never for AJ, but there was no way she could get enough of a head start to beat Roberto up the stairs. Just then, Layla, Amibeth's little shih-tzu, who had been sleeping in the kitchen, awoke, slowly ambled into the front foyer and bit Roberto in the ankle. Layla weighed ten pounds and the bite didn't break skin, but Roberto was startled. He slashed at the dog and missed, but the effort put his momentum toward the front door and away from AJ. It was enough of a distraction for AJ to make her move. Now or never became NOW!

AJ Golden on weakened legs, her hands now free, raced up the carpeted staircase and headed to her stepfather's office. She removed the duct tape from her mouth as she ran. Rodrigo Diaz spoke to his brother almost annoyingly, "Get her. Bring her back." Roberto Diaz was on his way holding the double edged blade that he had brought to the Miller home.

The Congressman's office was not as luxurious as one might have expected considering the acre of lawn and the colonial pillars that graced the home on Woodland Hills Lane. The office was merely a 10 x 10 carpeted room near the top of the stairs. It contained a small desk, a chair, two bookcases and the gun safe. It was a converted exercise room but the congressman did not like exercise, and Mary Nell did not like having the gun safe in the Congressman's larger downstairs study. "If we are going to have guns, they will be upstairs and locked away." The Congressman had no trouble with that. The upstairs office was about to be redecorated in grisly fashion.

As AJ reached the upstairs landing, Roberto grabbed at her right ankle, but her legs were wet with urine. She twisted away. He slipped on the stairs and AJ eluded his grasp. She reached the office before Roberto. The door to the Congressman's office was open. She raced in, closed and locked the door behind her, turned on the light and moved to the gun safe. Roberto started kicking at the door. She would have time enough for only one chance to try the combination. One chance was all she needed. She opened the safe and grabbed the shotgun as Roberto finally kicked the door open. He climbed over the desk and reached for the barrel of the gun to push it away.

Downstairs in the foyer Rodrigo heard the shotgun blast. He moved toward the stairs, then moved back toward Amy Elizabeth. It seemed best to kill the girl before seeing what had happened upstairs. Then he heard AJ screaming at the top of her lungs "NO. NO. PLEASE DON'T. PLEASE DON'T." Rodrigo knew that begging for her life would have no effect on Roberto. He moved back toward Amy Elizabeth. Amy Elizabeth who had previously gone numb began to cry, imagining her sister being raped—and worse.

Next door at the home of Doctor Steven Federoff, the man whose roof had been repaired by a crew containing the Diaz brothers, Adele Federoff awakened her sleeping husband. Adele Federoff was an insomniac. A clinical psychologist, she spent her late evenings ruminating about her clients, their problems, their jobs, their love affairs, and all the other things she couldn't change. She enjoyed helping people but felt she rarely made a difference. This night, one of her hobbies would make a great deal of difference. It was 11:45, a time when Adele Federoff was usually awake. "Steven, wake up, I think I heard a gunshot." Adele Federoff was fifty-nine years old and had never heard a gun fired in anger, but she shot skeet, a hobby not uncommon at the Highland Hills Yacht Club, and she thought she knew a gunshot when she heard it. She didn't believe it. A gunshot on Woodland Hills Lane. From the Congressman's house.

In the Congressman's office, AJ had started screaming almost as soon as the gun went off. She wasn't screaming to dissuade Roberto from raping and killing her. Roberto's guts and blood were splattered all over her and the small office. The shotgun had been pushed into his abdomen when she fired. Roberto was dead. AJ was screaming to distract Rodrigo in the downstairs foyer. She worried that if she didn't distract him, he would kill Amy Elizabeth. AJ kept screaming while she carefully locked the magazine of the Walther P22 in place just like the Congressman had shown her. It was surprisingly easy. Now came the hard part. She shut off the office light and moved into the hallway.

The front foyer was illuminated only by the large lantern light that the two men had brought to the Miller home. She could clearly see Rodrigo, and he could clearly see her. Obviously, he was more surprised. She held the Walther in two hands like she had done when her stepfather took her target shooting. The first shot missed as she was taking exceptional care not to hit Amy Elizabeth. She fired three more shots, aiming at the center of Rodrigo's chest. One shot shattered his left wrist, another missed completely. The third entered his body below the left clavicle and severed his subclavian artery. It was a lethal wound. Ordinarily it would have taken him several minutes to die.

AJ was unaware that Rodrigo had been lethally wounded. She placed the Walther on the floor at the top of the stairs and started down, holding the shotgun.

At this point, counting the shotgun blast, five shots had been fired. Steven Federoff got up and went to the window. The master bedroom of the Federoff home overlooked the Miller estate next door. There was minimal light emanating from the Miller home. He dialed 911, found a flashlight, and told his wife, "Stay here." He kissed her and began running toward the Miller home. He had reached Mary Nell's azaleas at the edge of the property when he decided that running toward gunfire was not an intelligent plan. He slowed down, and walked up the crushed stone driveway, trying to gather his thoughts. Walking towards gunfire does not seem especially intelligent either, but, as Amibeth says on her radio show, "You know how men are."

Inside the Miller home, AJ had not yet run out of adrenaline but she had run out of plan. Up to that point, her plan had been simple. Run upstairs, get the shotgun, shoot the first man who was likely to follow her up the stairs, do something to distract the second man so he wouldn't kill Amy Elizabeth, shoot the second man with the handgun while she was far enough away that she was safe, then get the shotgun, come downstairs, and shoot the second man. But the second man was just standing in the hall. He had dropped his knife at his feet and stood there facing her. He was unarmed.

Amy Elizabeth was still bound and gagged. Though she certainly appeared to have the upper hand, AJ had a problem. If AJ put down the gun and started to untie her sister, the man might take the opportunity to grab his knife and kill them both. If she didn't untie her sister, then there was no one to call 911. The nearest phone was in the kitchen, but she couldn't leave Amy Elizabeth alone with the man. AJ of course had no idea that Rodrigo had been lethally wounded. "Think. Think. Think." she told herself. This was like one of those video game situations where you seem to have no options. She had the shotgun, but sooner or later the man might realize that she was incapable of shooting someone who was unarmed. "Think. Think. Think." Sure she had a gun, and yes, the man had done some horrible things, but there had been a gun in the house in Kenton, Tennessee where daddy—the Reverend Nathaniel Golden—had done things and no one shot him. What was she going to do? For the first time since she had started up the stairs she was starting to feel scared. She was terrified.

Outside the Miller home, Steven Federoff was just as frightened. He heard screaming from inside the Miller house and a final shotgun blast.

According to the press reports, based on Amy Elizabeth's eyewitness account, Rodrigo had solved her dilemma for her. Either from stupidity or from macho bravado, he moved towards a twenty-one year old woman who was holding a loaded shotgun. Perhaps he was just falling forward because of losing three liters of blood into his chest. He reportedly staggered toward AJ, who lifted her shotgun to his jaw and sent most of his head into the ceiling of the Miller foyer. From the time AJ had started up the stairs to the time the final shot was fired, only 61 seconds had elapsed.

AJ's description of the final events would have been a bit different. "I couldn't think of anything to do! I couldn't untie Amy Elizabeth! I couldn't call for help! I was sure he'd kill me if he realized I needed help! So I did the only thing I could. I walked up to him, said 'Sorry!' I had to yell because I was a little deaf from the gunfire. I even told him 'Lo siento'—that's Spanish for I'm sorry, in case his English wasn't that good."

Whichever version of events you choose to believe, after firing the shotgun, AJ untied Amy Elizabeth. The adrenaline was gone. The carnage on Woodland Hills Lane, as the *Chicago Sun Times* would call it, was over.

Chapter Two

Steven Federoff considered what might have transpired inside the Miller home. There was no wind and the night had the silence of death. He was standing at the bottom of the stairs leading to the front porch when the door opened and he saw a naked figure covered in blood. In her right hand was the semi-automatic handgun which she had retrieved from the top of the stairs. AJ was willing to open the door while she was undressed, but not while she was unarmed.

Steven Federoff thought he was looking at a demon and was certain that he was going to die. He considered the irony that his great grandmother had escaped from the Russian Cossacks during the pogroms of 1908 and that his father had left Austria in 1936, before the Holocaust, only for him to be slaughtered in an American suburb. He was not an observant Jew but under his breath he started to say the shema. "Shema Yisrael Adenoi Eloheinu . . ."

He was stunned when the figure at the top of the concrete steps joined in ". . . Adenoi Echad." For AJ, who had experimented with hair colors throughout high school, had drifted through religions with the same ease. Events in the Golden household years ago had led her away from the Baptists. She had investigated Roman Catholicism, but stories of priests abusing children soured her on that idea. AJ knew that most of her Reform Jewish friends only went to services twice a year, and she knew the Shema.

"AJ? Amy Elizabeth? Is that one of you? It's me, Dr. Federoff. Did you shoot your sister?" Steven Federoff had no other logical explanation for the unearthly apparition on the front steps.

"It's AJ. I know who you are. Of course I didn't shoot Amy Elizabeth. But we need a doctor. Amy Elizabeth is hurt. She was raped. There were two men."

"Where are the men?"

"Dead."

Amy Elizabeth was sitting in the foyer wrapped in a blanket that AJ had taken from the foyer closet. Within the hour, at the hospital, Amy Elizabeth would be found to have two black eyes, two broken ribs, some shallow cuts, and what the doctors at Highland Heights Hospital would describe as moderately severe vaginal trauma. The police would use the term "brutally raped and beaten," as if there was such a term as "gently raped and beaten." Leaving the terminology aside, the physical trauma was less than one might have expected. The psychic trauma would be hard to evaluate.

Steven Federoff entered the Miller home and saw a horrific sight. There, feet near the living room side of the foyer, was the nearly decapitated body of Rodrigo Diaz. Most of his jaw and skull were splattered over the walls and ceiling. The shotgun had been in contact with his jaw when AJ fired. There was a larger mess upstairs where the shotgun had been jabbed into Roberto Diaz's abdomen before AJ had splattered his guts, blood, and life over herself and the walls of the Congressman's office. Steven Federoff took the Walther P22 from AJ and went upstairs to check that the man upstairs was dead. He turned on the light and decided not to bother checking for a pulse. He knew dead when he saw it.

Steven Federoff had served in Vietnam and had seen gore on many occasions. He kept his composure. He returned to the front foyer. "AJ . . . What the heck happened?"

AJ knew she had killed two truly evil men. She did not know that they were serial killers or serial rapists. She did not know that she had cleansed the earth of The Roofers. AJ shook her head and managed a weak smile. "The dragons broke into the wrong house and tried to kill the wrong princesses. They picked the wrong fucking house." It made no sense to Steven Federoff when he heard it. It made perfect sense when she explained it to him. Layla, thereafter lovingly referred to by AJ as her "shih-tzu attack dog" was back asleep in the kitchen.

At that point the paramedics arrived, placed Amy Elizabeth on a stretcher and loaded her into an ambulance. Only when the paramedics refused to leave without her, and she realized that her insistence that she was fine might be endangering Amy Elizabeth, did AJ climb in the ambulance under her own power. It was two minutes after midnight, Monday, the seventh of June. The aforementioned iconic photo of a beaten Amy Elizabeth on a stretcher with a bloodied AJ standing by her side with a thumb upraised was snapped by Adele Federoff who had rejected her husband's advice to stay home. Adele Federoff was one of those women for whom every birthday, anniversary, and vacation had to be interrupted by her posing people and asking them to smile. Amy Elizabeth was not smiling. The photograph won Adele Federoff a Pulitzer Prize in the Category of Breaking News Photography.

When Amibeth launched her career as a public speaker, after the press conferences that followed the events at the Miller home, the photograph was there to demonstrate that even on the worst day of your life, when you were flat on your back, and seemingly defeated, you could recover. Amibeth—one word, "No Y, there is no WHY."

It should be noted that AJ was not totally naked when she was seen by Steven Federoff on the front porch of the Miller home. Around her neck was a gold pendant with two small diamonds. Amy Elizabeth had an identical pendant which read T181. T one hundred and eighty one. It was a Golden family talisman that went back to the time the girls had grown up in Middle of Nowhere, Tennessee. The girls were certainly no longer in the middle of nowhere. They were in the middle of what would become a media firestorm.

The meaning of T181 was a mystery that, at the time, neither Amy Elizabeth nor AJ could explain. All Amy Elizabeth and AJ knew was the origin of the jeweled pendants. Twelve years earlier, when Andrea was seventeen—nearly eighteen, when Amibeth was ten, and when AJ was nine, the eldest Golden daughter had left Kenton, Tennessee. Andrea had returned only once, weeks later, to attend her father's funeral. It was not an act of daughterly respect. At the funeral she was heard to say, "I just came to be sure the son of a bitch was dead." Her whereabouts from that point on were unknown. The events on Woodland Hills Lane and the aftermath did not bring her back to the family.

At Reverend Golden's funeral, Andrea had given Amy Elizabeth a gold pendant. AJ's pendant was an identical copy, purchased by AJ years later after Mary Nell had married the Congressman and the family's fortunes had radically improved.

There has been considerable speculation about the pendants, especially after jeweled designer purses made out of faux Illinois license plates T181 became a fashion rage. One listed on eBay for $22,000, but that, of course, is because of the jewels. The meaning of T181 would remain unknown to the public for another six years, but there is no need to get ahead of ourselves. For now, let's just wrap up the unfortunate events on Woodland Hills Lane.

In 2004, Highland Heights, Illinois had a population of approximately 23,000 people. It had a small police department and, at night, only one police car. When Officers Janeway and Drover entered the Miller home, they became ill, and did what any civilian might have done. They vomited. However, being trained police officers they had the presence of mind to run down the steps from the Miller front porch and empty their stomachs in Mary Nell Miller's boxwoods, preserving the crime scene.

Realizing they were in over their head, not hard considering that what was left of Rodrigo Diaz's head was on the ceiling of the front hall, they called Richard Rogers, the Highland Heights Chief of Police. He called the Chicago Police Department, who in turn called the FBI. At this point it was not known that two serial killers who had crossed state lines were involved. However, the rape victim was the stepdaughter of a Congressman and the FBI agreed to help out, not that much help was needed.

The press coverage of the events on Woodland Hills Lane was limited by the fact that most news media have a policy of not identifying the living victims of sexual assault. Amy Elizabeth had been raped. AJ had barely a bruise. Two men, identities unknown, were dead. The early headlines read "2 dead, woman raped at Congressman's home." As facts emerged, media coverage was both fair and sensational. If that seems contradictory, consider the events.

The FBI profiling team arrived on Woodland Hills Lane on the morning of June 8th, thirty two hours after the unfortunate events. By then the details had been sorted out, and the FBI profilers came just to see if they could learn anything from the scene. The headline in USA TODAY read "Picked the wrong house" and the story had pictures of the twelve previous victims of The Roofers. In keeping with the FBI policy of not glorifying serial killers, there were no pictures of the criminals, the term "The Roofers" was never used again. They were simply The Diaz Brothers. AJ was pictured above the fold with the caption "Princess Slays the Dragons." Amy Elizabeth's college graduation picture was below the fold.

Amos Bunden, the lead FBI profiler, one of the highest ranking African Americans in the FBI, had been following The Roofers since they had claimed their seventh and eight victims. They had started their march of terror in Duluth, Minnesota, worked their way across that state, through Wisconsin, and finally into the northern suburbs of Chicago. The DNA, male pubic hair, semen, and a drop of blood had tied the cases together. After the eleventh and twelfth killings the FBI had generated a profile. The level of rage suggested that the killers were young men, probably between the ages of 21 to 30. The teamwork suggested that they were either related, possibly brothers or cousins, or as one agent had suggested, perhaps homosexual lovers with a hatred of women. For reasons never released, and profilers never discuss all their reasoning, the FBI had predicted that the two men were two lower class to lower middle class men of Latin descent, most likely laborers. The overall profile was accurate. The FBI had predicted, though not publicly, that they would be stopped only by a chance event or minor mistake—such a traffic stop—that might provide authorities with a match to a fingerprint. That part of the prediction was wrong, unless one considers invading the Miller home a minor mistake.

Joseph Apted, head of the Chicago office of the FBI, walked Amos Bunden through the crime scene. The crime scene tape had been removed. Congressman and Mrs. Miller were back from their Baltic Cruise. Amy Elizabeth and AJ were said to be in seclusion and out of the hospital. Apted showed Bunden the door where The Roofers had gained access from the rear of the house. He showed him where the girls' bedrooms were located, and the path taken as they were dragged to the front foyer. He then related the entire story of the attack.

Bunden had seen more horror than anyone should have to endure in a lifetime. It had cost him two marriages and his sense of humor. While serial killers seemed capable of anything, there were limits to what normal people could do. Bunden was a student of human capabilities. He was perplexed about AJ. "You're telling me that the girl made this plan while she was sitting there watching her sister being raped?"

Apted nodded.

"I'm not a betting man, but if that's true I suspect that she had seen some bad things before. No one could lie there or sit there and generate a plan like that unless they had a way to shut things out. Is the Congressman her biologic father?" Bunden was afraid that a political scandal might be about to emerge—or be covered up.

"I thought the same thing. No. The Congressman is the stepfather. He married the girls' mother three years ago. Until Amy Elizabeth and AJ were eleven and ten, they lived in Kenton, Tennessee. Their father was a minister. He died when Amy Elizabeth was ten and AJ was nine. There was an older daughter too. She was seventeen when the father died. She left home and never came back."

Bunden did not like to profile based on limited facts, but he speculated that all or some of the Golden girls had shared a bedroom and that bad things had happened there. "What did the Reverend die of? And please do not tell me that he died of an accidental gunshot wound while out hunting with one of his daughters." One problem of being a profiler of serial killers is that you see killers everywhere.

"No. He died of stomach cancer." There had been no autopsy, but that's what the death certificate said.

"Sorry. Sometimes I get carried away. Looks like you guys were thinking the same thing I was." Bunden paused. "Something else isn't right. You said that the girl told you she started screaming while she was loading the Walther. She said she had to distract the guy in the foyer. No one could think that up while watching someone rape her sister. No one."

"She didn't think it up. She got it from a video game."

"A video game? There are video games about serial killers?"

"No. *Dragons and Princesses*." Apted explained how AJ had played the game when she was ten and that on level 5, after you killed the first dragon, if you immediately went after the second fire breathing dragon, that dragon incinerated the princess before you got to him. But, if you distracted the second dragon and moved it away from the princess, then you could easily kill the second dragon and save the fair lady. AJ had told him that those events occurred on level 3, instead of on level 5, but no one is perfect. Remember, two of the four shots had missed and AJ was the one who forgot to set the alarm.

Bunden thought it over. "So she kept herself sane during an insane situation by pretending she was the prince rescuing the damsel in distress."

"Actually she thought of herself as a princess rescuing the other princess. These video games are gender neutral. Women can take the rescuer role. The avatar changes and . . ." Apted had obviously been looking at the game.

"Smart girl. Maybe we should recruit her to the FBI and give her the file on The Unforgiving." The Unforgiving was a case that had frustrated Amos Bunden and his Behavioral Analysis Unit for a decade. He had written about the case in his book, *Serial Killers Volume 2*.

Between December of 1993 and July of 1994, four men died of thallium poisoning following travel to Memphis, Tennessee. Forensic evidence had linked the four Memphis murders to a fifth case of thallium poisoning that had occurred in Atlanta six months before the Memphis killings started. There was strong circumstantial evidence that with respect to the first three murders, the killer was avenging attacks on women.

Code names are often attached to serial killers when they are the subjects of a manhunt. In 1992 the Academy Award for the best motion picture had gone to *The Unforgiven*. In that movie, Clint Eastwood portrayed a retired gunfighter who was hired to avenge a prostitute who had been attacked and disfigured by a client. The Bureau nicknamed the avenging killer who used thallium "The Unforgiving."

"You're still hung up on that case?" Apted asked. He had been the Special Agent in the Atlanta office assigned to the first of the five murders. Apted and Bunden had met during that investigation.

"I probably will be forever. Fortunately, for whatever reason, it's been almost ten years since she claimed a victim." Bunden was certain that The Unforgiving was a woman. "On a much happier note, when can I meet AJ? She might actually make a good agent."

Apted chuckled. "I thought the same thing, but she had no interest. She wants a nice quiet life. The FBI is not a possibility. You know, I hate to say it, but talking about recruiting her, we're starting to sound like that asshole Hamilton."

Jeffrey Hamilton was with the CIA. The Agency, or at least Hamilton, tried to recruit heroic individuals who in life or death circumstances had demonstrated unusual psychological skills. What the CIA called recruitment, the FBI considered brainwashing. Apted had seen Hamilton hanging out with the reporters on the front lawn of the Miller home.

Amos Bunden repeated his question. "When can I meet AJ?"

"You can't. At least not right now. She's gone."

"Gone where? What happened?"

"After her parents came home from their cruise, they had a run-in at the hospital and she left in her car. She's been gone a couple of hours."

Bunden sighed. "Girls!" Bunden had a daughter from his first failed marriage. "Look, I came here to see the crime scene for myself, to double check the forensic evidence, and to wrap up The Roofers once and for all. I'm going to talk to the police, and talk to the girl who got raped. What's her name?"

"Amy Elizabeth."

"I'll talk to her, and if AJ doesn't return by then, I'll just head back to Washington. I'd like to meet her, but it's not essential. It's all in the reports. I suspect she'll come back." But she never did.

Chapter Three

Amos Bunden did not know what had occurred when Mary Nell Miller, the Congressman's wife, returned to Highland Heights. Instead of comforting Amy Elizabeth she had screamed at her, "How could you let them do this to you? How could you let yourself be raped?" Then she had turned to AJ and said "You're going to pay for those repairs in the house. It's your fault too."

Mary Nell Miller was a narcissist. She cared more about herself, her gardens, and her front foyer than she cared about her daughters. Her daughters were used to the neglect. They disregarded everything Mary Nell said. Congressman Miller, who observed the scene at the hospital, thought his wife was having a hard time handling an impossible situation. As he learned more about the childhood of the Golden Girls back in Kenton, Tennessee, he decided that there were limits to standing by your woman. Six months after the attack on Woodland Hills Lane, after being re-elected to Congress, he would separate from Mary Nell.

If not for Mary Nell, and the fact that AJ could no longer stand to be around her mother, Amy Elizabeth would not have morphed into Amibeth. If AJ had stayed in Highland Heights, Amy Elizabeth and AJ would likely have done their best to resume their previous lives. The press would have quickly lost interest. But AJ went down the driveway in her black Mazda Miata, Illinois License plate T181, and life was never the same for Amy Elizabeth, or AJ, or—for that matter—for me.

As AJ drove down the driveway, she had no short term plan. She had no intermediate term plan. She did have a long term plan. Before the attack, she had entertained thoughts of being a writer or a doctor or an attorney. She had always worried about how she would react to the sight of blood. It hadn't bothered her in the least. She had decided to become a doctor, if only she could figure out how to pay for her senior year of college and four years of medical school without having contact with her family. That was going to be difficult, but she had solved harder problems.

While AJ was missing, Amos Bunden, the FBI profiler, reviewed his suspicions regarding AJ's traumatic childhood and considered what he knew of her capacity for violence. He worried that she might become a serial killer. Of course, he worried that everybody was going to become a serial killer. There were mornings when he looked in the mirror and asked himself if he was looking in the eyes of a serial killer. Somehow, a woman who says "Sorry" as she pulls the trigger doesn't strike me as a future serial killer. Then again, I am not a profiler, I am a private investigator.

Joseph Apted was worried about how AJ was going to handle the events on Woodland Hills Lane. He told himself that no twenty-one year old goes through what AJ had gone through without experiencing some negative consequences.

Mary Nell had no thoughts about AJ. She was just concerned about getting the house repaired before the next time she entertained the ladies from the garden society. And Mary Nell was concerned about the plate. One of AJ's errant shots had ricocheted and shattered a piece of Mary Nell's fine china. How could AJ do that? Under her breath, she kept muttering, "How sharper than a serpent's tooth it is to have a thankless child."

AJ drove on Woodland Hills Lane, turned onto Green Bay Road, eventually reached Skokie Valley Highway and turned south. She had no idea where she was heading. She passed the turnoff for Northwestern and went south on I-94. She drove through the city of Chicago, past Wrigley Field, and past the high rise condominiums. She contemplated stopping at the Art Institute to help her settle down, but traffic was backed up at the Ohio Street exit ramp and she kept driving. I-94 merged into I-90 and she saw signs for I-65 South. She knew I-65 went to Nashville, where Vanderbilt was located. She figured it was as good a place as any to get away from reporters. For the moment, she wanted to disappear. She wondered how Amy Elizabeth could like the attention. Then again, her older sister had wanted to be an actress.

I-65 it was. AJ hoped that she could register for summer school and get a head start on the fall. The young woman who had planned in detail her escape from The Roofers had no definite plan, but she was running on adrenaline again.

As AJ Golden drove toward Nashville, on Wednesday, June 9, a press conference was held on the front porch of the Miller home. The FBI confirmed that the two men slain by AJ at the Miller residence were serial killers, Roberto and Rodrigo Diaz, implicated in twelve homicides and rapes. Forensic evidence of their link to other crimes was presented. Details of the attack on Amy Elizabeth and AJ were not mentioned, only that there had been an attack and that in the course of events AJ had managed to get loose and get to her stepfather's guns. Joseph Apted concluded, "There is absolutely no doubt that we got the right men. Before I take questions, Amy Elizabeth Golden, the Congressman's oldest stepdaughter would like to say a few words." And thus began the transformation of Amy Elizabeth Golden, a tentative twenty-two-year-old, who appeared more a victim than a survivor.

"Hi. My name is Amy Beth Golden and I was raped. I was raped by a man who had taken part in the murder of twelve people. My heart goes out to those families and to their friends. I would just like anyone listening who has ever been raped or otherwise abused to know that there are people out there to help you. Please get help for yourself. Thanks to the people who sent cards and e-mails to AJ and me. I don't know if I can answer them all. I'll try." By report, she answered every single note personally. "And AJ, if you are out there and hear this, please come home."

Amy Beth. Two words. She had spoken them very slowly and distinctly. Never in her life had she been known as Amy Beth. Previously, it had always been Amy Elizabeth. Always.

Joseph Apted took questions, but other than clarifications about some of the forensic evidence there was only one theme to the questions. "Did something happen to AJ? Where's AJ?" The official answer was that AJ seemed to have taken time to get away. There was no official concern. AJ was an adult woman of twenty-one. Joseph Apted told the audience that the Miller family—or the FBI if she did not wish to speak to her family—would appreciate a call from her. AJ was driving, and not watching television.

By Friday's press conference, the situation was different. On Wednesday night, AJ and Layla had checked into a motel near the Nashville airport and AJ had gone to sleep. She slept almost the entire day on Thursday, getting up only to walk Layla and to drink enough water to avoid dehydration. She ate nothing. She learned that people were looking for her, so she cut her hair short and dyed it back to her natural color of red. She had never liked red hair; she regarded it as too flamboyant. However, there were no recent pictures of her as a redhead and she hoped that the disguise would buy her time until she could decide what to do. Most likely she would just head back home and face a life of finger pointing. Obviously, there were outcomes that would have been much worse.

Friday morning, as AJ checked out of her motel, Amy Elizabeth, more precisely Amy Beth, gave another press conference. With hundreds of cable channels everything gets covered, and because of the events which followed, this one would be re-run frequently. A few weeks ago I watched it as part of the Lifetime Biography, *The Amibeth Phenomenon*. Of course, it is a little early to do a definitive biography of Amibeth.

One hundred and five hours after the unfortunate events on Woodland Hills Lane, Amy Beth addressed America, speaking slowly, distinctly, and sounding very professional. She had been coached. "I'm Amy Beth Golden. I'm sure you know what happened to me but I'm going to say it, just to show that there is no shame in being attacked. I was raped. There is No Cause for Shame. Something horrible happened to me. It has happened to many women. There are people to help women like us, but there are not enough. Two days ago, I was a young woman with no plan in life. Well, now I have a plan. I am going to devote my life to help the victims, the survivors, of sexual abuse, physical abuse, and emotional abuse. Abuse is abuse. And if you have been molested, tell somebody. You are not

28

to blame for being abused." Then, as Mary Nell Miller's eyes widened in horror, Amy Beth went off script. It was off script as far as Mary Nell was concerned; it was planned by Amy Beth.

"Of course you have to tell the right person. You can tell a teacher, a counselor, maybe a parent—but maybe not a parent. Sometimes parents enable the abuse. I'm pretty sure that's the correct word." She knew it was the correct word. She had gone over the speech with an expert in the field of sex abuse.

Amy Beth continued. "When I was a child, my father, Reverend Nathaniel Golden started coming into the room where his daughters were sleeping. He would usually come once a week."

Mary Nell exploded from her seat shouting "You little bitch. How can you tell everybody?" The Congressman and two FBI agents had to restrain her. Chairs went tumbling over.

Amy Beth continued, calmly, as if oblivious to the commotion behind her. "Once a week, he would slide back the covers from his oldest daughter. He would put his hands where they had no business being. He would put his mouth where it had no business being. He would put his penis where it had no business being. And after he was done with his eldest daughter he would give each of his daughters a piece of candy and tell us to shut up because he would kill us if we told."

There were tears and pandemonium as the assembled reporters began to conclude that the girl who had been raped in the safety of a fancy mansion had evidently been raped repeatedly in the safety of her childhood bedroom. I watched the press conference that evening on the major network nightly news and was transfixed. I was expecting someone to move Amy Beth away from the microphone. However, Amy Beth had designed her talk so that to do so would be to side with the enablers; or maybe the only people who could have terminated the conference were too busy restraining Mary Nell. Amy Beth was one smart woman.

I remember thinking, as did many people, that she was talking about her own abuse. I did not realize that Amy Beth had chosen her words with great care and that when she said "oldest daughter" that she was referring to Andrea Golden, the daughter who had left the family nest years earlier.

Amy Beth continued. "He threatened to kill us if we told. We were scared. But Nathaniel Golden's oldest daughter told. She told her mother. Her mother called her a liar, even though in her heart she knew her daughter was telling the truth. She told a teacher. Daddy was a preacher. The teacher didn't believe her. She told the sheriff, but he just made a cursory investigation. No one wanted to believe her. Finally, she kept quiet." She paused just the right amount of time to let people digest her story. "So my message to people is to please listen. Try harder. Do better. I'm not saying that every claim of abuse is true, but at least listen and consider the situation." She took a deep breath—and so did the American public.

"My thanks to the people who have written to us. With your love I will make it through this just as I have made it through the things that happened in the past. I am a survivor. With your help, and with the help of the Lord, I will be fine. I swear I will devote my life to do everything I can to help people like us." She dabbed a tear from her eye, and finished with another tug on the heartstrings of America. "Enough about me. AJ, you saved my life. To me and to many people you are a hero. But, I know you, and I know you are probably very scared about all the publicity. If you are listening to this, please come home. I love you and I miss you. Congressman Miller loves you and misses you. Your friends love you and miss you." The omission of Mary Nell from the list was obvious. "We are all worried, AJ. Thank you everyone." It was shocking. It was engaging. It was heartfelt. It was sincere.

AJ was scared, but only at night. She kept waking up in the middle of the night, shaking in her bed. Sometimes she dreamed about shooting the Diaz brothers. Sometimes she dreamed about being awakened and dragged from her bed. Sometimes she dreamed about people pointing at her. That had happened at the hospital even before the tabloids had started calling her "Shotgun Sister" or "AJ Bang Bang". Sometimes she just stayed awake, afraid to sleep, afraid to dream. Since she had left Highland Heights, AJ had not contacted her sister, or anyone else for that matter. She was trying to figure things out on her own.

Major portions of Amy Beth's press conference were run on the national evening news. After all, her stepfather was a Congressman, two serial killers were dead, there was a tale of incest, AJ was missing, and Amy Beth was planning to devote herself to a worthy cause. "Brave woman," said the nightly news anchor. "We all wish her well. And in other news . . ." He probably assumed that was the last America would see of Amy Elizabeth, now morphed into Amy Beth. Several months later, Amy Beth would re-emerge in the public eye making the saddest personal appearance of her life, delivering a eulogy and completing her metamorphosis to Amibeth.

As AJ's disappearance became a national news story, photographs of AJ with blond hair were distributed along with a statement from Agent Apted of the Chicago FBI Office that AJ was not armed, not dangerous, just an agitated young woman, and that Congressman Miller wanted her home and was offering a small reward. To make it clear to everyone, including AJ, that there were no charges pending for the shooting of the Diaz Brothers, in case that was her concern, he added that the FBI also had a reward to give AJ. Twenty-two thousand dollars had previously been offered for information leading to the arrest and apprehension of The Roofers. The reward money was hers. He added that she was thought to be driving a black Mazda Miata convertible, Illinois License plate T181. AJ remained missing.

Apted was correct on one account. The Mazda had initially been parked in a corner of the motel parking lot, with the license plate backed against a dumpster.

That morning, AJ had driven the Mazda five miles to the Vanderbilt campus where she had parked on the top floor of the Vanderbilt Hospital parking lot. No one noticed the car or its driver. Apted was wrong on the other count. AJ was armed. The Walther had been collected as evidence at the scene and would not be returned to the Congressman until the following week. However, just beyond Indianapolis, AJ had stopped for lunch, found a pawn shop, and purchased a handgun. She had felt that she might need protection. Now, she was embarrassed that she had made that decision. She had no intention to fire a gun ever again.

There are no explanations for the events that happened on Woodland Hills Lane. Why did Roberto and Rodrigo Diaz, become rapist killers? Why did Amy Elizabeth invite The Roofers to go up on the roof to give an estimate? Why did AJ forget to set the alarm? How come Roberto Diaz never learned to tie good knots? How come AJ's blood alcohol was just high enough that her totally disinterested mother felt obligated to punish her and keep her from going to Curacao? Why did Layla, the shih-tzu, awake at exactly the right time?

Amibeth says that there is no WHY; things just happen—good and bad—and we have to make the best of them. Some religious zealots believe that every single event that happens is part of God's plan. Considering the twelve women who lost their lives to The Roofers, and all the other evil that has occurred since the dawn of time, I can't accept that as God's plan. Man has free will. We are the ones responsible. I take Amibeth's side on that one.

There is, of course, another explanation of the events, and I mention it because the person who would have given that explanation plays a major role in this story. That explanation is that since both Amy Elizabeth and AJ were born with Jupiter in Leo, they are protected by guardian angels. It sounds absurd to me, and it probably makes no sense to you. However, the woman who would have explained things that way was Andrea Golden, the oldest of the Golden sisters.

Guardian angels do not have to be dead and do not have to be mystical forces. Andrea Golden had been a guardian angel to Amy Elizabeth and AJ in their home in Kenton, Tennessee. Exactly what she did there remains to be told. Andrea Golden would have regarded AJ as a guardian angel to Amy Elizabeth in the home on Woodland Hills Lane. Andrea would have overlooked the fact that AJ had not set the alarm.

AJ had driven on I-65 to Nashville without a guardian angel. She arrived safely. Maybe the blood alcohol level of 0.00 had something to do with that. Or maybe she did have a guardian angel. Layla the shih-tzu was riding with her.

My name is Jonah Aaron. I am a private investigator in Nashville, Tennessee. Having failed at a few things in my life, that is one thing that I do relatively well. I tend to get answers to questions, even if they are not the answers my clients are seeking.

As I write these words in June 2010, I am thirty-one years old. Around Music City I'm generally known as the lucky guy married to Elana Grey. I don't mind being regarded that way. I am fortunate beyond measure to have her in my life, and if I am defined in terms of my famous wife, the former singer/songwriter who sang lead in Fireball, that is fine with me. Elana is a loving, spirited woman and I love her with all my heart and soul. We have a dog, and our first child is on the way.

I was twenty-five years old when AJ Golden arrived in Nashville. I was the one who figured out what T181 meant. I know what it concealed and what it eventually revealed. I played a role in the transformation of Amy Elizabeth Golden to Amibeth. As for AJ, you would not think it to look at me, but when AJ Golden arrived in Nashville I became her guardian angel.

I am nothing at all like The Roofers, but, I am a very dangerous man.

Chapter Four

Nashville in June is hot and humid. The sun shines most of the days; the neon shines brightly at night. Tourists come for Fan Fair, now renamed the CMA (Country Music Association) festival. They meet and greet the stars, take pictures, and get autographs. My younger brother, Barry, has a collection of autographed pictures of himself posing with more wannabe starlets than you would believe. He even dated one of them for a few months several years ago.

On Friday, June 11, 2004, the whereabouts of AJ Golden became a topic of national interest. The network news show, *America Tonight*, prepared a feature on Amy Beth, and on the topic of child sexual abuse in America. AJ and Layla visited the Vanderbilt campus and then stood in line for two hours at Fan Fair waiting to get a signed picture of bluegrass singer Alison Krauss. Even holding a shih-tzu, no one recognized AJ. She spoke to no one, including the many young men who tried to flirt with her. She only spoke to her favorite singer when she asked her to inscribe the picture, "To Abby Jo."

AJ was intending to go home. She knew what Amy Beth had said at the press conference. She wasn't sure that the truth always made one free, but with Mary Nell put in her place, AJ felt free of her mother. She would go to school where she wanted. The reward money wouldn't cover tuition, but it would help, and if the Congressman wouldn't pay the difference, she had no problem working part time.

Before heading home to Highland Heights, AJ decided to try and live out a tourist fantasy. She had always wanted to sing on a stage in Nashville. While Amy Elizabeth was the actress, AJ had sung second lead in the high school musical in Highland Heights. With all the talent continuously descending on Nashville, one does not just walk in off the street and get a job in a Nashville club. AJ was determined, but unsuccessful. After a few phone calls and several hours of taxi rides with Layla, she got hired as a waitress at Jerry's, a karaoke bar off Music Row. The owner promised that when the regular singer took her break, she would get to do two numbers on her own.

Of course, at a karaoke bar, all she had to do was walk in, sit down, sign up to do a song, and she could get on stage and sing it. But AJ didn't want to sit and do nothing while she gathered her nerve to go on stage. While AJ was a truthful woman, she was willing to stretch the facts a little. By working as a waitress, even if she never returned to Music City, she could always say truthfully, well sort of truthfully, that she had been paid to sing in Nashville. Her plan was to fill food and drink orders for a few hours, do her songs a little after eight, leave before nine, and get almost halfway back to Highland Heights by midnight.

AJ felt that waitressing would be, in her words, "a hoot." AJ had lost her southern accent in the eleven years since she had left Kenton, Tennessee, but she would occasionally use a phrase such as "a hoot" and might rarely use the term "y'all". As a born Southerner she knew enough to use it only as a pleural, and never as a singular as some northern transplants occasionally do.

Had she completed the shift as a waitress, I doubt that it would have been a hoot. Jerry Donegan, the owner of Jerry's, was notorious for occasionally requesting fellatio as a condition of either payment or further employment. Nothing was ever proven; it was always a "he said—she said" thing if anyone even bothered to complain. Most waitresses quit on the spot. Jerry didn't mind. It was easy to find waitresses. Rarely, a desperate woman complied, the alternative being unemployment, work in a strip club, or work in a massage parlor.

Jerry didn't care about his failed attempts to obtain oral gratification; to him, the occasional success made the practice worthwhile. Jerry had never confronted a woman with a loaded gun in her purse and whose recent experiences might lead her to take very unkindly to sexual harassment. AJ was not planning to complete her full shift, but she was planning to get paid. That would not have worked out well. Fortunately, for both Jerry and AJ, AJ had a guardian angel.

Things had not gone well for me in the spring of 2004. I had been involved in a shooting and my longtime girlfriend had broken up with me. The two events were not unrelated. Since I have said that I am a dangerous man, it might be assumed that I had done something illegal. That is not the case. According to the press, I was even a hero.

Why did Donna break up with me? I asked myself that question for over a month until I decided to move on with my life. I appreciate irony as much as the next person. If I had been killed in the East Nashville Shootout, as the press called it, Donna would have worn black and bemoaned the fact that the love of her life had been snatched away from her by deadly criminals. Instead, I survived and she decided that she did not want a man with my capacity for violence in her life. Some people need to see the world as a safer place than it truly is.

My fifteen minutes of fame had placed me in the public eye and I had as much work as an investigator as I could handle. Even if I had not been working steadily, I would not be worrying about my finances. At the age of thirteen, I had started working in a recording studio as an assistant sound engineer. I had even taken some courses in sound engineering at Nashville Tech. The job has always involved microphones, cables, dials, and levers. Nowadays it's also computers. It requires considerable interest in music, if not actual talent. My previous work experience is a tremendous asset when my investigative work puts me in contact with people in the music business.

I made more money than one might expect working the night shift when I was in high school and college, and my work ethic impressed my grandfather. He passed away in 2003, and since my father is a successful cancer specialist, Grandpa Aaron, elected to have the money skip a generation. I have empathy for people who are struggling paycheck to paycheck, but I am never going to be one of them.

Friday evening, I was sitting on the deck of my ninth floor condominium overlooking downtown Nashville and the Cumberland River, sipping a glass of a New Zealand Sauvignon Blanc and reading Amos Bunden's books on serial killers. Like half of America I was fascinated with the tale of Amy Elizabeth and AJ Golden. Though I didn't expect to cross paths with any serial killers, I thought that Bunden's work would be interesting reading. In addition to reporting some of his unit's brilliant solutions to complex cases, Amos Bunden had humbly noted one unsolved case that had baffled him, the case of The Unforgiving. I was in the middle of Bunden's discussion of how the cases were tied to women working for an escort service based on Lamar Avenue in Memphis when I got the call from Karen Bing.

Karen Bing was then and is now the karaoke emcee at Jerry's. It's a small rectangular venue with a stage along one wall and a bar at the opposite end of the room. The floor is covered with peanut shells and the spilled beer that gives the room its distinctive odor. It seats fifty and serves horrible food. In short, calling it "a dive" is to pay it a compliment. Karen is the one in buckskin, holding the microphone. She is the one who calls the guys and gals up on stage. She is the one who draws the customers to Jerry's, keeps the people moving and the beer flowing. She would also warn the waitresses about Jerry, and, unknown to her slimy boss, she would also call me whenever an obviously underage girl would be hired. I was, after all, a licensed private investigator, and I was willing to spend more time searching for runaways than were the police, who felt that they had better things to do.

At the time, Karen was my one and only operative. Karen had a remarkable ability to get people to spill their guts to her. She could get hired as a receptionist or personal assistant and play the role of bimbo to perfection. She was actually quite smart, having graduated from Belmont College two years earlier. She was adept at industrial espionage, and possessed a level of people skills that I suspected I would never attain.

Karen was hoping to be discovered and someday she may be. Karen was twenty-four years old, attractive, blonde, and busty, and that was five years before she got her breast implants. A woman has to try everything to get discovered, I guess, and given the choice of trading up on her truck or going for a pair of double D's, she would eventually decide against the truck. She was my friend—without benefits. Karen was more than capable of taking care of herself with Jerry. Karaoke singers who would work for minimum wage plus tips, stay sober, show up regularly, smell like lilacs, and maintain some decorum in the bar area were impossible to replace. She was also six feet tall and could beat the crap out of Jerry if it became necessary.

It was a quarter past seven. Karaoke Showtime started at 7:30. Until then, Jerry's was just a bar serving what might be mistaken for food. "OK, Jonah. Here are the keys to the house and to the guest house." She handed me a key chain with a large monogrammed B for Brandenburg. "Just leave them in the guest house Sunday night. I have my own keys and I'll be back Monday morning." Karen supplemented her income at Jerry's by being dog walker, house sitter, general helper, and surrogate daughter to Dr. Mona Brandenburg, a prominent Nashville psychologist. Karen received free rent in the guest house for her services, but free rent is not truly free. The Brandenburgs travelled frequently and the dog, the marine fish, and the plants could not be left alone for long. The three Brandenburg children were grown, and when Karen was in charge, and had to leave town on short notice, I was one of her backups. While Karen was reliable, Mona did not trust the Brandenburg estate to any of Karen's ditsy girlfriends.

Karen reviewed my assignment. "Detailed instructions are on the table in the kitchen of the big house in case you forget something. And set the alarm. The code is the same as always."

The detailed instruction book was the creation of Milton Brandenburg, a highly organized and extremely successful entrepreneur. After moving to Nashville in 1977, he had founded a talent agency and his firm represented some of the better known acts in the city. In addition to an occasional star who might be in the running for a Country Music Entertainer of the Year award, Milton managed a string of country bands that played weddings, anniversaries, bar mitzvahs, rehearsal dinners, and other local events. Over the years he had managed well known acts such as the Dana Twins, Robbie Mack, and Shelly Dixon. He would become most famous for managing the woman known as Amibeth. Many have said that Brandenburg Management is to Amibeth what Colonel Parker was to Elvis. I believe that some other individuals played an equally important role in the rise of Amibeth, but there is no point arguing with the conventional wisdom.

Since I frequently work for Milton Brandenburg, since he is among the very rich and very powerful in Music City, and since he is also my uncle—by marriage, I will simply say that while he may seem a bit unpolished at times, he is a great guy, and he is scrupulously honest. A detailed book of instructions is quite reasonable when someone like Karen is watching the house.

The book explained how to feed the dog, how to feed the fish in all three tanks in the house and in the pond. It listed which plants outside were not on the irrigation system, and needed to be watered. The book had a map of where all the indoor plants were located, along with watering instructions.

The book gave instructions for all the light switches in the house. For example, the outside lights could be turned on and off from four places inside the house. The book listed whom to call for problems with anything from air conditioning to electricity to plumbing. The front cover of the book said, "For major emergencies call my son, Brian," and gave Brian's cell number. When Milton Brandenburg was on vacation, he was totally out of touch to the world, a fact appreciated by Mona Brandenburg, and one of the reasons that their marriage had lasted thirty-one years.

Since Karen lived in the guest house, that's where she stayed when she was in charge. To her, the big house was complicated. I was planning to stay in one of the empty guest bedrooms in the big house. I liked the big house.

"Karen, I got it. Have a good time, and I hope it works out with Kenny this time, if that's what you want."

She nodded and gave a sheepish smile. Kenny, her on-again off-again boyfriend, had called at noon and asked her to drive to Birmingham at 2 AM, when she finished work, so they could fly to Orlando together for the weekend. Birmingham is two hundred miles south of Music City, and the fact that Kenny didn't drive to Nashville so that they could fly from Nashville to Orlando was indicative of the level of consideration that frequently made them off-again. But it was none of my business. If Karen wanted help with relationships, she could talk to Mona Brandenburg.

"So, what's the other thing. On the phone you said you had two big things to tell me."

"Oh yeah. Big thing. See the waitress over there, the one with the red hair and the small boobs."

To Karen, all women with the possible exception of Dolly Parton and a couple of exotic dancers on Printer's Alley had small boobs. The redhead was adequately endowed. In fact, the redhead, dressed in a blue denim shirt, a black leather skirt, black tights, and knee high, high heeled black boots was an absolute knockout. Her makeup was a trifle heavy. I guessed that she was eighteen or nineteen and trying to pass for twenty-one to look legal enough to serve alcohol, as if Jerry cared. She was overdressed for Jerry's. What was she doing in a dive like this? Hey, I was there, so I had no right to be judgmental, but I had to wonder. What was she doing working at Jerry's? "She is hard to miss. Are you pimping for me, now? I thought our arrangement was that I don't mess in your love life and you don't mess with mine."

"No! No! She has a gun in her purse."

Chapter Five

Karen could be a fool for a man, but she was smart. "How did you reach that conclusion?"

"When I warned her about Jerry, she said, and I quote, 'If he tries anything on me, I'll just shoot him in the head. He will have picked the WRONG waitress.' Her purse is heavy. I picked it up. Could just be a brick and she could be joking. I didn't have a chance to look inside. I know Jerry is slime, but if she kills him, she'll be in trouble, this place will close, and I'll be out of my main job. Can you please check it out?"

"Where does she say she is from?"

"Why does that matter?"

"I have a reason. Do you know where she's from?"

"Up north."

For Karen, there are only eight places in the world: Nashville, Memphis, Knoxville, Birmingham, down south, up north, out west and somewhere foreign. The latter also includes, as best as I have determined, Canada, Alaska, the Dakotas, Wyoming, and Idaho.

"Jonah, what do you think? Could you stick around? Oh, no, I know THAT look."

"Huh?"

"You are mentally undressing her. Look I know she's cute, but she could be dangerous!"

I wasn't mentally undressing her. I was trying to imagine what she would look like with long blond hair, like in the pictures I had seen. It was a skill I had learned in searching for runaways. If Amos Bunden saw serial killers everywhere, like many people in America, I was starting to see AJ everywhere. If you took the redhead, gave her long blond hair, gave her less makeup, took away the smile, and gave her the bland expression that newspaper photos always have, you would end up with AJ Golden. Then again, you could probably take any number of women, go through the same steps, and convince yourself that you were gazing at AJ. I assumed I was imagining the resemblance. "OK, I'll stick around and see if the shooting starts."

"Just keep it from starting . . . Jonah, get the dreamy look out of your eyes . . . During my first break she is going to get up, do two numbers, and quit. She doesn't need the money, so she probably won't even go to the back room with Jerry. Then again, she said something about really wanting to be paid—on principle. You know Jerry. OK. It's seven-thirty. Showtime. See ya."

I watched Karen belt out a few up-tempo numbers, and watched a few hopeless hopefuls go up on stage and give it their best. I considered doing my best Dwight Yoakum impersonation, and thought better of it. But the waitress was incredibly hot, and she might have a gun in the purse. I was glad to stick around.

Time dragged, during which I did manage to get the waitress's attention, order a hamburger which turned out to be overcooked, flirt with her a little, and give her my business card, the one that said "Jonah D. Aaron, Talent Agent." I actually had been a talent agent. It was one of the things at which I wasn't very good. The card was helpful in finding underage runaways, and was a conversation starter.

The conversation was limited to her telling me she had been at Fan Fair half the day, me telling her that she "cleaned up real well," as we say in the south, and her telling me she had to see if someone else's order was ready. I thought it was a wonderful start, and the more I looked at her, the less likely I felt that she was AJ. But she was hot. I know I said that already, but it bears repeating.

At a quarter past eight, the waitress, whoever she was, went up on the stage and did two Alison Krauss ballads, not exactly the type of material that appeals to the usual crowd at Jerry's, but it was Fan Fair week, the place was packed with tourists, and she got polite applause. I was applauding like mad, stopping only to give her a thumbs-up sign. I walked over to where the steps from the stage returned to the main floor and took her hand to help her down.

She smiled at me. It may not have been a million dollar smile, but it was close. "Well, I'm glad somebody liked it."

"Well, you look fabulous, and you have a clear clean sound."

She shook her head and held up two fingers. "Two songs in this town and I already found a talent agent who is going to tell me how great I am to try to get in my pants. No thanks."

"No. No. I was going to say that your voice . . ."

Jerry was yelling, "Hey, you, waitress, get back to work." I told him to be quiet and continued talking to the waitress/singer, thereby increasing Jerry's chance of staying alive through the night. He has never thanked me, but he doesn't know the whole story.

"No. No. I was going to say that when I look at you and watch you sing, you are fabulous. But when I close my eyes and listen . . ." At least I had her attention; she wanted to hear where this was going. "But when I close my eyes and listen, and that's the best way to assess the commercial potential of talent, you have one of those clear pretty voices, perfect pitch, that either sang first female lead or second female lead in the high school musical. Your sound is too sweet; there's no edge. There are thousands of you. You're much too classy to be waitressing in a place like this and you look like you could be anything you want, a doctor, a lawyer, an architect. There's just something amazing about you. Personally, I could watch you sing all night, and I know you didn't ask for my advice, but . . ."

"But, don't quit my day job." She smiled more than I expected.

"Don't quit your day job . . . But as a hobby, you could have a lot of fun singing. You are good."

She laughed. "I sang second lead in my high school musical before I went to college—but it was a big high school, second lead was an accomplishment. I just figured this might be the only time I'd be down here in Music City and I wanted to get up on a stage so I could someday tell people that I sang on a stage in Nashville. Look, I have to settle up with the owner and head for home. So are you really a talent scout?"

"Actually I'm not a talent scout anymore. It's an old card. Look, you don't have to get back to work or settle up with Jerry." I took her arm, not hard enough to frighten her, but enough so that she turned around. "First of all, if you have clothes like that you don't need the money. Jerry's a pig. If you keep working, he'll make an obscene pass at you when you try and settle up. I suspect you can take of yourself, why bother proving it? Let me buy you dinner. It'll be simpler for everyone."

"Thanks but no thanks—for the dinner invitation. You're sweet, but I have to start driving home. If I leave soon, I can get almost halfway home by the time I stop driving. Sorry."

I tried to hide my disappointment. Think. Think. Think. I had run out of ideas.

She looked at her watch, "Look I'm sorry . . ." She looked at the card I had handed her, since she had forgotten my name. "Jonah. I sort of came down here after a fight with my folks and it's time to go home . . . If you're not a talent scout, what exactly are you?"

"Private investigator . . . What did you have the fight about? The fight with your parents." I was expecting her reply to be, "None of your business," but asking a question was worth a try. As long as she kept talking she might not walk out the door and out of my life.

"I burned down the high school gym. See ya." She turned around and started walking back to where she had been waiting on the crowd.

I recognized the line immediately. "Well, Buffy welcome to Sunnydale. Other than the Hellmouth it's a wonderful place." In the television pilot of *Buffy the Vampire Slayer*, Buffy comes to Sunnydale after she burns down the high school gym in order to incinerate a group of vampires. I had a Buffy poster in my office for years—until I replaced it with a No Cause for Shame poster. "Good luck whoever you are. Have a good life."

To my surprise, she turned around, walked back to me, and kissed me on my cheek. "You made me laugh. A few days ago I thought I might never laugh again. No one ever gets stuff like that. I always say that whenever someone asks me why I'm in trouble with my folks. Not that I'm always in trouble with my folks." She was more animated than she had been on stage.

"Maybe I just get you. Why don't you give me your number, I'll call. Unless you want to reconsider dinner."

She looked me over before responding. "OK. Dinner it is. I hope you know a place better than this piece of crap. Keep this up and it may be breakfast too." She had never been that brazen before, but it had been a very unusual week. "I'm Abby Jo Golden, but everyone calls me AJ." She seemed surprised when I nodded and took it in stride. "I got to get my stuff in back and then we're out of here." She kissed me softly on the lips. "Back in a couple of minutes. If you don't run away, now that you know who I am, Mr. Investigator, the night is ours."

Why would I run away? From the moment I met AJ, there has only been one moment, on the Caruthersville Bridge over the Mississippi River, when I wished that I had. But what is one moment?

Chapter Six

Just as I started to think that she might not be coming back, AJ emerged from the back room, with Layla in a carrying case. "Sorry. I had to do some girl stuff." The heavy makeup was gone. "All my other things are in the trunk of my car. You can take me back there—eventually." We walked out of Jerry's and into the warm night. The humidity was low and it wasn't uncomfortable. "Are you any good as an investigator?"

"Good enough, usually."

"You know if this goes well tonight, we could be an interesting couple. We sure as heck would be a great looking couple." She laughed. "And if it doesn't work out I might hire you to find my sister."

I looked puzzled.

"My oldest sister, Andrea. I know where Amy Elizabeth is. She . . . Forget it. This is a date. I don't want this to seem like you're auditioning for a job."

"Sounds good. I need a girlfriend a lot more than I need work. I have steady work."

She looked at my hand, checking for a ring. "Can't believe you need a girlfriend. Are you married—or engaged—or living with someone? If you are, tell me now, and no hard feelings."

"No! Completely unattached right now."

She looked me over again. "OK. You look honest and I think I'm a great judge of character. I believe you. Where are we going for dinner? Obviously, I don't know the city."

I suggested The Grille. "New American Cuisine. Sort of elegant and casual at the same time. Does that sound ok?"

"Works for me."

"It's a six block walk. Nice night for walking. Are you up for it?"

"I usually run three miles a day. I ran track at Northwestern, but you probably know that." I nodded. "I can walk six blocks. Lead on."

In addition to the good food, the tables were far enough apart and the ceilings were high enough that it was possible to have a conversation. I wanted to get to know this woman. We talked about a number of things that night. While we didn't agree about everything we at least showed that we could listen to each other.

For example, she felt that running an hour a day would add two years to one's life. I pointed out that if you ran an hour a day, by the time you included taking a shower, and the time spent buying running clothes and shoes, it would all add up to about five hundred hours a year. If you did that for fifty years, you would have spent about two and a half years running, and you would be half a year behind, plus you might have two artificial knees. She thought I was funny. I loved the way she laughed. We agreed that if she stayed in Nashville we would go running together.

I mentioned that I had run a bit when I played college football. She asked if I was any good and chuckled when I told her no. I had walked on at Vanderbilt and played on special teams, covering punts and kickoffs. I was so far down the depth chart that until my senior year, I rarely went on the travel squad.

"You look like you could still play. And if you were a marginal player, at least you played in the best football conference in America." Any woman from a Big Ten school who is willing to recognize the superiority of the Southeastern Conference is a gem. Of course, she had been born in Tennessee.

We split a Caesar salad. I asked her what she wanted to be when she grew up. She told me that she was an English major, and had always wanted to write screenplays. However, she liked science, and having decided that she needed to be able to support herself, she was hoping to become a doctor. I told her I suspected she could handle that, but that she shouldn't necessarily give up her dreams. "My father wanted to be a writer, but he felt he wasn't very good at it, so he became a doctor. He enjoys his work, but I never saw him as happy as when he had his first short story accepted."

"How old was he when he had the story published?"

"Fifty-four."

"I think I better go to med school, unless you know someone who is going to pay for my meals for the next thirty-three years."

I said nothing for a moment but just looked at her.

"What?"

"Nothing. I was just thinking that if I get to sit across the table from you, it might not be a bad deal."

She asked what I was going to be when I grew up. I pointed out that I was grown up. I had my own condo, my own car, a steady job with a good income, and I was financially independent. I added that all I needed to complete my life was a girlfriend. She asked how her audition was going. I told her wonderfully. She looked very happy.

She said that what she liked about medicine was that you were always solving problems and helping people. I said that being an investigator involved many of the same things—defining a problem, gathering information, redefining the problem, getting more information . . . but I agreed that in the scheme of things doctors were more important than investigators. She liked that I conceded the point. Then she humbly admitted that while I was already an investigator, she was only pre-med, and there was no guarantee that she would become a physician.

We shared my rack of lamb, and her duck. Suddenly, our conversation morphed into a discussion of waste in health care. She had taken an elective on health care economics and was concerned that the cost of health care could bankrupt the country. My father is a physician who had educated me about inappropriate testing by doctors and wasteful delivery of health care in futile situations. This was not a real live Buffy the Vampire Slayer like one of the tabloids had said. This was an intelligent beautiful woman, and for one evening, she was my date—even if she was headed back to Chicago and I might never see her again.

We decided to skip dessert. She offered to split the check; I pointed out that I had invited her. She didn't put up an argument. All the while Layla stayed relatively quiet in the carry-all.

There was one topic we didn't discuss—the night on Woodland Hills Lane. I figured that she would talk about it if she wanted to, and that if she didn't want to talk about it, we would enjoy our first date and hopefully pick back up when she came back in the fall, if she came back. During dinner she had called Amy Beth and told her sister that she was getting a very late start back home. She planned to stop off somewhere in Indiana, and she wouldn't be home until Saturday afternoon. A cab drove us back to the Vanderbilt garage where she had left her car and I accompanied her and Layla to the top floor.

"Jonah, you are charming. You are funny. You are smart. You are not what I expected from an investigator."

"I get a lot of that."

"I bet you do." She looked me over. I must have looked sad. I was calculating the odds of seeing her again. If I didn't, I expected that I would spend the rest of my life reading about her in the papers and telling people about my one date with this fabulous woman. "Jonah, I probably shouldn't say this, but you make me think about staying in Nashville instead of going back home. Thank you for an absolutely lovely evening." We kissed. Her lips were the softest I had ever encountered. "Bye, Jonah. Here's my cell number. Call me."

"You don't have to go back. You can stay here, get an apartment. Go to school in the fall. You have the reward money."

"Yeah. Twenty-two thousand dollars. Eleven thousand dollars a head . . . Actually, eleven thousand for the head, and eleven thousand for splashing the other one's guts all over the upstairs office." She started to tremble. She grabbed me and pulled me close to her before I could even make a move to hold her. "Sorry. I almost made it through one complete day without falling apart. I'll be ok." She opened the door of her Miata.

"Are you sure you're ok to drive?"

"I'll be . . . You have a better idea?"

"I do. The place I'm house-sitting is huge—five bedrooms. Plus, it has a guest house if you want to be completely alone. I'll be glad to take you there. You can spend the night and reassess the situation in the morning."

She nodded. "Thank you." She handed me her keys and started blotting the tears from her eyes. "Could you please drive?"

I had left my car near Jerry's. We drove there to get my duffel bag from the trunk, then drove down West End Avenue past half a dozen churches and two synagogues. We turned onto Belle Meade Boulevard, then onto Chickering Road and finally onto Chickering Lane. We rode in silence as we finally approached the gated driveway. "Where are we?"

"The middle of Belle Meade. It's a part of Nashville and one of the wealthiest zip codes in Tennessee. As soon as we go through the gate, up the little hill, and around that curve you'll see the house." The house was about seven thousand square feet, with six colonial style pillars on the front porch. Magnolia trees lined the last fifty yards of the orange gravel driveway. The air was thick with the smell of honeysuckle. From the front porch it was impossible to see the street.

"Who lives here?"

As we went up the driveway, I explained about the Brandenburgs and how land and housing was much cheaper in Nashville than up north.

"Wow. Just the two of them, and Karen in the guest house. Do they take boarders?"

"They might like to. All three kids are gone. They have two guest bedrooms downstairs and three guest bedrooms upstairs. They're hoping for grandchildren someday—but none yet. Are you seriously thinking about staying in Nashville?"

"Not really." She exhaled softly. "Imagine growing up in a place like this. Quiet. Plenty of space. It would be nice."

"It's beautiful in the summer. The driveway is a bitch in the winter. That's why it's crushed stone. It's a fantastic place—except for going down the driveway in the winter."

"You know the Brandenburgs?"

"Milton Brandenburg is my uncle, and Brian, their oldest son, my cousin, is my best friend. He's in med school. I spent a lot of time in this house growing up in Nashville. They're a very loving family."

"And your family. Do they live in a house like this?"

"Similar. Different architecture. It's not a colonial, more like a Frank Lloyd Wright house. We passed it a while back, but you can't see it from the road."

"Wish I would have known. I would have ordered something more expensive for dinner . . . I'm joking. And where do you live?"

"I have a condo in The Gulch—nice part of town halfway between downtown and Vanderbilt. If I didn't have to house sit, we could be there. I take responsibility very seriously. I agreed to watch the house; I'm going to watch the house."

I turned off the alarm and turned on the lights as we entered the foyer that led to the thirty foot by twenty-five foot living room and its twenty foot ceilings. Large abstract paintings graced the walls.

"Keep Layla in the carry-all until Buffy sniffs her out." Buffy, the cocker spaniel, came to greet us. "Don't pet her!" It was too late. Buffy, in a typical cocker act of submission to AJ, peed on the marble floor.

"Stay here. I'll get a paper towel."

As I walked away, I heard AJ say, "That's ok girl. I peed in the front foyer once. No big deal."

I gave AJ the full house tour, except for the master bedroom. That was off limits. We settled in the recreation room. The wall opposite the TV was covered with gold records.

"Is your uncle a musician?"

"He's a promoter, and a very good one. I've seen him make something out of next to nothing. He's very good."

I put on an Alison Krauss CD and we cuddled.

Baby, now that I found you, I can't let you go.
I'll build my world around you, I need you so . . .

"Do you want to talk about it? What happened last week?"

"Not right now. Maybe tomorrow. I think I ought to get some sleep."

"Do you want to take a look at the guest house? See if you want to stay there."

She shook her head. "I don't want to be alone out there . . . Jonah, can I stay with you? I don't mean sex. I just feel safe with you. Could you just hold me tonight? I've been having trouble sleeping."

"Sounds fine. Let's walk the dogs and settle in for the night."

"Look I'm sorry, but I have to ask. I don't know where this is going between us. You're funny. You're charming. You're respectful. You wear really nice clothes. You're not gay are you? I mean it's ok if you are."

"No. I'm not gay. Three months ago I was on the verge of getting engaged to a woman I had dated for almost four years. Then she decided that she didn't want someone like me to be the father of her children some day in the future. That's why I am totally unattached. Until I saw this beautiful redhead at Jerry's tonight, I really hadn't been very interested in dating again."

"What happened?"

"I saw you and found you irresistible."

"No, I mean why did you and she . . . ? None of my business. But I want to know."

"Can we talk about it in the morning? There's probably nothing more boring on a first date than a guy who talks about his ex. Tomorrow is our second date." At least until she took off in the morning. "We can talk in the morning."

"Works for me."

After we had walked the dogs and picked up after them, we headed to one of the guest bedrooms. She dressed chastely for bed in a Northwestern University Track Team t-shirt and a pair of running shorts. I propped up two pillows and lay on my back. She put her back up against me and folded my hands around her waist.

"You make me feel very safe, Jonah."

"You are safe." She was also fast asleep.

Chapter Seven

For the first time since the events on Woodland Hills Lane, AJ slept through the night. In the morning, after she made a phone call to Amy Beth, we walked the dogs, then went for a three-mile run before it became unbearably hot. I expected her to hit the road after breakfast; I was going to miss her.

We raided the Brandenburg refrigerator and AJ cooked us an omelet with cheese, mushrooms, pepper, and onions. She said she could cook anything I wanted, as long as I wanted an omelet or pancakes. While we were eating out on the Brandenburg's patio, she asked me, "What's the agenda for today? Or did you have something planned?"

"Agenda? I thought you were leaving."

"Changed my mind, if that's ok with you."

"Better than ok. It's wonderful. No plans until tonight. I'm getting together with friends, my brother Barry and Brian Brandenburg, the one whose . . ."

"parents own this place."

"Right. You can come along. I'd love to have you. How long are you planning to stay?"

"In Nashville? Maybe forever. How long can we stay here?"

"We have to be out of here by Sunday night. If you want to stay at my condo . . . How long are we talking about?"

"With you? Just until I find a place for me and Amy Elizabeth."

"Amy Elizabeth? Is she coming to Nashville?"

"Probably. No reason for me go home, except for Amy Elizabeth. No reason for her to be there instead of here. Her friends are in Maine where she went to college. She can make friends here as well as in Highland Heights. Be good for her to get out of the house. Anyway, when I told her about meeting you, she said she didn't want to be the reason that I had to leave."

"That's sweet. Look, you can both stay with me for a while if you want. It's not as big as the Brandenburg's, but there's room. I can suggest some areas where you should look for an apartment."

"As long as it's where you can find me. You're interesting."

"You don't really know me."

"Know enough to decide that it's worth my staying in Nashville. Not like I'm changing my whole life around because you took me to dinner. I was coming here anyway in the fall—probably. It's just that I feel safe with you and I want to get to know you better."

We were both very quiet for a while. I asked the first question. "If we're getting to know each other, do you want to talk about what happened last Sunday?"

"If you tell me afterwards why your girlfriend broke up with you."

"Deal."

We moved to the recreation room. AJ put a throw pillow behind her head and reclined on the Brandenburg's teal-colored leather sectional. It probably cost more than many people would pay for a small car. Her feet were resting in my lap. She paused before starting. "I can't figure where to begin . . . OK. Last Sunday night, I almost went to Nashville. And if I did, I would have been dead."

I looked at her like she was speaking a foreign language.

"Sorry. I do that sometimes. Say things that make no sense unless you know what I'm talking about. Amy Elizabeth and I had our own language, a shorthand, so we could talk without anyone knowing what we were saying. Sometimes we just whistled part of a song. Anyway, you heard Amy Elizabeth on TV yesterday? You heard what she said about my father?"

"Hard to miss."

"I never told anyone! In fact, if she hadn't spoken out, I probably never would have. When we were growing up, whenever daddy came in the room, we would just go somewhere in our minds, pretend we were somewhere else. Andrea said that in her mind, she went to Graceland. She'd never been there, but she imagined it. Amy Elizabeth said that she went to Memphis. There was this place on the water that she liked. Anyway, daddy never touched Amy Elizabeth or me. But we just went somewhere in our mind when he came in the room. I went to Nashville. The Grand Ole Opry. Music Row. The Parthenon. Places I had never been. I'd just seen pictures."

"There were three of you, right?"

"Right. Andrea, Amy Elizabeth, and me. Daddy only messed with Andrea—but we were there."

"I thought your father . . . maybe did things to all of you." I was trying to remember what I had heard.

"No! Amy Elizabeth said that daddy did things to his oldest daughter. Not to her. Not to me. Never. Andrea would have done something if he tried anything with us. I think that's why she stayed as long as she did, to make sure he wouldn't do anything to us. She didn't leave until he got too sick to try anything with Amy Elizabeth or me. Of course, before then she had made it stop with her."

"What happened?"

"One Sunday after church, when Andrea was fifteen, mama went to a neighbor's house. The three of us were home with him. I guess he looked at her funny, or something. I don't know. We were sitting there and she went and picked up a rifle and walked over to him and said "Daddy. The Bible says, 'Thou Shalt not Kill,' and the Bible says, 'Honor Thy Mother and Father.' But the Bible also says, 'God helps those who help themselves,' and God help me, if you ever touch me again, or if you ever touch Amy Elizabeth or AJ once, I swear to God I will take this gun and kill you."

"What did he say?"

"It was eerie. He told her that she shouldn't take the Lord's name in vain, and how the thing about 'God helps those who help themselves' isn't in the Bible. He said that she should know scripture better than that, being a preacher's daughter. But he got the message. He never touched her again; and he never touched any of us."

"It's not in the Bible? 'God helps those who help themselves'?"

"Nope. The Bible is full of how God helps the weak. It's from Benjamin Franklin. In fact it actually goes back to Aesop, the fable guy. Sort of the ultimate mix of the American spirit and American belief, but it's not in the Bible. Anyway, now you know what I meant about 'going to Nashville.' Pretending I was somewhere else."

"Got it."

"So, last Sunday, when the men broke in and ripped off our clothes and took us to the front hall . . ." She stopped to grab a tissue. "I'm ok."

"Do you want to stop?"

"No I want to talk. All I could think was that after all these years, our turn was finally going to happen, and that we didn't have Andrea to protect us, only these." She touched her T181 pendant and told me the story of its origin. "Anyway, I started to go to Nashville in my head, and then it hit me, this wasn't going to be just a rape. We were going to DIE. Well, I wasn't ready to die. I don't believe in Heaven—or Hell. I figure this life is the one chance you get, and I wasn't going to give it up without trying. I had spent my whole life figuring out that if I worked hard, got really good grades, I could make something of myself, despite coming from a crazy family. I would have been valedictorian at Gibson County High School if we had stayed in Kenton. Not that I was an all work no play type. But I had plans, I'm good at making plans. So I figured out what to do, and I did what had to be done. G-H-T-W-H-T. It went ok until the end."

"Wait. G-H-T-W-H-T?"

"God helps those who help themselves. It's like a mantra for Amy Elizabeth and me." Then she told me about her run up the stairs, getting the combination right the first time, getting the shotgun out of the gun safe, shooting Roberto Diaz as he moved towards her, facing Rodrigo Diaz, and telling him she was sorry before she killed him. "Not sorry now, though; I've had five days," she counted them off on her fingers, "to second guess myself, and there isn't anything else I could have done except get killed."

"I can understand that—the second guessing."

"You probably can't, but it's ok to say that. And that's the whole story. I'm not really a female Rambo or a Xena or a Buffy, like one of the tabloids said. I'm just a twenty-one year old woman who did what I had to do to stay alive. I trust my instincts more, now. I believe that I am going to be somebody. I believe Amy Elizabeth and I are both going to amount to something. We didn't end up being the girls who died before they even ran the opening credits." I knew what she meant without her having to clarify. "Thank you for letting me talk, and for listening. And don't worry, if I stay with you a long time, I may never bring it up again. Not fun to hear about, I'm sure. Why are you smiling?"

"Just thinking about that 'stay a long time' part.'" I leaned over and kissed her on the lips. She kissed back; then pushed me away.

"Not the time. Too soon."

"Sorry. I mean all that stuff just happened to you, and . . . Look you're just too pretty for your own good. I'm sorry."

"No! No need to be sorry. Not too soon that way. Too soon, as in you owe me a story." She threw a toss pillow at me.

"Huh?"

"Your time to share. You told me that you were going to tell me why your girlfriend decided she didn't want someone like you to someday be the father of her children. Did you cheat on her?"

"No. I didn't cheat on Donna. If I wanted to fool around I would have broken it off. That's just the way that I am."

"Did you hit her?"

"Of course not. If I was in a relationship with a woman, I would never hit her. Never have. Never will. You want to keep guessing or do you want me to tell you my story?"

"You wouldn't hit a woman in a relationship? Does that mean you would hit a woman?"

"Look. I'm an investigator. Maybe you see me as very gentle because I spent last night in bed with you and just held you. That was what you wanted, and that was what you got. My mother raised me to be a gentleman, but that doesn't mean that someone can push me around because she doesn't have a Y chromosome. Sometimes I get in rough situations. If a woman, a stranger, does something physical with me, I get physical back. Women are human beings—no more, no less—and I treat them that way. Sorry if that offends you."

"Doesn't bother me at all. Growing up with my parents telling us they loved us—when daddy did what he did to Andrea and mama let it happen—hypocrisy really pisses me off. I'm all for women getting to be doctors, or lawyers, or politicians, or homemakers—whatever they want to be. I'm all for equal pay for equal work, but women shouldn't be allowed a free pass to screw up just because they are women. Anyway, you were with your girlfriend for four years. That's college, right?"

"Since junior year."

"And all of a sudden she decided that you were not the one she wanted to be with. I don't get it. What did you do?"

"I killed two people." I said it in the same tone that one might use to announce that he had forgotten to mail the rent check.

"No. Quit joking. Don't make fun of me."

"I'm not making fun of you. I killed two people and Donna decided that she didn't want a man who could be that violent in her life anymore. She's a second year law student and she knows exactly what she wants to do with her life. Nice job. Nice condo. Nice husband. Nice kids. Nice everything. She didn't mind that I had a carry permit for a gun. It just never crossed her mind that I actually knew how to use it and would use it if I had to. She thought it was an affectation, like a piece of macho jewelry. She never took me being an investigator very seriously."

"What happened?" she looked a little afraid, but she wasn't reaching for her purse, the one with the gun in it. I took that as a good sign.

"Long version or short version?"

"However you want to tell it."

Chapter Eight

"I was working on a case involving counterfeit CD's. My client owns a small retail store, not far from where we had dinner last night. He had bought a big lot of CD's by Tim McGraw, Kenny Chesney, Rascal Flatts, Alan Jackson—artists like that. He didn't care that they were probably counterfeit. In fact he denied knowing they were counterfeit, but I didn't believe him. The CD's were poor quality. That was the problem. He wanted his money back. Not my job to judge him, about buying the counterfeits. I figured I could go by, talk to the guys who sold him the CD's, and get some sort of settlement. So I tracked the guys down—didn't take long—and found them at a warehouse in East Nashville. I tried to negotiate a refund. I was escorted out by three large but not particularly frightening guys. Still, there were three of them and one of me. No major damage. Having no obvious options, I convinced my client to go to the police. He had six thousand dollars invested, so he took my advice. The police invited me to tag along. Basically they wanted to show off how real police do their jobs—impress me."

"Doesn't sound violent to me."

"I'm getting there. We went back to the warehouse and parked outside. Two police cars and me in my Lexus. Not a bad neighborhood at all. Not Belle Meade, but not bad. Anyway, the four real police went inside for what they thought was a simple fraud bust. Four police, three men and Patrolwoman Debbie Lafferty. Twenty-nine years old. Mother of two." I took a deep breath. "I was told to wait outside. They didn't want me in the way. No problem for me. I just wanted to be able to tell my client that the guys who ripped him off were going to jail. What no one knew, what no one had any way of knowing, was that the counterfeit CD's were being used get start-up money for a meth lab in Rutherford County. These people had long criminal records and were not going to go easily."

AJ looked like she wanted to hear more.

"So, I was standing there in the parking lot, leaning against the hood of the squad car, getting some dust blown into my eyes when 'BLAM!' And again. And again. And again. I had no idea how many shots were fired. Later, they said it was ten shots in a room no bigger than this."

"What did you do?"

"I radioed for backup. I had seen cops use the police radio; I knew how to do that. I told them officers were under fire. I unholstered my gun. I went in. I had never fired a gun at a live target before—even an animal."

"Very brave or very dumb." She smiled when she said dumb.

"I went in. There were three bodies in the reception area—one cop and two of the bad guys. All dead I would find out later. Another one of the bad guys, one of the three who had tossed me out the day before, was bleeding from a shoulder wound and standing over two wounded police officers, about to execute them." I raised my index finger as if it were a weapon. "BAM, BAM, BAM. I put three bullets in his chest before he even saw me. He went down. Dead. The two wounded police officers ended up in the ICU at Vanderbilt and survived. For that I got a medal from the Chief of Police and the gratitude of the Police Department—which is rather helpful, since I'm an investigator."

"Were you scared?"

"No time. Not until afterwards when I thought about what I had done."

"Boy, can I ever relate to that. What happened next?"

"When the guy I shot fell to the ground, I could see down the hallway. Thirty feet away from me was the fourth and last perp, holding a gun to Debbie Lafferty's head. Lafferty was being used as a shield. They were moving toward the back door. I figured that if the perp got Lafferty outside, Lafferty was going to be dead. There was no need to have a hostage once they left the building. There were no cops out the back door. I had to keep them in the building until backup came."

"What did you do?"

"What would you do?"

"What do you mean what would I do? You were the one who was there."

"Well you have more tactical experience now, than I had then. I had none. I was winging it. What would you do?" I figured she would toss the pillow at me, but instead she analyzed the situation.

"Hmmn . . . . The perp has got a gun at Lafferty's head. How far away were they?"

"Thirty feet. I had a revolver. It's pretty accurate within fifteen to twenty feet, if you have a decent target to shoot at. But I didn't. The perp was blocked by Lafferty."

She thought it over. "I would probably run . . . Told you I wasn't Rambo. But in your shoes, if I were a guy, I'd walk towards them trying to get nearer. And I'd look for a way out of the hallway in case the perp turned the gun on me, and I'd try to get the perp to put down the gun."

"Exactly." I took her hand and kissed it. "I walked toward them, saying something like 'Lower your weapon. You don't have to make this worse than it already is.' Obviously it was pretty bad. Six people, three cops and three perps were critically wounded or dead. We're talking lethal injection type bad here, but I figured that maybe the perp didn't know that at least one cop was already dead."

"Go on."

I had intentionally left out one important detail. But, since the story goes better without the detail, I continued. "So the perp, who looked just as scared as Lafferty was, said 'One step closer and I blow her head off.' I considered my options. I had a target about six inches by six inches on the perp. A head shot." I held up my hands to show the size target I had. "The rest was all Lafferty. They were almost out the back door, so I fired my gun, and I hit her, right in the forehead. Dead instantly."

She sat up straight. "You killed Officer Lafferty? A mother with two children?"

"No. I shot the perp, a woman named Janice French, a woman with three children and eight arrests. A woman, a person, who was holding a gun to the head of a police officer. The guy I shot in the reception area was her husband. The kids went to child protective services, if that matters."

"You didn't tell me the last perp was a woman! I thought you shot Lafferty!"

"Makes a more exciting story when I leave out the fact that the fourth perp was a woman, doesn't it? It's a better story when you think I shot Lafferty? Give me a break. I've had four months to deal with this story. If I can't joke about it, just a little, by telling the story that way, I don't think I could handle it."

She got up and kissed me. "Jonah Aaron, we are a match made in Heaven."

"Only if Heaven is a place where you take target practice."

"Not just because of that. Because of your sense of humor—if you can call it that." She was smiling. "And no wonder you weren't intimidated when you found out who I was."

"I was impressed. We both just did what had to be done. Anyway, that's why I'm totally available. Donna's gone. She's not coming back. Looking down the barrel of a gun, literally, has made me a little more serious about things. The way I look at it, there's no sense being with someone unless you think the relationship has a chance to be something. Otherwise, why waste your time? Anyway, you looked marvelous last night, and I thought you were interesting even before I knew you were AJ Golden."

"And now?"

"You are definitely not a waste of time. I don't know you all that well, yet, but I am certain that my life will be interesting with you in it."

"Thanks. So what do we do today? What are the choices?"

I thought it over. "There's a crafts fair in Centennial Park. We can take the dogs. That would be fun. We could just hang out here. Or I could take you to Heaven."

Almost as soon as the words were out of my mouth, her T-shirt, bra, shorts, and panties were in a pile on the floor. She had the cutest little shaved red landing strip of a pubic patch. In a minute, we were both naked on the recreation room rug. There was fierceness to her kisses that I probably should have expected. She seemed intent on devouring my tongue. I ran my hand over her breast. Her nipple hardened in response; she moved her hand toward my erection.

Suddenly, she pushed me away. "Not on the floor. Bad memories of last week. You have a condom somewhere don't you?"

"Bedroom."

"Race you back there."

She won, partly because she was a track star, and partly because I was admiring the view.

We fell in bed and embraced.

"Jonah, I will never be sorry about this. Whatever happens . . ."

"AJ, can we talk later?"

"Good idea."

Heaven it was.

Or, as AJ said afterwards, as she regained her breath, she rode the fire wave.

"Amy Elizabeth . . . calls it that . . . . The fire wave . . . . Was I . . . too noisy?"

"No such thing . . . . Noisy is hot."

"Never thought of . . . . myself as hot . . . Cute yes; . . . hot no . . . Whoa!"

"You're hot . . . No doubt about it . . . It was like getting into this quiet lake . . . and then finding out that there was a rip tide . . . and a waterfall . . . and an underwater volcano. I just went with the flow. Where did all that energy come from?"

"Been-a-long-time." She was still catching her breath.

Past was past. I did not want to speculate.

"High school."

"High school?"

"Yeah." She rolled off me. "High school. After growing up in that family, I wanted to know if I was . . . normal. It was ok back then. Today was a lot better than ok."

"You are fabulous. It was your energy that got to me. You look beautiful naked by the way."

"Thank you. Hey, you want a picture of me naked?"

"What? You took a glamour shot once or something?"

"Or something. It's a really cool picture. My energy shows through, but I'm too tired to get up and look for it. Maybe later. Can we rest up and do that again?"

"In a while." I held her close and kissed her forehead. For several minutes she lay with her head on my chest, and said nothing.

"Jonah. Having you hold me now, this is nice, too. Like when you just held me last night . . . God, I could get used to this . . . We have to talk. I have to say it right . . . Look, this may come out jumbled. Please don't hold it against me."

"OK."

"First, I am not into being picked up by strangers—even cute ones—and going to bed with them. I have never done that before. It was a crazy week and this morning, I figured if we ever had a chance at being something, we should get all the dumb game playing out of the way. I'm glad we did."

I started to say something, but she placed a finger on my lips.

"Second, I have problems with 'relationships.'" She held her fingers up to make little quote signs. "With every boy I've been with—and there haven't been that many—I've been so scared that they would dump me, that I got all clingy. Lots of phone calls and stuff. It wasn't like I was a stalker or anything, and I was only seventeen, but I guess I made them break up with me. If I start doing anything like that, just tell me, please."

I nodded.

"Three. I don't trust people. You know me enough to know why. The fact is, you know more about me than anyone I have ever been with. I don't know how long this will last. Just promise me that if you decide you want to be with someone else that you tell me and we try to stay friends. Don't cheat on me."

"OK." I doubted we could ever become "just friends," but at that moment I wanted to stay with her forever. I nodded.

"Four . . ." I was starting to wonder how long the list was going to be. "Four, do you want a little encouragement?" She started kissing her way down from my chest.

I wasn't sure I needed all that much encouragement. It had been a long time for both of us. Suddenly she stopped. "Mmm. You were going to say something before I started on my list."

"Nothing. You got very serious after that, and I was serious when I agreed with you. I don't want to change the mood. It was unimportant."

"Come on. What was it?"

"Well I was going to explain . . . Before, when I told you about the shooting at the East Nashville warehouse you said we were a match made in Heaven."

"Yeah. I remember." She propped herself up on one elbow.

"Well I said something about how that was true if Heaven was a shooting gallery."

"I remember that. So?"

"So when I said that I wanted to take you to Heaven, all I meant was that I would take you for target practice. I read the papers. You missed on two of four shots from ten feet. That is atrocious shooting. I wasn't even thinking about sex when I said 'take you to Heaven.' I just meant target practice. Next thing I knew, you were naked."

She played back the scene in her mind. "Oh-my-God. You mean this is a mistake. You really didn't want to . . ." she looked in my eyes, saw me smiling, and started to laugh. "You're joking. You're joking." Playfully, she punched me in the shoulder.

"Of course I'm joking. Did I seem like I wasn't interested?"

She was giggling and shaking her head. "God. You bring the fire wave and you make me laugh." She started whistling three bars of a tune I didn't recognize. "Ta-da-Ta-da . . . Ta-da'-da . . . ta-da-da-da."

"What song is that?"

"It's my secret." She went back to licking her way down my body. From what I had learned about her, I had a feeling she was very good at keeping secrets. So was I for that matter. No sense pushing the point; we had better things to do.

Chapter Nine

At the crafts fair I bought AJ a pair of gold earrings as a getting to know you present. She bought me a belt with a jasper stone buckle that she caught me admiring. Every time I did something she liked, she smiled and then whistled that little phrase—Ta-da-Ta-da . . . Ta-da'-da . . . ta-da-da-da. "Not gonna tell you." From the way she said it, I figured it couldn't be bad.

Layla and Buffy had a great time as well. Layla was afraid of any dog bigger than she was, which meant just about every dog she saw. Layla's attitude was that the best defense was a good offense. She showed her fear by leaping toward other dogs before they could even growl at her. Since she was on a leash, she didn't bite any of them, not that all ten pounds of her could inflict any damage. The third time it happened, AJ ended up apologizing to a man whose medium sized dog, cowering behind him, was a pit bull.

As we walked, AJ told me about Amy Beth's plan to speak at high schools and colleges, talking about her experiences, talking about abuse, about date rape, and about treating people with respect. It wasn't an original message, but Amy Beth felt she would have credibility and that people would listen. Amy Beth wanted to do something useful, and she saw it as a form of therapy. As far as I was concerned, the best way to do therapy was to do therapy. Then again, I had grown up with Dr. Mona Brandenburg, a psychologist, as my best friend's mother.

That evening, while Amy Beth was in Highland Heights, packing, I took AJ to The Green Hills Sports Bar to meet my friends—my younger brother Barry, Brian Brandenburg, Barry's girl of the week, and Brian's fiancée, Melanie. It was nowhere near as elegant as the night before, but the food was above average, especially the burgers, and The Green Hills Sports Bar had one special attraction.

We were in the parking lot before going in. "When you introduce me, please don't tell them I'm AJ Golden. Not tonight. It's too complicated." The crawler on the cable news station that we had watched as we got ready to go out had said, "FBI Agent Joseph Apted says AJ Golden 'on vacation with friends and sorry for the misunderstanding.'"

"Don't say another word. I understand. What should I call you? Abby Jo?"

"No. Not even that. Can I just be . . .?"

"Red. How about Red?"

"Works for me."

We walked into a room packed with tables. Sports memorabilia and flat screen TV's filled the walls. I found our group and made introductions.

Brian and his fiancée Melanie had recently completed the second year of medical school, and had been spending nearly every waking moment studying for studying for National Board exams. Neither of them had been out in the sun recently. Melanie's black hair and dark red lipstick gave her the dramatic look of a 1940's starlet. Brian was naturally thin, and looked like he needed to put on twenty pounds and get out in the sun. I was certain he would do both when exams were completed.

Brian stood up to greet AJ, and gave her a quick peck on the cheek. "Good to meet you, Red. Jonah, is she any good?"

"Jonah, what did you tell them?" AJ was blushing.

"Brian means are you good at bar trivia. Some people come here for the beer and the games on TV. Some people come for the food. We come to play bar trivia."

My brother Barry joined in. "Play bar trivia? Others come to PLAY bar trivia. We come to WIN bar trivia. Red, this is not a game, this is a passion. The only reason I play with Jonah instead of against him is because . . . Well, did you ever hear of Cain and Abel? It would be worse."

Barry is two years younger than I am, and except for his light brown hair, could almost pass for my twin. Except when he is playing bar trivia, Barry looks completely relaxed, as if he doesn't take anything seriously—which he doesn't. It keeps everyone from taking him seriously. I always felt that would be an asset if he chose to be an investigator. However, Barry had absolutely no idea what he wanted to be when he grew up, assuming that he someday chose to grow up. In the fall, following another change of his major, this time to Communication Studies, he would start his sixth, and hopefully, final year at Vanderbilt. Since his major marketable skill was being able to talk to women who wanted a career in the music business, I suspected he would eventually go to work for Milton Brandenburg.

We enjoyed our beers, food, and conversation. AJ whispered in my ear, "I like your friends."

"They like you."

"Except for Melanie. She doesn't like me."

"She's good friends with Donna. She'll get over it." I suspected that sometime during the evening Melanie was going to take a picture on her cell phone and send it to Donna. Not my problem.

At the same time, Brian and Barry saw me whispering in AJ's ear and said, "Get a room guys."

And then the game began. Same rules as always. Teams up to six players. Twenty questions. First prize was a ten dollar gift card. The team captain, Melanie, would write down an answer for the team if we disagreed. That was it. A lot of questions are easy, and everyone knows the answer. Some questions are difficult. But we are professionals, at least that was our team name.

Barry knows sports and old rock and roll trivia. Brian knows science. We all know current events, but Melanie knows that best. Barry's date of the week usually knew Barry—but not much that we all didn't know. Since Donna left me, we had a gap in geography. I know music and more miscellaneous general knowledge than I care to admit. It was helpful in solving problems. Of course knowing that the driest desert in the world is the Atacama desert in Chile doesn't help with investigations, and we were all glad that Red knew that one since none of us did.

"How did you ever know that?" Brian asked her.

"Took Spanish last year. We read about it . . . Sorry. Lo siento . . ."

"Don't be sorry. That's one we get right that no one else does." I squeezed her hand.

We knew we had nineteen right. We had no idea what poison came from jimsonweed. It turned out to be atropine. Brian and Melanie were embarrassed. "Hey, we're only second year med students. We can't remember everything." We traded answer sheets with a team of six coeds from David Lipscomb University, listened to the emcee read the correct answers, enjoyed hearing the other teams groan, and figured we had won. We had nineteen correct, the girls from Lipscomb had six, most of the other teams had ten or eleven. A group of tourists in from New York for Fan Fair had nineteen as well; they had missed the Atacama desert.

"Way to go Red." Barry surprised her with a quick kiss on the lips. "She's your date but she just saved our butts. Playoff time. Bear down."

AJ looked at me and pointed at Barry. "Is he always this way?"

Melanie said, "Worse. You're seeing Barry on his best behavior. But way to go, Red." Melanie gave AJ a high five.

The emcee was back at the microphone. "Playoff round. One question at a time until one of the teams gets it right and the other one misses. Our two teams are New York/New York and our hometown Professionals. The first category is music trivia and it's a hard question. Who is the oldest living member of the Grand Ole Opry?"

I looked at Barry; he looked at me. We all looked at each other. "We don't know but they won't know either." New York/New York was mumbling amongst themselves. "We'll get 'em on the next question."

AJ took the paper from Melanie, and scribbled something. We passed it around.

Melanie nodded. "I'll go with Red's answer." Barry's date had said nothing since the game started.

The emcee was back at the microphone. "Time to read your answers. Team New York/New York what do you have?"

The captain, a thin middle aged man with sandy hair, stood up and said, "Roy Acuff?"

The crowd and the emcee groaned. "Sorry, New York/New York. Roy would be 101 if he were still alive, but he died years ago. The Professionals. Do you know the answer for the win?"

"We're not sure, but we're going to guess Hank Locklin." Melanie gave the answer. At least I knew who he was.

The emcee looked surprised. "That's right! Way to go guys . . . and gals. Hank Locklin. He recorded "Send Me the Pillow that You Dream On," "Please Help Me I'm Falling In Love With You," and a ton of other songs, and that's it. Enjoy yourselves everybody and drink responsibly." He shut the microphone and canned music began to play.

"Yes! Yes! Yes!" AJ was giving fist bumps to everyone on the team. "That was fun. When do we play next?"

Barry answered for the team. "Next Sunday. Not tomorrow. Next Sunday."

AJ looked at me. "Was that presumptuous? I sort of invited myself."

I gave her a hug. "Of course you're back next Sunday. We need you."

"Beginners luck. But I do know a lot of stuff." Seeing her smile, one would never have imagined how her week had started. Across the table Melanie snapped a picture.

We sat around talking for a while. Brian and Melanie finally left to go back to their place. Before we left, AJ and Barry's date went to the ladies' room; Barry and I waited at the table. "How did you meet her? When did you meet her? She's fabulous. And does she have a sister?"

"Yes, she does have a sister, but . . ."

"Just joking. About the sister, that is. She is fabulous though. She is funny, she is smart, and she looks hot."

"All of the above. She was singing karaoke at Jerry's when I went to pick up the key from Karen so I could house sit for the Brandenburgs. She was here for Fan Fair."

"You have all the luck. Karen called me to house-sit, but I was too tired from standing in line all day at Fan Fair to drop by Jerry's. I got a bunch of autographs, and you got Red. How long is she here for? You said she was here for Fan Fair."

"Hopefully, forever. She's transferring to Vanderbilt."

"She met you and she's . . ."

"No! She was planning to transfer to Vanderbilt. That was her plan from the very beginning."

Barry paused and ran something through his mind. "That's a song lyric. My plan from the very beginning. Ike and Tina Turner, 'I Think It's Gonna Work Out Fine.' Tina sings ninety percent of the lyrics, and that's one of the small parts that Ike sings."

That's Barry. Obscure songs. Obscure lyrics. I remembered the song—after he said that. "Hey, help me with this. It's a melody I can't get out of my head." I whistled the tune that AJ had been whistling in bed and at the crafts fair. Ta-da-Ta-da . . . Ta-da'-da . . . ta-da-da-da.

He played it over in his mind, then shook his head. "Sorry. No idea at all."

AJ and I stopped by the Bluebird Café for the late show before returning to the Brandenburg's. We walked the dogs in the yard, then I checked something on the Internet from Milton Brandenburg's office while AJ got ready for bed.

While I was on the computer she came up behind me and asked, "What are you looking up?"

I answered without turning around. "The stuff I didn't know tonight at trivia. Poisons and antidotes. Don't get too much of that in Music City. Someone wants to kill someone, they usually use a gun. This is the only way to learn. Miss something; study it. For instance, do you know what the antidote to anti-freeze poisoning is?"

"No idea."

"Alcohol. Ethylene glycol is what's poisonous in antifreeze, but it has to be metabolized to oxalic acid in order to kill someone. The enzyme that does that binds tightly to alcohol, so alcohol keeps the enzyme from working on the ethylene glycol. That's kind of neat. It means that if two guys drink antifreeze, the one that's drunk is the one that's going to survive. That's kind of interesting."

"Ooh. I have a smart boyfriend." She hugged my neck from behind.

"Just reading Wikipedia. Whatever else we are going to be, if we keep playing bar trivia we are going to be fountains of useless information. Next time I have to face down someone holding a gun I'm going to try boring them to death with facts like that."

"Might work" She kissed the back of my neck. "You're funny."

I turned around. "And you're . . . naked."

"It's warm in here, even with the air-conditioning, and you've seen it all. I didn't bring anything sexy to wear when I came down here. You," she kissed me on the lips, "were not part of the plan."

"You have a plan for everything?"

"I am completely out of plans. Just wish I could come up with some way to help Amy Elizabeth. Anyway, here's that picture I wanted to show you. The one where I'm naked. Amy Elizabeth wants to make it into some kind of poster."

I was speechless as I stared at the picture that Adele Federoff had taken from the front lawn of the Miller home. Finally, I said, "Not exactly a glamour shot, this is obviously from . . . that night."

"Obviously! Isn't it fabulous?"

"You think so?" I wasn't sure that fabulous was the right word.

"Yeah. I'm naked, bloody—not my blood, by the way—and triumphant. And Amy Elizabeth is dazed, looking up at me and starting to recover. She keeps saying she's a survivor, not a victim. Anyway, she says the picture shows how you can bounce back from the worst moment of your life. She's sort of 'in love' with that concept. It's her new mantra. She says she wants to put the photo on a poster, but I don't see how you could do that. What do you think?"

I was trying to imagine the picture in a different format. "Well, my first thought was that it was kind of gross. The nudity sure isn't erotic or obscene. It is sort of artistic. Can't even tell you are naked. I thought you were wearing a bloody t-shirt."

She pointed at the picture. "Naked. Left nipple. That's part of the problem."

"But it is kind of neat the way you seem to be looking at each other in a loving sisterly way."

"Yeah," she drew the word out so that it seemed to contain three syllables. "Do you want to know what she was saying to me when that picture was snapped."

"What?"

"She was saying, 'Idiot. It was your job to set the alarm.'"

I couldn't help but laugh. "Really?"

"In the house, she thanked me for saving her life. But that's what she was saying when the picture was snapped. I still think it's a cool picture, but to do it as a poster, you'd have to do it vertical, not horizontal."

"And the problem with that is?"

"I'll show you." AJ sat down at the computer, opened her e-mail, and downloaded a copy of the pictures that Adele Federoff had sent to her before she had left Highland Heights to travel to Nashville. She found the entire uncropped photo and printed it.

Despite the horror shown by the picture, AJ approached the situation objectively, as a problem in geometry and public standards. "If you run it horizontally, you can trim the photo without showing the nipple and still have enough of a picture. My right breast is behind Amy Elizabeth. That's what the Highland Heights paper did when they ran the photo. But, if you try and do it vertically, which is what you have to do to get anything big enough to put on a poster, my coochie shows. If only I had taken the time to put on a pair of panties. But I was so sticky from the blood that I didn't want to put on anything until I had a shower. Any ideas?"

We looked at the picture in silence. It had a surreal beauty. Life pulled from the edge of death. Triumph. Two sisters looking lovingly at each other—even if what was being said wasn't loving. Hell, you had to love someone to say something like that at a time like that. "Maybe unsolvable. Too bad. The more I look at it, the more I think it's a great picture, and no one is ever going to see it."

"Unless they get the Highland Heights Times. Circulation 1250."

"Fortunately, I have the real thing to look at. And you are extremely beautiful."

"And you are very sweet. Let's go to bed. Learning about poisons can wait."

"Poisons starting with letters S through Z, or go to bed with my amazing new girlfriend? I pick you."

"I told you I had a smart boyfriend . . . And guess what? You get a reward for being smart."

Chapter Ten

Sunday morning, AJ and I drove over to my parents' house to swap cars. Amy Beth was arriving that afternoon with several suitcases and I needed to borrow a car with better trunk space than AJ's Miata or my Lexus SC430. We could have taken both cars, but AJ wasn't confident about her ability to navigate around Nashville.

I get along ok with my parents. My father Melvin is a medical oncologist at the Vanderbilt Medical Center. If you let him get wound up telling stories or discussing sports, he can talk your ear off. His patients love him, which says something, since he was often the one breaking very bad news.

My dad has a simple philosophy of life. Treat people with respect. Don't spend money you don't have. Pray that you don't outlive either your brain or your money. To my knowledge, no one in the Aaron family had outlived their money. My great aunt Lillian had spent her final years in a nursing home, not recognizing her children, and my father considered it a tragedy beyond measure. One reason my dad could handle being a cancer doctor is that he knows that everybody dies of something and at least if you die of cancer you are likely to die while your brain is working, and you are still a person. My dad is as sharp as ever, but worries when he misplaces his keys or his glasses.

With me, my dad is usually a man of few words. "Take the keys. Leave your car and your keys in case something comes up. Bring my car back by tomorrow night."

"I'll have it back later today."

"Good."

AJ got out of the Lexus and into my father's Volvo sedan. I was almost headed down the driveway when my mother came outside. My mother is an interior designer with an eclectic group of clients. She decorated the Brandenburg house, which had appeared in Architectural Digest, and she decorated my condo. That's about as eclectic as you can get considering that the budget for the Brandenburg house was likely twenty times what I spent. I had no idea if Barry had spread the word that I was seeing someone new, but considering that my mother's priorities in life are grandchildren, grandchildren, and grandchildren, in that order, I was hoping to get away before my mother met AJ.

"I was looking out the window, Jonah, and just happened to see that you had someone with you in the car. Are you going to introduce me to her?"

"Of course, Mom." I introduced my mother to 'Red' and vice versa.

"Jonah, may I have a word with you, privately?" Her tone made it sound as if the future of the republic depended on what she was about to say. With my mother I never have any idea what to expect. Maybe she had noticed that AJ was wearing a Star of David around her neck and she was going to say something about that. I smiled at AJ as I walked about fifteen feet from the car.

In a very low whisper, my mother said, "Jonah, it's burnt orange. It's not red. You should know colors. You come from a family where interior design and color are very important."

"It's a nickname. Did you ever hear of anyone nicknamed 'Burnt Orange'?"

She thought it over. "Good point. But people should know their colors. Do you know how many clients tell me they want blue when they really want teal?"

"I get the point. Bye, mom."

"Nice to see you with someone again, Jonah." I waited for a "but" that never came.

"Nice to see you too, Mom." AJ had brought me luck. I had completed a conversation with my mother in which I had not been referred to as her underachieving investigator son. We headed to the airport before my luck changed.

If someone had told me that the woman that AJ and I met at the Nashville Airport that afternoon was destined for either fame or fortune, I would have laughed. Of course, it would have been impolite to laugh in the presence of a woman who was transported in a wheelchair from the arrival gate to where AJ and I were waiting at the exit from security. Amy Elizabeth was physically and emotionally drained. Amy Elizabeth hugged her sister, gave me a weak handshake, and managed to walk to baggage claim. "The Congressman packed everything for me. I didn't have the energy. I hope I brought what you wanted, AJ." I suspected that she had; she had brought herself.

Sunday in Nashville meant minimal traffic, and it took only twenty minutes to get to The Gulch. Amy Elizabeth stayed in the car with AJ while I made three trips to take the bags upstairs to my condo. We went to my parents' house to swap the cars and went on to the Brandenburg's to spend what I figured would be a lazy afternoon house-sitting. It didn't work out that way. Milton and Mona were back early, and they were arguing.

"Milton, to fly up to Chicago because this girl, this woman, won't take your phone calls is insane. WHY you want to sign her up is beyond me. Why you think YOU have a snowball's chance in hell of signing her is way beyond me, too." I had no desire to listen to an argument between the parents of my best friend, especially when they appeared to be arguing about some performer Milton wanted to represent. However, I wanted to say hello and drop off the keys before we were out the door. AJ was taking Amy Elizabeth on a brief tour, showing off the house where we had spent much of the weekend.

"Didja really see her, Mona? Stage presence. Can't teach it. Can't fake it. Some moron's gonna sign her. He'll set her up for some talks or for a bit part on TV. One of dose criminal investigation shows. Six months. History! Forgotten! If I sign her, she and I will figure out what she really wants. BANG! A once-in-a-lifetime act. Da girl is a friggin' natural. I can help da girl." Twenty seven years in Nashville and most of the time Milton sounded like he had left New York yesterday.

"Help her? I thought business is business. All of a sudden you're Mother Teresa?"

"Ah, forget it. Weekends are not for work. Isn't that what you always say? But you're da psychologist. You do dat work with kids who been abused. I can help dat girl."

Mona Brandenburg thought it over. "OK. But if you get in to see her, PLEASE tell her to get some therapy. I'll give you a list of names. People in the Chicago area who could work with a celebrity rape victim and not be bragging about the fact that they were the ones treating Amy Elizabeth Golden."

"Deal. I'm off to da airport. Bye."

I didn't believe what I was hearing. As far as I was concerned, AJ was the only one who felt that her sister had some sort of career ahead of her. Now Milton Brandenburg was seeing something I couldn't see. It had happened before with country singer Skylar Jones. I wasn't buying into it, but it wasn't for me to argue. Amy Beth's tour of the house, directed by AJ, had reached the kitchen a few moments earlier and they had heard the latter part of the discussion.

"Don't pack. Milton and Mona, there's two people I would like you to meet. This is my girl friend A . . ."

AJ interrupted. "Hi. I'm 'Red,' I'm Jonah's friend. Thanks for having him house sit. This place is incredibly lovely." And before Mona Brandenburg could offer thanks, AJ continued. "And this is my best friend in the whole world, Amy Elizabeth Golden from Highland Heights, Illinois. She's down here visiting me."

"Good to meet you. Gotta run . . ." Then he realized what he had heard. "You're friggin' yanking my chain aren't you?"

AJ shook her head.

"You're not joking. You're not joking are you, Red?" He shook hands with each of them. "Amy Elizabeth, can we move to my office down the hall? We gotta talk."

"Absolutely. Because I have some really cool ideas and you sound like you understand what I want to do better than I understand what I want to do. I have this idea of going on stage in front of this giant poster, but I can't figure out how to make the picture into a poster, and . . ." She was talking a mile a minute.

"I don't know what you wanna do, but I can listen, and I know show business. Hope dat don't offend you, calling it show business. You got a serious message but marketing it is show business. We can figure it out."

"Not offended at all. Where do I sign?"

Milton Brandenburg gulped. "I think you might wanna talk to an attorney, or to your family, or to someone first."

"I don't have an attorney. I don't trust my mother. I already used too much of Congressman Miller's time. The only person I trust is . . . 'Red.' She trusts Jonah and she told me Jonah said good things about you. So, give me a pen, show me where to sign, and let's get to work."

Over the next hour, while Red and I visited with Mona Brandenburg, Amy Elizabeth and Milton accomplished the following. Amy Elizabeth agreed to be in therapy for at least three months before doing any more public speaking. Amy Elizabeth wanted to 'make a move' while she was in the public eye. Milton convinced her that it was better to wait. Her mental health really did come ahead of his twenty percent.

While Amy Beth wanted to speak for free, Milton convinced her that if people paid nothing they would figure it was worth nothing and that a ten dollar fee would reduce the chance of getting rude hecklers. She would, after all, be speaking at college campuses or high schools. Milton hadn't decided which venue was most appropriate.

After a phone call and a fax, Milton purchased the rights to the photograph from Adele Federoff. She had retained all the rights to the picture when she had let the Highland Heights Times publish it. No one had ever paid for one of her photos and she was thrilled that Milton offered her $500 for her photo. She didn't even pay attention to the fact that Milton Brandenburg, who recognized the commercial potential of the picture, had thrown in a license fee of one dollar for every copy of the picture that was made. In the long run, the five hundred dollars would be dwarfed by the royalties.

Over the ensuing weeks, the photograph would be digitally modified. AJ's offending left nipple would be blurred out, and the blood on her upper chest, under her chin would be given a smooth curve, making it appear as if she was wearing a t-shirt. AJ hadn't chosen to put a pair of panties on over her bloodied torso, but the digitally created panties looked almost real—but somehow never looked quite right. Before the first posters were printed, Milton had an idea. Layla was digitally placed in AJ's left hand. Layla covered up AJ, and most of the not-quite-right-panties.

As we walked to the car to go out to dinner with the Brandenburgs, I asked AJ about something that had been bothering me, "What's with all this 'Red' stuff and you being her 'best friend', not her sister?"

She squeezed my hand. "No big deal. Amy Elizabeth wants to be a star. I want to be nearly invisible. Plus there is a Plan B. And if we have to go there, it will be messy if everyone down here knows me as AJ Golden. Trust me. This is best for everyone."

"What's Plan B? What's Plan A for that matter?"

"Just trust me. Nothing bad. Doesn't matter if I'm AJ or Red. What I am is YOURS!" She threw her arms round me and kissed me. I had found a woman who was smart, funny, hot, ambitious, and who liked me. I suspected that she would get bored with me; she was only twenty-one. But it was likely to be wonderful while it lasted.

Plan A and potentially Plan B had to deal with how to get Amy Beth back in the public eye after what would be at least a three month absence. Fame is fickle. If Amy Beth took several months to get her head together, there needed to be a way to get her back in the public eye before her first performance. Over dinner with the Brandenburgs, I learned how I fit into the picture.

Milton Brandenburg had finished a toast to Amy Elizabeth and turned to AJ and me. "I don't wanna influence your decision, but as a finder's fee, for getting Amy Elizabeth to me, I'm gonna give a share of my commission to da two of ya. Two and a half percent of everything to 'Red' and two and a half percent to Jonah." It was a sweet gesture which I figured amounted to two and a half percent of next to nothing, but he didn't have to do it. "For taking on da case of finding Andrea Golden, I'll pay your usual fee of $500 a day plus expenses, maximum of ten days, plus, a $2000 bonus if you find her—regardless of whether or not she goes with da plan. Whatta ya say?"

"What if she's dead? I mean with everything that's happened in the last week she hasn't come forward, hasn't made a phone call, and hasn't sent an e-mail. Right?" AJ and Amy Beth nodded.

"You get da fee for your time no matter what. If she's dead, and you prove it, you get da bonus as well."

I thought it over. No leads. The woman had been gone twelve years. All I had to do was find Andrea Golden and—best case scenario—convince her to tell the story of her life after Kenton, Tennessee as a means of propelling Amy Beth back into the public eye. Overall, the plan made sense, but finding Andrea Golden was going to be nearly impossible. I looked at Amy Beth. I looked at Milton. I started to shake my head. This was likely to be a colossal waste of time.

Then I looked at AJ. If I turned it down, all I would be was a rich kid playing at being an investigator. One week earlier, against all odds, AJ had raced up the stairs and had pulled off an incredible feat. How could AJ respect me if I ran from a challenge?

"I'll take the job—but there a condition. I'm dating 'Red', and Amy Elizabeth is her friend. My ability to get work in this town depends on keeping things confidential. You're the one hiring me, Milton, so ordinarily I would tell everything I learn to you and only you. But in this case I don't want to end up in a position where I learn something that you don't want me to share with the ladies. As long as

I have your permission to tell them whatever I learn, then I'll take the job. I don't want to tell them something and then have you feel that I broke a confidence. As you know, Milton, sometimes when I work for you, there are secrets that have to be kept." It is always good to plan ahead.

Milton knew exactly what I meant. "Not an issue. Fine with me."

As we left the restaurant and walked to the car, AJ squeezed my hand. "You think she's dead, don't you? Amy Elizabeth and I figure that she's dead."

"It would explain a lot of things, but you never know. I never jump to conclusions. What I do know is that we have to get back to my place so I can find out everything you know about Andrea. You two are the only leads I have."

"Works for me. And I finally get to see your condo."

Chapter Eleven

AJ and Amy Elizabeth were admiring the view from my living room. "You can see half the city from here."

"Not quite, but it is a great view." My condo was on the ninth floor of an eleven story building. Doctors, lawyers, and a few successful young songwriters lived there. My friend Skylar Jones, the Country Music Association nominee for best new act of 2002, lived on the tenth floor. The living room had glass windows that extended from the floor to the top of the twelve foot ceilings on the north and east walls. The west wall had a fifty-two inch flat screen plasma TV. The condo had three bedrooms and three baths. The master bedroom had two walk-in closets and a master bath suite with a steam shower and a Jacuzzi tub. The furniture was all Scandanavian modern. I had regarded it as a great starter place for a young couple. In the previous four months I had spent more time alone in the condo, watching television or reading, than I cared to remember.

"Jonah Aaron, do you really live here? This place is spotless, and everything is put away." Amy Elizabeth would forever call me Jonah Aaron, as if there were another Jonah in the room. Maybe she just enjoyed giving everyone else two names when she was about to have only one, Amibeth. "The only person I know who could live like this is AJ. She's a neat freak, too." Amy Elizabeth wandered over to the sofa sectional where I was sitting.

"I just like being organized."

AJ was still at the window. "What's that river called?"

"The Cumberland."

"How high is that bridge over it?"

"I don't know . . . Twenty feet. Thirty feet. Why are you asking?"

AJ paused before answering. "Plan B . . . If finding Andrea doesn't pan out I was thinking about jumping off the bridge."

"What? You're kidding aren't you?"

"Not for real. I was thinking of faking a suicide. Then, instead of using Andrea's story as a way to get Amy Elizabeth back in the public eye, Amy Elizabeth could give this really beautiful eulogy for me and launch her career that way, and . . . What's the matter Jonah? You think it's crazy?"

"You have . . . interesting ideas. This is just a bad one. It's only thirty feet high, so unless they found a body, they wouldn't even assume you were dead. Thirty feet is height of the high platform in the Olympics. Not that many people have jumped into the Cumberland, but when they do, they either survive or the body washes up. Plus, there are homeless people who camp out on the bank of the river, downtown. People would see what really happened, and the police would find them. And there are people like us in the condos who have a view of the bridge. I think that's enough reasons for now."

"OK. I'll keep it in mind. But it's a really great eulogy. Amy Elizabeth could finally apologize for stealing my boyfriend when I was in the ninth grade."

"AJ, he wasn't your boyfriend. You had smiled at him three times in study hall and he had never said a word to you. I have nothing to apologize for."

AJ thought it over. "Let's work on Plan A."

Before we could get to work, Amy Elizabeth said, "That's fine. But I'd like to see where I'm staying, first. Which bedroom is mine?"

The condo had a master bedroom, a guest bedroom, and a third bedroom which was empty. I pointed to the guest bedroom. "I put your suitcases in there. It really isn't decorated much. And please don't tease me about the poster. It's a collectible."

Amy Elizabeth entered the guest bedroom and turned on the light. "AJ, come here. You have to see this."

AJ entered what had become her sister's room, and a broad smile filled her face. "Boy, that brings back memories. We had that poster of the Dana Twins on the wall of our bedroom in Highland Heights. And yours is autographed. Where did you get this?"

"Long story. Let's just say I got the poster as a gift and leave it at that. How old were you back then?" I didn't feel like doing the math.

"I was fourteen; AJ was thirteen." Amy Elizabeth was tapping on the glass that covered the poster. "Ours wasn't autographed. An autographed poster must be worth a fortune now, since they're dead."

AJ immediately contradicted her sister. "They are not dead!" Then she looked at me and said quietly, "Well, no one really knows. I like the other version of the story better."

"Me too. And my autographed poster isn't really worth that much. Most people have almost forgotten all about them."

As pictured on the poster, the Dana Twins, Richie and Stevie, were androgynous twelve-year-olds who had four consecutive top ten hits between December 1995 and August 1996. According to rumor, their parents were Christian fundamentalists whose objections to their boys performing in public had limited their career to two CD's and a pair of grainy music videos. The Dana

Twins never made a personal appearance and never gave a single interview. Reliable information on the Dana Twins was meager, to say the least.

During the time that the Dana Twins were popular, teen-aged girls argued over which Dana Twin was the cutest. With their identical blonde Beatle mop haircuts, white sports jackets, and Roy Orbison style sunglasses, it was impossible to tell them apart. Brian Brandenburg and I were juniors in high school when the Dana Twins were at the peak of their popularity, and since Milton Brandenburg was their manager, girls assumed we had inside information about the duo. We always told the same story. We claimed that the Dana Twins didn't exist and that their sound had been created by an imaginative sound engineer playing in a studio. It was a perfectly plausible story, but no one ever believed us.

On the way to what would have been their first concert performance in Reno, Nevada, the Dana Twins, if there were Dana Twins, vanished on the night of June 12, 1996, a date that was said to be their thirteenth birthday. The most widely accepted explanation for the end of the Dana Twins career was that a private plane carrying them from Seattle, Washington to Reno, Nevada had crashed near the Washougal River in Washington state, and that there was a cover-up to protect the sensibilities of their young fans. No plane wreckage was ever found; no bodies were ever recovered. However, since this is the same general area where the noted airplane hijacker, D. B. Cooper, disappeared, that scenario is not beyond the realm of possibility.

Other fans, AJ Golden apparently among them, believed the story that their parents had changed their minds and had decided that show business was an inappropriate place for their children. According to that theory, with adolescence approaching, the family arranged to have the children disappear dramatically without having people point to the twins and ask, "Didn't you used to be . . .?" If that were true, it was a great career move. Two of their four hit singles, reached the top ten after they disappeared. While most fans expected that someday someone would find the skeletons of those cute little boys, or what was left of their airplane, as of June 2004, that hadn't happened.

I had no idea if anyone was still searching for the Dana Twins, but I was about to embark on a search for another teenager who had apparently vanished from the face of the earth in the 1990's, Andrea Golden. Amy Elizabeth, AJ, and I were back in the living room of my condo, and I was in full investigator mode. "Why don't the two of you tell me everything about Andrea? In fact why don't we start with Mary Nell and The Reverend and their families? Maybe there is someone, a grandparent, or an aunt or uncle, who might know something."

At the same time, both women said, "Isn't anyone."

AJ added, "Except for us, and Mary Nell, all the family is dead."

Amy Elizabeth nodded her agreement.

The story of Mary Nell and Nathaniel Golden was fairly simple. Mary Nell Johnson was raised in Appleton, Wisconsin, south of Green Bay. She was an only child and was born when her parents were in their late forties. Mary Nell hated the cold weather and had come south to go to college at Union, a small Christian school in Jackson, Tennessee. Jackson is a modest sized city a little less than two thirds of the way between Nashville and Memphis on Interstate 40. Mary Nell's parents had died shortly after she graduated college and Mary Nell had worked as a secretary, on campus, where she met Nathaniel Golden.

The Reverend had received his calling to the ministry in his early thirties. His father owned a car dealership in Jackson. There had been a brother who had died in Vietnam. The Reverend's mother had passed away when he was five, and he had been raised by Grandpa Golden—as the girls called him. Grandpa Golden was still alive when Mary Nell, AJ, and Amy Elizabeth had left Tennessee shortly after the Reverend's death, but he had died shortly thereafter. Considering Andrea's experiences with her father, and considering that Grandpa Golden had a reputation as a strict disciplinarian, AJ and Amy Elizabeth doubted that Andrea would have contacted him. It didn't matter, since it was, literally, a dead end. The only interesting fact that I learned was that Nathaniel Golden had a large life insurance policy that facilitated the purchase of a nice home in Highland Heights, and eventually led to Mary Nell's meeting James Miller, who had been a first-time candidate for Congress in 1998. The two had married in 2001.

"What was Andrea like? I mean what did she like to do? What did she want to be?"

Amy Elizabeth answered first. "Well, remember, Jonah Aaron, she was seven years older than me, eight years older than AJ. We didn't have the same friends. All I remember is that she read a lot—mysteries mainly. I remember her reading those old English detective novels, Dorothy Sayers and Agatha Christie. Then she started reading all the detective fiction she could get her hands on—John D. McDonald—the Travis McGee mysteries, Robert B. Parker, and who was that other one AJ?"

"Sue Grafton. Andrea was up to 'H is for Homicide' when she left . . . Do you think Andrea could have become a writer? They say that the way to become a writer is to read a lot, and she sure had something to write about."

"Anything is possible. It would be ironic if I was hired to find someone and they were hiding in plain sight, writing fiction under a pen name. Probably not very likely."

Amy Elizabeth chimed in. "A lot happier thought than thinking that she's dead."

"Exactly. But what did she want to be when she grew up?"

They answered simultaneously. "OUT OF KENTON." And they laughed. "Home of the white squirrels." They could tell by my expression that I was lost. AJ explained. "There are four places in the United States that call themselves the home of the white squirrels. Kenton, Tennessee is one of them. I don't know about the others, but when all you have to brag about is a bunch of albino squirrels—well you don't have much to talk about."

"I get the picture. But back to Andrea. When did she leave? The papers said it was when she was seventeen. In my mind I've been visualizing this high school dropout, and you're telling me she was an avid reader. Not that people who read books can't drop out of school, but AJ told me that the abuse stopped at fourteen. What am I missing?"

AJ looked at Amy Elizabeth. "We may as well tell him."

Chapter Twelve

"High school was hard for Andrea. She had a 'reputation'. She got around. And around. And around . . ." AJ made a circular motion with her index finger. "Once she accused daddy and no one believed her things were horrible." AJ paused. "And then there was the abortion." AJ whispered the last word. "She was sixteen. It wasn't Daddy's baby; that stuff stopped at fourteen. I told you about that time with the rifle. It was some boy. One day she was pregnant and in tears that her life was over. Next day, after a trip to Jackson, everything was fine. Mama might have killed her if she knew about the abortion. That's not a figure of speech. Mama wasn't pro-life as much as anti-abortion. If she wasn't anti-abortion, I don't think any of the three of us would have seen the light of day. Anyway, I don't know who took Andrea to Jackson. It wasn't the boy. Andrea told us that much."

Amy Elizabeth continued the tale. "But Andrea wasn't a dropout. She skipped a grade before we were even born. She must have been really good in school before Daddy started messing with her. Anyway, she graduated in June of '92. Then she took a job in Jackson. She bought this car, an old beat-up Plymouth Satellite. The color was sassy grass green. That was Andrea. Sassy. Grass—smoked a lot of pot. Not sure about the green. It took every penny she had. And she went to work in Jackson. But she came home every night, at first. I think she wanted to be sure we were ok. We told her we were fine, but she kept driving back to Kenton every single night. It was like fifty miles each way. The gas must have cost nearly ten dollars a day, and she couldn't have been making that much. She could have stayed with someone in Jackson. Lots of girls went to Jackson when they graduated high school."

"What was she doing in Jackson?"

The women looked at each other. Amy Elizabeth answered. "We have no idea. Working somewhere. I think it was a glass company, but I don't know which one. And then Daddy got sick, right about the same time. Andrea had been working in Jackson a couple of weeks. I know it was that long because graduation was on Flag Day, June 14. Andrea started working in Jackson right after that, and by the Fourth of July, Daddy was too sick to go to the town square to see the fireworks.

He had these bad stomach pains and his hair fell out. Mama never said cancer, but we knew. The lady down the block had cancer, and went to Jackson for the chemotherapy, and her hair fell out, so we knew what it was." You didn't have to have a father who was a cancer specialist to know what she was talking about.

AJ took over the story. "After the Fourth of July, Andrea quit coming back home at night. Daddy died July 25th. It sounds cruel to say it, but it was one of the happiest days of our lives—me and AJ, I mean. I don't know how Mary Nell felt about it. But at least we knew we didn't have to worry about him coming into one of our beds—ever. And the last time we saw Andrea was at the funeral. She came back to Kenton for the funeral."

"When she gave you the pendants, right?"

Amy Elizabeth answered. "She gave ME a pendant. AJ bought hers just a couple of years ago."

I did a rough calculation in my head. "Wait. Did she still have the car at the funeral?"

"Sure. She drove in. She made a comment about wanting to be sure he was dead, spit in his face right in the casket, and took off. We followed her to the parking lot. That's when she gave me the pendant, kissed us both goodbye, and took off in the Plymouth."

"What's the pendant worth? I hate to talk about money, since it's got sentimental value, but what's it worth. Any idea?"

The women looked at each other, smiled, and sang in sing-song harmony. "Been there, done that, got the t-shirt."

"We thought of that too. We had it appraised at $1400. And where on earth does a seventeen year-old girl with no money and a high school education come back a couple of weeks later with a pendant worth $1400? Not many explanations. Right, Jonah?"

"You figure she was a hooker or a stripper."

They nodded. I nodded back. There were other possible explanations, but none as likely to explain how Andrea had paid for the pendant. That would certainly fit with a girl who had been sexually abused between the ages of ten and fourteen, but there was no point jumping to conclusions.

All sorts of information is available on the Internet. I had software that could help me find birth records, death records, some marriage and divorce records, and professional license information, but there was no registry for teenage prostitutes and no one in the business was likely to remember a girl from twelve years ago even if she had the habit of reading detective novels. If they did remember her, they weren't likely to admit it.

"Give me a couple minutes. I want to look for something on the internet. I have some investigator software."

"What are you doing?" AJ and Amy Elizabeth moved behind me and watched over my shoulder as I worked on my portable computer.

I googled Andrea Golden and found over a thousand listings, most of which turned out to be related to the events on Woodland Hills Lane and Amy Elizabeth's press conference. I ran my locator software. I had no idea how good the records were for middle of nowhere Tennessee before 1992. It was better than I expected. I found birth records for Andrea, Amy Elizabeth, and Abigail Josephine Golden. I found a death report on Nathaniel Golden. I found no death certificate for Andrea Golden. At least it didn't look as if she had died in Tennessee. Of course, if she had met a bad end, the body might not have been found or even identified. I set the software to run on all fifty states. In the morning I would ask my friends in the Nashville Police Department to check their data bases for information on Andrea. The warehouse shooting made it easy to call in a small favor.

"The T181 thing. Any idea what it means?"

Amy Elizabeth looked at AJ. "You tell him. I'm tired."

"We have searched the internet for hours. As a lark, we even had one of the Congressman's aides look into it for us. He spent two days on it. Nothing. T181 is a scientific calculator. Don't think that's it. There is Japanese currency that was issued during World War II for use in Australia that has a T181 code. There is an archeological site in Hawaii called T181. Never checked it out. If you want to take us to Hawaii, we'll go." The girls giggled. "There's a piece of scientific equipment, T181, that analyzes raw radar data. Oh, and of course, Tennessee Highway 181 is located forty miles west of Kenton. It's the Great River Road. Before we left Tennessee, when we were kids, we had the older sister of one of our classmates spend half a day driving us up and down that road. We didn't see anything that seemed relevant. There were houses, a fruit stand, and a gas station. And there was no reason for Andrea to be on that road. It wasn't the direct route to Memphis, or anywhere we could think of going. Middle of nowhere to the middle of nowhere. We're pretty sure that's not it, but it isn't that far from Kenton, so who knows?"

T181 seemed to be another dead end. "Did Andrea say anything when she gave you the pendant?"

AJ answered. "G-H-T-W-H-T!"

"God helps those who help themselves."

"Right, Jonah. That's what she said. Then she got in her car, and that's the last we ever saw of her. Not a phone call. Not a post card. Nothing. There was one thing that was strange. Andrea hated Mary Nell as much as she hated Daddy. But when she came to the funeral, before doing her thing and saying that she wanted to be sure he was really dead, she walked up to Mary Nell and hugged her and they had a good cry. Andrea told her not to worry, that things would be fine. It was . . . spooky."

"Maybe Andrea knew about the insurance. The whole family-what was left of it—was going to be able to get out of Kenton."

"Maybe. It was just so strange. I mean I never saw Andrea hug Mary Nell. Anyway, that's all we know. Right, Amy Elizabeth? Did all of this help you Jonah?"

"Not much. I guess I have a place to start. Glass businesses in Jackson. See if I can find the one where she worked and see if they have a forwarding address for her. Can't be that many of them."

Amy Elizabeth was falling asleep on the loveseat. AJ shook her gently, escorted her to her bedroom and then came back to me.

"You may be stuck with us a while. This place is so nice, it's not going to be easy leaving it. It wouldn't be easy leaving you." She gave me a hug.

It looked like this was going to become a very long first date. I wasn't about to complain. "Let's go to bed. I'm going to be on the road early tomorrow. I'm going to drive to Kenton."

"I'm going to miss you."

"I'm going to miss you too . . . What's so funny?"

"It's eleven fifty-three on Sunday night. I was just thinking where I was exactly a week ago tonight. I didn't miss either of them." She pointed her index finger like a gun. "BANG. BANG."

"Hard to miss at pointblank range with a shotgun."

"Lo siento . . . I've come a long way . . . And you've been a big help."

"My pleasure." I kissed her lightly. "Hang on. Got to check the computer before we go to bed."

My software had quit searching for death certificates on Andrea Golden. There were six women named Andrea Golden who had died in the United States between 1992 and 2004. None of them was close to the right age. The data base was incomplete but it was an encouraging sign.

A good night's sleep, and off to Kenton. Or so I thought. While I had been checking the computer AJ had changed out of the tailored shirt and blue jeans that she had worn during the day. "AJ, where did you get that?"

She was wearing a diaphanous, floor length black nightgown. The deep v neck went to her waist. "Bought it three years ago. I was saving it for a special occasion. I had Amy Elizabeth bring it down from Highland Heights. This may be as special as it's ever going to get. Me and you. And you could be gone a whole week. I wanted you to see me in it."

If I didn't come back until I found Andrea Golden, I would probably be gone forever. Fortunately, Milton had only offered to pay for ten days. "The memory of you in that nightgown will keep me warm at night. Thank you for calling us special."

"We are special." She flashed a wicked smile and pulled the nightgown over her head, walked over and gave me a very friendly kiss. "How about the memory of me without the nightgown?"

"For a woman who hadn't had sex in years, you are turning out to be very amorous."

"I'm making up for lost time."

I put my hands on her shoulders, looked her in the eyes, and began to softly and very slowly sing the words from the Dana Twins first hit song, a remake of the 1960's so-called bubble gum hit, "Yummy, Yummy, Yummy."

> Girl you're such a sweet thing.
> Good enough to eat thing.
> And that's a-what I'm gonna do.

AJ interrupted my singing. "Jonah! That was such a sweet and innocent little song the way those little boys sang it. You made that sound absolutely erotic like you were going to . . ." She paused. "I was twelve years old then. I'm grown up now. I like your way much better."

I suspected that I might be getting a late start to the middle of nowhere.

Chapter Thirteen

According to Brett Phillips, author of the eponymous Brett's blog, the MAJOR CITIES in the state of Tennessee are Memphis, Nashville, Chattanooga, and Knoxville. In addition, Jackson, Murfreesboro, Clarksville and Johnson City are CITIES with a population of more than 50,000 people. There are about forty SMALL CITIES in Tennessee with a population between 10,000 and 50,000.

TOWNS are defined by Brett Phillips as having at least one traffic light and either a McDonald's or a Dairy Queen. A SMALL TOWN has no traffic lights, but does have a four way stop; it may or may not have a Hardee's or a Dairy Queen. A VERY SMALL TOWN has no stop lights, has a four way stop, but no fast food restaurants. A REALLY SMALL TOWN has no four-way stop signs, just a stop sign where the highway intersects the main street of town. Occasionally very small towns and really small towns have signs stating, "You are now entering . . . ." and "You are now leaving . . ." The proximity of those signs determines where the really small town stands on the Phillips scale, but I don't remember the details except that it includes such factors as whether or not there is a post office, a hardware store, and/or a gas station.

I have nothing against small towns. People in small towns are courteous to visitors, regardless of what they may say behind our backs when we leave. Despite the view of a recent vice presidential candidate, I don't believe that small town America is any more or less American than urban America. It is just different.

I present the Phillips scale of towns for two reasons. First, I thought about it as I drove from Nashville past a number of small towns on the way toward Jackson on Monday morning. The hills of Tennessee are lovely, but as AJ and Amy Elizabeth would say, "Been there, done that, got the T-shirt." I had taken the drive many times; it was incredibly boring.

Secondly, Brett Phillips plays a major role in the story of Amibeth, and with the traffic moving seventy miles an hour and nothing happening, this is as good a time as any to introduce him. Brett Phillips grew up in Memphis, Tennessee; his parents were dentists. His father was African-American, his mother was Korean. If you imagine a young Tiger Woods without the golf talent and without the girlfriends you have the general idea. In 1981, at the age of nine, he started his first business, buying and selling baseball cards. I suspect that people in Memphis laughed at the handsome young man who wore a business suit to the ubiquitous card shows that graced the shopping malls of America in the 1980's, especially when everyone else considered a shirt with a collar as being overdressed.

Brett's motto, as printed on his business card, was simple, "Buy at a penny, sell at two pennies; do it a hundred million times; retire a millionaire." Selling one hundred million baseball cards in the 1980's would have been difficult. First of all, buying a hundred million baseball cards at a penny each would have cost a million dollars, and Brett Phillips started his business with a little over eight hundred dollars. The true business model was simple, "Buy low, sell high," which was more easily achieved, especially in a hobby where some of the people who bought and sold the cards also published the price guides that said what the cards were allegedly worth. Buying a baseball player's first card for a quarter or a dollar, and then selling the card for ten or twenty dollars when the player became a star, was an easy way to make money. Of course, if you didn't get out at the right time, you ended up with a lot of worthless cardboard.

Brett Phillips figured out how to time the market to his advantage. Since he knew that the dealers wrote the price guides, he realized that baseball card prices would never go down, they would simply go flat. As he later explained it to me, "When the hobby publications started talking about football cards instead of baseball cards, it meant that baseball cards were dead and it was time to get out."

It was a story I heard many times, because Brett Phillips was my roommate at Vanderbilt during my junior and senior year. At Vanderbilt, where many students came from money, Brett Phillips was a self-made millionaire. It is relatively easy to become a millionaire in Belle Meade, Tennessee. All one has to do is to inherit several million dollars from a parent, screw up, and be left with a million dollars. Brett Phillips made his own money.

Brett didn't make a million dollars buying and selling baseball cards, but by the time he got out of the hobby in 1990, the same year in which he graduated high school, he had run his eight hundred dollar investment into nearly a quarter of a million dollars. The real money came from what he did next. Instead of going to college, like anyone else in his social strata with his good grades would have been expected to do, he went to work.

On Sunday evening, AJ, Amy Elizabeth and I had speculated that there weren't many jobs around Kenton, Tennessee in 1992, that would have enabled Andrea Golden, with only a high school education, to make enough money in a few weeks to buy the jeweled pendant that she had given to her sister at their father's funeral. In 1990, Brett Phillips left Memphis, Tennessee with a high school education and became a multi-millionaire. He took his mathematical skills to Redmond, Washington where he spent eight years writing software code for a very well known company. I would tell you the name of the company, but as Brett once stated in his blog, "If you don't get money for product placement, why give anyone free advertising?" However, Brett dropped the phrase, "Bill Gates made me a wealthy man," into enough conversations that people knew exactly where he had spent his years between high school and college.

Before he returned to college, Brett had started writing his blog about life, technology, and the randomness of the universe. Even before I met him, I had started reading his blog because he was one of the first people in the country to explain winning strategies for fantasy baseball and fantasy football leagues, strategies based on mathematics. Mathematics is one of the few things at which I am good. While most college jocks at Vanderbilt majored in human and organizational development, I majored in mathematics. Of course, anyone looking objectively at my record as a special teams player for Vanderbilt football would likely conclude that I was not a college jock, but that is another matter.

Brett Phillips graduated from Vanderbilt at the age of thirty-one, winning the Founder's Medal for being first in the class of 2002. I graduated in the top quarter of the class which was good enough for me. After graduation, Brett returned to the Seattle area and went to work as a self proclaimed "consultant and problem solver." That means that he occasionally needs a licensed investigator to deal with issues that are more physical than mental. I have been employed by him on several occasions. More importantly, I still read his blog religiously, including the humorous reminiscences about life on a high school basketball team travelling to what he defined as small towns, very small towns, and really small towns in Tennessee. He was, in 2004, among the funniest writers of whom no one had ever heard. Ironically, the fact that almost no one read his blog ended up working to his advantage.

It was nine thirty when I got to Jackson. There are fourteen listings in the phone directory under glass. The largest company is Thompson Glass, three miles north of Jackson on Highway 45. I went there first, hoping to find that Andrea Golden had worked there and—if I was really lucky—finding that she had left a forwarding address. I had my story, which is to say my convenient lie, worked out long before I reached Jackson.

Thompson Glass occupies a medium sized warehouse. Yellow paint was flaking off the brick exterior. I parked in one of the three spaces marked 'Visitors Only". The heat in the parking lot was merely uncomfortable on the way to being unbearable. The receptionist behind the counter was occupied with a customer on the phone when I arrived, but finally was able to give me her attention. "How can I help you, sir."

"Well, maybe I can help you." I handed her a business card reading 'Jonah Aaron, Location Scout, Brandenburg Entertainment.' With nice paper and a good printer one can create a business card that says just about anything and I carry a wide variety of cards in my glove box. "You heard about that shooting up near Chicago, the one where the Congressman's daughter got assaulted?"

"Who didn't? That poor girl. Glad her sister got 'em though. They're from around here. The girls, that is. Kenton. About sixty miles up the road."

"I know. That's why I'm here. Brandenburg Entertainment has an option on a movie based on the lives of the Golden sisters and I'm trying to find out what I can about the oldest Golden sister, Andrea."

"Didn't know there was a third one."

"Well there is, and the third sister, Andrea, might have worked here. At least that's what we heard. The movie is going to get shot in Nashville, for the most part, but we figured that if we do a scene about the time that Andrea Golden worked in Jackson, we might as well be accurate. That sign outside, the one that says 'Thompson Glass' would look real nice in the movie, but we need to know if she worked here. It would have been 1992, twelve years ago. Do your records go back that far?"

"I'll check in back."

I waited, examining a University of Tennessee football schedule for the upcoming season and a listing of events at Union University in Jackson.

"Sorry. The records go back to 1986, but we have no record of an Andrea Golden."

I showed her Andrea's high school graduation picture, one that Amy Elizabeth and AJ had given me the night before. She shook her head. I thanked her for her time.

"You come on back, you hear," which is Southern for 'Goodbye and thanks for wasting my time.'

That was so much fun, at least compared to the one hundred and twenty mile drive to Jackson, that I tried the other glass companies before heading to Kenton. At the ninth stop, Pilson Automotive Glass, I got a hit. Maureen Templeton, the sixtyish year old woman with horn-rimmed glasses, who was the receptionist, secretary, and billing clerk had worked at Pilson's for over twenty years. She didn't recognize the name, Andrea Golden, but she agreed to check. It's amazing what people will do for the chance that a movie studio will camp out in their parking lot. She came back with a thin manila folder.

"Andrea Golden worked here from June 15, 1992 to July 1, 1992. Miscellaneous clerical. Means that she did odd jobs around the office here." She pointed to a girl seated at a large grey metal desk, implying that she now held what was once Andrea's position. "Can't tell you more than that."

"Wonderful! That sign out front will look fabulous in the movie. If we go ahead with the picture, I'll be back for a release. Is there a forwarding address by any chance?"

She shook her head. "There's a note here that she was paid in cash—guess she had no social security number—and picked up her pay personally after she was fired. No forwarding address.

"Fired?" That was interesting. How does one get fired from a job that requires almost no skills? "Does it say why she was fired? Just curious."

"Loitering in unauthorized areas. That's our phrase for going where she shouldn't have been." She whispered so that the girl at the other desk wouldn't hear. "Some of the young girls who have worked here chase after the men on the work floor and use the chemical storeroom as a place to uh . . . get together if you get my drift. We keep it locked now. The state got on us for worker safety, but back then some of the girls used to fool around with the men in the storeroom. Can't say for sure that was it, but . . . more than likely that's why they let her go."

Now I knew where Andrea Golden had worked in Jackson, and it was a dead end. I thanked Maureen Templeton for her time. It was only eleven thirty. I could get to Kenton by half past noon. I was no nearer to finding Andrea Golden than I had been when I had left Nashville but this was fun. I was even starting to look forward to seeing the movie about the Golden girls until I realized that I had invented the whole thing.

In his blog, Brett Phillips once discussed travelling to a basketball game played at the University Tennessee Martin campus, a place he described as being twenty miles from the middle of nowhere. The middle of nowhere, at least the West Tennessee version of same, was described by mathematics major Brett Phillips in the following manner. "Bisect the segment of US 40 that runs west southwest from Nashville to Memphis. You will find a point on the Nashville side of Jackson. Draw a perpendicular line from that point to the northwest corner of the state of Tennessee near Reelfoot Lake and the New Madrid fault. Bisect that line, and you have the middle of nowhere." If you travel to that location on the map, you will find yourself in a charming little community with an area of two square miles, and a population just over thirteen hundred. Kenton. Tennessee.

Chapter Fourteen

I drove north on Highway 45, passing the Gibson County High School along the way. I passed the public square and saw the sign 'Welcome to Kenton, Tennnessee. Home of the White Squirrel. Established 1872.' A large white squirrel was pictured in the top center of the sign. I contemplated making up a story that I was researching a movie on giant killer white squirrels, but I doubted the story would be necessary. This was small town America. People loved helping strangers.

I continued six blocks to Easter Street, passing two small restaurants in the process, and made a right turn. If I had gone one more block on Highway 45 before turning off, I would have passed the sign saying "You are now leaving Kenton."

I drove two blocks on Easter, made a left turn, and there it was, a small ranch house, probably a thousand to twelve hundred square feet, where AJ and Amy Elizabeth had grown up as part of Mary Nell and Nathaniel Golden's dysfunctional family. I knocked and from inside I heard a woman's voice. "We don't want any."

"I'm not selling. I'm trying to find out something about Andrea Golden, a girl from the family who used to own this house."

"Don't want any. Go 'way."

It took seven houses before a middle aged man came out on the porch to talk. I explained that I was looking into the whereabouts of Andrea Golden. "You a reporter?"

"No. Private investigator."

"Some reporters came by over the weekend. Everybody's sick of talkin', 'specially when they don't have anythin' to say. Reporters ask questions and it's like we knew what was goin' on in the Golden house and did nothin'. Truth is, once that girl started talkin', a lot of people stopped goin' to his church. Got very empty 'round there. People didn't know what was true, but they didn't want their kids there. I sure didn't want my kids there."

"Do you have any idea what happened to Andrea?"

He shook his head. "No. I just remember her showin' up at the funeral. She said what a lot of people were thinkin'. We came to see that he was dead too, so we could move on. And we have. There's been a lot of talk since . . . since what happened up north, and no one knows anythin' about Andrea. Heck, we didn't even know where the rest of the family had moved. As soon as Reverend Golden was in the ground, the house went up for sale, and in a couple of months, they was gone."

"Can you think of anybody who might know anything?"

He thought it over. "Try the high school. Someone might know somethin'. I do remember some things about those girls growing up though."

"What?"

"They almost never stayed in the house. They were always outside, sittin' on the porch readin'. Rain, shine, summer, winter, they did not like bein' in the house. Can't blame 'em."

"I can understand that."

"And one other thing. The little one. Abby Jo. Cute little tomboy. Whenever the kids played tag, she could run down anyone, even the older boys. She was quick."

"She ran track at Northwestern."

"I read that. Not surprised. She was the only happy one. Andrea kept to herself until she was about fourteen, then it was always boys, boys, boys. Not to speak bad about a girl whose daddy was inappropriate, but she had round heels. The middle one, Amy Elizabeth, always walked around with a frown on her face. But Abby Jo, she always looked like no matter what life threw at her, she knew she could handle it. Let me tell you a story."

We sat on his front step and he continued, "One day, Abby Jo and Amy Elizabeth and two boys were walkin' home from where the school bus dropped them off. The girls must have been eight or nine; the boys were likely ten and eleven, the Sharkley brothers. Not bad boys. Little wild. Anyway, one of the Sharkley boys started throwing pebbles at the two girls. Nothin' huge. Just the kind of stupid things kids do. I was out waterin' the lawn. Before I could say anything, one of the pebbles, guess it was a big one, hit Amy Elizabeth in he forehead and she started to bleed. Abby Jo got ticked off. She started hittin' the boy and when he ran, she took off and chased him down. That girl could run. She beat the crap out of him."

"Girls have been known to do stuff like that."

"She did a good job. Gave him two black eyes. That boy outweighed her by thirty pounds. That girl could take care of herself, and she had a lot of anger in her, a whole lot of anger."

"She's mellowed." At least I hoped so.

"Yeah. I guess even if you got mellow you still would go after two guys planning to rape and kill you and blow them to pieces. I just remembered that story about the Sharkleys when I heard about what happened. Anyway, good luck finding Andrea. You know how to get to the high school?"

"I passed it on the way up from Jackson. Just have to double back."

"Why are you lookin' after all these years?"

"The girls want to find their sister."

"Well, seein' that they been in the news, she knows where they are. Looks to me like she don't wanna be found."

I had to agree. "You're right. If she's alive, that's true, but I'm thinking she may be dead. I'm just trying to find out what happened to her."

"Good luck. When you see the girls, tell them Hal Jennings said hello."

"I'll do that."

I was in the middle of nowhere and learning absolutely nothing. There was an unsatisfying symmetry to that. Detective work may sound exciting, but, as Brett Phillips says about solving problems, it's mostly collecting information, reassessing the situation, figuring out what information is needed next, gathering more information, and doing it over and over until an answer smacks you in the face.

The only thing that hit me in the face was that I was hungry. I drove back to Trenton for a late lunch. While Kenton is classified as a really small town, Trenton not only meets the Phillips criteria for being called a town, it is also home to the world's largest collection of teapots. I had no interest in the teapots, but if the matter ever came up at bar trivia, I had the answer.

I stopped at a diner and had a cheeseburger and fries for lunch. The girl behind the counter looked much too young to have any useful information regarding the whereabouts of Andrea Golden, so I didn't ask.

The Gibson County High School was in summer session, and the building was open when I went to the main office around half past two. I introduced myself to Rosemarie Burns, the principal's secretary, and told her that I was trying to track down one of their alumni. I asked if she had a current address for Andrea Golden. She politely refused to help until I told her that an unnamed relative needed a bone marrow transplant and that Andrea was her last chance. Patient confidentiality made it impossible for me to tell her who the patient was. She eyed me suspiciously. "Just so happens that AJ and Amy Elizabeth Golden are in the news, and you come looking for their sister? Just a coincidence? I doubt it."

"Look, the doctors didn't even know that there was a third sister until they heard about it Friday at the press conference. If you don't want to help, I understand. The patient will probably die anyway, and Andrea has a right to her privacy. Frankly, I'd just as soon go home myself. I'll tell them I tried."

She looked appalled at my laziness in the face of a life and death situation. "Wait. I'll see what we have."

She returned in a minute shaking her head. "Nothing. But was Andrea in the college prep program?"

"Well, I know she didn't go to college directly after high school. If she did I wouldn't be here, I'd be talking to them. But she might have been in the college prep program at some time."

She looked me in the eye trying to judge my sincerity. In being an investigator, sincerity is critical. If you can fake that, you can fake anything. "Well, all the college counselors are new since 1992. The old ones have moved away. But if she was in the college prep program, then Grace Rogers might know something about her. Grace was the secretary in the counselor's office and she knew more about the kids than anyone."

"Great, where's her office?"

"Oh, she doesn't have an office. She took a leave of absence three years ago when her father became ill. But she's still in the area; lives in Trimble. Let me call and see if she's home and if she knows anything."

I tried to think of where Trimble was and whether it was back towards what I regarded as civilization. Then I realized that since Kenton was the exact middle of nowhere, any direction from Kenton had to be towards civilization. The secretary returned. "Just spoke to Grace. She said she remembers Andrea Golden and that she'd love the company. She'll be expecting you."

She started to draw me a map. I had planned to use the GPS, but when the directions became 'After the rusted out 1954 Pontiac, take the dirt road to the right, cross the bridge, and take the first left—can't miss it, it's the house with the light yellow shutters' I decided that a GPS was useless. I thanked her for calling Grace, and for the directions. I hoped that Grace wasn't just lonely and, more importantly, I hoped she might have something useful. I doubted it, but I had nowhere else to go.

I doubled back four miles on Highway 45, going about half way back to Kenton, and took Highway 105 west past acres of tobacco. It was twelve miles until I saw the sign proclaiming that I was entering Trimble. In two tenths of a mile I saw the rusted out Pontiac, made the appropriate turns and five minutes later I was in the driveway of a house with yellow shutters. A middle aged African-American woman wearing a black dress with white polka dots was waiting at the front door. "Mister Aaron, thank you for coming by. We don't get many visitors. Come on in."

It wasn't difficult to discern why Grace Rogers got few visitors. A large hospital bed took up most of the space in what had been the combination living room/ dining room of the small home. A television was located at one end of the room, but by the looks of things, Mr. Rogers was unaware of what was on the screen. By the smell of things he needed to have his diaper changed. Evidently, the smell no longer bothered Grace Rogers.

"Daddy, this is Mr. Aaron. He came to ask me some questions about one of the students at Gibson County."

I reached out to shake his hand. He made no response.

"Daddy is having one of his bad days. Been having more and more of them lately. Some days he doesn't even know me. Other days he sort of does."

"They told me you took a leave three years ago."

"That was after he had the last stroke. His high blood pressure finally caught up to him. His heart is strong though and his kidneys are good enough that he doesn't need dialysis yet, and . . . and you really aren't that interested are you."

"Not disinterested though. Sorry for your trouble. Looks like a lot of work."

She nodded. "I'm private duty nurse, cook, maid, companion, all in one. It's a labor of love. He was a wonderful father."

"Do you have help?"

"Can't afford any. It's cheaper for me to do everything than for me to work and pay for what he needs. Some days I think I'm going to shoot myself, other days . . . Today's a good day; he's quiet."

At times, I may be able to fake sincerity but I couldn't fake the absence of nausea. "Can we go talk outside?"

"Sure. The smell. I'm sorry. I guess I just don't recognize it any more." We walked back to the front steps and sat down. There was no porch. "Rosemarie said you were trying to find Andrea Golden. Something about a transplant? I hope it isn't for one of her sisters."

"No. Not them. Don't worry about that. Do you have any idea what happened to Andrea?"

She looked at the round for a few moments, considering what to say before she spoke. "I knew that little girl like she was one of my own. She was the sweetest, saddest, most troubled girl I ever met. Just horrible what her daddy did to her. Then no one seemed to believe her, or at least not enough to do anything about it. When she was fifteen, she got pregnant. She had no business having a baby; she was a baby herself."

"Guess so."

"Absolutely. Imagine being almost sixteen, a sophomore in high school, pregnant by some boy who denies it's his. End of the world. She knew she couldn't raise a baby. She couldn't tell her parents. I think if I hadn't helped her, she would have killed herself."

"What did you do?"

"I drove her to Jackson, to the hospital, for the abortion. What else could I do?"

I thought for a moment. "Wasn't there a parental consent law back then?"

"Um-hmnn. I told them I was her mama."

"But you're . . . Go on with the story."

"I know. I'm black. She's white. But I was an adult, and no one asked. In a way, it might have been better if someone had asked. The courts in Jackson would have stepped in, and maybe something would have happened. Reverend Golden might have ended up in jail. The state might have had all three girls in foster care. Anyway, once she got her problem taken care of, she didn't quit messing with boys, but she was careful. Never got pregnant again and she had some hope that her life might work out. She was such a sad girl. It almost made me stop believing in God, but then God came and struck down her daddy. I remember hearing about how his red hair was falling out—I guess from the chemotherapy. He was such a good looking red haired devil before that. That's exactly what he was—a devil. And by the time he died he looked exactly like the devil he was, all shriveled up and bald. I tell you Mr. Aaron, the Lord has strange ways."

I had a rabbi in Sunday School who used to say exactly the same thing whenever we asked him to explain anything miraculous from the Bible. I doubted that striking down Nathaniel Golden was the direct work of the Lord. Not to second guess the Almighty, but his timing seemed less than optimal. "Do you know what happened after she graduated?"

"I know where she went. She went to Memphis. I have no idea where she is now. I kept writing but after the first time, she never wrote back. I think she wanted to put Kenton and everything about it way behind her. At least I hope that's why she never wrote back." She went inside and returned with a well worn address book.

I copied the address in Memphis, 645 Lamar Avenue, B-6, and thanked her for her help. Lamar Avenue sounded somewhat familiar. I had been to Memphis several times in my life and I assumed that I had passed Lamar Avenue on one of those visits. In any case, I had my first lead for Andrea Golden's life after Kenton. Grace Rogers' father was moaning and she started back inside. "Good luck to you Mr. Aaron. If you find her, give her my love. Somehow, I have always felt that things worked out for her. Maybe that's just crazy optimism on my part. Maybe I just want to believe that I helped her by doing what I did. I don't know." Her father was moaning again and she vanished inside.

I went back to my car and headed for the main road. I was momentarily more depressed over seeing a man who had obviously outlived both his mind and his money than I was happy about getting—possibly—a step nearer to Andrea Golden. Grace Rogers' father made me realize how sheltered my life had been. Which was worse—being fifteen and pregnant in a dysfunctional family where your father had raped you repeatedly and where your mother let it happen, being middle aged with nothing to wake up to but a father whose illness had stripped him of most vestiges of his humanity, or being Grace Rogers' father, oblivious to the world around him? On that note, I turned onto Highway 3 toward Dyersburg and eventually turned west on US Highway 155. I headed to the Great River Road, officially known as Tennessee Highway 181, and perhaps the answer to the meaning of the T181 pendants.

I was just short of the Great River Road when I remembered when I had heard of Lamar Avenue. In Amos Bunden's book, he had mentioned that two of the victims of The Unforgiving had used an escort service on Lamar Avenue. I tried to remember other details of Bunden's unsolved case. Five victims. Four men poisoned in Memphis, one man poisoned in Atlanta. Thallium. 1993-1994. A killer who was avenging abused women.

I was looking for a teenage girl who left home after being raped by her father, a teenage girl who AJ, Amy Elizabeth and I suspected of having been a prostitute. I now had evidence that she came to Memphis in 1992 and that she lived on Lamar Avenue. I assumed that Lamar Avenue ran for miles. There was no reason to assume that Andrea Golden had anything to do with an escort service on Lamar Avenue, but it didn't take much to realize that this search might end very badly.

Chapter Fifteen

As any trivia buff knows, the Mississippi River is the longest river in North America. Most trivia buffs do not know that the lower Mississippi River, the part south of the junction with the Ohio River, has twenty bridge crossings. The Caruthersville Bridge carries US Interstate Highway 155, also known as Route 412, across the river from Tennessee to Missouri. In April 2005 I would experience the worst moment of my life after crossing the Caruthersville Bridge as part of what can best be regarded as an elaborate publicity stunt. In June 2004, however, when I was searching for Andrea Golden, I didn't cross the bridge. Just before Interstate 155 became the road across the Caruthersville Bridge, Tennessee 181 branches off. The road runs north for approximately eight miles and south for approximately twelve miles. For that twenty mile stretch, Tennessee 181, is also identified, due to its proximity to the Mississippi, as the Great River Road.

AJ and Amy Elizabeth had once traveled up and down Tennessee Highway 181 looking for a clue for the meaning of the jeweled pendant. They had come up empty, but they had been pre-teens at the time. There is always a role for a fresh set of eyes, especially when the first set of eyes might have seen something but missed its significance.

In June, the western part of Tennessee has daylight until just a little before 9 P.M. That gave me plenty of time to retrace the path that AJ and Amy Elizabeth had ridden years earlier. Unfortunately, the hour I spent on the Great River Road revealed nothing of interest other than the fact that the southern boundary of Tennessee 181 was the Moss Island State Wildlife Management Area. It is supposed to be a great place for fishing, but as a city boy, as of 2004 I had never been fishing. It would not be until I married Elana Grey that I would occasionally participate in what I considered exotic activities like fishing, hunting, parasailing, skydiving, and line dancing. My trained eyes detected nothing on Highway 181 that would explain the meaning of the pendant.

I finished my tour of Highway 181, and headed back toward Highway 3 to finish the one hour and forty-five minute drive south to Memphis. I called

AJ from the road and learned that both she and Amy Elizabeth had enrolled in the summer session at Vanderbilt. Amy Elizabeth had decided that it was time to get serious about her career, though the exact nature of what she and Milton Brandenburg were planning remained fuzzy. AJ was enrolled in introductory physics, a required premed course that she lacked. I didn't understand why doctors needed to know anything about physics, but then again there were a lot of things I didn't understand.

That AJ was able to enroll at Vanderbilt was no surprise. She had previously been accepted for the fall term. That Amy Elizabeth was allowed to enroll reflected the connections that Milton Brandenburg had as a member of the Vanderbilt Board of Trust. Amy Elizabeth had, as if by magic, become a graduate student in the Counseling program; her tuition money was a cash advance from Milton Brandenburg.

I didn't like talking while driving an unfamiliar road so I promised AJ that I would call her back after I arrived in Memphis. Despite starting classes, she and Amy Elizabeth were going to a movie. They were planning to see 'Angels from Rikenny,' the hit sci-fi film of the summer.

It was much too late to follow up on the address I had obtained from Grace Rogers. I had left my copy of Amos Bunden's book at home, and the only book store I tried didn't have it in stock. They volunteered to order it for me, and have it in a week. That was pointless. To compensate for lunch, I ate a healthy meal before I checked into a hotel.

It was a little after eleven when I called AJ. Amy Elizabeth and AJ had both enjoyed the movie, but, like me, they thought that Hollywood had diluted a serious message by amplifying the love story between the female leader of the aliens and the leader of Earth's task force. AJ had read the original short story when she was a sophomore at Northwestern. "Hollywood makes everything into a romance. It's pathetic. It's a serious story about the possible end of civilization. The aliens come and give us a medicine that cures heart disease and cancer, and people end up living so long they get demented and society goes broke."

"And then they develop the virus to wipe out all the old people, and the virus mutates and wipes out everybody."

"Well that was depressing, but did they have to make it a love story? It's as if the people who make movies think that people can't consider a serious idea."

"True, but how many people would see it without the romance and the special effects?"

"Good point. I'll remember that when I write a screenplay. Of course, now that my life has changed from being a violent story with serial killers and become a hot romance, I'm not complaining in the least." There was a long pause.

"Are you still there, AJ?"

"Yeah. I was just thinking. You and me, that's almost romantic comedy material. We had a meet-cute after all."

"Huh?"

"You know. Boy meets girl in a cute sort of way. The only way our meeting would have been cuter was if I got pissed off when you told me I couldn't sing well enough to be a success and poured a pitcher of beer over your head."

"Anything that cute would not have led to us going out to dinner. Plus, doesn't the girl in the meet cute usually have a boring fiancée who takes her for granted or something?"

"Usually. We fail as romantic comedy material. We were both unattached and there is no impediment to the relationship."

"Which is much nicer."

"Got that right," AJ started to giggle. "I like our way better. In romantic comedies they spend an hour and a half of movie time, which is several months or even a year of story line, before they hook up. 'AJ Rides the Fire Wave' isn't a rom-com title, but it's a lot more fun. And despite what she who shall not be named always told me, having sex does not get in the way of getting to know someone. We're doing fine."

"She who shall not be named? It sounds like you read the Harry Potter novels."

"Obviously. You too?"

"Yeah." We talked for a couple of hours, about books, about summer school, and about growing up in Kenton and Belle Meade respectively. At 1 AM we decided it was time for sleep.

"I hope you're not disappointed, Jonah. You picked up a girl at a karaoke bar and you ended up with a pre-med nerd for a girlfriend, someone who would rather study or read than be a party animal."

"A beautiful, sexy, and smart pre-med nerd with a great sense of humor. Anyway, my days as a party boy are behind me. You're almost perfect for me."

"Only almost?" She sounded disappointed.

"Yeah. You're there and I'm here. If you were here you would be perfect—except for your calves. You have the calves of an athlete, not a model. No big deal. You look absolutely fantastic as far as I'm concerned. I wouldn't change a thing about you."

"Considering that I'd never have made it up the stairs last week if I had the calves of a model, you'll have to settle for that."

"AJ, there is something wrong about combining any consideration of you and the concept of settling in the same sentence."

"Smooth, Jonah. Very smooth. Good night. Talk to you tomorrow, sweetie. Happy hunting."

We ended the call, and I fell asleep thinking about how nice it was, after several months of being alone, to be living in a world that contained AJ Golden.

Chapter Sixteen

In the morning, I left the hotel without checking out of my room. I had no idea how many days I would be staying in Memphis. I got to the address on Lamar Avenue a little after seven AM and found an attractive apartment complex, Lamar Village. It reminded me of the apartments about a mile south of Vanderbilt on Hillsboro Road where my brother Barry lived. The six two-story brick buildings were designated A through F. All of the apartments opened to the outside and there was a large swimming pool in back of the buildings. I had no idea if these buildings had been there in 1992 or if they had undergone remodeling in the interval, but if Andrea Golden had lived here in 1992, she had lived relatively well. I wasn't expecting to find Andrea Golden, but I started with apartment B-6 anyway.

People throughout the complex were getting ready to go to work. Charles Yang, the Oriental man in B-6, kept the door latched while he opened it, but he was friendly enough. He and his wife both worked as research assistants at St. Jude Children's Research Hospital. He had lived in B-6 for three years and had never heard of Andrea Golden.

From inside, I could smell the bacon sizzling on the stove. Charles Yang excused himself to join his wife for breakfast. He politely closed the door. I hadn't expected to find anything, and he hadn't slammed the door in my face. I was off to a reasonable start. Like Charles Yang, all of the residents on the first floor had been there for five years or less. No one had ever heard of Andrea Golden.

In B-12, the apartment directly upstairs from B-6, I hit paydirt. Martha and James Holloway had been at Lamar Village since 1990 when they moved to Memphis to be near their grandchildren. Mrs. Holloway appeared to be in her seventies. She didn't recognize the name Andrea Golden, but when I showed her Andrea's picture, the recognition was immediate. "Why that's Candy." She undid the latch and invited me into her apartment. Her husband was seated at the breakfast table reading his newspaper and occasionally jabbing his fork at a stack of pancakes. He was dressed in a shirt and tie. "James, this young man is looking for Candy, the girl who used to live downstairs. You remember her, don't you? She was one of those models who lived here when we first moved in." James Holloway gave a facial gesture somewhere between a smirk and a smile when his wife used the word 'model.'

"They weren't models Sarah. They were . . ."

"Shussh. Don't say it. They were sweet little girls and they got dressed up in those pretty little dresses, like prom dresses, nearly every night and went out. Candy was the nicest of them. She was the only one I ever gave our key to. She used to water our plants when we went on vacation, and she came up almost every day to talk and read her horoscope in the Commercial Appeal. She even did a full horoscope reading for me based on how the planets were aligned when I was born. Didn't make much sense, though. She decided that James and I were a bad match and we've been together forty-six years."

I looked around the apartment. I saw a fig tree, a dieffenbachia, a couple of coleus plants and something that I suspected my mother would have identified in an instant. To me it was just a plant. "How long did Candy live here in Lamar Village?"

"A couple of years. She was gone by . . . let's see, the end of July '94. That's when my father passed away and we had to go to Baltimore. We came back to Memphis on August first. I remember that date because it would have been his eighty-first birthday." She paused to check a mental calendar. "I asked Candy to check on the plants while we were away that time and she said she couldn't because she might be gone by the end of July. She was. Gone for good. I had asked her to leave an address but she never did. They were the sweetest girls, those models."

James Holloway was shaking his head. "For heaven's sake, Martha, quit calling them models. They were call girls and you know it. And the gentleman has a right to know it, if he's looking for her."

"Why do you say that they were call girls?"

"Well, it wasn't like they propositioned an old man like me. I was sixty-eight years old back in 1992. They were always on their best behavior around the complex. You rarely saw them during the day, except in the summer when they were sunning themselves at the pool. None of them had a regular job. There were usually three of them sharing the apartment. They worked evenings, and they had these really large guys with moustaches who drove them to their 'modeling assignments'. The men drove these old beat up Oldsmobiles. The guys here in the complex used to joke about the cars and call them the 'hookermobiles'. The girls and their drivers would usually come back around midnight, sometimes later. Those Oldsmobiles had bad mufflers; you could tell it was them."

"Did men come around here on a regular basis?"

"No way. I think that would have raised a stink. No, the girls went out nearly every night and we just looked the other way. A couple of the girls had regular boyfriends come around, but that was it. No one else ever visited them here . . .

except for that woman who came by once a week to collect the money. Those girls weren't models. I guess today you would call them escorts."

"Was there ever any problem with the police?"

"Never. We never complained. No reason to. They were a lot quieter and a lot nicer than those college boys who lived in Building A when we moved in. The girls downstairs never bothered anyone. We never bothered them. Frankly, they were ideal neighbors, quiet and polite, but they weren't models. Then, one day they were all gone. The FBI came by once, while those girls were still living downstairs, but I have no idea what that was about. I'm not sure if that was when Candy was here or if that was after she left."

"FBI?"

He nodded as he spoke. "Mmm, hmm. I remember the badges. F-B-I. Not sure what it was about. They were asking the same sort of questions you are, but not just about Candy, about all the girls. Never found out why."

Some of my investigative work in Music City involves looking for underage girls who leave home—often with good reason—to try and make it as a singer or songwriter in Nashville. The ones without talent, that means ninety-nine percent of them, usually go home. Unless they have someone to support them, the ones that stay become waitresses, strippers, or prostitutes. By professional necessity, rather than personal need, I knew a lot about prostitutes.

If you are a moralist, a whore is a whore. If you are a realist, you have to recognize that there are several levels to being a whore. At the bottom rung of the ladder are the streetwalkers. Often drug addicted, they have an occupational risk of getting in a vehicle and disappearing. The next rung up the ladder is in-call, the massage parlor girls. Despite the fancy names on the outside of the buildings, names like Executive Spa or Upscale Gardens, the basic job is the same, the working environment is generally clean, and the pay is a little better. The next highest rung is outcall, the escort services that generally cater to traveling businessmen and professionals. The limited screening of clients is such that the element of danger is never totally absent but the fees are higher, and the operation is lower volume. Some of the women have day jobs as secretaries or the like. Others are divorced housewives trying to make ends meet in the face of inadequate alimony and child support.

From the story the Holloways were telling me, in 1992, on the basis of her good looks, or by knowing somebody who knew somebody, Andrea Golden had entered the world of prostitution at a relatively high level. Unfortunately, there is no license required to be an escort. There was no way for me to use this information to track Andrea Golden. If she had ever been arrested in Memphis, she would have been fingerprinted and she would have made the national criminal data base. However, since my computer software and the software used by my contacts in the Nashville Police department had found nothing, Andrea Golden had apparently never run afoul of the law, or if she had, she had been using an alias.

The only fact that didn't fit was the FBI. The FBI wouldn't care about a local prostitution ring. Maybe there was a tie to human trafficking. Eastern Europe was notorious for exporting young women to work in American brothels—but not to work in escort services; the girls in escort services had too much freedom. James Holloway had talked about the girls in B-6 sunning themselves at the pool. That didn't sound like girls who were being held prisoner. Then I remembered the story of The Unforgiving. I had to get another copy of Amos Bunden's book and read about the escorts on Lamar Avenue.

"Is there anything you can tell me about Candy? What she liked? What she wanted to do in the future?

"No. Not really. She never talked about herself much. Such a sad story though. No family. Her parents and her brother and her sister were killed in that fire. She only survived because she was out baby-sitting that night."

"Fire?" I showed Martha Holloway the picture again to be sure we were talking about the same girl.

"Oh yes, that's Candy. I remember thinking about how that girl with such a pretty name and such a pretty car had such a sad life. I remember that car of hers. It was an old light green Plymouth. Very snazzy."

It wasn't the wrong girl. Candy had invented a personal history that erased her family when she put Kenton, Tennessee in the rear view mirror. That was another piece of bad news for me. If she was trying to erase all connection to her past, she might very well have succeeded. "The woman who came by once a week, the one who picked up the money, is there anything you can tell me about her?"

"White woman. In her . . . I don't know, late twenties, early thirties. Hard for me to tell about ages in young people. Average looking. Not tall, not short."

That narrowed the field to thousands of women in the Memphis area. I thanked the Holloways for their time and resumed knocking on doors, completing a sweep of Buildings A, B, and C by a little after nine fifteen. No one else could provide any information about Andrea Golden. I considered skipping Buildings D, E, and F, but given the lack of a good lead I decided to knock on all the doors. Most people had headed for work, and the few people who were home had all been living at Lamar Village for less than the decade that Andrea Candy Golden had been gone.

I headed for the office of the rental agent for Lamar Village. Someone had signed a lease for apartment B-6 and that person might know where Andrea Candy Golden had gone. Unfortunately, the rental agent informed me that her firm had managed the property only since 1999. Earlier records did not exist. I was almost at a dead end.

In college I had played on a football team that won twelve games and lost thirty-two. Our record in the Southeastern Conference was a dismal four wins and twenty-eight losses. I was used to losing, but that didn't mean I had to like it. I made another stop at a bookstore before going back to my hotel. Amos Bunden's books had sold out. Having the stepdaughter of a congressman kill two serial killers was evidently good for sales of Amos Bunden's books.

It was too early to call the west coast but when I returned to my hotel, I e-mailed Brett Phillips before going back to sleep. Lamar Village wasn't that far from the part of town where his parents lived. Brett would have been twenty-two in 1992. Whoever drove the 'hookermobile' might be about that age. I wondered if he knew someone who had bragged about being the driver for a bevy of escorts. It seemed like the kind of job someone in their late teens or early twenties would brag about. I doubted that Brett was going to be able to help me, but it seemed that he was all I had. I didn't have much.

Chapter Seventeen

I napped until noon, then went to the hotel's health club and ran three miles on the treadmill. If I was going to be dating a woman who had run track in the Big Ten, I figured that I better get in shape to run with her. While I didn't see any health benefit to running, my Saturday morning experience had convinced me that the rewards of running a few miles with AJ made it worth the effort.

I was stuck in Memphis until I heard back from Brett and I was temporarily done searching for Andrea Golden. In the lobby I read through the brochures on local tourist activities. On previous trips, I had walked Beale Street, and I had seen the ducks walk through the lobby of the Peabody Hotel. I had been to Graceland when I was a kid, and I didn't want to do that again. I decided to tour the National Civil Rights Museum.

On April 4, 1968 Dr. Martin Luther King was assassinated as he stood on the balcony outside his room on the second floor of the Lorraine Motel. The motel and some adjoining properties had been converted into a museum which opened to the public in 1991. I visited the exhibits dealing with the Montgomery Bus Boycott and with lunch counter sit-ins in the South. I saw the tributes to the Supreme Court decision Brown vs. Board of Education, to the integration of the University of Mississippi by James Meredith, and to Freedom Summer and the three college students who were killed by the Klan in Mississippi in 1964 for trying to get African Americans registered to vote. I stood outside the replica of Dr. King's Birmingham, Alabama jail cell and wondered if I cared enough about a political cause that I would ever risk my life or go to jail for it. I doubted that I would. I wondered how AJ and Amy Elizabeth felt about civil rights having grown up in Kenton, Tennessee. AJ and I hadn't really discussed politics. After two and a half hours I completed the tour and came to the Visitor's Book.

The majority of the events commemorated at the museum occurred ten to fifteen years before I was born. The tour had been a moving experience and I wanted to write something profound. I looked at what other people had written. Most people had just signed their names and listed their home city. A few had written a few lines about being black in America or about what Dr. King had meant to them. I stared at the page for a minute, then wrote one simple statement documenting my only personal tie to the Civil Rights Movement and signed my name.

> My parents met participating in Freedom Summer 1964.
> May The Dream live on.
> Jonah Aaron, Nashville, Tennessee June 15, 2004

It was the best that I could do. It was time to go back to my hotel, contact Brett Phillips, and consider wrapping up the investigation of Andrea Golden. And then, thinking about the visitor's book, and what had brought me to Memphis in the first place, I had an epiphany. The more I thought about it, the less absurd the idea seemed.

At the Civil Rights Museum's main information desk I found a listing of other Memphis attractions. Graceland closed at 5 P.M. I called the main number and eventually was connected to a woman who said that she would be glad to help if I came by in the morning. It was already ten minutes to five.

I had remembered Saturday morning and AJ telling me that whenever the Reverend Golden had come into the girls' bedroom at night, that she, AJ, had gone to Nashville in her mind and that Andrea had mentally gone to Graceland. It wasn't a big jump to assume that when Andrea had gotten to Memphis, she had gone to visit the real Graceland. Maybe she had gone again before she left. It might have been her last chance.

Would Andrea Candy Golden have signed her name in the visitor's book at Graceland? Maybe. What would she have written? Anybody's guess. Perhaps, if I were lucky, seeing all the names and cities written in the book, Andrea Golden might have written something that would tell me where she was going. Maybe she had signed the book "Andrea Golden, Los Angeles" or "Andrea Golden, New York." Any location other than Memphis or Kenton could put me back on the trail.

I checked my cell phone as I left the museum. I had missed a call from Brett Phillips. I called him back.

"What do you have?"

"Other than a crazy former roommate, trying to find a prostitute who has been missing for over ten years? Not much. Did you really think that I was going to come up with something?"

"No, but desperate times call for desperate measures. It was worth a try. I really didn't think you'd come up with anything."

"Never underestimate me, Jonah. I did come up with something. I found two guys who know the name of the woman who came by to collect the money. They wouldn't tell me over the phone but I set up a meet between you and them for eleven tonight at a place near the airport. Lazy Muskrat. Figured you could handle that. The guys are Alan Campos and Tommy Harper. Big guys. Moustaches. They like to wear black. They'll be at the bar."

I jotted down the names. "Fine, what else did they tell you?"

"They told me that the woman you were looking for is now a real estate agent. No name. You have to get that from them. Sells expensive houses. I told them you were in a hurry to get out Memphis, and they agreed to call her office and set up an appointment for tomorrow morning at nine. They said they wouldn't clue her in as to what it's about, but who knows?"

"No big deal. Even if they told her it's about Candy and Lamar Avenue, being unable to surprise her is better than having nowhere to go. How did you find them?"

"Well, a magician doesn't reveal how he does his tricks, but since we work for each other at times, I'll tell you. I started with the Robertson brothers. They used to do collections for me . . ."

"Collections? You were dealing baseball cards, not drugs. What collections?"

"A bad check is a bad check no matter what you're selling. Since I was a kid at the time, some people figured they could stiff me, so I used the Robertson brothers. Terry and Tony. They were two years ahead of me in high school and I helped them with their math and science homework. We're still in touch. Big dudes. Six feet four, six feet five. Linemen on our high school football team. No moustaches by the way. Clean shaven. Gentle as lambs off the football field, but they were very big and very scary, especially if they came and knocked on your door at night. They were kind of the opposite of you. You look like the college educated gentleman that you are, and you could probably kill someone with your bare hands."

"Probably. You know I was trained by an ex-Navy Seal. But I never hurt anyone badly with my bare hands."

"Sort of proves my point, though. Most people don't bother to get that kind of training. Anyway, after I helped them make it into college, during the summers, when they were home from UT, Terry and Tony Robertson did all sorts of miscellaneous jobs. They didn't drive the girls on Lamar Avenue, but they did drive some other girls. The real job isn't driving by the way. The real job is waiting outside so that they can come knock on the door if the girl signals that there is trouble and so that the girl has to leave at the end of the allotted time even though part of her act is telling the guy that he's the most fantastic guy she's ever been with and that she'd like to stay forever."

"Thank you for educating me. All the runaways I ever found were working massage parlors. I don't know much about escorts."

"No problem. Anyway, no matter whom the girls are working for, the guys driving escorts end up going to the same hotels, and since they sit and wait while the girls go inside and do their thing, they get to know each other. I called the Robertsons; they recognized the descriptions of the big guys with moustaches."

"And they found them? After all these years?"

"That part was easy. Terry and Tony Robertson graduated from UT, went to law school in Knoxville, and practice criminal law back in Memphis. They represent Tommy Harper and Alan Campos. They were the big guys with the moustaches. They drove the girls on Lamar Avenue. These days, Harper and Campos allegedly provide muscle for an alleged small time hoodlum."

"Alleged? Alleged?"

"Well, remember I got this from a pair of criminal attorneys. They love the word alleged."

"Got it. Go on."

"Well Harper and Campos remembered Candy all right. Said that after she got her boob job she was one of the most impressive looking women in Memphis. Anyone called the service for a blond with big jugs, they got Candy. She was a big money maker." The Holloways hadn't mentioned the boob job, not that it mattered. "Harper and Campos also said that Candy was a bitch. It seems that most of the girls gave out discount samples to the drivers since the girls didn't have to split that money with management as long as management didn't know. And no one was telling. But Candy never sold anything for less than full price. A true professional."

"You have to admire her for that."

"Damn straight. She made herself more marketable with the boob job and she had standards. If General Motors, Chrysler, and Ford had that kind of work ethic, then Toyota wouldn't be kicking our asses. Of course General Motors, Chrysler, and Ford are getting killed by cost of health care. Did you know that health care costs per every car made in America exceed the cost of the steel in the same car?"

"I read it on your blog a few years ago. But can we stick with Candy Golden?"

"Sorry . . . Anyway, Harper and Campos had a few other things to say about your girl, Candy. First, she was always trying to get them to have a full astrological reading. She offered the reading at half price. I guess in the astrology business she was an amateur. But they weren't interested."

"Fits with what I know about her."

"Second, they had no idea where she was from or where she was going. They did remember that she had lost her family in a fire. At least that's what she said when anyone asked where she was from."

"That's about as true as her name being Candy."

"You're kidding me! A hooker who doesn't use her real name. I don't believe it. Sorry, I just had to say that."

"You're excused."

"And, finally, Harper and Campos told me that girls came and went all the time. Candy lasted a little more than most by their estimate. All the girls who were working back then are long gone. There were just two or three girls at a time. A small operation. Boss lady, whatever her name is, liked it that way. Under the radar so to speak."

"A small business. You know, small businesses create the majority of new jobs in America."

"Right, Jonah. Anyway, they said they'd meet you at eleven tonight, and they were going to set you up at nine tomorrow with the boss lady turned real estate agent."

"And you accomplished all this in six hours."

"Couple of phone calls. That was easy. Knowing who to call. That's always the hard part. Actually it was fun talking to them. They were obviously sitting around with nothing to do when I called. By the way, I sensed something when Harper and Campos talked about the boss lady. They didn't like her. Obviously, there was no body language to read over the phone, but there was something funny in their tone of voice."

We talked about what was going on our lives. He congratulated me on having a new girlfriend. Nothing was new in his social life.

"Hey, Brett, I almost forgot to ask. The guy you had me talk to when I was in Seattle three weeks ago. Did that work out the way I said it would?" Brett Phillips had a client whose daughter was being stalked by an ex-boyfriend. There was an order of protection, but, as always, the police couldn't do anything until something happened. Until I intervened, that something was likely to involve her body ending up in a body bag.

"Yes, it was a truly wonderful conversation you had. Sometime you have to explain how a guy has a simple 'conversation' with you and ends up with two black eyes and a dislocated shoulder."

"Easy. You can only talk to people in the philosophical and emotional space which they occupy. I read that phrase in a blog somewhere. Anyway, I had to move him to the right philosophical and emotional space so we could have a simple conversation. He didn't want to be moved. That's where the two black eyes and the dislocated shoulder came from. After that he was a very attentive listener."

"Must be. He came by my client's house to apologize, and said he would never have anything to do with my client's daughter ever again. My client said he sounded like he meant it."

"Guess that means I don't have to come back out to Seattle. I enjoy seeing you but now that I have this gorgeous redhead staying at my place, I'd rather be in Nashville."

"Staying with you? I thought you just met her."

"It's complicated. Thanks for the help. I've gone from no options to two possibilities." I told him about my reasoning regarding the visitor's logs at Graceland.

"You know that might work. You're looking for a girl who talked about astrology and who has a spiritual attachment to Elvis. Like I always say about solving problems . . ."

"Always think about a problem logically, but when that doesn't work, think outside the box."

"Talk to you later."

I stopped at two bookstores on the way back to my hotel. Both were sold out of Amos Bunden's book. Fortunately, one of the clerks had just finished reading his personal copy. He sold it to me for twenty dollars, double the retail price. I began looking at the chapter on The Unforgiving before returning to my hotel. I ended up reading it twice.

Chapter Eighteen

Amos Bunden told the story of The Unforgiving in exquisite detail and with a touch of irony, but the basic facts were these. On December 12, 1993, a salesman named Elmer Jones, became ill on a flight home from Memphis to Tucson, Arizona. The flight was diverted to Albuquerque where Mr. Jones was hospitalized and eventually died. Five months later, in May of 1994, a lawyer from Little Rock, Arkansas named Mario Grancliff died in his hotel room while attending a trial in Memphis. Both men had died of thallium poisoning. The diagnoses were missed when the victims were alive, and if not for toxicology studies done as part of the autopsies, the cause of death would never have been determined. In fact, had the homicide detective investigating Mario Grancliff's death not remembered an earlier phone inquiry from the Albuquerque Police Department regarding Elmer Jones, the two cases would never have been linked.

Bunden explained that thallium was odorless and colorless and took several days to weeks to have the maximum effect. The major symptoms of thallium poisoning were hair loss, abdominal pain, gastrointestinal bleeding, and neuropathy—abnormal sensations in the fingers and toes.

There was no apparent connection between the two men. However, an investigation revealed that both men had a history of violence toward women. Elmer Jones had been accused of assaulting an alleged prostitute in 1981; an ex-girlfriend of Mario Grancliff had a restraining order out against him. Of greater interest, phone records revealed that both men had called the AAA Absolute Angels Escort Service while in Memphis. The phone number for the escort service led the police to the Lamar Village Apartments.

Two of the three women who shared the apartment, identified by Bunden as "Candy Christian" and "Emma Roualt," claimed not to remember meeting either of the victims. The third, a teenager named "Lolly Hayes," freely admitted dating Mario Grancliff. She said that she had consensual sex with him and that he had gotten 'a little rough.' Lolly passed a lie detector test denying that she had done anything to harm Mario Grancliff. According to the lie detector test, Emma was lying about not meeting Elmer Jones, but she was telling the truth when she denied harming him.

Candy, described as being the most sophisticated of the three women, declined to take a lie detector test though she stated that she had never met either Elmer Jones or Mario Grancliff. She held to that statement when informed that it was a crime to lie to an FBI agent. Bunden reported that Candy had what he regarded as a perverse sense of humor. When asked if she knew anything about thallium she had said, "Of course I know about thallium. In Season Three of the original Star Trek, Captain Kirk got trapped in the Thallium Web." The episode, Bunden noted, is the Tholian Web. Bunden was convinced that Candy had been toying with the investigators. That was the last question she answered before requesting an attorney.

There was no forensic evidence linking any of the women to Elmer Jones, and Lolly had been going to school in Massachusetts at the time that Elmer Jones had been in Memphis, a fact that was easily verified. The school records revealed that Lolly was only sixteen years old.

Before Memphis detectives proceeded further with their person of interest, Candy Christian, a critical piece of evidence was found. A thumbprint had been detected on the metal clasp of Mario Grancliff's briefcase. It did not match Grancliff's fingerprints, and it did not match the fingerprints of any of the three women residing in the Lamar Village apartment. However, the fingerprint matched a fingerprint that had been found in June 1993 in the room of Yuri Yevtushenko, a member of a visiting Russian trade delegation who had also died of thallium poisoning.

Yuri Yevtushenko had developed abdominal pain and gastrointestinal bleeding while in Atlanta. After he had been hospitalized, he developed tingling in his fingers and toes which progressed to paralysis. Since Yevtushenko was bald, he couldn't show the complete triad of thallium poisoning—abdominal pain, neuropathy, and hair loss. As a result, a rare condition such as thallium poisoning was never considered. As in the other cases, the diagnosis was made only when toxicology studies performed as part of the autopsy revealed elevated levels of thallium. The FBI had investigated Yevtushenko's case at the time he became ill, and had reached a dead end. Now, with three victims in two states, the Behavioral Analysis Unit of the FBI was called in.

Since Yevtushenko was a visitor to America, out of courtesy to the Russian authorities, the Atlanta police had treated his hotel room as a possible crime scene from the time he was hospitalized. With one exception, fingerprints taken from Yevtushenko's suite at the Ritz Carlton Hotel could be matched to the hotel staff or to Yevtushenko. That one exception was the fingerprint that linked his death to the cases to Mario Grancliff and presumably to Elmer Jones.

There were many individuals who might want to see Yuri Yevtushenko dead. However, none of them seemed to have had the opportunity to kill him. During the period from 1986 to 1991, Yevtushenko had been a suspect in a series of sexual assaults in the Soviet Union. One of the cases involved a group of American tourists. None of the cases had gone to trial. In the cases involving Soviet citizens, witness intimidation had been suspected.

In 1988, Marsha Bowen, Ann Taber, and Colleen Brand, all twenty one years old, had traveled to the Soviet Union as part of a group of sixteen college seniors, members of Kappa Delta sorority at the University of Florida. On the third night of the trip, the three young women were kidnapped while walking home from a Moscow night club at two in the morning. They denied being raped, but police suspected otherwise. After twenty four hours they were taken to a deserted Moscow intersection and released without their clothing. They were found by a taxi driver who drove them to the authorities.

When the women described one of the kidnappers as a man who was well over six feet six inches tall and bald, the police had no trouble identifying one of the hoodlums who had kidnapped Marsha Bowen and her friends. Yuri Yevtushenko was arrested. However when the student group cancelled the remainder of their trip and returned to the United States, the charges against Yevtushenko were dropped for lack of a prosecuting witness.

When Yuri Yevtushenko was killed, the three kidnap victims, as well as the other thirteen members of the tour group were interviewed and fingerprinted. There was no match to the unexplained fingerprint found in Yevtushenko's suite. With no suspect, the murder of Yuri Yevtushenko quickly became a cold case. Since symptoms of thallium poisoning can be delayed, the authorities initially weren't even certain that Yevtushenko had been poisoned in Atlanta. The trade group had first visited Newark, New Jersey. Not until the fingerprint in Yevtushenko's Atlanta hotel suite was linked to the other killings did the authorities conclude that Yevtushenko had been poisoned in Atlanta.

When the fingerprint from Mario Grancliff's briefcase linked Yuri Yevtushenko to the Memphis killings, the FBI again interviewed the sixteen students who had been on the trip to the Soviet Union. None of them lived within three hundred miles of Memphis. Their fingerprints had already ruled them out as suspects in Yevtushenko's murder, but the FBI is nothing if not thorough. The FBI checked for any family links to Memphis or Atlanta. Nothing panned out.

A single unexplained fingerprint connected with cases of thallium poisoning could not be a coincidence. However, no connection could be established between Yevtushenko and the Lamar Avenue escort service. Amos Bunden emphasized the fact that if such a link could be established, the case would likely be solved. No link had ever been found.

While the FBI did not have a suspect they had a theory. The first three victims of "the thallium killer" all had a history of violence toward women. It appeared that someone was exacting revenge. Everyone associated with the escort operation was interviewed and fingerprinted by the FBI. This included the drivers who delivered the women to their assignments, the man who held the lease on the Lamar Village apartment, and his associates. No match to the telltale fingerprint was found.

The Behavioral Analysis Unit generated a profile, but it led nowhere. The killer was organized and intelligent and appeared to be motivated by revenge. Unlike many serial killers, this killer was not a sadist; the killer did not watch the victims die. The fact that the killer was not present at the time of death meant that the killer did not take sexual pleasure in the killings.

Amos Bunden noted that the BAU had never before seen a serial killer who was avenging separate crimes. Since the killing involved poison, and since most killers who use poison are women, the BAU gave the following profile. The killer was a woman, twenty-one to fifty years old. Since the killer had no trouble gaining access to the men, they postulated that she was well educated, well groomed, and probably a professional of some sort. They did not exclude the possibility that the woman was an escort. The BAU postulated that the killer or someone close to the killer had once been sexually assaulted.

Because of the use of thallium, Amos Bunden further speculated the woman might work in the pharmaceutical industry, the electronics industry, or the glass industry, employment that would give her access to thallium. A search of those industries did not yield a viable suspect. No one was identified who tied the Yevtushenko case to the other killings.

I stopped to think about what I was reading. Obviously, the FBI search hadn't connected the escort named Candy with the girl named Andrea Golden who had briefly worked at Pilson Glass. Andrea had no social security number when she worked in Jackson, and she had been paid in cash. Her name never would have come up in any computerized search of employees. Just as obvious to me, the FBI had never learned "Candy's" real name. My search of the national criminal data base hadn't found Andrea Golden. Candy had been fingerprinted. I was certain she was "in the system." She just wasn't in the system under her real name.

As the FBI was reaching a dead end in its investigation, in early August 1994, two more men died of thallium poisoning after returning from business trips to Memphis. Each of the men had stayed at the same hotel near the Memphis airport. Review of the phone calls made from the men's hotel rooms and on their cell phones revealed that none of the men had called an escort service. However, the bartender at the hotel bar where the men had been staying reported that the men had each met a well-dressed woman at the bar during his stay at the hotel. While Bunden's profile of the killer was vague, the woman fit the general parameters.

The bartender described the woman as average. In his chapter, Amos Bunden pointed out how irritated he gets when a suspect is described as average, but this woman was indeed average. She was five feet three inches tall. She weighed about one hundred and twenty-five pounds. She had short brown hair, eyes that were either green or brown—the bartender wasn't certain, and no visible marks or tattoos. Her figure was unremarkable. A sketch artist was called in. A drawing was made. The woman indeed appeared average. Her actions were anything but average. She had killed five men and she had changed her modus operandi. Instead of avenging women who had been abused, she was apparently trolling for victims.

Since there was the usual delay in making the diagnosis of thallium poisoning, the hotel rooms of these last two victims had been cleaned and little fingerprint evidence was available. However, one print that was identified in one of the rooms matched the fingerprints of the person who was suspected of killing Yuri Yevtushenko and Mario Grancliff, and who had presumably killed Elmer Jones. The FBI felt that it was reasonable to assume that all five men had been killed by the same woman.

Since the killer had changed her pattern, and the murders were becoming more frequent, the FBI felt that the killings would escalate. However, to the surprise of the Behavioral Analysis Unit, the killings stopped and never resumed. As of 2002, when Amos Bunden published Serial Killers, Volume 2, the killer of Yuri Yevtushenko, Mario Grancliff, and the other men had not, as best as could be determined, killed again.

Serial killers generally do not stop killing. Amos Bunden discussed the reasons that serial killer would stop killing before being caught. A serial killer might be arrested and sent to prison for an unrelated crime, or a serial killer might die—or be killed by the authorities—before their identity as a serial killer was confirmed. Another, and less likely possibility, was that the killer became incapacitated and might therefore be unable to continue killing.

Given that Yuri Yevtushenko was a foreign national, it was also possible that the killer left the United States to ply her trade in a country where her activities were not as easily detected. Amos Bunden's final speculation was that since thallium can be absorbed through the skin, this serial killer might have been sloppy and accidentally exposed herself to thallium, in which case she might have died. While it was very possible that a death due to thallium might be undetected, there was no evidence to confirm this hypothesis.

I had no reason to tie Andrea Candy Golden to thallium. She had worked in a glass factory, and had been fired for being in the storeroom, but that was hardly convincing circumstantial evidence. How would she even have heard of thallium or considered using it as a poison? Furthermore, the killer was described as average. Andrea Candy Golden, after her boob job, was anything but average looking. I didn't know when she had undergone plastic surgery, but she had left Memphis in July of 1994, so obviously it was sometime before then. Also, she had been fingerprinted and her fingerprints weren't a match to the killer's fingerprints.

Candy Golden wasn't The Unforgiving, but I had a depressing thought. She had been missing since 1994 and we had initially presumed that she might be dead. The Unforgiving may well have had something to do with the girls on Lamar Avenue. AJ and Amy Elizabeth said that Candy was smart and was always reading mysteries. What would she have done if a mystery landed in her lap? It was pure speculation on my part, but if she attempted to solve the mystery, that might not have ended well for Andrea Candy Golden. Was she an undiscovered eighth victim of The Unforgiving?

Chapter Nineteen

As I read Amos Bunden's chapter, I tried to come up with a viable suspect. James Holloway had told me that the men in the complex had joked about the "hookermobile." The idea that one of the men in Lamar Village had acted as a protector seemed plausible until I came to the end of the tale. The killer was definitely a woman, and in any case, how would one of Candy's neighbors be tied to Yuri Yevtushenko?

The only woman at Lamar Village who had even remembered the girls in B-6 was Martha Holloway. She didn't look the type to go racing off to Atlanta to poison Yuri Yevtushenko even if she had some connection to one of the Kappa Delta girls. Martha was over seventy. In 1994 she had been over sixty. She wasn't the woman in the hotel bar.

The woman who collected the money from the girls in apartment B-6 had been described as "average looking." Bunden's chapter on The Unforgiving reported interviewing "everyone with any connection to the escort service." The FBI might have interviewed her, or might not have even known about her. It wasn't clear. There was no reason to exclude her as a suspect. Of course, if she had done it, there would have to be some connection to Yuri Yevtushenko. I suspected that I would never get within miles of The Unforgiving, even if she were still alive.

As Amos Bunden stated, the key to the case was the link between Yuri Yevtushenko and the killings in Memphis. However, all sixteen women on the Moscow trip—not just the three who were kidnapped—had been interviewed and fingerprinted. There had been no match. Their families had been interviewed, and nothing suggesting a tie to Memphis, or Atlanta had been noted. I decided to leave The Unforgiving to Amos Bunden and concentrate on the search for Andrea Candy Golden.

After dinner I made what would become my daily call to AJ whenever I was on the road. Her cell phone went to voice-mail; I called my condo.

"Aaron residence."

"Hi sweetie!"

"I'm not your sweetie."

"What did I do wrong? I'm not even there?"

I heard laughter at the other end of the line. "Nothing wrong, Jonah Aaron. This just isn't your sweetie. Sweetie is out shopping for food. This is Amy Beth. TV dinners don't cut it. We decided that as long as we're here, we'll take care of the food, the cooking, and the cleaning."

"Sounds fair."

"AJ is in charge of the cleaning. My approach to keeping your place neat is to close my bedroom door."

"A fine strategy. My brother had the same approach when we were growing up. How are you doing?"

"Tired, but getting some energy back. Classes are good."

"I heard about you enrolling. What are you taking?"

"Two seminars. Consequences of Childhood Abuse with Brenda Styne and Violence Against Women with Norma Warren."

"That's a heavy load isn't it?"

"Well, if I'm going to do anything about abused women, I have to start somewhere. I've taken all the basic courses. I was a psych major. The reading is the hard part. I'm not used to this much reading."

"Welcome to Vanderbilt."

"No kidding. With all the work, and the way I feel, I may never go on a date again. I might as well go into a what do they call it . . .?"

"A convent?"

"Yeah, but the Shakespeare word. I was in Hamlet up at Colby. A nunnery. Hamlet says to Ophelia, 'Get thee to a nunnery.'"

"You were Ophelia?"

"Tried out for Ophelia. Ended up playing Gertrude, Hamlet's mother . . . Someone had to do it. Not like there are fifty year old college students."

"You don't have to explain to me. I couldn't even get a bit part the one time I tried out for a play. You know a nunnery has a double meaning. It's Elizabethan slang for a brothel."

"And my sister's investigator boyfriend knows this how?"

"Took a Shakespeare course as a junior. Got an A minus."

"Fascinating. Any other skills I should know about?"

"Investigating. Bar trivia. Defensive back playing touch football. Well read. And I could still get a job as a sound engineer. I was really good when I was younger. That's about it."

"My sister might argue about that. She says you have other talents, but speaking of sisters, did you find out anything about Andrea?"

"I confirmed that she worked as an escort and I found out that she had a breast augmentation. When I started out yesterday morning she had been missing since 1992. Now I've got her story through July of 1994. Unfortunately, at that point the trail goes cold. Got a couple of ideas; neither one is great."

I heard a loud sigh. "A call girl with a boob job. Guess it's hard to think much of yourself when your own daddy makes you a sex object. Men! What is it about having a Y chromosome that makes human beings into pigs?"

"You think the world would be a better place if there were just women?"

"Not really. Some men are ok, Jonah Aaron. In fact, I have met some very reasonable men. And you haven't messed up yet, for example. Of course, you've only known my sister for five days. You might turn out to be a worthwhile human being."

"Thanks. I'll try not to mess up; I think your sister is fabulous."

"Please try. My sister doesn't have that much dating experience. Of course, that's probably to her advantage. You realize what dating is don't you?"

"I'm not sure where you're going with this."

"Divorce practice. You meet someone. You get to know them. You become intimate with them. Then you end it. You learn that people of the opposite sex are replaceable. You eventually get married and wonder why it doesn't work. How can it, when you have spent your whole adult life learning how expendable people of the opposite sex are. Dating is practice for divorce."

"So are you advocating celibacy, abstinence, or arranged marriages?"

"God, don't get me started on that crap, Jonah Aaron. The big thing wrong with that abstinence education shit is that people have hormones. They convince these girls to sign these damn pledges and then instead of thinking about sex with some intelligence they have to pretend to get 'swept away' by the moment. They don't plan and they don't use birth control. You know where that leads. Idiots!"

"Agree with you there. Hey, have they ever done a study comparing results of abstinence education versus contraception education."

"Just a couple. They found a trifle less sexual activity but more pregnancy and more STD's in the abstinence education group. It doesn't work."

"Interesting. You are a fountain of knowledge and cynicism. That's a compliment. I like to consider myself a smart cynic, too. I have to be cynical in a business when I often get hired to prove that a spouse is cheating. I am starting to like you, Amy Elizabeth. Don't take that the wrong way."

"I didn't take it the wrong way. My point about dating is that AJ is an absolute gem, and I hope you appreciate it."

"I'm not going to argue. Look, tell your sister that I called. Have her call me when she gets in."

"Will do, but one thought for the night, related to my other sister, Andrea. What's the difference between a hundred and fifty dollar call girl and a college girl who sleeps with a guy she doesn't like because he took her out a couple of times and spent a hundred and twenty bucks on her?"

I thought about it for a minute. "Not sure where you are going. What's the difference?"

"Thirty bucks. Good night, Jonah Aaron."

I chuckled. "OK, Miss Cynic. Good night."

AJ called around nine and we talked about what we had been doing. I learned that the Reverend Golden had taken the entire family on a tour of the Civil Rights Museum when it opened.

"What? You thought daddy was a fire breathing monster?"

"Sort of."

"He believed that you should judge people by what was in their hearts not by the color of their skin. He never preached that non-Baptists were going to hell. I think he had listened to that part of the Bible about taking the beam out of your own eye before removing the speck from your brother's eye. He wasn't all bad. He just had one major flaw."

"The kind of flaw that kept him from being father of the year."

"Yes it did, but people are complex."

"That they are."

We talked for a while longer before we called it a night. I had to drive out to the Lazy Muskrat and figured I'd need at least a half hour to get there. I wanted to be on time. Harper and Campos were bigger than me. No point in making them angry.

The Lazy Muskrat is a country music bar about ten minutes from the Memphis airport. Being from Nashville I had been in my share of similar places. There wasn't a Phillips scale for them, but I had a simple one. The more days per week with live music, and the brighter the lighting, the higher the class of clientele and the safer the environment. The other rule is that the later at night it gets, the more dangerous the situation. The Lazy Muskrat was dark and had a jukebox playing Shania Twain as I entered. There were no posters regarding live music on the weekend. I would never take AJ to a place like this, but it was three minutes before eleven o'clock and I was fine. At two AM, I wouldn't have felt comfortable in the place without a bodyguard.

Harper and Campos weren't hard to find. Black shirts, black jeans, and the moustaches were a giveaway. As promised, they were seated at the bar.

"Nice place." I lied as I walked over and shook hands. "I'm Jonah Aaron. Which of you is Campos and who's Harper?"

The one on my left answered. "The place is shit. They should call it 'The Dead Muskrat.' And do you really give a damn which of us is which?" He didn't crack a smile as he asked the question.

"Not really. Making conversation. If the place is shit, why do you come here?"

"'Cause we've been coming here for a long time."

Good a reason as any. "I hear you have a name for me."

The one on my right nodded, and blew some cigarette smoke in my direction. If that was going to be his way of showing how tough he was, this would be easy. "Yeah, college boy, we do. But what's in it for us?"

A hundred dollars seemed more than fair. Bargaining was the same in the Lazy Muskrat as when Brent Phillips had been dealing baseball cards in the Memphis shopping malls. I took a fifty dollar bill out of my wallet, placed it on the bar between them, but kept my hand on it.

The one on the right spoke without looking at me. "A hundred seems fairer."

"Fifty seems fair since I have no way to know if you're telling me the truth."

Smoke blower stood up. He was about four inches taller than me and outweighed me by seventy pounds. Forty pounds of it was fat and in his gut. I wasn't worried. Of course, there were two of them. He looked down at me with what I assumed was his best glare. "Are you calling me a liar, college boy?"

"No, I'm just saying that I don't have a way to know if the name is any good, and I don't have a way to get a refund once I walk out of here. Therefore, fifty seems fair."

The one on the left, who turned out to be Harper, had been sitting quietly drinking his beer. "Kid has a point, Alan. He won't know 'til tomorrow if the name is any good, and we got somewhere else to be tomorrow night."

"But it is good. We even made him an appointment. Told her we had a friend from Seattle looking for an expensive house just so she'd see him early in the morning. And how are we gonna split a fifty. You got change, asshole?"

The "asshole" comment was directed to Tommy Harper not to me. One thing I didn't need was to have the two of them fighting. "Tell you what. How about I give you fifty each, you use the money to buy me a beer, you tell me the name, and we all go home happy." I reached in my wallet for another fifty.

That earned a nod of the head from both of them. "Sit down college boy. The name you want is Janice Pettigrew. She's a real estate agent at Drexel and Bishop over on Ford Parkway."

I drank my beer and we talked a little about Janice Pettigrew, a little less about Candy—Brett Phillips had covered that topic—and a lot about baseball. Campos and Harper were Red Sox fans—don't find many of those in Tennessee—and since I was a Cubs fan we commiserated about the fate of our respective franchises. At the time, the Red Sox hadn't won a World Series in eighty-five years; the Cubs hadn't won a World Series in ninety-five years. I commented that anyone could have a bad century. They hadn't heard that before, and it got a good laugh.

By the end of the evening, I agreed to root for the Red Sox if and when they made it to the World Series. Campos and Harper agreed to root for the Cubs if they ever made it to the series, not that any of us expected that to happen. As I started to leave the bar, Campos motioned for me to wait while he took the final sip of his beer. "Watch out for Janice Pettigrew, college boy. There was always something about her. Gave me the creeps."

"Thanks for the heads up. Good talking to you." It was five minutes to midnight and I needed to get a good night's sleep before meeting with a woman who gave Alan Campos, all six foot five inches and two hundred and fifty-five pounds of him, "the creeps."

Chapter Twenty

In the morning, I drove to Janice Pettigrew's office at Drexel and Bishop. Up until this point, my search for Andrea Golden had carried me nowhere near trouble. Potentially, Janice Pettigrew was a lot of trouble. When I played special teams football at Vanderbilt we gave up a lot of touchdowns. It seemed like our opponent was always kicking off to us. Every time we went on the field to receive a kickoff, our special teams coach would yell, "Watch for the onside kick!" No one ever tried an onside kick against us. Why try a trick play on special teams when you didn't need it to win a game? But the point stayed with me as an investigator. One needed to consider the unexpected. In my line of work what one didn't consider could get one killed.

On the surface, Janice Pettigrew was a respectable realtor. Under the surface, she had an interesting past. I was going to pull the scab off that past, and remind her of her connection to an escort service. It was also possible that she was the serial killer known as The Unforgiving and that she was responsible for the disappearance—even the death—of Andrea Candy Golden. I wanted to guarantee, as best as I could, that her response would not be violent. I sat in the parking lot until I had seen several people enter the building. If my interview degenerated into a confrontation, the presence of witnesses was likely to help. At five minutes after nine, I entered Drexel and Bishop and was directed to her office. The door and external wall were glass. We were visible to everyone in the building. Good.

Janice Pettigrew was expecting me and stood to greet me with a handshake and a warm smile. She was slim and looked to be in her late thirties or early forties. She was wearing a dark blue blouse, a black skirt, and heels. She had dressed up the outfit with what I regarded as a stewardess scarf. She certainly fit my image of a professional realtor. "You must be the man from Seattle, the man looking for a three bedroom house with lots of land." Campos and Harper had obviously gone to the trouble of inventing a reasonable cover story for me.

I was wearing a sports jacket and tie, dressed as if I was didn't understand the Memphis heat. It enabled me to carry my revolver in a shoulder holster. I was prepared for the unexpected. I shook her extended hand and pretended to be surprised. "I think there's a mistake. I handed her my business card on which was printed "Jonah Aaron, Private Investigator." On it I had scribbled the following note: "Andrea Golden, Candy, Lamar Avenue, 1992-94. I need your help." I added the last part so that she wouldn't think this was a shakedown.

She leaned over and with her right hand reached across her body toward the upper left drawer of her desk; I reflexively reached inside my jacket. She stood up straight and smiled. Her response was exactly what mine would have been in her situation. Deny everything. "I'm sorry, but I have no idea what this is about. Who is Andrea Golden? Who is Candy Lamar?" She intentionally read the card incorrectly, but the slight pause before responding, and the smile, had given her away. She knew it said Candy and Lamar Avenue, not Candy Lamar.

I took back the card. "Sorry. I guess you're the wrong Janice Pettigrew. I'll let them know. This is going to make the movie more complicated. Sorry for the inconvenience." I turned and started to walk out of the office. Hopefully, now that I was willing to leave, she would want to know who "they" were, and what movie was now more complicated.

"Wait. Please sit down."

Moving a person to the right philosophical and emotional space does not necessarily involve throwing punches. Sometimes it just involves an appeal to curiosity. "Sure. What can I do for you?"

"For starters, what's this about?"

"I'm just trying to find someone who has been missing a while. You did recognize the name and the address, didn't you?"

"Never heard of Andrea Golden. Candy and Lamar Avenue I know. Look, can I get us some coffee? Or something?"

"Coffee would be fine. I take sweetener and cream—milk if you have it."

"Take mine the same way. I'll get us some coffees." She walked out of the office at a deliberate pace. As soon as she was out of sight, I moved around the desk, peeked in the upper left drawer, and saw a handgun. I returned to my side of the desk before she returned with our coffees.

"What movie are you talking about?"

I had just one small task to take care of before getting down to business. "How many people work here?"

She looked around the office as she counted. "Thirteen. Why are you asking?"

During the distraction I switched coffees. There are many things at which I am terrible. Dancing and basketball are two of them. Sleight of hand, the simple magic that entertains children at birthday parties, is something I have been superb at since I was thirteen years old. Janice Pettigrew didn't notice the switch. "Someday I may really need to buy property in Memphis. Just wanted to know how big a firm this was. Thirteen. That's good. Did you know Candy's real name?"

"If I did at one time, I certainly don't remember now. She was Candy. It's not like I had to fill out a W-2 on her. She was an independent contractor. What she did when she went on dates was her business, not mine. What is this really about?" She sipped her coffee very slowly.

"Just trying to locate her. The coffee is very good by the way." I actually had no idea how good the coffee was. Even though I now had the cup she had made for herself I was only pretending to drink it.

"We buy the beans at Starbucks. Thanks. I have no idea where she went when she left Memphis." She still looked worried, but panic was no longer part of her repertoire. "What kind of movie?"

"You heard about that shooting near Chicago, and the two men who broke into the Congressman's house?"

"Who didn't?"

"Andrea Golden, the woman you knew as Candy, is the older sister of the two girls who were attacked."

"You're kidding?"

"No. And don't worry about the movie. Candy's years on Lamar Avenue won't be in the movie. I just have to find out what happened to her."

She gave a deep sigh of relief. "Wish I could, but I can't help you. I don't know where she came from. I can't remember how she found me in the first place. And I have no idea where she went when she left. Just like all the girls on Lamar Avenue. They came, worked for a while, and went on their way. I wasn't that close to any of them."

I wasn't sure if I should believe her. She had no reason to lie, but she had no reason to tell me the truth. "Damn. I was hoping you knew something. What can you tell me about her? Even if you don't know where she went, maybe you know something that would help me. I know it's been ten years."

"You know, you think the past is buried and then something like this comes along." She tapped her left hand on the desk. "OK, I'll tell you what I remember. You'll have to figure out what to do with the information. Candy worked for me for two years. She was the most reliable employee, I mean the most reliable independent contractor, I ever had. She worked whenever she was supposed to work. She never turned down a client because he was too old or the wrong color. She never stole. She never set up a repeat date with a client on her own time so she wouldn't have to split the money. She was the perfect escort. Perfect attitude."

"Which means what exactly?"

"No pretensions. No fantasy that a client would turn out to be Prince Charming and run away with her. She saw each client for exactly what he was—a penis attached to a wallet."

I had never heard the expression before. If I had actually been drinking the coffee I would have choked on it. I pretended that I was. She smiled at my supposed discomfort as she continued. "Candy listened to the clients; she talked to the clients, but she never lost sight of that fact. She knew how to get the money, do her thing, and leave. She was not a romantic. And she told the best story. I really hated to lose her."

I could see why. She may not have been a whore with a heart of gold, but other parts of her anatomy had a Midas touch. "She told the best story? What do you mean by that?"

She savored her coffee before answering. "Candy was a pro at generating sympathy. The men were objects to her, but she wanted to try and be a real person to them. Or at least seem like a real person. She had this story about losing her family in a fire and telling the clients that she was working as an escort to get enough money to go back and finish college. Finish college? She had never set foot in a college classroom in her life. But, the story made her seem older, and when the story didn't earn her a tip, on the way out of the room she would ask for a donation to the volunteer fire department in her home town. That girl was a piece of work."

If Janice Pettigrew didn't know Candy's background, how did she know she hadn't dropped out college. No sense pushing that point. "Why did she leave?"

"Two reasons. First, she got bored. She was a smart girl. For the other girls, the job was about—pardon my language—fucking and blow jobs. Candy did that, of course, but for her, the real job was relating to the client, or pretending to. She once told me that the key to the job wasn't sex; it wasn't even about faking orgasms to make the guy feel like a stud. Candy once said that the key to the job was faking an interest in the client. It was too easy for her. Somehow, she learned to be an actress at an early age. She got bored."

"And the second reason?"

"She hit her number."

"The lottery?"

She waved her hand in a negative motion as she sipped her coffee. "No, not that number. Her target. The only way to survive in this business is to get out at the right time, before it really gets to you. Right after she started to work she told me that when she hit her goal, she was going to leave. Candy told me that she thought it would take her about two years. I don't know what her target was, never asked, but it took her two years, just like she said."

"Any idea what she was saving for?"

"No idea. I know she didn't stay in Memphis and start her own escort service. I would have known if she did that. After she quit, I never ran into her, so I'm sure she left town."

"How much money are we talking about as her number?"

"No idea. But she worked for two years. She never used any drugs. She wasn't supporting a worthless boyfriend or his drug habit—a lot of girls are working to do that. She never bought a fancy car. Probably never spent very much on anything." She exhaled slowly as she did a mental calculation. "I bet she left here with maybe $100,000, maybe $120,000, plus whatever she collected for the volunteer fire department . . . Hmmn . . . I just thought of something. Graceland. She loved that place. She was always going to Graceland. Not that it would cost much but you asked about what she was like. Guess that doesn't help much."

It didn't. I already knew about Graceland. Considering the gun in the drawer, the interview had gone well. Unless Janice Pettigrew was a fantastic actress, she wasn't The Unforgiving. There was no reason to think that she might have avenged the girls if they were attacked by a violent client. She had essentially said that the girls were expendable. One came, one went. Why would she bother killing someone because he had abused a girl who put herself in harm's way? If she had motivation, I didn't see it. On the other hand, I didn't see why she gave Alan Campos the creeps. I was missing something. "One last question. Is there some bad blood between you and Alan Campos?"

She chuckled. "You could say that. My father is Herbert Kane. I'm Janice Kane Pettigrew. I'm not ashamed, and it's on the Internet, but I don't advertise that."

I could see why. Herbert Kane was a Memphis mobster. An alleged Memphis mobster. He was famous enough that living in Nashville, two hundred miles away, I immediately recognized the name.

"The apartment on Lamar Avenue was in the name of a company daddy controlled. There was a problem in the early nineties and the FBI investigated. Alan got picked up. He gave the FBI my name. I had been completely under the radar. The girls didn't even know my real name. I got called in to the Memphis office of the FBI. It got leaked to the papers. Daddy was irate. Let's just say Alan took a beating for it. It's a long time ago."

That was the problem. It was a long time ago, and I had no way to connect it to the present. "Thanks for your time, and don't worry. This ends here."

She smiled weakly as I turned and left her office. When I was out of her line of vision I emptied my full cup of coffee into a potted plant. It was almost ten o'clock and already eighty-five degrees. It was going to be another ninety-degree scorcher in Memphis. I called the hotel and told them I wouldn't be back. I asked them to bill my credit card. I set the GPS to 3764 Elvis Presley Boulevard and headed to Graceland. After that, I would either be leaving on the trail of Andrea Golden or heading home.

Chapter Twenty-One

Elvis Presley, "The King," died on August 16, 1977, a little less than two years before I was born, which explains why I am not much of an Elvis fan. Among the classic acts, I much prefer Dwight Yoakum, Martina McBride, Patty Loveless, and Faith Hill. My parents had been teenagers in the late fifties and early sixties when Elvis was at the peak of his popularity and they both loved Elvis. In the early nineties, shortly after our family moved from Chicago to the Music City, my parents, my brother Barry, and I made the two-hundred-mile pilgrimage to Graceland, a colonial style mansion similar to the ones that we found around us in Belle Meade.

On the outside it looked like the homes in Belle Meade. The inside is another story. If you have never been there, go. It is a truly American experience. The name Graceland makes the estate sound like the stately home of an American king. According to critics, however, the inside of the house can best be described by adjectives such as gaudy, garish, tacky, and tasteless. My mother, the interior decorator, took the tour, and despite her love of Elvis declared that she had just visited America's unofficial monument to white trash style and that it was decorated like an elaborate whorehouse. My mother has exquisite taste. My father said nothing. Barry, who was ten years old asked "What's a whorehouse?" I felt terribly sophisticated since I was twelve years old and knew the answer to that question.

I remembered visiting the graveyard, the room with all the television sets, and the room with the animal skins. What I also remembered was signing the visitor's book when we left. Barry had written "Neat place, but Mom was disappointed. Barry Aaron, Nashville, Tennessee." That was actually a pretty profound analysis for an eight year old even though he misspelled both disappointed and Tennessee. The more I thought about it, the more I was sure that I was about to visit Andrea Golden's favorite place in the city of Memphis.

Fortunately, for my aesthetic tastes, I had neither the need nor the desire to tour the mansion. I parked the Lexus and headed to the administrative offices where I found Wendy Mason and introduced myself.

"You're the investigator that called yesterday as we were closing?"

"Guilty as charged."

She pointed to a box in the corner of the room. "Might be a little musty. They were in the basement. But we never throw anything away around here."

I thanked her and shook her hand. When she opened her palm she found a one hundred dollar bill. I was going to be there a long time and I would rather she spend the day looking at me as if I were a rich eccentric rather than an idiot. I usually don't care what people think, but since I was starting to regard myself as a bit of an idiot for trying this, I liked the image of a rich eccentric. Plus, I planned to bill the hundred to Milton Brandenburg.

"You're very generous. There were more books than I thought, by the way."

"How many?"

"Twenty-one."

I winced. "Twenty-one?"

"We get 600,000 visitors a year. The only private home in America to have more visitors is the White House. And they only have the President. We have the King." It was a line I suspected she repeated several dozen times a day. "And we have twenty-one books."

Thank goodness Andrea had left Memphis in July of 1994 and not August, the anniversary of Elvis' death. That would have meant even more visitors and more books to review.

My grandfather Herbert Aaron had been a certified public accountant in the days before computers and computer spreadsheets. He had always referred to the work he did by hand, with a crank handle adding machine, as 'dumbbell work.' Unless I got very lucky very quickly, I was going to be a dumbbell for a day or a day and a half. I didn't want to check back in to a Memphis hotel. Hopefully, I could do it all in one day. I chose a book at random and began turning the pages. Most people signed their name and listed their home city. Some gave full addresses. Comments like "Beautiful!!" and "Elvis lives!!" filled page after page. This was the Emperor's New Clothes come to life. Never did I see the words 'gaudy, garish, tacky, or tasteless.' Then again, if I was signing a book at Graceland, with Elvis fans waiting behind me to sign their names, what comment would I have made?

After reading through a few pages line by line, I started looking only for the letters A for Andrea and C for Candy. I finished the first book in twenty-seven minutes and started on the next. During my review of the fifth book, Wendy Mason and I got to talking. My dedication to my case or my hundred dollar bill had generated a friendly attitude. It was easy to talk and scan the books at the same time. She had worked at Graceland for four years. She was married and had an eight year old son and a six year old daughter. The fact that I was a trivia buff eventually came up and for the rest of the afternoon, whenever Wendy Mason was in the office, she amused herself by demonstrating how little I knew about Elvis.

For example, how many Number One hit records did Elvis have? I guessed fifteen, the answer is eighteen. What was his first Number One record? I got that one right—Heartbreak Hotel. What was his last Number One record? I had no idea that it was Suspicious Minds. What record was Number One on the charts for the most weeks? I guessed Hound Dog. The answer was Don't Be Cruel, eleven weeks at number one. Meanwhile, I continued my dumbbell work.

I worked straight through lunch. Whenever Elvis finished a concert, the stage announcer said "Elvis has left the building." Wendy Mason made it perfectly clear that while Elvis might leave the building, none of the books was going anywhere. I guess she was afraid that some other idiot investigator might come along one day and want to check if another twenty year old call girl had left an important note in the visitor's books. I was getting cranky.

At four o'clock, as I was finishing my thirteenth book of the day, Wendy Mason started asking questions about the B sides of Elvis's greatest hits. "What was the B side of Little Sister?"

"No idea."

"His Latest Flame. What's the B side of Jailhouse Rock?"

"I have no idea." I could feel my brain melting. I had probably lost ten points off my IQ since the morning had started." I had eight books left to go and I wasn't going to finish. "Can I please take these books home? I'll send them back." I didn't want to stay overnight in Memphis and come back in the morning.

"Sorry. Nothing leaves the building. What was the B side of Don't Be Cruel."

I knew that one. My father had the old 45. "Hound Dog!"

"Very good."

"Fantastic!"

"I wouldn't get that excited. A lot of people know Hound Dog is the B side of Don't Be Cruel. They were both Number One hits."

"Not that. THIS!" A good idea is a good idea whether or not it works, but this had actually been a good idea. Maybe I was getting the hang of the investigator business. In purple ink, in the middle of a page three quarters of the way through the book, was the following notation:

7/22/1994
Dear Elvis: This is my twenty-third and last trip to Graceland.
Thank you for looking over me the last two years. "Candy" is
leaving the building.
Ha! Ha! I *HEART* YOU!!!
Andrea Golden, 122 Sycamore Street, Morristown, TN
P.S. Feel free to drop by.

Morristown? I had been trying to guess where Andrea Golden might have gone. New York, Los Angeles, Chicago, Houston, and Miami had come to mind.

Despite Janice Pettigrew's assertion that Candy had gotten bored, I had the image of a glamorous woman, older than her years, who had graduated to a more upscale city and a better paying clientele. Morristown, Tennessee was not on my list of likely destinations. What was in Morristown that would have motivated Andrea Candy Golden to move there? I knew one thing. I was going to find out.

After I found the note from Andrea, Wendy Mason left the office and asked me to wait for her. She returned with a bag from the gift shop. "I bought you a present out of that hundred dollars you gave me."

I opened the bag and found an Elvis Trivia Game. I couldn't help but laugh. In my best Elvis voice I said "Thank you. Thank you very much." She didn't even laugh. I guess everyone does an Elvis impression when they're at Graceland. "That was nice of you. I think I'll give it to my parents. They're the Elvis fans in the family."

"Well, it was nice having you. I thought you were crazy until I saw that note. Good luck finding her."

"I'm going to need it. Do you have any idea what's in Morristown, Tennessee?"

"I don't even know where it is."

Morristown was more than four hundred miles and seven hours away. There was no way I could get there that night, and no reason to try. I would drive home to Nashville and sleep in my own bed. Now there was a pleasant thought, especially considering who else was sleeping in my bed. I had been staring at the visitor's logs for so long that I had almost forgotten why I was looking for Andrea Golden, let alone who her youngest sister was. My brain was switching back on after all the numbing dumbbell work. I would be in Nashville by eight.

On the radio, Amibeth says that in the long run, successful relationships depend on friendship as well as on fire and passion. It's true. AJ and I had been building a friendship with our long late night phone calls, but as I drove home from Memphis I was thinking about the potential for fire and passion.

Chapter Twenty-Two

When I left Memphis, my plan was to spend Wednesday night in Nashville and head to Morristown on Thursday morning. After spending the night with AJ, I had decided to take a long weekend in Nashville, and resume my travels on Monday. Milton Brandenburg was my client, but I was under no obligation to work nine to five, five days a week. Andrea Golden had been out of touch with her family for twelve years and, assuming Morristown held some answers, a few more days wouldn't matter.

Also, I wanted to assess my situation. After three days on the road, I realized that I wasn't just trying to prove to AJ that I was a competent investigator. I was still trying to prove it to myself. Four months earlier, in an East Nashville warehouse, I had shown that when lives were on the line, I could use a handgun. As a result, people took me seriously as an investigator, as if that were a logical train of thought.

I had read some books on detecting, and I had a mentor, a retired investigator named Kyle Ford. However, things had changed with the advent of the internet, and the books, as well as Kyle's training, seemed outdated. The tedious search through the visitor's books at Graceland had been successful, but was that an intelligent plan or merely a ridiculous idea that went well? And then there was the matter of Janice Pettigrew. My sleight of hand with the coffees, was a cute display of skill, but since I didn't drink the coffee anyway, what was the point? Even though I had tracked Andrea Golden to Morristown, I had serious doubts about my skills as an investigator.

After AJ left for school, since I wasn't traveling to Morristown, I decided to study the place on the world wide web. By the Phillips criteria, Morristown was a small city, population around 25,000. I checked the aerial map for Sycamore Street. I didn't want to drive an eight hour round trip on Monday only to learn that the address I had for Andrea Golden was now a shopping mall. It was an apartment building. Monday was going to be another knock on the door day. Hopefully, someone would be as helpful as Martha Holloway had been on Lamar Avenue.

What else could I do on the internet? Andrea Golden had lied about the family fire and about returning to college, but perhaps she did intend to go to school. I searched the internet for "Morristown Colleges." Three schools came up on the page—the Connors School of Beauty, Tusculum College, and Walters State Community College.

The Connors School of Beauty was on Main Street in Morristown. Being a beautician sounded like a reasonable career move. From the internet, I couldn't tell if it had even existed in 1994. For that, a simple phone call would suffice. I wrote down the number and made a note to call.

Tusculum College, established 1794, was the oldest college in Tennessee. Now there was a useful trivia answer if I ever heard one. But while it came up on an internet search of Morristown colleges, the main campus was in Greeneville, there was simply a downtown Morristown extension campus near the beauty school. That would be easy to check out.

The third and last school listed for Morristown Tennessee was Walters State Community College, a school that was located in Morristown, at 500 South Davy Crockett Parkway. Now, there was a true Tennessee address if ever I heard one.

I checked Google Maps to find out where Davy Crockett Parkway was located. It was only one street over from Sycamore Street. Starting at 122 Sycamore Street, one could walk through a grassy area and be on campus.

I called the Alumni Office at Walters State Community College, and told them that I was checking out a resume'. Andrea Golden had applied for a position, listing attendance at Walters State. I told the clerk that I needed to check the reference. After a few minutes I was informed that no one by that name had graduated from WSCC as they referred to themselves. I asked if they could please check if Andrea Golden had ever enrolled at Walters State.

After another wait, I was informed that Andrea Golden had enrolled in the General Studies program at Walters State in the fall of 1994, transferred to the Nursing program in 1995, and completed her R.N. training in 1998. At that time her name was Andrea Butler. Presumably she had married during her time in Morristown. Thank you, Walters State. Thank you, Elvis Presley.

I had spent three full days in West Tennessee and moved two years along the trail of Andrea Golden. I looked at my watch. Without leaving my condo, I had moved ahead four years in thirty seven minutes. That was when I hit a temporary dead end. I went to the site of the Tennessee Nursing Registry. Andrea Butler had obtained a nursing license on May 2, 1998, which would have been about the time she graduated from Walters State. The license had expired on May 2, 2000 and had never been renewed.

Why would that happen? She could have moved to another state, had a child and retired temporarily, made another career change, or, perhaps she had died. I checked for death certificates on Andrea Butler and came up empty. A search through birth records and divorce records was similarly unsuccessful.

Speculation could wait. I had already done enough work for what I had intended to be a day off. I decided to get back to a loose end that I had remembered on the drive from Memphis to Nashville. Poisons. Bar trivia from the previous Saturday. It was time to finish the list of poisons from S to Z; I had to check out the two drugs on my list.—sotalol and thallium.

Sotalol is a beta blocker, a drug that is used to slow a rapid heart rate or treat high blood pressure. In high doses it stopped the heart. Why was that even on the list as a poison? Any drug could kill you as an overdose.

The last drug on the list was thallium. Until I had started reading Amos Bunden's book, I had never heard of it. Now, I considered myself somewhat of an expert on the drug. Still, it was worthwhile to see what Wikipedia had to say about the poison.

> **Thallium** is a chemical element with the symbol **Tl** and atomic number **81**. About 70% of its use is in the electronics industry, the rest is in the pharmaceutical industry and in glass production. The odorless and tasteless thallium sulfate has been used in rat poison and as an ant killer but was banned in the United States in 1975. Because of its use for murder, thallium has gained the nicknames "The Poisoner's Poison" and "Inheritance Powder". Agatha Christie, who worked as a pharmacist, used thallium as the agent of murder in her detective fiction novel *The Pale Horse,* the first clue to the murder method coming from the hair loss of the victims. Other symptoms include abdominal pain, gastrointestinal bleeding and neuropathy. Were it not for the fact that thallium does not decompose and can be identified for decades in the bodies of its victims, it would be a perfect undetectable poison.

I dropped my head into my hands. No wonder the girls hadn't deciphered the meaning of T181. It wasn't T181. It was capital T, lower case L, then the number 81. Tl81, not T181. It was hard enough to tell them apart in print. As a piece of jewelry, the two would look the same. Andrea Golden had been a fan of mysteries. She had read English detective novels. She had worked at Pilson Glass and had been fired for being in the chemical storeroom. I saw no conclusion other than the fact that Andrea Golden had poisoned her pedophile father and bragged about it in a way that no one had recognized—until now.

G-H-T-W-H-T. God helps those who help themselves. Andrea Golden had helped herself and the sisters she was leaving behind. I had no real proof, but it made perfect sense. Before I told AJ and Amy Elizabeth anything I wanted to consider how this related to the case of The Unforgiving.

There was fingerprint evidence that showed that Candy was not The Unforgiving, but it seemed hard to believe that it was just a coincidence that both Candy and The Unforgiving had been associated with the Lamar Village Apartments. If Andrea Candy Golden had used thallium to kill her father, she might have even brought some leftover thallium with her to the apartment on Lamar Avenue. If she bragged to her sisters by giving them a pendant advertising what she had done, maybe she had mentioned thallium to someone else. Was she an accomplice, or had she unwittingly provided The Unforgiving with an idea? Maybe she had no connection to the crimes other than that. At the age of eighteen, Andrea Candy Golden had gone from living in the middle of nowhere to being in the middle of everything.

But I had no idea whom had she told about her lethal magic trick. With respect to the identity of The Unforgiving I had reached a dead end. And I had another problem. AJ and Amy Elizabeth had told me that their father had died of cancer. When we had discussed his illness, we had blamed his hair loss on chemotherapy. Did Nathaniel Golden have cancer? Was he really poisoned with thallium and did that explain his hair loss? Maybe he had cancer and had been poisoned with thallium—but if so, why poison a dying man?

Death certificates were public records and I had software that gave me access to all death certificates in the United States. According to the death certificate, Nathan Golden had died of stomach cancer on July 25, 1992. No autopsy had been done. The death certificate was signed by Dr. James Hall of Trenton, Tennessee. An Internet search revealed that Dr. Hall was a family physician, still practicing in Trenton at the age of seventy-four. I considered calling up Dr. Hall and asking him if he remembered the case. The problem was, how could I get him to tell me anything?

I wasn't certain that I would be going to Trenton, but if I was even considering a return trip to the home of the world's largest teapot collection I needed some information about death certificates before I hit the road. The perfect person to give me some of those answers was my father.

My father didn't see patients on Thursday morning or Friday morning. It's one of the benefits of an academic career that involved research and teaching. I called and caught him at his desk. Without telling him details of my case, I asked him about the accuracy of death certificates.

"Depends."

"On what?"

"If there's an autopsy, and if the results are back when the death certificate is filled out, then it's probably accurate. Otherwise, it depends on how hard it would be to make the right diagnosis."

"There's no autopsy in the case I'm working on, Dad."

"Well, in that case, the death certificate might just be a best guess. What diagnosis did they make?"

"Stomach cancer."

"And what do you suspect?"

"Thallium poisoning."

There was a long pause. "Interesting. Missing thallium poisoning is very possible. Most doctors never see a case, never think of the diagnosis, rarely even get a test for heavy metals as we call them. Missing thallium poisoning is easy to believe."

"But why put stomach cancer on the death certificate?"

"Well, ordinarily, to put cancer on a death certificate, you would want to have a biopsy of the tumor. But, maybe the doctor just wrote his best guess. He had to put something. Or, there's another possibility. Maybe the patient had one of those cancer insurance policies that only pay for cancer. Perhaps the doctor was trying to help the family get the policy to pay. Probably wouldn't work though, the insurance company would want a pathology report. At least that's been my experience."

"Thanks dad. That's actually a big help."

"You're welcome. Sounds like you have a case more interesting than the stuff I see. Most of what I do is routine after thirty plus years."

"Well, it's not routine, but it's confusing. And before I forget, Happy Father's Day. Have a great cruise." Sunday was Father's Day and my parents were leaving Saturday to spend two weeks in the Western Mediterranean.

"Stay safe, Jonah."

"You, too."

I re-read Amos Bunden's chapter looking for ideas. Amos Bunden had speculated about why the killer had stopped. Maybe the killer hadn't died, been disabled, or left the country. A killer using guns, or knives, or a garrote wouldn't run out of weapons. However, if the killer had gotten their supply of poison from Andrea Candy Golden, with Andrea no longer working for Pilson Glass, perhaps the killer had simply run out of thallium.

Chapter Twenty-Three

I took Layla for her morning walk around the neighborhood, and then went down to the exercise room on the second floor to work out before heading over to the Sundown Grille to meet Barry and Brian for lunch. We saw each other whenever we played bar trivia, but that was with the ladies. Our weekly lunches were men only.

I did forty-five minutes on the Olympic rowing machine and was hot and sweaty when I ran into my upstairs neighbor, Skylar Jones, the country singer. Skylar was going in as I was going out. She and I have been friends for years. She was dating Ricky Stone, the guitar player in her band, and I suspected that if he ever cut back on his drinking, they would get married. Since I had broken up with Donna, Skylar had been trying to fix me up with her younger sister, her hairdresser, and the divorced songwriter with whom she had co-written her last hit. I had gone out with Skylar's personal trainer, once. Nothing had clicked.

"Hey, Jonah, I got another girl for you."

"Thanks, but no thanks. Not looking right now."

"This one's different. This one is cute, funny, and smart. I know you like smart."

"That was the problem with Valerie? She was nice, but I didn't see it going anywhere."

She poked me in the ribs. "You could have some FUN Jonah. It's been months since you broke up with Donna. Live a little. Not everything has to 'go somewhere.'"

"I know. Nothing against fun. I picked up a girl Friday night at Jerry's that I thought might be fun. Turned into something very different."

"Sorry it didn't work out. But this girl I met . . ."

"No. Worked out fabulously, unbelievably fabulously. Funny. Sexy. Smart. A lot more than fun. That's the point. I'm seeing someone."

She looked as if she were trying to decide if I were making up an imaginary woman to avoid a fix-up. Skylar knew me well enough to know that not every word that came out of my mouth was the truth. "Oh. Well good for you. I hope it works out, and if it doesn't work out, you can call my friend." she looked in her purse for the number. "Her name is Elana Grey. I think you and she have a lot in common."

"Thanks, but not interested. Fix your friend up with someone else. When are you leaving on your tour?"

Skylar walked over to the stairmaster. "Not like she's desperate. She gave me her number so I could call her, not so I could find her a guy. For all I know she has a boyfriend." Skylar stated her work-out. "I don't know her that well, but I met her and I thought of you. Anyhow, we leave on our west coast tour next Wednesday. Twenty cities in twenty-four nights. Then Rickey and I are taking off for a month in Maui. Then ten days on tour in the Midwest. Then back in the studio for my new album September 1."

"I'll see you when I see you. Have a great time, and if my new redheaded girlfriend and I don't work out, I'll get back to you."

"See, I know you like redheads. Every time we're walking around The Gulch, you always look at the redheads. Elana's got red hair too."

"Good for her. I'll keep it in mind. One woman at a time for me, Skylar. Have a great tour!"

"Thanks. Singing is fun. Touring is a bitch."

"So I've heard."

As I left, she waved goodbye and stated to concentrate full time on her workout routine.

I called Karen Bing on my way to lunch. She was spending the day in the studio cutting a couple of songs and taking a lunch break. Maybe this time something that she recorded would actually get released. I asked her to call the Walters State Alumni Office and see what she could learn about Andrea Golden beyond the fact that she had become Andrea Butler. I was afraid they would recognize my voice, and Karen was great at getting information out of people. I had no idea what kind of story she could come up with, but she was a smart woman. I had nothing to lose by having her call.

And then, having accomplished far more on what I had intended to be a day off, I went to lunch. It is not true that women bond by getting together to talk about feelings and relationships while men bond by sitting and watching sports events. Brian, Barry, and I bond by getting together to talk about a wide variety of topics—like professional sports, college sports, fantasy sports, and sometimes even high school sports. Just kidding. Men do talk about relationships. At the time though, Brian was engaged to Melanie, Barry had his flavor of the month, and it had been four months since my relationship with Donna had ended unceremoniously. Discussing women had fallen off our agenda.

While I was unsure of my skills as an investigator, it seemed better than being a perpetual student. Barry was in summer school and hoped to get his undergraduate degree in May 2005. If he stayed on schedule, Brian would finish his fellowship in a medical specialty in 2012. Brian said that he and Melanie, who was one of the fifty-eight women in a class of one hundred and four medical students, hadn't given up sex to study for Board exams, and then pretended that he couldn't remember the last time they had done it. Since they had the time for bar trivia, I assumed he was only pretending to not remember sex.

As the only one with a real job, I got to discuss my cases as much as I could without breaking confidentiality. The guys were amazed that I had spent six hours reading visitors' logs at Graceland in order to track down someone who had vanished from the face of the earth. They were astonished that I had actually succeeded in my plan. I had to admit that even if it was a ridiculous idea, it had worked out amazingly well. I did not say a word about the thallium, or that the woman I was searching for was Andrea Golden.

After we ordered, the conversation turned to sports. Brian and Barry share a fantasy baseball team and were gloating over their success. "Two words for you big brother—Adrian Beltre. The guy's a stud." Beltre was having a phenomenal year in real baseball and Barry and Brian were collecting the benefits of his statistical accomplishments. In fantasy baseball terms, they were getting the advantage of Beltre's $33 performance for the minuscule investment of $11. In a fantasy baseball League, all of the fantasy owners get the same amount of money to spend. If one gets better statistical performance for his or her money than all the other guys and girls in the league, he or she wins. The game is basically played for ego and bragging rights. As AJ and Amy Elizabeth would say, I had been there, done that, and got the T-shirt. I also had six first place trophies in the closet for the experience.

I am not bragging when I mention the six trophies. With ten teams in a league, if one plays in up to four leagues at the same time for seven years, the law of averages says that one should win almost three times. I am a recovering fantasy baseball addict. If I ever decide that my life is incomplete without an all-consuming hobby that keeps me up past midnight in order to see box scores from the west coast baseball games, I hope someone shoots me.

As it is, I accept the fact that I will never again be able to name the closers and setup relief pitchers for every team in the major leagues, as I once could. I can no longer name the top five prospects in every minor league farm system. As far as I am concerned, crack cocaine is probably a cheaper and safer hobby than fantasy baseball. I have no idea how many marriages and relationships have been destroyed by fantasy baseball as compared to crack cocaine but I would bet that the numbers are close. For the record, I have no personal experience with cocaine; I'm just using it as a point of reference. With regard to fantasy baseball, as of June 17, 2004, as I sat on the patio of Sundown Grille with Barry and Brian, I had been sober for five years, eight months and ten days.

We were enjoying the Nashville sunshine and our appetizers, when Brian asked if he could expect to see 'Red' at Sunday night trivia.

"Absolutely!"

"Good! By the way, my dad told me that 'Red' turned out to be a friend of the famous Amy Elizabeth Golden and that Amy Elizabeth was in Nashville and living at your condo."

Before I could reply, Barry said "WHAT?" loud enough to be heard in my dad's office four blocks away. "You are dating 'Red' and you have this attractive, wounded blonde living at your condo? That is insane. What does 'Red' think about this? Does she even know that Amy Elizabeth Golden is crashing at your place?"

"Of course she knows, Barry. 'Red' is staying there too. Amy Elizabeth is staying in one of the other bedrooms."

"Other bedroom? Other bedroom? My brother has gone insane. Unless you put a sleeping bag in the empty third bedroom, that implies that you and 'Red' are living together in the master bedroom."

"We're not living together. She's just staying with me until . . . Well, I don't really know until what. It's sort of indefinite. She was going to look for an apartment, but we were talking last night, when I got back from Memphis, and things are so comfortable that . . . Well, she's staying. But we aren't living together."

"And the difference is what, big brother?"

"Her name isn't on the mailbox and her voice isn't on the answering machine. Basic distinction."

Brian had been listening to us without saying a word. He finally joined in. "So you go to sleep with her every night, and wake up with her every morning, and it's ok with you that she has a friend visiting with you in what is your place, but which appears to be 'sort of' her place, but you aren't living with her?"

"Exactly! And it's not like we're inseparable. I was out of town three days and two nights. She and Amy Elizabeth were at the condo. I didn't take her with me or anything."

The entrees had arrived. Being highly unimaginative, we had all ordered the chicken quesadillas. Barry was resting his face in his open palms. He finally looked up. "You dated Donna for years and she never spent more than a couple of nights in a row at your place, and you have known this woman since . . ."

"Friday."

"Friday. And you are . . . Let me see. You met her Friday. You started having her stay with you, but not actually living with you, by . . ."

"Sunday."

Barry shook his head. "Should I tell mom and dad to cancel the cruise, so they don't miss the wedding? You met her Friday. You were living with her by Sunday. At this rate you'll be engaged in a few days, married by the end of the month, and have a baby by New Year's."

New Year's was six months away. No baby by New Year's. "Of course not. We're not even living together . . . Never mind. It's just that she's obviously gorgeous.

She has a great sense of humor. I enjoy being with her. She enjoys being with me. We're getting to know each other." What was their problem?

"Well, at least he didn't say they were soulmates," Barry said to Brian. "If he had said that they were soulmates, I would have run to the bathroom to puke. Then I would have gone to hire one of those guys who rescues people from cults."

"Come on, guys. I do not believe we are mystically meant for each other. Relationships require adjustments. We're just trying to adjust, and it's easier to adjust if we're spending a lot of time together. So far, so good."

"I bet it's good. I mean, I have no complaints about Melanie, but 'Red' certainly looks hot. I just hope you don't come home from a trip and find dead bodies and blood in the condo because she turns out to be a psychopath, or all your furniture sold and the condo empty because she's a sociopath. You have to admit, you don't know that much about her."

I was too distracted thinking about Mary Nell and Congressman Miller coming home to find crime scene tape around their house to respond. When I said nothing, Brian changed the subject and we spent the remainder of the meal discussing Adrian Beltre and Brian and Barry's fantasy baseball team.

Chapter Twenty-Four

Having accomplished far more than I had hoped during the morning, I started the afternoon by reading a Robert B. Parker detective novel. My plan was to improve my problem solving skills by studying how someone else solves a problem. One reason I had doubts about myself as an investigator was the fact that I lacked a credible sidekick. Parker's hero, Spenser, has Hawk, a six foot six inch sculpted African-American buddy who is comfortable with all kinds of guns. The closest I had to a professional associate was Karen Bing, who was six feet tall and terrified of weapons.

I had read fifty pages when Karen called a little after three and delivered a rapid fire report. "Hi Jonah, I have to get back in the studio in three minutes, but I found out what you needed to know. I called that school, wherever it is, and spoke to a woman, and told her that your inquiry was not authorized, and that you had been canned, and that I personally wanted to call Andrea Butler and her husband and apologize to them. She asked around the office and found someone who remembered them. The husband's name is Bradley Butler, he was one of her teachers. He left wherever it was to enter the doctoral program in psychology at University of Chicago in June of '98. His wife Candy Butler, no one there called her Andrea by the way, went with him, and nobody knew what happened after that. That's it. Bye."

Karen hung up before I could thank her for her efforts. Considering the kind of cases that I handled as an investigator, maybe having Karen Bing as an associate was better than having Hawk.

The Illinois registry of psychologists listed a Bradley Butler with an office in Wilmette, Illinois. He had graduated from the University of Tennessee in 1991, had obtained a Masters Degree in Psychology from UT in 1993, and had obtained his doctorate from the University of Chicago in 2003. The timing was consistent with teaching at Walters State during the time the woman I now considered Andrea Candy Golden Butler would have been there.

Before I called Bradley Butler to check on his wife, I looked at the Illinois nursing registry. There was no Andrea Butler and no Andrea Golden. I wondered if she had divorced him and remarried. I searched the registry for an Andrea with middle initial B for Butler or middle initial G for Golden. There was an Andrea B Cain who was first licensed as a R.N. in Illinois in August 1998, with a license renewed in 2002 and still active. Her degree was from Walters State Community College. I had found Andrea Candy Golden Butler Cain.

There was no phone number or address in the registry, but I had more than enough to use my people finder software. Andrea Butler Cain, 506 North Lake Shore Drive, Apartment 3206, Chicago Illinois. I knew enough about Chicago to recognize a classy address when I saw it.

I googled the address and learned three important facts. The condo resembled mine. It had scenic views of the Chicago lakefront. It was for sale. All I had to do was contact the real estate agent, pretend to be a prospective buyer, and we would be in the apartment, and, eventually, in touch with Andrea. But then what? Andrea Candy Golden Butler Cain hadn't left any forwarding information along the way except for her message to Elvis. She didn't want to be found.

I had been trying to find her to create a story for Milton Brandenburg to use to promote Amy Elizabeth. We had a story, but I didn't see how it was usable. I was happy for myself, for finding her, and even happier for the woman who had been born Andrea Golden. After a horrific childhood, and a stint with an escort service, she had a respectable career and a husband. I wasn't sure how AJ and Amy Elizabeth would react to learning that Andrea was alive, apparently well, and that "T181" was, symbolic of the fact that she had used thallium to poison their father. And, of course, there was the little loose end of the serial killer known as The Unforgiving.

I waited until we were seated at dinner before I told them. AJ had heated up some frozen pasta and frozen cauliflower with cheese sauce. It was not true that she couldn't cook, just that she couldn't cook very much or very well. I couldn't complain. My repertoire was TV dinners and restaurants.

"Come on Jonah, what's the big announcement?" AJ was watching me pour the wine, an Italian Pinot Grigio. "Just a little bit. I have an exam tomorrow, and I don't really drink anyway."

"Excuse me? I read the newspapers. You got a DUI, once."

She banged her fist on the table. "This is so unfair. My life is a goddamn open book. You want to know about the DUI? I'll tell you about the DUI." She was spitting out the words. "I don't drink. Unlike some of my girlfriends who go out and get loaded so they have an excuse to fool around, I don't have any more than an occasional glass of wine . . . The DUI? We won a track meet and went out to celebrate. I was the designated driver. I had nothing to drink but a pitcher and a half of what I thought was fruit punch. Except it wasn't fruit punch. It was sangria and I didn't know it. What? You thought your girlfriend was a closet alcoholic?"

"No. I thought maybe you had cut back since then. Or maybe you just overindulged one time. I'm sorry."

She glared at me for a moment. "Not your fault. It just comes with being AJ Golden and having my whole life all over the papers. That's why I don't want to be her . . . Come on, you said you had big news." She tried to smile.

I thought about AJ's desire for privacy. Shooting the Diaz Brothers had made that impossible. "Ladies, I have a toast. To Andrea Candy Golden Butler Cain, your sister. I found her. She is a nurse, and she is married to her second husband, well, the second one that I know of, anyway."

"WHAT?"

"WHAT?"

"I thought you were taking the day off, Jonah Aaron. That's fabulous. To Andrea." Amy Elizabeth raised her glass to her lips and took a sip.

AJ got up and raced over and gave me a hug and a kiss. "I have a smart boyfriend. I have a smart boyfriend." In a voice a little above a whisper she added, "Even if he did think I was an alcoholic." She laughed. "How did you find Andrea? When we left for school this morning you were talking about going to Morristown on Monday."

I went through the sequence of events that I had used to find Andrea Candy Golden Butler Cain. "Dr. Eric Cain is a cardiologist. That marriage is on the books by the way, but the bride listed her name as Andrea Butler, that's why I didn't find it when I did my computer search Sunday night. The marriage to Bradley Butler must have occurred somewhere that the records didn't reach the internet, maybe out of the country. By the way, I don't know if Andrea has any children from either marriage. I couldn't find any record of children, but that doesn't mean that there aren't any."

"AJ, we could be aunts. Where are they? New York? Florida? C'mon tell us."

"Chicago. Lake Shore Drive."

"Jonah Aaron, that is thirty miles, forty five minutes from where we have been for the last five years. And she never called us . . ." Her voice trailed off.

"Ladies, she may not have known—at least not until the attack on Woodland Hills Lane. She might have assumed you were in Kenton. I don't know."

Amy Elizabeth waved her hand in a horizontal motion. "She knew. Mary Nell Miller the Congressman's wife was all over the society pages. Mary Nell is not a common name. She couldn't have missed it." She paused. "Well, she might have. Not everybody reads the society page. I always do, but you don't do you AJ?"

"Never."

"Well, maybe she didn't know. But after I was raped, she couldn't have missed that. She does not want to be in touch with us."

"Looks that way, ladies."

AJ and Amy Elizabeth were digesting the information. Neither of them was touching the food.

"When can we see her? Did you set something up to go and visit?"

I took a deep breath before continuing. "Unfortunately, there is some other news. The reason you couldn't figure out what T181 means is that it isn't T181." I gave them a printout of the information on thallium with the 'Tl' and '81' in boldface. I wanted them to draw the conclusion themselves.

"Oh-my-god. She killed daddy. Amy Elizabeth, Andrea killed daddy. She poisoned him with thallium." She tried looking at her own pendant, which was difficult to do as the chain was short, and the letters and numbers were upside down. She walked over to examine her sister's pendant. The two women embraced and started to cry.

"AJ, she killed him to protect us. She knew she had to get out of there and she wanted to make sure we were safe. If it wasn't for us, she could have just left. No wonder she doesn't want to have anything to do with us and wants to put it all behind her. Andrea killed daddy!" Her mascara was running down her face as she and her sister shared an embrace. "Turnips. It must have been the turnips, Jonah Aaron. Daddy loved turnips and the rest of us hated them, especially mama. But mama always made him turnips for dinner. If Andrea poisoned the turnips she would know she wouldn't hurt anyone else. Of course it could have been the whiskey . . ."

I interrupted the speculation. "Whiskey? I thought Baptists weren't supposed to drink."

"Not supposed to rape their oldest daughter either, sweetie."

Amy Elizabeth had stopped crying and was blotting the tears with the back of her hand. "Excuse me. I have to put my face back together," She headed toward the bathroom.

AJ came over and hugged me. "Are you sure you still want us here?"

"Of course I do. Why wouldn't I?"

"Daddy was a rapist, mama is a narcissist, and our older sister is a murderer. I'm not sure I'd want to hang out with us."

"Well, I want to keep you around. You are fabulous and Amy Elizabeth is . . . Amy Elizabeth. What other people in the family did doesn't count against you."

Amy Elizabeth had come back in the living room and was making a call on her cell.

AJ eyed her suspiciously, "Who are you calling?"

"Milton. He has to help us decide what to do."

AJ glared at her sister. "I know he's your agent but you can't tell him. This is private."

But it wasn't. "I'm sorry, but Milton already knows. He's the client—remember. I already told him. He's coming over at eight. There's some more information, but I want to wait until Milton gets here to talk about it." For the time being, I was going to sit tight on the information about The Unforgiving.

When Milton arrived, we all agreed that the pendant was a symbol for thallium and that Andrea Golden had poisoned her father. Neither of the girls remembered their father actually being diagnosed as having stomach cancer—they had just assumed that was the diagnosis after he lost his hair just like the woman down the block who was getting chemotherapy. In fact, they didn't remember Nathaniel Golden ever being in the hospital. Nathaniel Golden hated hospitals and had died at home.

AJ and Amy Elizabeth wanted to go see Andrea but they wanted everything to do with thallium to remain buried in Nathaniel Golden's grave. On the other hand, Milton thought that Nathaniel Golden's death from thallium poisoning was a lucky break for Amy Elizabeth. "If we can play it right da publicity would be unbelievable. Fantastic." Whenever he said fantastic, he spread the first syllable over a few seconds so that the word came across as FAN—tastic.

Milton regarded the situation as "great theatre." The way Milton saw the situation, Andrea might be willing to tell her story, especially if he could arrange it that there would be no legal repercussions. After all, her father had raped her repeatedly. Milton saw the killing as a selfless act done to protect her sisters. If it didn't meet the legal definition of justifiable homicide, it was close, and in the interval since the crime, Andrea had apparently become a productive citizen.

Milton wondered out loud what District Attorney would take a woman to trial for murdering her abusive father especially when she had sought help from the authorities and been turned away? "Dey go after Andrea, den public opinion is gonna crash down on 'em. Dey ain't gonna do it." Milton saw it as a win-win proposition for everybody—except Andrea. "How are da people in her new life gonna react to findin' out she killed her daddy? Dat's da question?"

With Milton wanting to go public with Andrea's story, I could no longer sit on the information about The Unforgiving. Very slowly I outlined the story of the serial killings that had been associated with the girls on Lamar Avenue. I went over the evidence that Andrea was not The Unforgiving but that she was almost certainly tied to the mess, possibly by providing the thallium, or by giving someone the idea of using it.

As I was telling the story, I could tell from the expression on Milton's face that this was the end of the line. A prosecutor might not go after a woman who poisoned the father who had raped her, especially when she was seventeen at the time. The story of a serial killer put matters into a different light. Milton removed his checkbook from his jacket. "Jonah, you had a great week. You found a woman I figured would never be found, and you also found out about something that could have come back to bite us all in the ass. You started Sunday night." He counted the days on his fingers. "Sunday. Monday. Tuesday. Wednesday. Thursday. Dat's five days. Twenty five hundred bucks plus expenses and a bonus of two thousand. Forty-five hundred for less than week's work. Will a thousand cover your expenses?"

I nodded.

"You ain't done bad. You found her, but at dis point, no way to bring dis out in da open. It's over. I ain't gonna hurt no one, let alone da sister of my client just to make a buck." He turned to AJ and Amy Elizabeth. "My lips are sealed. Da past stays buried. Dis bit with Da Unforgiving, dats a little too much. We'll figure out a Plan B." He handed me a check for fifty five hundred dollars.

I knew Milton would keep the secret, but I was not comfortable with the way the situation had been resolved. When AJ and Amy Elizabeth and I had first discussed a Plan B, AJ had talked about faking a jump off a bridge into the Cumberland River. I thanked Milton for the check. "The question right now is whether we go see Andrea."

"Considering dat she don't wanna see you, why go? And if you do go, why are you going?" He looked at me. "Are you going up dere to find out what happened with dose murders? She ain't going nowhere. My suggestion is to wait a while. Just saying."

AJ gave me a hug as Amy Elizabeth saw her agent out of the condo. "You know how I've been saying all week that I have a smart boyfriend?"

"Mmm, hmm."

"Right now I think I wish you weren't so smart. We all might have been better off not knowing about The Unforgiving. Why did you smile when I said that?"

"I'm smiling because you said you wished I wasn't as smart. You didn't say that you wished I wasn't your boyfriend."

"If I didn't have to study for an exam tomorrow I'd show you how happy I am that you are my boyfriend. You did more than I hoped for. You found my sister and she's alive. If she doesn't want to see us, maybe that's because she thinks she has something to lose. And that means she has something in her life that matters to her. And that's good." She looked at her watch. "Got to study." She gave me a very wet kiss. "Not your fault Andrea did what she did." She looked at her watch again. "No. It's study time. There's tomorrow, and the weekend, and hopefully a whole lot more after that." She kissed me again then went to sit in the Eames chair in the corner of the living room. "You know, not to complain or anything, but if I could get a desk and put it in that empty third bedroom, that would be great. I'd have a comfortable place to study, I would never mess up the living room, and I could stay here forever."

I didn't say anything.

"Oh, God. I just messed up big time didn't I? I had no business saying that—assuming that you would want me to stay a long time and that I would need a desk. I'm sorry. Lo siento. Lo siento. Say something, Jonah! I told you the first time we were together that I can get too clingy. It's just that I like being here with you. Say something, please."

"Two Danes."

"Is that code for something? What does that mean? I'm sorry."

"Nothing to be sorry for. Not code. It's a store. Two Danes. Great Scandanavian furniture. A little expensive. I can afford it. That's where most of this stuff comes from. Do you want to go shopping with me tomorrow night, or Saturday, or do you want me to pick out a desk myself. What do you want to do?"

"You're not angry that I talked about staying here forever."

"Not angry. The third bedroom's empty. You're here. You need a place to study. You need a desk; it'll keep the living room neat. I have money. What could be simpler?"

"Nothing I guess, but we've been together less than a week. I was tired and sort of both happy and upset about Andrea when I said it. I wasn't thinking. You don't have to be buying me furniture."

"I know. I'm not. I'm buying furniture for the condo. You're just going to be the only one who uses it seeing as how we're on this long first date." I smiled.

She thought it over, tilting her head from side to side like a metronome as she thought about it. "In that case, we go shopping together. Gotta study." She got up, gave me a peck on the cheek and went back to the chair.

I sat on the sofa reading my detective novel and looking up every once in a while to gaze at the redheaded angel who was staying at my condo. I finished the book a little after one. Spenser solved his murder case after depositing a pair of dead bodies in a Boston parking garage. AJ was fast asleep. I thought about waking her up and walking her back to bed, until I remembered the last time someone had awakened her from a sound sleep. I decided not to startle her. I let her sleep in the chair.

Chapter Twenty-Five

In the morning, AJ headed off to Vanderbilt. I kissed her goodbye, wished her luck on her exam, and called Dr. Hall's office in Trenton. An answering machine told me that the office opened at 8:00. I left a message explaining that I was investigating a problem with some medical records, that the case was an old one involving Nathaniel Golden, and that I would appreciate being called as soon as the office opened. I hoped that he wouldn't dodge the call.

To my surprise, a little after eight, Dr. Hall's receptionist, Martha Gomen, called to inform me that Dr. Hall would see me that day if I could catch him during his lunch break, at eleven. It would be about a two and a half hour drive to Trenton. I showered, put on a clean sport shirt and a clean pair of jeans, decided against taking my gun, and left the condo before eight thirty. My curiosity had gotten the best of me. Why was stomach cancer listed on the death certificate?

Despite being a medical sub-specialist, my father had taught me to respect primary care doctors. While my father knew a great deal about the diagnosis and management of patients with different types of cancers, primary care physicians had to deliver babies, do minor surgery, and see patients with a myriad of common medical complaints—and some patients with serious problems masquerading as common medical problems. There was no way the breadth of their knowledge could possibly match its depth.

I felt guilty about the fact that I was about to waste Dr. Hall's valuable time with one of my concocted stories, but not guilty enough to stay home instead of heading to Trenton. I listened to CD's by Skylar Jones and by the Dana Twins while I drove and made it to Trenton by eleven.

Dr. Hall's waiting room was as crowded as a department store on the Friday after Thanksgiving. It was filled with pregnant women, coughing children, geriatric patients, and a couple of teen-aged boys whose mother told me they were there to have stitches removed. Dr. Hall was running late. I introduced myself to Mrs. Gomen, a short, wiry woman with long dark braided hair and tired eyes. Over the course of an hour, the waiting room emptied out. A little after noon, Mrs. Gomen told me that the doctor could see me.

Doctor Hall was seated behind his desk eating what smelled like a tuna fish sandwich. He looked every day of his seventy-four years. What was left of his grey hair was professionally styled, and he was wearing a Tommy Bahama shirt and a pair of blue jeans. His white coat was tossed casually on one of the two chairs opposite his desk. He motioned for me to sit down on the other chair. "Are you any relation to Doctor Melvin Aaron at Vanderbilt?"

"He's my father."

"Good man, your dad." He chomped on his sandwich. "He gave a lecture to the Academy of Family Practice a couple years ago on how we have cardiac resuscitation in the hospital all backwards. Outside the hospital, that's another thing. Some people who have a cardiac arrest can be saved. But for patients in the hospital, he said that instead of resuscitating everyone unless they decided in advance that they didn't want it, we should resuscitate nobody except patients with cardiac arrhythmias and totally unexpected deaths. He said that if we can't keep them alive when they're alive, we can't keep them alive when they're dead. The statistics he showed on the results of in-hospital resuscitation opened a lot of eyes. Sure convinced me to talk to people about being less aggressive."

"Sounds like my dad."

"Yeah. The problem is that people want everything done. With all they hear about advances in technology, it's difficult for people to accept that the death rate is one hundred percent." He finished the last bite of his sandwich. "Of course, in a big medical center the doctor has an advantage."

"What's that?"

"If a doctor at a big medical center suggests that it's time to stop treatment and be made comfortable, the patient might listen. If I tell someone he needs to stop treatment and be made comfortable, he decides it's time to get a second opinion. I can't blame them. I probably wouldn't trust a family practice doc like me if it was my life on the line. Anyway, you didn't come here to talk about your dad and terminal care. Martha said you were investigating an insurance problem. Is that right?"

"Basically. It's a case from long ago. They sometimes give the young investigators cases with loose ends to see what we can learn. There really isn't a major problem. The case is Nathaniel Golden, you probably don't even remember . . ."

"I know the case. Just so you know, the Golden family never brought that little girl, Andrea, in to see me after she was nine. Her mother kept her away from doctors. I pulled the charts on the whole family last week after I heard Amy Elizabeth talking on television. I was worried that I had missed the signs of abuse. I never had a chance to see them."

"Nathaniel Golden?"

"For what it's worth, I looked at his records too. Saw him three times for stomach pains. I had no idea what was going on. The last two times, I told him and his wife that they should go to Jackson to be seen by an internist. They finally did. There's a report in the chart from the Emergency Room in Jackson where they did a CAT scan. It showed nothing. They recommended admission for testing, but he refused."

Dr. Hall handed me the chart containing the report. The bottom line was all I needed to see. "No abnormality detected." If Nathaniel Golden had died of thallium poisoning, the CAT scan would have been normal. If he had stomach cancer, the CAT scan would almost certainly have shown a tumor. I looked at the billing records in the chart. The diagnosis "abdominal pain" had been crossed out and replaced with "stomach cancer."

Dr. Hall anticipated my follow up question. "I know. There was no proof of cancer, but they had a cancer-only policy. I had no diagnosis, so I filled out all the forms as stomach cancer. Just trying to be helpful. Does your company want the money back after all these years? It's all of ninety dollars for three visits."

"No. I think the company just sent me here so I could be educated on how things work. I suspect that if it was a larger amount they wouldn't have paid without a diagnosis in the first place. I saw the death certificate, it said stomach cancer."

"Same thing. I told Mary Nell that she needed a pathology report to get the CT scan covered by the cancer insurance, but she was hoping that a death certificate would do."

His explanation made perfect sense, and I didn't want to waste his time. "I'll let you get back to work. Sorry to bother you. Thanks for the education."

"Say hello to your father for me."

"I'll do that." As I left the office I noted that the waiting room had filled up again.

Mary Nell had taken Nathaniel Golden to Jackson. The only thing she had helped to cover up was the sexual abuse of her daughter. Despite what the death certificate said, Nathaniel Golden had died of thallium poisoning.

I headed back to Nashville. After I passed Jackson and got on Interstate 40, I called AJ on her cell phone. "Hi-ya. Sweetie. How'd your exam go?"

"So-so."

"Sorry to hear that. With Milton over and all the talk last night you didn't really get a chance to study. And it was your first test at Vanderbilt. You'll do better next time. Anyway, maybe you're worried about nothing. When do you get it back? Maybe you did better than you thought."

"I know how I did. They posted the answer key. I'm going to end up with a ninety-six."

She was truly disappointed. "Only got a ninety-six? And you're unhappy?"

"I should have done better. I'm hard on myself when it comes to grades."

"Sounds like it."

"Yeah. When I was in the fifth grade I used to come home with hundreds on all my tests, and you know what Mary Nell said?"

"Probably said something like, 'How many other kids got a hundred?'"

"How did you know that?"

"Your mom and my mom and dad evidently went to the same school of child rearing when it came to having your kids get good grades."

"But you love your folks and I hate my mom."

"There are other variables in that equation."

"I love it when you talk math."

"It was the only way in which my folks were over the top. And in case you haven't looked around, Mary Nell is nowhere near Nashville. It doesn't matter what she thinks."

"Yeah. It's just going to take a while getting used to not have to listen to her crap. I am never going to have to put up with her again. Never."

"Not if you don't want to."

"By the way, Amy Elizabeth and I were looking at your friend's blog. Bret Phillips. She loved it. She says she needs a philosophy of life for when she has her radio show and she wants to use his."

"Excuse me for asking, but what about her philosophy of life."

"Oh, Amy Elizabeth can be funny, maybe even witty, or over the top, but she doesn't have an original idea in her pretty little head. Her philosophy of life used to be 'See boy, date boy, decide boy doesn't have enough money, repeat cycle.' She needs more than that if she is going to be on the radio playing the wise Amibeth. That's one word by the way. No Y. A-M-I-B-E-T-H. The wise all-knowing Amibeth, that's who she wants to be on the radio. It's her new persona. She starts Monday on the Vanderbilt radio station by the way. Milton says it will be good practice. Anyway, Amy Elizabeth and Milton Brandenburg want to buy the rights to Brett Phillips' blog."

"I'll give him a call and try to put the two of them together. It might even be become more than a business relationship."

"Good. Maybe she'll fall in love with him and move out. She is being obnoxious today. She's a little bit too much into herself. Living with her is like having a chaperone around."

"What's the problem?"

"Sister stuff. No big deal. She was criticizing the clothes I was wearing. Said I looked too casual. I was taking an exam for heaven's sake. I told her to give it a rest. It'll be fine."

"I'm going to call Brett. I'll have him give her a call." I looked at the GPS. "See you in an hour and a half."

"Bye, Jonah. Drive safe. Bye."

Southerners, even those who do well academically at top schools, often use adjectives to modify verbs. She was off the phone before I could tease her about it. Drive safe indeed. The word is "safely."

I called Brett and told him about Amy Elizabeth's interest in his blog. I explained that the fabulous woman I had told him about was AJ Golden.

"Did you tell her about the shooting."

"Of course I told her. She wanted to know why Donna ended everything. She was relieved to find out that was all it was."

He laughed. "All it was? You found the only civilian woman on the planet whose reaction to that shooting is 'No big deal. I killed two people just last week, myself.' Since you're telling her everything, did you tell her about the Dana Twins?"

"No. And there were no Dana Twins."

He laughed. "You didn't tell her about Huetter, Idaho, and the harpoon gun? I mean, shooting two meth dealers is impressive, but Huetter, Idaho, that story is incredible."

"I have never told anybody that story. The only reason you know is because Kyle Ford told you when we went out drinking. And he knows because he was there. Milton still talks about making a movie about the Dana Twins. I don't see how he can, but there are a lot of things I don't understand."

"You and me both. I'll give Amy Elizabeth Golden a call tonight. I wouldn't mind if people ended hearing my philosophy of life, even if they heard it from some rape victim."

"Don't call her that. She keeps saying she's a survivor, not a victim. Save yourself a fifteen minute tirade."

"I'll remember that. It'll be a short phone call."

After dinner, before AJ and I left to buy the desk, Amy Elizabeth got a phone call from Brett Phillips. When we returned from shopping they were still on the phone. It was a build it yourself desk. AJ and I had it assembled by eleven. They were still on the phone. They were talking at midnight when AJ and I went to bed to celebrate our one week anniversary.

Afterwards, I held AJ in my arms, listening to her heart beat, and concluding that I was the luckiest man on the face of the earth.

"You are a great problem solver, Jonah."

"I like to think so, but what problem are you talking about."

She brushed her hair off her face. "My problem. I told you that I used to get all flustered and worried if a guy was ever going to call me again." She kissed me. "This way I don't have to worry. I like it. Is it really ok if I don't look for an apartment? Is it ok with you if I stay here?"

"Let's keep seeing how it goes. Have you heard one word of complaint from me?"

She shook her head, and kissed me. "Good night, Jonah."

We snuggled up like spoons. "Night, AJ."

I couldn't hear what was being said, but I could tell that Amy Elizabeth was still on the phone with Brett Phillips. If Amy Elizabeth's philosophy of life was "See boy, date boy, decide boy doesn't have enough money, repeat cycle" she had reached the end of the line. When I was addicted to fantasy baseball, I would routinely spend several hundred dollars to finance teams with corny names like The Nashville Daze, The Music City Wonders, and Jonah's Whales. If Brett Phillips wanted to buy a baseball team, he would put together a small syndicate and buy the Seattle Mariners.

Chapter Twenty-Six

The trip to Chicago's Lake Shore Drive was put on an indefinite hold until it could be a happy family event not marred by our concerns over the Memphis thallium killings. Andrea was married, hopefully happily married, and that information would have to suffice. Other than telling Milton what I had learned, I never even considered telling anyone, including the FBI, what I had discovered.

Andrea Candy Golden Butler Cain became less and less of a topic of conversation at the condo. We developed the habit of singing her name to the tune of ACGBC, the musical notes they represented. This is, after all, Nashville.

AJ and I settled into a very comfortable relationship, though we occasionally joked that we were on a "long first date" and not actually living together.

"Sweetie, do you think that maybe we should tell people that I have a drawer at your place or something, so they get the idea we are a serious couple?"

"I think all our close friends know that by now. I think they know you have more than a drawer," and we burst out laughing. From the time AJ and I had started our "first date" at my condo she had her own closet and a complete bureau in the master bedroom, her own sink in the master bath, and her own medicine cabinet above her sink. One advantage of having a large condo, was that we never had arguments over "her space" and "my space." That is not to say that we had a squabble free life.

Mona Brandenburg says that successful relationships depend not on the absence of arguments but on the ability to argue respectfully, and when we argued, we did that. Despite the fact that under exigent circumstances we had shot and killed four people between us, we were even-tempered individuals—even-tempered individuals who took target practice together at least once a month.

I did not mind that my experience in the East Nashville Warehouse served in part to define me. I was a man, and the shootout made me look competent. It brought in business. I had more than enough to do, and, financially I was doing well, even before Amy Elizabeth became Amibeth and I started to collect the two and a half percent of her income that Milton had given me. AJ, on the other hand, did not wish to be defined as the shooter of The Roofers. Her sixty-one second run had been necessary; it had saved her life. It was not who she was.

Sometime in July, AJ showed me her Montana Driver's License—Elfleda Anastasia Something or other—from Bozeman, Montana. I finally realized why people in Nashville and at Vanderbilt had no idea that she was AJ Golden. On paper, she wasn't AJ Golden.

"What is that driver's license about?"

"Simple. You know I don't want people knowing I'm AJ Golden. Amy Elizabeth has been telling us that sometimes people shout out 'Where's AJ? Bang! Bang!' when people recognize her on the street. That's not for me. It's like chalk on a blackboard to my ears. So, when Milton was getting Amy Elizabeth into grad school, I had him get the name on my official records changed. Milton is very powerful at Vanderbilt."

"Board of Trust powerful."

"Yeah. So he had this name someone wasn't using. It's a beautiful name it means . . ."

"Noble beauty. It doesn't quite express how hot you are, but noble beauty is fine."

She wrinkled her nose as she looked at me. "How do you know what an Old English name means? Is that trivia stuff? You're smart but you're not that smart."

I couldn't argue the point. "You don't even know where your own name comes from. That's funny in a way."

"Huh?"

"Skylar Jones. Elfleda Anastasia is Skylar's real name! No wonder you don't look like the picture on the license. That's Skylar Jones at seventeen. That's what she looked like when I undiscovered her. Her father is a super rich banker from Bozeman, Montana. He sent her to Nashville just before her seventeenth birthday with enough money to get by for about a year. You're going to need to get the picture changed."

"Cross that bridge when we come to it. Undiscovered? How exactly do you undiscover someone?"

"Easy. I saw her singing at a charity fundraiser for abused children. She had been in Nashville eleven months. She had one month to go on her failing plan for fame and fortune, and that was the best gig she could get, appearing for next to nothing at a charity function."

"Was she any good?"

"I sure didn't think so. Flat and flat. Her chest and her voice. But she was cute and her original songs were very good. She always could write. Of course singing under the name Elfleda didn't help. I was telling her she should give up singing and become a songwriter, when Milton walked by and said "Sweetie, with voice lessons and a little body work you could be a star. Your stage presence is F-A-N-tastic and you are having so much fun up there, everybody loves you—even if you drop a few notes." I had been talking in my natural manner, but I dropped into an impression of Milton's deep bass voice and his accent, "But we gotta change da name."

"He said that?"

"I was right there undiscovering her, telling her she had no future as a singer, and Milton saw something nobody else did and discovered the rising star who may yet be one of country music's biggest acts of the decade. She turned down the breast augmentation. You can tell that if you've seen any pictures, or if you've run into her. But she took the voice lessons. Milton signed her on the spot. I was there when she signed the contract on top of her piano at the charity fundraiser."

"Her piano?"

"That was the other thing. Elfleda played the piano. Not a guitar. She's good at the piano. I have, I guess we have, a standing invitation to come upstairs and sing. She's one floor up. We should do it sometime. Anyway, that's how I know that Elfleda means 'noble beauty.' She told me. Milton decided that since she was from Montana it should be Sky Something. She chose Skylar. Skylar and I have been friends ever since—even before I gave her a heads up on the condo upstairs."

"Did you and she ever hookup? No big deal if you did. It was before we met."

"No. I was a twenty or twenty-one year old Vanderbilt junior, and she was a seventeen year old high school dropout. Actually, she was home schooled. She has a GED. Even then, I wasn't into relationships that were dead end deals. I like things with a long term potential. She's always been just a friend."

"Seventeen? She was like sixteen when she came to Nashville. That's almost child abuse. Who sends a sixteen year old girl to Nashville by themselves to be a star?"

"Not by herself. Mama was there, sitting in the corner, knitting, being a chaperone and making sure nothing happened to her angel, while Daddy was back home in Bozeman. By the way, save that Driver's License. It's a collector's item. If you don't want to sell it on eBay, give it back to Skylar."

AJ went quiet for a while. "You told ME I had no chance of making it as a singer."

"Obviously, I am a better investigator than I am a talent scout. But that was before I knew you were AJ Golden. If you channeled your inner AJ and got some spunk in your voice, instead of trying to be a clone of Alison Krauss, like you doing that night at Jerry's, you could front a band that did parties. I don't think you could be the next Skylar Jones but I bet you could do something like that."

"Not interested anyway. Gotta keep up the grades. But I love to sing."

I took her hand and kissed it. "Five years from now, whatever happens to you and me, whenever you and the man who is the special person in your life have friends over, you will be able to amaze people with how good you are. And the man in your life, he will be one very lucky man."

"You're sweet." She kissed me and began whistling. "Ta-da-Ta-da . . . Ta-da'-da . . . ta-da-da-da."

"Excuse me for asking, but now that I've seen that ID, I have to ask. What do they call you at school?"

"Right now they call me 'Elfie' or 'Red'; I'd like to be AJ. It's just that I don't want to have to sit in class and be worried that if I give a right answer to a question, someone will shout out 'Bang Bang, Nailed that one.' I know I'm AJ; you know I'm AJ. Amy Elizabeth knows I'm AJ. The fewer people that know, the better."

In late August I found out that Brian Brandenburg knew that the woman I was living with was AJ Golden. After a successful Saturday night of bar trivia at The Sports Bar, AJ was in a mood to sing. Barry and his date had headed back to his apartment. Brian, Melanie, AJ, and I had gone to Jerry's.

AJ and Melanie were starting to bond, so instead of performing solo, AJ joined Melanie in performing some numbers by the Dixie Chicks, including the suggestive "Sin Wagon" with its reference to "mattress dancing." Melanie can't hold a tune, and singing without Melanie would have been addition by subtraction. As it was, accompanied by Melanie, it was hard to tell that AJ had a much better voice for up-tempo songs than she did for ballads. Despite the dissonance, the two women had a wonderful time.

Despite our protests, the two women convinced Brian and me to get up on the stage. We decided to perform two songs that we hadn't sung together in years, "Yummy, Yummy, Yummy" from the first Dana Twins CD, and "Dangerous Man," the big hit from *Dana Twins 2*. The thought of those cute blonde boys being "dangerous" was one of the reasons the song had been such a gigantic hit. The fact that the boys disappeared the day the record was released didn't hurt sales either.

> I know that you know that I know that you know that I know (drum riff) what you did last night. But I can keep a secret, I can keep a secret. I can keep a secret. You know that I can. You think I'm a sweet boy. You call me your boy toy. But maybe, baby, maybe I'm a dangerous man.

If I am allowed to brag for a moment, we then received something that I had never seen previously at Jerry's, a standing ovation. Except for an oblivious drunk couple pawing each other in a back corner of the room, we were a hit. Of course, as they say in show business, "If you can make it in New York, you can make it anywhere. If you can make it at Jerry's, you can make it at Jerry's."

Brian turned to me, and under his breath whispered, "Oh, shit. What do we do now?"

"Laugh it off! Wave to our fans and sit back down." I smiled and did exactly that as the Saturday night crowd of about forty people shouted for an encore. "What do you think is going to happen, Brian? Do you think the headline in the Tennessean tomorrow morning is going to read 'Dana Twins Back from the Dead at Jerry's last night?'"

"Of course not, but we shouldn't have done that. If my father hears about this . . ."

I shrugged my shoulders. "It's eight years. We'll tell him we were just trying to revive interest."

Melanie had an expression six degrees beyond shock on her face. She had known Brian only for the two years she had been at medical school at Vanderbilt. "I had no idea you could sing. That was actually amazing. Uh, how old were you guys in 1996 and is there something you want to tell us?"

I answered for both of us. "We were seventeen in 1996, and we are not the blonde boys on that famous poster. We just spent a lot of time imitating the sound back then. I was shocked we were still any good. But there were no Dana Twins. There was just a brilliant sound engineer playing around with computer equipment." It was exactly what Brian and I had said back in high school.

"I've heard that before from Brian. No way."

AJ decided to parody my first assessment of her performance at Jerry's the night we had met. "Well, looking at you, I thought you boys were cute. In fact, I'd take you home," she pointed to me, "and jump in bed with you right now. But the choreography was god awful. Of course, when you close your eyes, and just listen to the sound, and that's the only way to truly assess the commercial value of talent, I'd swear we were listening to the Dana Twins, especially the second album when their voices were just starting to change."

I chuckled and began to cough. "Well, too bad there is no market for Dana Twins impersonators like there are for Elvis impersonators, but I'll take you up on the 'take you home and jump in bed with you' part."

AJ and Melanie headed for the rest room while Brian and I settled the tab.

"Jonah, I have to apologize."

"For what. I got up there too. We probably shouldn't have done that, but so what? That was . . ." I tried to think of a synonym for stupid. "That was a lot of fun!"

"No. Not for that. For a couple of months ago. For saying that you and she were rushing things. You may have been, but I hope you and she stay together. She's witty, she's a knockout, she's wild about you, and she's got spunk. It takes spunk to kill two serial killers."

Now it was my turn to look shocked. "Where did that come from?"

"My dad left some papers lying around from the time he got 'Red' into Vanderbilt. I told him to be more careful. Clients come to the house. Someone else could see. Anyway, I hope you stick with AJ."

I shook my head. "I've been thinking about asking her to marry me, if things keep going well, except that she'll say, 'No.' We get along great. We like the same kind of things. But she's applying to medical school all over the Ivy League. Her grades and test scores are out of sight. She's going to be able to go anywhere. My job depends on connections. I know everyone I have to know here in Nashville. It would be difficult but not impossible to move. But I have thought about it. I could start over."

"Plan to move East, or beg her to stay. I guess it's not for me to say, but do not let her get away."

"Look, this is going to be the greatest year of my life, with the most fabulous woman I am ever going to meet, after which I can become like all those cynical detectives who are loners, and who stare at their liquor, moping about the lost love of their life. Except," I looked at the glass on the table in front of me, "instead of hard liquor, I am going to be drinking white wine."

Before I could say any more, Brian pointed out that the women were headed back in our direction. "Just remember, if you stick with AJ, then you'll have the fabulous Amy Elizabeth in your life forever. That woman is into herself a little bit, wouldn't you say?" He started laughing at his own comment. "She's exactly the opposite of you and me. Unlike us, every time you're with her, you get the impression that her aim in life is to be a rock star."

AJ heard the last part of the conversation. "Rock star? Were you guys talking about my good friend Amy Elizabeth?"

"Who else, Red? They call it Music City, but it's Country Music City. Not like there are a lot of rock stars here."

Chapter Twenty-Seven

While the relationship between AJ and me was relatively smooth, the relationship between Brett Phillips and Amy Elizabeth was the polar opposite. After a series of extended phone calls and e-mails, Brett Phillips came to Nashville to visit Amy Elizabeth in early July. He stayed in a hotel. The night he met her, Brett Phillips told me that he had met "the most phenomenal woman he had ever met." Two weeks later, as I drove him to the Nashville airport he told me that she was "a bitch, an opinionated idiot who was impossible to be with." As soon as he got back to Seattle, he called her on the phone and they talked for more than six hours. Suffice it to say that Brett Phillips earned a substantial number of frequent flyer miles over the years visiting his on again and off again companion.

It was because of Amy Elizabeth that we eventually got back on track with the case of The Unforgiving. By September, when Brett Phillips was about to make his fourth trip to Nashville, Amy Elizabeth decided that it was absurd to have him stay at a hotel, and have her shuttle back and forth. She thought it was even more ridiculous to have him stay with us. They wanted privacy. Amy Elizabeth, the woman who AJ now called in jest "our first child", got her own apartment near Belmont University, halfway between our condo and Vanderbilt. It was pleasant, it was convenient, and it had three flights of stairs. AJ and I helped with the suitcases and the boxes.

We had finished the move, and Amy Elizabeth had just put her message on the answering machine. For the record, our answering machine now said "You have reached the home of Jonah and Red . . ." We were living together.

Since AJ had teased Amy Elizabeth about being "our first child", Amy Elizabeth proposed a toast to her new parents. "AJ and Jonah, I would say that I love you like real parents, except that you both know the story and that would not be a complement. I hope I can do you proud. Thanks for letting me stay at the condo, and thanks for your help with the move. Sorry to be leaving, but Brett and I really don't need chaperones, so this is where we are going to be. Here's to you guys."

"Here's to you and Brett, and may you have as smooth sailing in your life . . ." AJ and I both thought of it at the same time. "CHAPERONES! How did we not think of that?"

AJ had called Amy Elizabeth her chaperone sometime during our first week together. We had talked about Skylar Jones having her mother as a chaperone during her first year in Nashville. We had missed it then; this time we figured it out.

In his book, Amos Bunden had emphasized that the FBI had interviewed and fingerprinted all sixteen Kappa Delta girls who had been on the International Student Understanding trip to the Soviet Union, not just the three women who were abducted. There was no mention of the chaperones or anyone else who might have been affiliated with the trip. No parent in their right mind would send a group of college girls to the Soviet Union if the group didn't have at least one chaperone.

Having decided that it was worthwhile to investigate the chaperone, or chaperones, for the Kappa Delta trip to the Soviet Union we needed a plan. We couldn't just call up International Student Understanding, ISU, and ask for the names of the people who were in charge when three women were kidnapped. I doubted that would be productive. We needed a cover story. I couldn't come up with one of my movie ideas. Three American women going to Russia and being attacked didn't sound like a marketable movie plot for the post cold war era. It was Amy Elizabeth who came up with a solution.

"How does this sound? I'll call up ISU and tell them that I'm in graduate school, studying how women react to their friends being attacked. I'll tell them that I'm planning a project about that tour of the Soviet Union in 1988. I'll tell them I want to talk to the girls and their chaperone, since the chaperone would probably be the best one to tell me how the girls reacted at the time. I bet they'll tell me who the chaperone was. After all, I'm Amy Elizabeth Golden, I'm sort of famous, and I was raped. Being raped has to be good for something, and since I'm going to try and cash it in for everything it's worth, I may as well start now."

AJ was not the only Golden sister capable of making a plan. Amy Elizabeth called the ISU office in Gainesville, Florida. She pumped her fist in the air as she hung up the phone. "Yes! Margaret Romanov was born in the Soviet Union, speaks fluent Russian, and, according to ISU, was the only chaperone for the trip in 1988. Better yet, she's been in assisted living for almost ten years. Amos Bunden said that the killer might have stopped because she became too ill to kill people. I don't know when she went into assisted living, but the timing could be right."

AJ asked two relevant questions. "How old is she? And why is she in assisted living?"

"I asked, but they didn't remember. They're going to call her and ask if she'll talk to us."

Margaret Romanov called us back several hours later and informed us that she was delighted to assist Amy Elizabeth with her Master's Thesis. I was impressed with my girlfriend's sister's ability to tell lies. There was, of course, no master's thesis. I began to believe that Amy Elizabeth had a chance to succeed in show business.

Unfortunately, Mrs. Romanov didn't want to discuss things except in person. We set up a meeting for the following day in Jacksonville. We agreed that only Amy Elizabeth and I would go. AJ had an exam coming up and it was Amy Elizabeth's imaginary project that we were supposed to be discussing.

We took a direct flight in the morning and scheduled a return flight in the afternoon. Amy Elizabeth would ask most of the questions, and I would take notes. I would be introduced as a classmate working with her on the project. From Amy Elizabeth's point of view, I was going to Jacksonville to provide protection. We felt there was a high likelihood that Margaret Romanov was The Unforgiving.

We arrived in Jacksonville, picked up a rental car, and drove to the Palmetto Extended Care Center. Between the front door and the elevator, we passed a library, a game room, and a TV room. All three rooms were filled. If not for the occasional woman in a nurse's uniform, the place would have seemed like a retirement community. The people at Palmetto Extended Care hadn't outlived either their money or their minds.

Our suspicion that we had found The Unforgiving lasted only as long as it took us to reach Margaret Romanov's room. We were welcomed by a white haired woman who reminded me of my grandmother on my mother's side. In her mid-seventies, with hands crippled by arthritis, Margaret Romanov had been in her sixties when The Unforgiving killed five men. Still, I hoped she might be a useful source of information.

After greeting Amy Elizabeth and me, and after consoling Amy Elizabeth about the attack on Woodland Hills Lane, Margaret Romanov informed us, indirectly, that we were not as clever as we thought. "It's nice to have a visitor, even if it is about that horrible trip so long ago. The last time anyone talked to me about it was when those young men from the FBI interviewed me. Let me tell you, having grown up under Communism, they scared me. They even took my fingerprints. Scared the devil out of me." Amos Bunden and his team hadn't overlooked the chaperone; he just hadn't bothered to mention it in his book. Amy Elizabeth looked at me and stifled a laugh.

We had apparently come to Jacksonville for nothing, but Amy Elizabeth knew that we had to complete our charade. Mrs. Romanov had volunteered to be helpful, and we were going to give her the joy of helping. Amy Elizabeth started with her list of prepared questions. "Thanks for meeting with us. My first question is this. How did the other girls react to their friends being kidnapped?"

"Once the three girls were released, everyone was extremely supportive. All three girls had been raped, but they refused to be examined by the Soviet doctors;

they didn't want the rapes to be reported in the American papers. I'm sure you understand how uncomfortable and embarrassed they felt about the whole thing."

Amy Elizabeth nodded.

"Anyway, when they didn't want to be examined, and didn't want to report being raped, I knew they'd never be able to testify. When they wanted to go home, I felt it was the right thing to do. Marsha, Ann, and Colleen didn't want to make the other girls leave early on their account, so we took a vote. It was sixteen to nothing to return home immediately, and we did. The tour only had four more days to run at that point, but still, the girls all agreed to go home."

Amy Elizabeth had a list of questions. The next one was supposed to be about whether Mrs. Romanov had kept in touch with any of the girls. With Margaret Romanov not being The Unforgiving, she instead decided to practice the role of Amibeth and try and comfort Mrs. Romanov. "That must have been hard on you, being chaperone for the girls and having them get into trouble."

"You have no idea what I had to go through, dealing with those corrupt police officials . . . Oh, you mean did I feel guilty about the fact that they got into trouble. Look, you don't understand what happened. And if you're going to interview the girls, you need to know." She paused, trying to think of the right way to phrase what she wanted to say. "ISU wasn't your usual tourist group. The idea was to meet the people and promote international understanding. The girls were expected to learn a little conversational Russian before the trip. There were scheduled meetings with government officials, and social get togethers with Soviet students who spoke English. At night the girls went to restaurants and even clubs in the company of a Russian guide. Marsha, Ann, and Colleen's guide was Dmitri. They were at a local club and the girls saw some students they had met earlier that day. They got on the dance floor together, and the boys offered to show them 'the real Soviet Union.' The girls waited until Dmitri went to the men's room and they took off with the boys."

"They weren't kidnapped walking home?"

"Hardly. That was just a story put out by the American embassy to put the girls in a good light and to get back at the Soviets for the way they handled things. Anyway, Dmitri had seen the boys on the dance floor, and he recognized them. He and I went to the police. As you might expect, the police had a good idea of who had taken the girls. They asked for $100,000 to speed up the investigation."

"A bribe."

"More than a bribe, dear. The police were collecting a ransom for the kidnappers. They were in on it. And Dmitri may have been in on it too. I was never certain. Anyway, there was a joint American-Soviet pipeline project under consideration back then. I lied and told the police that my Congressman was on the Committee reviewing the appropriation and that the whole project would be killed because of their little scam. I emphasized the world 'killed' when I talked to the police.

Amy Elizabeth interrupted. "Your implication being that the Russian higher-ups would have them killed for kidnapping the girls and getting the project cancelled."

She smiled. "I would never threaten anyone. I was just a kind little old lady." Then she chuckled. "I lived in Leningrad until I was seventeen. I knew how to deal with those bastards. At the end of the day, ISU paid a 'finder's fee', $20,000, and that night the girls turned up naked in the streets. I spent a whole day in that police station, talking to the police, phoning the American embassy, and dealing with ISU. It was the hardest I ever worked. I think the stress made my arthritis worse, but I got those girls back alive."

Amy Elizabeth and I were impressed. Not only was she not The Unforgiving, she was a hero. Before Amy Elizabeth could ask if she had stayed in touch with the girls, I had a question. "While you were with the police, how did the girls hold up? Their friends were missing. You were away from the hotel. I would think it would be terrifying."

Mrs. Romanov picked a picture of the tour group off of a bedside table. "I took this photo out when I knew you were coming. In this world, you have to be able to delegate." While she pointed to a short brunette in the front row, I counted the people in the picture. There were seventeen women, sixteen sorority girls and Margaret Romanov. "Janie Boston was the sharpest girl in the group. When Dmitri and I went to the police, I put Janie in charge. It was a good choice. I suspect Muffin wouldn't have been any help at all. She just would have gotten the girls angrier and angrier. That was the last thing we needed."

Amy Elizabeth and I had the same question. "Who's Muffin?"

"They never told you about Muffin? There was another ISU tour group at the hotel. They were travelling in the opposite direction. We started in St. Petersburg and ended in Moscow. They were starting in Moscow and ending in St. Petersburg. Their group was from . . ."

I was hoping she would say Memphis.

"Chicago. They had eighteen girls and two chaperones." Mrs. Romanov clearly took pride in the fact that her group had only required one chaperone. "Ordinarily I would have borrowed one of their chaperones and put her in charge when I had to be away from our hotel. Unfortunately, the older one, Brenda McElroy—I had known her a long time—needed to stay with her group. They were leaving that morning for St. Petersburg and she had to go with them. The younger one, Muffin, stayed at the hotel with the Kappa Delta girls, but she was useless. The only reason she was on the trip in the first place was because her parents owned a travel agency and they got her a discounted ticket to work as a chaperone. She wasn't a full time ISU employee. Mousy little girl. I could tell she wouldn't do well in charge. Janie ended up comforting her."

"Comforting her?"

"I didn't know it when Barbara assigned her to stay behind with our group, but I got to talk to Muffin before she left for the airport to catch up with her group in St. Petersburg. She'd been in a bad marriage and had been beaten by her husband. When the girls went missing, Dmitri had told us about a tall, bald man that he suspected of being the leader of the hoodlums that had kidnapped the girls. Muffin's ex-husband was tall and bald. It brought back memories for her. Muffin wasn't much help, but you can't blame her. She had had a rough life."

I wasn't interested in her rough life as much as I was interested in finding her. She sounded young enough to be The Unforgiving. Amy Elizabeth had the same thought. "Jonah, that's someone else we should interview. Mrs. Romanov, do you remember her last name or do you know how to get in touch with her?"

After all these years, I expected she wouldn't. "It was Mancini. I remember because at one time there was a Mancini's restaurant a couple of blocks from my apartment in Gainesville. I remember asking Muffin if she was related to the Mancini family, but she wasn't. Her parents owned a small travel agency, not a restaurant. But you can't interview Muffin, she's dead."

"Dead?"

"Yes. Poor girl. I forget how I heard about it, but she was killed in an auto accident. It was several years after the Moscow trip."

The rest of the interview consisted of Amy Elizabeth asking about the girls on the trip. The only person Margaret Romanov had stayed in touch with was Marcia Bowen. We hadn't learned much about the girls on the tour, and Mrs. Romanov wasn't The Unforgiving, but we had a new suspect. I gave Mrs. Romanov a business card, one that listed no occupation, just my e-mail and cell phone. I asked her to call if she thought of something important.

As soon as we left Mrs. Romanov's room, Amy Elizabeth turned to me and said "Three hours to our plane. Let's find an internet connection, and find out more about Muffin Mancini."

Chapter Twenty-Eight

We headed for a Starbuck's we had seen on the drive to the nursing home. The internet search was completely frustrating. We couldn't find a Mancini Travel Agency anywhere in the United States. We found no record of a fatal accident involving Muffin Mancini. Considering that Muffin might have been a nickname, we checked for fatal accidents involving anyone named Mancini. No luck. We tried every alternate spelling we could think of and found nothing. All we found was Mancini's Restaurant in Jacksonville. On the way to the airport we called ISU. They no longer had records for individual trips, but they had a master file of employees and of the individuals who had ever travelled as part of an ISU tour. They used the list for fund-raising. There was no one named Mancini on the list. We returned the rental car, and barely made our plane.

We spent the hour and a half flying to back to Nashville wondering why Margaret Romanov would have misled us. "Maybe Mancini wasn't her real name, Jonah Aaron. Maybe Muffin was travelling under an alias."

"She had to have passport. It was a trip out of the country. The Russians are paranoid. The names would have match up. Whatever name she gave the ISU group would have to match the passport."

Amy Elizabeth thought it over. "What if she was a spy?"

I knew that I was paranoid at times. Maybe it was contagious. "You're kidding, aren't you?"

"No. Think about it. Muffin was a spy. She was in the Soviet Union when three girls were kidnapped and raped. The girls came home to the United States and didn't testify. The justice system over there couldn't do anything. Muffin couldn't do anything because she was stuck with her cover as a tour chaperone. Several years later, one of the rapists came to the USA as part of a trade delegation. Muffin got the information that he was here in the states. She tracked him down, and that was the end of Yuri Yevtushenko. Maybe she was some kind of trained assassin for the CIA."

I had to admit, it wasn't that unreasonable. Then again I watch too much television. "And the other four men? The Unforgiving's other four victims. How do they fit into the picture?"

"I'll work on it. Maybe those four men were all part of some plot and she set out to eliminate them." Before I could even comment, she thought about what she was saying. "Guess not. Wanna do a crossword puzzle?"

"Good idea."

By the time we arrived in Nashville, we had agreed to try and track down Barbara McElroy, the other chaperone on the other tour—assuming there was a Barbara McElroy, and assuming there really was another tour headed in the opposite direction of the Kappa Delta tour. It appeared that our trip to Florida had been a waste of time.

Although Amy Elizabeth's theory that Muffin Mancini was a spy didn't make sense, it had one inherent advantage. It potentially eliminated the connection between the escorts on Lamar Avenue and The Unforgiving. I dropped Amy Elizabeth off at her apartment and went home to AJ.

Before I could report on the trip, AJ asked, "How was your lunch in Jacksonville?"

"We didn't eat lunch. We just ate snacks on the plane. Aren't you going to ask if Margaret Romanov is The Unforgiving."

"I know she isn't. She's seventy-six years old, and she sounded really nice. I talked to her for half an hour. She called here."

"Why did she call? And why were you asking if we ate lunch in Jacksonville?"

"She called to apologize. She said she told you the name of the wrong restaurant. Mancini's is in Jacksonville. It's Mancuso's that's in Gainesville. Or maybe it's the other way around. She said she gave you the name of the wrong restaurant. If you didn't eat there, it's no big deal I guess. How was the trip?"

So much for CIA conspiracies. "It just got a lot better."

The internet is more helpful when one has the right name. We found a Mancuso Travel Agency in Memphis, located four miles from the Lamar Village Apartments. The internet confirmed that Muffin Mancuso, a pharmacist at Baptist Hospital in Memphis, had been killed in a collision with a tanker truck carrying gasoline on August 14, 1994. That was around the time that the killings had stopped.

AJ and I talked it over with Amy Elizabeth and the three of us decided to send an e-mail to Amos Bunden. We titled the e-mail "Information about the Unforgiving?" In our message we stated that we had read his book, started thinking about who might have been missed in the official investigation, and since he didn't mention the chaperones, we had gone off in that direction and discovered the name of someone who might have been overlooked. We didn't mention our connection to Candy or the meaning of T181.

For three days we kept watching for an e-mail response. When none was forthcoming, we sent the same message. This time we entitled the e-mail "AJ Golden, Information about the Unforgiving." We heard back in twenty minutes. To this day I am convinced that Amos Bunden had a crush on AJ.

Amos Bunden had never heard the story of the second chaperone, one who had been "borrowed" for the day, a chaperone who had been abused by her husband, who had lived in Memphis, and who had died around the time that "The Unforgiving" stopped claiming victims. At that point, the FBI took over.

They obtained pictures of Muffin Mancuso and showed them to the bartender at the Memphis Airport Hotel. He agreed that the woman in the picture looked like the woman he had seen in the bar. It was hardly a positive identification, but it was a starting point.

Fortunately, there was forensic evidence to help identify Muffin Mancuso as a killer. Female epithelial cells had been recovered from the sheets in Mario Grancliff's room in Memphis. Amos Bunden hadn't mentioned that evidence in his book, and at the time, the authorities were not certain that the cells had any connection to the case. DNA had been extracted from the cells.

When Muffin Mancuso was killed in the automobile accident, no DNA had been collected. She had been burned beyond recognition, and she had been identified as Muffin Mancuso because it was her car and because of the dental x-rays provided by her dentist in Memphis. She had been in the ground for a decade. The FBI considered having the body exhumed so that DNA could be obtained.

In the end, the FBI took a simpler means of confirming the fact that Muffin Mancuso was The Unforgiving. Her parents were still alive. They did not wish to have their only daughter's remains disturbed. Her mother and father agreed to have their DNA tested. Each of them was a fifty percent match to the DNA found in Mario Grancliff's bed. The female DNA from Mario Grancliff's bed belonged to their daughter, Muffin.

Thallium may not be the easiest poison to obtain, but it is not tightly regulated. The FBI didn't know how Muffin Mancuso had obtained the thallium. We had a hunch but we didn't have proof, and we had no obligation to share our suspicions. The FBI concluded that Muffin Mancuso had motive, means, and opportunity to be The Unforgiving. On the basis of the forensic evidence, the case was closed.

Everyone seemed satisfied except Amos Bunden. He argued that the body should be exhumed because the dental x-rays provided by the dentist, the x-rays which matched the corpse, might not have really belonged to Muffin Mancuso. Nearly a decade after Muffin Mancuso had been buried, it seemed that the dentist could not be located. Amos Bunden was concerned that anyone clever enough to elude the FBI while they murdered five men could have faked their own death. The Bureau disagreed and gave Amos Bunden two weeks of paid vacation to assuage his paranoia. Having once read a Sue Grafton mystery in which dental x-rays were intentionally exchanged, leading to the misidentification of a corpse, I thought Amos Bunden had a point. Of course, no one asked me.

There was no reward for solving the case of The Unforgiving, but in the long run, I got something much better, a consulting relationship with the FBI. Memphis, in the western part of the state, and Knoxville, in the eastern part of the state, have FBI offices. Special Agents from those offices come to Nashville when there are major problems, but for routine matters, the FBI sometimes calls on me.

With The Unforgiving identified, and the case closed, we agreed that there was no point in delaying the family reunion. The chance that Andrea's story could be used to promote Amibeth was nil, but AJ and Amy Elizabeth wanted to see their sister. We were curious about Andrea's ties to Muffin Mancuso, but we felt no pressing need to explore the matter. That was ancient history. If it came up during our visit, it came up; if not, we were content to leave it buried.

Amy Elizabeth and AJ hoped that the reunion with Andrea would be "tears of joy and lots of hugging." I heard that phrase over and over for days before Amy Elizabeth finally got the nerve to call ACGBC. I doubted it would be "tears of joy and lots of hugging," but they had grown up with Andrea. Maybe they understood something that I didn't. Frankly, I thought they had "rocks in their head," my mother's favorite expression for having a really poor assessment of a situation. I said nothing other than to say that I hoped it went well.

Amy Elizabeth finally got up the nerve to make a phone call to Andrea. AJ sat nervously on the couch at her sister's side. The call was on speaker phone.

"Hello."

"Andrea. Is that you? This is Amy Elizabeth. AJ is here with me."

"I'm sorry. Who is this?"

"Andrea, it's your sister Amy Elizabeth. AJ is with me."

She spoke in a monotone. "I'm sorry. I have no sisters. They died in a fire. The whole family died except me. I was out babysitting or I would have died too." Then showing some emotion she nearly screamed "AND MY NAME ISN'T ANDREA. IT'S CANDY. YOU HAVE THE WRONG PERSON."

Amy Elizabeth handed the phone to AJ.

"Andrea, this is AJ, Abby Jo. We love you. We want to see you. We don't want to hurt you. We love you."

"HURT ME? YOU'LL WRECK MY MARRIAGE. ERIC WILL LEAVE ME. YOU HAVE THE WRONG PERSON."

AJ started to cry and handed me the phone. I was afraid Candy Cain was going to hang up. "Mrs. Cain, my name is Jonah Aaron. I'm a private investigator working with these two women." You can only talk to people in the emotional space that they occupy. It was a lesson that Amy Elizabeth would remember when she went on the radio as Amibeth and fielded phone calls. "Mrs. Cain these women have a crazy story that their older sister killed their father with thallium, gave them a necklace that said 'TL81' to brag about it, and then went to work on Lamar Avenue in Memphis before she became a nurse. As a favor to me I would really appreciate it if you would meet with them to tell them they have it wrong."

There was silence at the other end of the line. Then she spoke very softly, "How did you find me?"

"Elvis told me."

Again in a monotone, she replied, "Elvis is dead."

"You wrote him a note in the visitor's book at Graceland. I found it."

"You found . . ." there was another long silence, but the line wasn't dead. "May as well get this over with. Once. I will see you all exactly once. Eric is going to be at the hospital until noon this coming Saturday. Come by at ten. I assume you have my address already if you're any kind of investigator."

"We have the address. Your sisters want to say hello. They love you. Can I give them the phone?"

"Ten o'clock Saturday. That's soon enough. ONCE!"

The line went dead.

I wasn't going to bet on tears of joy and lots of hugging.

Chapter Twenty-Nine

We flew to Chicago on the early flight and took a taxi to the building on Lake Shore Drive. The women were wearing dark suits with white blouses, dark panty hose and black low heels. They looked like the "penguins" I saw coming for medical school interviews at my father's office. I wore a dark sports jacket so that I wouldn't look out of place. I did not bring my gun.

The Cain condominium had been on the market for eighteen months. I assumed that the asking price of $799,000 might be high for eighteen hundred square feet, even in Chicago. That was not the problem. It was the style in which it had been decorated. The first hint of what lay ahead occurred as we got off the elevator. A woman who lived on the thirty-second floor had ridden up with us. As we got off the elevator and headed to the Cain condo, she mistook us for prospective buyers. "If you're headed for the Cain's I have to tell you something. It's really a nice place. Just try to imagine that the walls are blank, and that the bedroom is totally redone . . . They had a party at Christmas last year. I saw it. Unbelievable. Just pretend that the walls are blank."

"Thanks for the heads up."

The woman had stopped at her condo and was opening the door. "Excuse me for being nosy, but which of you is the real estate agent, and which of you is the couple that might be moving in."

Amy Elizabeth and AJ answered at the same time, "I'm not a real estate agent."

She gave us a funny look. "Well in that case, the three of you might want to keep the bedroom as it is." She continued in a whisper "Mirrored walls and ceilings."

We laughed and continued to 3206. The woman who greeted us was not Andrea Candy Golden Butler Cain. "Hi. I'm Janie. I work with Candy at CMI, Chicago Medical Institute. She asked me to come for moral support. She's getting dressed. She couldn't figure out what to wear. I'd offer you some food, but she said she thought you wouldn't take anything for some reason." ACGBC had some insight. "Feel free to take a look around."

It was hard to avoid looking around. The ceilings were twelve feet high. The entire north wall of the seven hundred and fifty square foot living room was custom wallpapered in a pattern showing the four musicians I recognized as the late 1970's, early 1980's glitter rock group Night Shadow. The pattern repeated so that there were eight outrageously dressed individuals in white faced makeup on the wall. Night Shadow was before my time, but I had seen some of their old music videos. Night Shadow was less successful than Kiss, but they had had several hit records, the most notable single being "A Boy's Best Friend Is His Mother." The video had started with a view of the sphinx and dripped with Oedipal allusions.

The east wall contained a montage of autographed photos of the group's members, autographed guitars, an autographed drumhead, and three framed and matted autographed vinyl albums. I couldn't help but admire the album cover from *A Boys Best Friend*. It was in mint condition. As Brett Phillips had taught me, collectibles such as baseball cards and record albums must be in mint condition to have real value. Fortunately the same rules don't apply to people.

The west wall of the Cain living room was glass with superb views of the city—the Cain's couldn't mess that up. In fact, I momentarily felt a twinge of jealousy towards people who got to live in the bustling city of Chicago. Then I thought of the Chicago winter, said thanks that I lived in Nashville, and continued to tour the condo.

The south wall of the living room contained a fireplace over which hung an eight foot high photograph of a man in his forties, dressed in full Night Shadow regalia, including the whiteface makeup, in the company of a much younger woman who was carrying a bouquet of roses and who was falling out of a black dress that reminded me of the nightgown AJ had worn the first night she had spent at my condo. The edges of the extremely deep V neck, which almost reached her pubis, were attached to each other by three large silver rings. AJ and her sister had similar taste with one major exception. I doubted that AJ would get married in a dress like that. It was a wedding photo.

My first thought was that Dr. Eric Cain was the ultimate Night Shadow collector and that he occasionally dressed up in Night Shadow regalia like Star Wars devotees dress up as Luke Skywalker or Darth Vader. Then, I looked at the wedding picture more closely, went back to the autographed album cover of *A Boys Best Friend* and realized that Eric Cain had been part of Night Shadow. I wondered what his medical office looked like and whether or not he stuck his tongue out at patients. No, that was the vocal group Kiss. Night Shadow didn't do that. I had forgotten what Night Shadow was known for. Then I remembered. Their bass guitar player had multiple arrests for indecent exposure on stage. Well, we couldn't hold that against Eric Cain. He was the vocalist.

Janie took a seat in a small chair near the fireplace. "Please make yourselves comfortable. Candy will be out in a minute." We took a seat on the sofa. "If you get a chance, go see the bedroom. Kind of weird, but whatever turns you on, that's what I say."

AJ and Amy Elizabeth were so happy that their sister was alive with a roof over her head that they made no comment about the décor. AJ just held my hand tightly, pointed to the picture over the fireplace, and whispered in my ear. "I know it's early in our relationship, but I just want to reassure you that if we ever get married I will NOT wear a wedding dress like that."

"Good idea." I started to imagine the two of us standing up in front of our friends. The way things were going, it might actually happen.

And suddenly, there she was. ACGBC. I don't know if it was because I expected a grand entrance, a flamboyant style of dress, or if I expected someone taller, or older, but she was not what I expected. Andrea Cain walked in wearing a pair of baggy blue jeans, and a loose grey sweater that showed off no cleavage. She was wearing flats, and a modest amount of makeup. She was thirty years old and looked it, no younger, no older. And yes, there were tears of joy and lots of hugging.

After AJ and Amy Elizabeth settled down, Andrea looked at Janie and said, "You can go. I'll be ok. Thanks for coming over."

"Are you sure?"

"It's fine." She watched Janie leave. "She and my friend Gail Riley are the only ones in the world besides you who know who I am. They don't know about the thallium, but they know I was Andrea Golden. I'm not Andrea Golden anymore; I'm Candy Cain. I know it sounds like a hooker name or a porn name, but Eric likes it. It keeps up his bad boy, ex rock and roller image. By the way, he has absolutely no idea how I earned the money to go to nursing school. I told him my family died in a fire and that I got some insurance money, and I have never, ever mentioned anything about what happened in our bedroom in Kenton, let alone in Memphis. That's the reason I've stayed away from you guys. Sorry to keep you waiting. I couldn't figure out what to wear today, so I dressed like I would on any Saturday morning. Hope I'm not too casual."

In unison, we answered, "You're fine."

"Hey, I'm being rude. Can I get you guys something to eat or drink?"

We politely declined.

She went to the refrigerator and brought back a shrink wrapped twelve pack of bottled water, opened it, and handed us each a bottle. "Fresh from the store, unopened, and thallium free. I am actually a reasonable hostess when I'm not so nervous. Ladies, you didn't introduce me to your escort." She smiled at the use of the word in its proper sense. "I assume this is your investigator, or does he belong to one of you?"

I introduced myself. "I'm Jonah Aaron. It's nice to meet you, finally."

AJ piped up, "He's my boyfriend!"

"Good for you AJ. You were always such a studious tomboy that . . . well, I worried about you. Good for you. He's obviously smart if he found me. If he has a talented tongue and brings the fire wave, he's a keeper."

AJ's face turned a shade of red that almost matched her hair. "Andrea, don't embarrass me. Anyway, the answers are yes and yes, and he makes me laugh." She squeezed my hand.

"Sorry. I'm just used to being very direct about sex. Look, I know all about you, but I assume you want to know about me? What do you want to know? Mind if I smoke?"

AJ asked the first question. "What do you do, as a nurse? I assume you work with patients."

Candy exhaled deeply, began talking and got on a roll. She went non-stop for almost two minutes. "I used to work with cancer patients in the cancer unit. It was sort of depressing, but I liked it. The patients were the nicest people. That's where I met my best friend, Gail Riley. She's a doctor. She's been my friend since I came to CMI, but she's married so I had Janie come over today. Anyway, I'm a research study nurse. I register patients for research studies, I explain the risks and benefits, and I get the consent forms signed. Then I make sure that all the follow up studies get done so they can see if the drugs are working. It's really exciting." She was getting animated. "We did a study of this drug called imatinib. It used to be that if you had chronic myeloid leukemia, you had to have a bone marrow transplant. Now they have this drug and you take a pill a day and you can go twenty or twenty-five years or more, maybe even be cured by a pill. No need for a transplant and all those complications. All I did was keep the data organized, but I was part of that big national study. That's something I am proud of."

"And now we have a new group of drugs, so new that they only have numbers. 884-something is the first one. Dr. Venapalli in Dr. Riley's lab came up with it. I may have had a crazy life, but when I am a study nurse, everything goes the way it should and everyone likes me—the doctors, the patients, the other nurses. On one study, they even humored me and let me check whether or not there was any relationship between the patient's sign of the zodiac and whether or not the medication worked. There was no correlation, but they let me look. That was neat. You know, Eric always says, assume nothing. There might have been a correlation. And CMI is such a wonderful place. Even when we sell this place so Eric has less of a commute to Evanston Hospital—he's been Chief of Cardiology there for a year—I'm going to keep working at CMI."

It was Amy Elizabeth's turn to ask a question. "Eric, is that him on the walls and in the wedding picture?"

"That's him. We're well matched. I think he probably had as many women when he was in Night Shadow as I had men in my two years in Memphis, but we never talk about it. It's like the past never happened. And it has to stay that way.

He thinks my family died in a fire, so does everybody, except for Janie and Gail. Bradley left when he found out. Do you know about Bradley?"

My turn. "Only that you married him while you were at Walters State."

"Right. Bradley taught psychology at Walters State. He is a very sweet man. He is also gay. Ninety-nine point nine percent gay. At Walters State I always wore loose sweaters, loose sweatshirts, and baggy warm up pants. I lived a sexless life and I hid my assets. I had the boob job when I was in Memphis. GREAT investment by the way." She pointed at her chest. "Bradley was in the closet. He wanted a woman to make him look respectable. Morristown is a small town and there had been rumors that he was gay. I didn't mind that we almost never did it. He put a roof over my head and paid my tuition. We went to movies and restaurants. We looked like a couple. He had his male friends. I had a vibrator. Anyway, after one of the rare times that we actually did it, I felt especially close to him and just like an idiot, just like the stupid seventeen year old who gave you that pendant, I started talking about how I had earned the money to go to nursing school, and about daddy, and about high school in Kenton. I never got to the thallium part. He got up, got dressed, left me and never came back. We got a divorce. I guess that there is no point in having a wife to make you look respectable if she turns out to be a whore who was the high school slut who used to have sex with her daddy." She almost started to cry. "Anyway, we were living in Chicago by then and I suspect he realized that up here no one gave a damn if he was gay, so he left me."

"Bradley was going for his doctorate. I was a nurse at CMI. Anyhow, there I was, an old woman of twenty-five, I had been through a lot, I had just been abandoned by the man I loved, loved in mostly a non sexual way, but I truly loved him. He treated me like a queen, kind of ironic since he was a queen," we all laughed slightly, "but anyway, I had been abandoned because he found out who I really was. I was devastated. That's why I will NEVER tell Eric anything, and that's when Eric killed me."

Chapter Thirty

I was drinking a sip of water and nearly choked.

"Eric killed you?" AJ asked. "What are you talking about?"

"Well, he didn't kill me. Well he did. But I bounced back. At that time, I had no idea that he had been in rock and roll, not that it would have made a difference. All I knew was that he was this sweet cute older cardiologist that a number of the nurses had a crush on. He had never been married. I even suspected that he was gay. My gaydar was off one hundred and eighty-degrees on that one." She chuckled. "Anyway, he was an old man of, let's see, Eric is forty-seven now, so he was forty-two then, I was twenty five. Bradley had left me a couple of days before. I stopped Eric in the halls of CMI. He was Dr. Cain to me at that time, not 'Eric.' I told him I needed to renew my amitryptilene prescription, my antidepressant, and that my doctor was out of town." She took a long drag on her cigarette then continued. "He didn't schedule an appointment; he didn't do a medical interview. He figured I was a nurse and it was ok to give me a prescription for the drug. I got the prescription filled. Then I went home-and-took-the-whole-bottle. Medically speaking I should have died." For the second time she almost started to cry.

"What happened?"

"Well forget the wallpaper, forget the guitars, forget the record albums. That is not who he really is. Eric Cain is just a sweet little boy who never grew up in some ways, but he is a devoted caring doctor, and a very good one. After he wrote that prescription, he got worried, as he should have been, and he called to see if I was ok. He had tracked down the numbers of my cell and my home phone. I didn't answer of course; I was too busy dying. So he drove three miles from CMI to where I was living at the time. He got himself let into my building by the superintendant. He stood outside my apartment door, and kept calling me on my cell to see if I was ok. He heard the phone ringing inside the apartment. He got worried, and had me paged by the CMI operator. Then he heard the pager beeping inside the apartment. He knew I wouldn't go anywhere without the pager. He got the super to let him in. He was a doctor after all and he said it was an emergency. And there I was. Naked. My boobs pointed towards the ceiling, my legs spread apart, smelling of strawberries."

"Strawberries?" AJ and Amy Elizabeth asked the question at the same time.

"Yeah. I had this thing about flavored douches and lubricants in those days. I figured my body might smell pretty rotten by the time they found it, so I sloshed the stuff all over myself. I assume I actually looked pretty fabulous at the time Eric found me—and I must have smelled delicious. Strawberries. To this day I can get Eric turned on by eating a strawberry in front of him." She laughed. "Anyhow, I was almost dead. Barely a pulse. Barely breathing. But I hadn't turned blue. Eric saw that I had a chance and started pounding on my chest and breathing for me. That's an interesting first kiss, huh? And he had the super call 911."

"And you came around obviously."

"Eventually. My heart didn't start up at first, but Eric kept me alive until the paramedics got me going. I was in the ICU at CMI unconscious for three days. My heart stopped seven times. Eric never left my side. He was so guilty about giving me that prescription. The ICU staff is great, but there is an advantage to having a cardiology attending by your bedside, especially when your heart stops seven times. And that is how we met."

I didn't say anything, but I thought that she had a better story than my tale of going into a karaoke bar to pick up the keys so I could house-sit and seeing a beautiful waitress.

"So you started dating after that?" Amy Elizabeth was interested in how relationships happen.

"Oh, no. That would have been a little inappropriate. He said hello to me in the halls whenever we crossed paths. He always said how sorry he was. Nothing happened between us. Then one day, about a year later he ran into me in the halls, literally. He got off an elevator, realized he was on the wrong floor, turned around suddenly and BANG knocked me down."

AJ jumped when Candy said the word "BANG."

"He had played hockey in college, and he started joking that he deserved a two minute penalty for roughing. I had no idea what he meant; I knew nothing about hockey. So he explained it. He offered to take me to a hockey game, and I went with him, but I didn't like hockey—at first. Also, I didn't really see it as amounting to much. So nothing happened. Then a few months later, he had two tickets to see Springsteen. The woman he had asked had come down with the flu. They weren't in a serious relationship. I figured, what the heck, who turns down a chance to see Springsteen. We had a great time. We came back here. I saw a whole different side of him, and we have been together since. Our third anniversary is in two months. By the way, whenever I tell the story in front of Eric, I say that he said 'five minutes for roughing,' just so he can correct me and say that roughing is only two minutes. He gets such a kick out of that." She flashed a smile.

"Anyhow, that's how we met. Eric can't find out about my past. I know that he has a past too. I suspect he wouldn't leave. He might even think it was 'cool' that he was getting for free what eleven hundred and twenty-three men had paid for." She rattled off the number as casually as if she was telling her age. "But probably isn't the same as certainly. I am not going to take the risk. I wouldn't kill myself if we split. I would never ever do that for the third time. But I do not want to lose him. I do not want him finding out that I even KNOW the famous Golden sisters. If he heard that I was having lunch with one of you, or if he found an e-mail that I was writing to one of you, well it might be worse than if he found out I was cheating. He knows my name is Andrea, but to him I am Candy, that's what everyone at work calls me. He's a very smart man. If you were in my lives he would eventually figure out that I was Andrea Golden. And now that blabbermouth over there," she looked at Amy Elizabeth, "told the world about Daddy and me, it would almost certainly be a disaster. This is going to be it. What else do you want to know? We have about half an hour until I have to worry about Eric coming home."

AJ had picked up on the number. Not the eleven hundred and twenty three men, the statement that she wouldn't try killing herself for the third time. "When was the other time? You said you wouldn't try killing yourself for the third time. One was when you split with Bradley and Eric gave you the pills. When was the other?"

She bit her lower lip as if she was going to get into territory she didn't want to traverse, and took another puff of her cigarette.

"Let me tell you about Memphis. You're not coming back, so I guess this is my one chance to share. The night of the funeral, after I gave you the pendant and hugged Mama and told her goodbye forever and not to come looking for me, I drove to Memphis. I had no idea what I was going to do. After I quit working in Jackson, I had worked as a stripper in Memphis. I had no tits back then. You must be . . ." she looked at her sisters, "Amy Elizabeth you are a 32-B and AJ you're a 32-C." The girls nodded. "Anyway, I had less in those days than Amy Elizabeth has now. Tips were bad and I was turning tricks to keep afloat. I probably would have ended up dead in a couple of months. On the way back from Daddy's funeral, I went to a bar, the kind that wouldn't let an underage girl in the place. But remember, I was really dressed up nice for Daddy's funeral. I looked twenty-one. I was so dumb that I didn't realize that it was a lesbian bar. This woman started talking to me, Muffin Something. I don't remember her last name. Muffin took me home with her. It was my first time with a woman and I loved it. If I hadn't had to support myself, I probably would never have had sex with a man ever again."

"Muffin set me up with some friends of hers at Lamar Avenue. They were lesbians too. Fuck girls for fun, fuck men for money, that was the motto. Lots of escorts are like that. Muffin used to come around every once in a while. She wasn't serious about me, but I was serious about her." She lit another cigarette before continuing. "Anyway, Muffin broke it off. She said I was too young for her. She had found out I was only eighteen. She was past thirty I think. She had thought I was twenty-three. Remember I was real dressed up at the time we met. And it wasn't just the age thing. I was immature. I admit that. I was clingy and needy and all the other shit. When she left I felt so bad that I decided to kill myself."

"I didn't have any pills. I didn't have a gun. A knife struck me as messy for my roommates to clean up. I liked them. I wasn't sleeping with any of them, but why make a mess in the house. You two grew up in Mama's house. You understand why I would be concerned about making a mess."

AJ broke in to what was becoming a monologue. "Goddam right I understand. Mary Nell cared more about one of her damn dishes getting broken and blood getting on the walls than about Amy Elizabeth being raped or me being . . ." She paused. "Sorry. Didn't mean to get so angry. Go ahead." She took a deep breath. "I'm ok Jonah, I really am. Go ahead, Candy." It was really interesting in a way. You could say "The Roofers" or "The Diaz Brothers" and AJ took it in stride. If you said "Mary Nell" she almost exploded.

Candy continued. "So, I took the one thing I had—an entire vial of thallium. It must have been more than ten times what I used to kill Daddy. I knew a lot about thallium by then. I knew I'd get sick to my stomach and go in a coma. I figured that even if it was a painful way to die, maybe it was what I deserved. Nothing happened. I thought God had spared me or that the thallium had expired."

"Nothing happened?" AJ was skeptical. "Thallium does not expire. It lasts forever."

"Let me say this another way. I took what I thought was the thallium and nothing happened to me. I was so dumb that at first I thought it was a miracle. What had happened, of course, was that someone had taken the thallium and replaced it with sugar so I wouldn't notice. I thought it tasted real sweet and sugary going down. How was I supposed to know what thallium tasted like? I had never taken any. All I had done was put in the turnips. I knew no one else EVER tried the turnips."

Investigator AJ was on a roll. "How did anyone know you had thallium? How did anyone know enough to steal it?"

"Good point. I had stolen this tube of thallium powder, about so long," she held her index fingers two inches apart, "and so fat around." She formed a circle about an inch in diameter. Lolly and Muffin found it in my purse one time and thought it was cocaine. They were about to snort it when I walked in and stopped them."

I began to speculate what would have happened if she hadn't stopped them.

"I had to tell them what it was to keep them from snorting the stuff, and I told them about Daddy. I'm sure Muffin stole my "magic disappearing powder.""

That's what I called it. I wasn't planning to use it ever again, but it made me feel safe. Muffin had a lot of anger. Her husband had beaten her and, well let's just say she had a lot of anger. Muffin was still sleeping with Lolly at the time that the police interviewed Lolly. Great irony don't you think. She dumped me because I was too young and started to date a girl who turned out to be even younger. Of course Lolly always seemed older. She had been all over half the country with a man old enough to be her father. Pervert. I was a naïve eighteen year old, and Lolly was a wise old woman of fifteen or sixteen. Anyway, Lolly was in love with Muffin and she never told the cops anything about Muffin when they questioned us about those other deaths. Lolly thought Muffin was some kind of mystical creature because of her 'magic eyes.'" She made quotation marks with her fingers when she said the phrase.

"Magic eyes?"

"She had one green eye and one brown eye. Muffin told everyone that it was a sign that she had magical powers. Lolly believed it. She thought maybe it was a sign that Muffin was some sort of divine creature." She made a snorting sound. "Now that I'm a nurse I know it's an insignificant medical variation called heterochromia iridis, one eye a different color than the other. Probably one in every fifteen hundred people have it. They say Alexander the Great had it. Dan Aykroyd, the actor has it." Candy paused for a moment. "Where were we? I kinda got lost there."

Amy Elizabeth got us back on track. "We were talking about the police interviewing you and the other girls and no one mentioning Muffin."

"Right. Look, I was nineteen. I was afraid of getting busted for prostitution. I was terrified of getting arrested for killing Daddy. The last thing on my mind was volunteering that I really did know about thallium. Police were the enemy. I hated guys who got rough. If someone was killing guys who got rough with one of us, I was all for it. But that was then; this is now. After I went to Walters State and got my head on straight, I thought of going to the police, but Muffin was dead. If you knew her last name you could look it up, and check it out, but I don't remember her last name. Her car skidded into a tanker truck loaded with gasoline. She was killed instantly. It was right after I left Memphis. I didn't find out about it until months after the funeral. Like Daddy used to say . . ."

The girls spoke in unison, "The Lord has strange ways!"

"The law couldn't get her. I didn't have the courage to turn her in. She was my first real love. But that was it. Now you know all about the first time I tried to kill myself. Never again, no matter what happens. But just because I wouldn't kill myself if Eric leaves, that doesn't mean I want to take a chance that he gets details of my past life, my past lives. I'm not going to tempt fate and risk throwing away what I have with Eric."

She looked at her watch. "C'mon stand up and give me a goodbye hug." And that was it. Andrea Candy Golden Butler Cain had come into our lives for part of one morning and was saying goodbye. Amy Elizabeth and AJ kissed their sister. I handed her a business card and told her to call if she ever needed help.

As we walked toward the door, she looked at AJ and Amy Elizabeth and started to laugh. "You know, both of you look just like all those medical school and intern applicants that I see around the hospital all the time. Black suits and white blouses. You aren't planning to go to medical school, are you?"

Amy Elizabeth answered first. "Not quite. Right now my plans are for some kind of radio show."

ACGBC smiled. "You always wanted to be a star. You probably will be. I'll keep my eye out for you. I bet you'll be impossible to miss. And what about you, AJ?"

"Med school. I'm just starting to work on my application."

"Good luck. You'll get in. You were always the smart one, and knocking off two serial killers makes you a star too. You know, I said I knew all about you guys from reading the papers, and then I spent all our time talking about me. I should have asked more about you. I'm sorry. But you have to go." She was smiling as the door closed, and for six years that's the way that I remembered her.

We didn't know how Eric Cain would react to learning that his wife was an incest survivor and a former prostitute, but we respected the fact that Andrea Candy Golden Butler Cain didn't want to find out what his reaction would be. It took AJ and Amy Elizabeth a while to realize that Candy Cain meant what she had said about no further contact. Her cell phone had caller-ID and she never picked up when AJ or Amy Elizabeth called. All the calls went to voice-mail. She never returned a call.

AJ and Amy Elizabeth never called the condo again since Candy had not wanted Eric Cain to know that she even knew the Golden sisters; he might overhear. They tried calling her at work; she was always too busy to take a call. Finally, the girls recognized that ACGBC couldn't be a part of their lives. She had pulled herself up from a horrible situation, and Amy Elizabeth, the proponent of No Cause for Shame recognized that even if you could bounce back from the worst experiences of your life, success could be fragile.

I'm not saying that we never thought about Andrea Candy Golden Butler Cain, but we all had other things to do. I had my work. AJ and Amy Elizabeth had school. AJ and I had each other.

AJ applied to nine medical schools and was accepted at all nine even though her personal essay was a bit weak. It left out all the information that would have identified her as AJ Golden. AJ chose Vanderbilt over several places in the Ivy League. We continued playing bar trivia, and going to dinner, movies, concerts, and football games. We played tennis and ran together. Whenever I had a challenging case I ran it by her and her advice was generally solid. She discussed her coursework with me. I could see us staying together forever, and I thought about giving her a ring for Valentine's Day. We had been together eight months by that time, but with Plan A having fallen apart, Plan B was looming in the future and I wanted to put Plan B behind us before making any lifetime plans.

As for Amy Elizabeth, Milton's original plan was that she would start her speaking tour in the fall of 2004. As time passed, Milton delayed the tour till April 2005. Amy Elizabeth would have almost two semesters of graduate school under her belt at that time. Milton felt she would be more likely to sound like she knew something if she actually knew something—a radical idea for talk radio.

Milton hired a speech therapist to help Amy Elizabeth redevelop a trace of the southern accent she had lost moving from Kenton to Highland Heights. He hired a drama coach to improve her flair for the dramatic. To get her used to hecklers, he took her on the road to comedy clubs where, wearing a dark wig and horn rimmed glasses, she performed under the name of Robin Coleman and developed a sense of comic timing and improved her stage presence. She was performing under an alias because as Milton said, "Gotta be an alias. Can't mess up da brand name for when she's Amibeth."

Most importantly, Amy Elizabeth learned to do the one thing she had never done in college. She learned to work. She developed even more ambition and realized that it would take effort, not just the happenstance of having been raped, to be a success.

Milton had most of it planned in advance, including the two labels of designer clothing. One would be called "Sixty-one Seconds" in honor of AJ's run up the stairs that culminated in the death of the Diaz Brothers. It would be sold in specialty stores. The other label would be sold at Target and would be named after whatever bridge we ended up using.

Yes, we were heading toward a bridge. Barry had quoted the Ike Turner lyric that first night of bar trivia, "the plan from the very beginning." It was the backup plan from the very beginning. Ten months would have elapsed between the events on Woodland Hills Lane and Amibeth's speaking tour. People have a short attention span. We needed a way to get people's attention.

Without Plan B, I suspect that the tour would have fallen flat, and that Amy Elizabeth, sadder and wiser from the whole experience, might have gone on to be a therapist. Had Plan B been executed as it was designed, Amibeth would likely have been a moderate success. As it was, what I call the glitch on the bridge led to The Amibeth Phenomenon and the creation of the Queen of Talk Radio. Just a little glitch on the bridge.

Chapter Thirty-One

Plan B involved convincing the world that AJ had committed suicide. In all likelihood, the memorial service, with Amibeth delivering the eulogy, would be televised, and people would turn out for what Milton now called "The Amibeth Experience," the launching pad for the Amibeth call-in radio show. A suicide hoax may not seem like a rational means of promoting a psychologist, but while Amibeth was more than performance art, she was about to become a part of show business.

In early April of 2005, as we were working on Plan B, the proposed Amibeth Radio Hour had no sponsors. Only six radio markets had expressed interest in carrying the show, and the only large market willing to run the show was Chicago. I had no idea if this level of interest was par for the course in launching a new venture. Milton said everything was fine but he looked worried. He was risking his reputation more than he was risking money. I owned two and a half percent of Amibeth, which I still considered two and a half percent of nothing, but I didn't care about the cash. Everything I did, I did so AJ could help her sister. If it mattered to AJ, it mattered to me.

As for the Amibeth Experience, the live show was going to open in Knoxville the night of April 15. If all went as planned, the eulogy for AJ would be Wednesday morning April 13 in Highland Heights. That would mean two days for the interest in Amibeth to boost ticket sales for opening night. AJ planned to skip her memorial service, but we had suite tickets for opening night.

The Amibeth Experience would start with a forty-five minute performance by Fireball, a group of studio musicians that Milton had assembled. Tickets for The Amibeth Experience were ten dollars a seat. As Milton told AJ and me he wanted a group "Good enough dat people feel they got dere money's worth if Amibeth sucks—and not so good dat people go home talking 'bout da band." He of course never said a word to Amibeth suggesting he doubted her ability to be a star. He told Amy Elizabeth that there was absolutely no doubt that she was going to FAN-tastic!

For a while it looked like Fireball would be an instrumental group only. It took until April 12, after the events at the Caruthersville Bridge, for Milton to

179

select a lead singer for the band. Everyone he had auditioned before that date was either not good enough or was too good. Finally, he found someone who was just right. Milton heard her singing a song that she had co-written and ended up changing the name of the group to Fireball featuring Elana Grey.

Not having a lead singer for Fireball until three days before the show opened was the least of Milton's problems. The ten venues for The Amibeth Experience had a total of just under 140,000 seats. Before the execution of Plan B, fewer than 11,000 seats had been sold. Considering the rental fees, the travel expenses, and the small fee to Fireball, Milton looked like he was going to take a bath. On the other hand, if The Amibeth Experience sold out, the gross would be almost one million four hundred thousand dollars, and the radio stations would come on board.

The University of Tennessee, Northwestern University, The Ohio State University, Penn State, the University of Connecticut, Yale, Harvard, the University of Washington in Seattle, the University of Southern California, ending up at Vanderbilt's Memorial Gym. Ten cities in thirteen days. For many of the schools it would be a brief escape during exams. It all hung on Plan B.

Plan B, a variation of AJ's idea of faking her death at the Cumberland River, was more complicated than one might imagine. We needed to have a believable suicide without a body.

First, we had to define a location. We needed a bridge high enough that anyone jumping off of it would be presumed to be dead. The fake jump needed to occur when traffic on the bridge was minimal. We needed someone reliable, someone not affiliated with me or AJ or Amibeth or Milton to think he saw AJ jump, but not so many people to see the action that anyone would notice that it was not a person who had plunged into the river.

None of the bridges in Nashville were suitable for what we had in mind. There are two bridges that cross the Mississippi River at Memphis. The Memphis-Arkansas Bridge carries Interstate 55 across the Mississippi; the Hernando DeSoto Bridge carries Interstate 40 across the river. Traffic across each bridge averages 40,000 to 50,000 cars a day. Even at night, there is too much traffic for what we were going to attempt. On the other hand, the Caruthersville Bridge carrying Interstate 155 and US 412 across the Mississippi has daily traffic of only 10,000 cars a day. That's four cars in each direction every minute, but, of course, fewer at night. It was more than one hundred feet above the water. It was our Goldilocks Bridge; just right. Since it had opened on December 1, 1976, no one had ever survived a fall from the Caruthersville Bridge. AJ's faked jump was scheduled for 2 AM on Sunday April 10.

The plan required two cars. AJ would drive her Miata to the bridge. After the fact, the Miata would be found to contain her clothes and a suicide note. AJ was going to run out of her car naked—to maximize the chance of being seen. Something that resembled a naked woman would have to be seen going off the bridge. Before anyone got near enough to the scene to know what was actually happening, AJ would be in the second car, and would eventually leave the bridge in the second car, mission accomplished.

There were a few logistical problems. AJ had to been seen coming out of the car, she couldn't be seen while she was tossing something off the bridge. She couldn't be seen getting in the second car. The solution required a little bit of geometry, but we figured it out.

At the critical moment, AJ was going to race out of her car on the driver's side. I was going to be following close behind and pull in front of her. AJ was going to run between the two cars—in front of her car, and behind mine. Crouching between the cars, AJ wouldn't be seen by anyone in a car coming from behind us, specifically by the person who was going to "witness the suicide." AJ was going to catapult something over the railing. That something was going to be visible going into the river while AJ got in the trunk of my car. There was no problem, except for one thing.

"I am NOT going in the trunk."

"AJ, there isn't a choice. We need someone to report the jump. The Observer has to see you get out of your car on the driver's side, and see something go in the water. They can't see you get in my car. If you go to the driver's side of my car, they will see you. If you run around to the passenger side of my car, they will probably see you, especially if the observer car has someone in the passenger seat."

"Get somebody else. It doesn't have to be me. Get somebody else. I am NOT getting in the trunk of your Lexus. I hate small spaces in the dark. I know it's my plan, but forget it."

"Come on. The fewer people who know the truth the better. We don't need an actress to pop out of your Miata and then hope she never sells her story to the tabloids. It will only be for a few minutes while I con the observer into being the one who waits for the cops while I drive us off the bridge."

AJ was adamant. "NO! Did you ever think that maybe I spent a couple of years in a dark space called my bedroom hearing bad sounds and that maybe I panic in small dark spaces. I am not getting in the trunk of your Lexus. That thing is tiny. No way. If the best we can do . . ."

"What about an SUV?"

"That would work. No it wouldn't. I might not be able to get the back door closed from inside. Someone would see me in the back of the SUV. Not an SUV. Get somebody else."

"What about Amy Elizabeth? She would keep her mouth shut."

"No way. Same problem for the same reason. She's even more claustrophobic than me. She won't get in the trunk. I won't even bother to ask her."

And so, for several thousand dollars, we hired a computer animation engineer, a brilliant young man from Orlando, Florida who was one of the hottest video game designers in the country. He ran computer simulations for us and reached the same conclusion. AJ—or whomever we would use—had to get in the trunk. Otherwise the plan wouldn't work. We were stuck.

"What if we used a regular car with a bigger trunk and a flashlight in the trunk?"

"Hmmn. What car?"

"Barry has a Toyota Camry. It has a bigger trunk than my Lexus sport coupe. Barry would never sell the story to the tabloids."

"What year is the Toyota?"

"Does it matter?"

"What year?"

"1999."

"OK. Amy Elizabeth had a '98. Basically the same thing. Not a problem."

We had wasted money on a consultant just so we could end up using my brother's car. The trunk of the '99 Camry struck me as a small dark space even with a flashlight. I should have asked why it was better, but I didn't want to dwell on AJ's claustrophobia. Instead I looked on the bright side. My girlfriend was a lunatic who was planning an insane hoax, but she was also capable of compromise. The Camry would solve another problem. Our "passenger" would fit far better in the Toyota than in the Lexus.

Something had to go over the bridge. In early April, AJ and I went shopping at Hollywood Hustler, an adult store that has been called "The Gap of Porn." While AJ purchased lingerie, I searched for a blow up doll that would meet our needs.

AJ found the experience arousing. "My God, Jonah. This one has a vibrating vagina. I don't vibrate."

"But you're much prettier, and you make neat noises when you get excited. Plus . . ."

"Quiet. People can hear us." I looked around. Two college students quickly turned away, laughing.

I started whispering. "Well, you do make neat noises."

"I know I do. Let's get Nurse Nancy."

"I vote for Britney."

AJ looked at the two boxes and whispered "Nurse Nancy has a vibrating mouth and Britney doesn't. They both have three openings. And Nurse Nancy is only twelve dollars more. Nurse Nancy is the better buy."

"We're not going to use her as a sex toy! She's going over the bridge. Britney has blonde hair. The world knows AJ as a blonde. You're getting out of the car wearing a blonde wig. Whatever goes over the railing has to be blonde if you are going to pull a long term disappearing act, 'Red.' In the dark, Britney will look more like you."

"Sorry. I wasn't thinking about the hair. C'mon let's pay for Britney. I already paid for my stuff. Wait until you see what I bought."

"I'm sure you will be very sexy tonight."

"Tonight? Who's waiting until tonight? They have a dressing room right over there."

"Can you wait 'til we get home?"

"I'll try."

We were only five blocks from the condo, and she did look fantastic for the thirty seconds that she had the lingerie on. After AJ proved to my satisfaction and her own that she was hotter than a $39.95 sex toy, we added a total of twenty pounds of concrete to Britney's arms, legs, and breasts to prevent the doll from blowing back onto the bridge supports after she went over the railing. It would be ridiculous to drive almost two hundred miles in each direction to fake a suicide only to have someone discover a blow up doll wrapped around the bridge supports when the sun came up. Milton hired a discreet engineering consultant who calculated that the blowup doll would either sink immediately, never to be seen again, or else turn up as a flat-chested quadruple amputee, sans concrete, somewhere in Louisiana in late April or early May. Either way, no one would ever associate the sex toy with AJ's faked suicide.

AJ was an athlete and could easily push a twenty pound blow up doll over the railing of the bridge. The problem was how to do it without being seen. The solution was elegant. Sex toy dolls come with oral, vaginal, and anal openings; they are sex toys after all. We took the handle of an old broom, painted it black so it wouldn't be seen at night, and with minimal engineering, had a long rod that could be placed in Britney's butt. AJ could kneel between the two cars, and, as if she were tossing a javelin, launch Britney over the railing.

"Jonah, we can't call her Britney."

"That's her name."

"Come on. She has a stick up her ass and she's flying in the night. She looks like a witch. We should call her . . ."

"Mary Nell."

"Mary Nell." AJ gave me a high five for my insight. The insanity was fun. The plan was complete. I started to believe that nothing could go wrong.

Chapter Thirty-Two

Amy Elizabeth's eulogy for AJ was the one thing we couldn't control. AJ was worried that Amy Elizabeth would giggle her way through the eulogy. After all, AJ was going to be alive and watching on television, while Amy Elizabeth lamented her dead sister. AJ had no idea how good an actress Amibeth was or wasn't.

"You know if it wasn't for the fact that I'd be dead, I'd go over the railing just so she would be appropriately somber. We're going to do all this for her and there's a fifty-fifty chance she's going to mess it up."

"Don't go over the railing!"

"Course not, sweetie. That's Plan Z. Out of the question. There is a Plan X and Plan Y however."

"Which are?"

"Plan X. I knock her out the morning of the memorial service, wear six inch heels to make me look five-ten, add a part to the eulogy that I dyed my hair red in honor of my sister AJ, who was a true redhead, and give the eulogy myself. If I wore sunglasses, as if I were hiding my tears, no one would know it was me. That's Plan X. Then there's Plan Y. After the bridge, we don't tell her that I'm ok. We hide out somewhere and Amy Elizabeth will be worried that I may be dead. That would keep her from giggling."

"That would be cruel."

"I know. But it might be necessary. I'm not ruling out Plan X or Plan Y. Knocking her out and doing the eulogy myself might be best, except if I did that, I'd have to ride in the funeral car with Mary Nell. NO!!!"

"And she'd know it was you?"

"Are you kidding? She will be so wrapped up in how SHE looks on TV, that I could tell her I was really AJ, and she wouldn't hear a word. No, the problem is that I would have to be with Mary Nell and that's not worth it for me. If Amy Elizabeth can't give a simple eulogy, she isn't going to go far as Amibeth. May as well find out now what she can and can't do. We stick with Plan B."

We ran dress rehearsals on the Brandenburg driveway. AJ could get out of the car, take Mary Nell from the trunk of Barry's Toyota, launch Mary Nell over the line that represented the top railing of the bridge, get in the trunk herself and get the trunk down, but not latched shut, in 4.9 seconds. I would have to slam the trunk shut before I drove off. That was going to be easy to remember. My code name for the trip was Jonah Slammer.

On the weekend of April 2nd and 3rd, AJ and I drove to the Caruthersville Bridge to confirm what the traffic was like on a Sunday morning at 2 AM. We identified what we regarded as our staging area short of the bridge. We identified an all-night gas station at the Missouri end of the bridge as the place where I was going to let AJ out of the trunk. We calculated that as soon as we were about three hundred yards ahead of what we called "The Observer," AJ could pull over, stop, and do her thing. Then, I could get into my act convincing "The Observer" that he had witnessed a tragedy, and that he should be the one to notify the police.

We were in countdown phase. On Saturday morning April 9, Day Zero, Barry organized a co-ed touch football game to calm our nerves and keep our mind off that night's event. Several of the men had played varsity ball with me at Vanderbilt. It was a zero-zero tie until we had the good sense to start throwing the ball to our former Big Ten track star. Fifteen minutes and three touchdown passes to AJ later, the game was over.

Barry drove us back to the condo. "See you tomorrow night at trivia. It's finally Day Zero." He whispered the last words even though no one was in earshot and no one would have known what it meant. "Toyota's yours. I'll take the Lexus. Trade back tomorrow night. Good luck guys." He hugged us both.

AJ looked at me as Barry drove away. "Great game. Great day. Great day to be alive."

"Absolutely. Let's get some rest and then go watch Mary Nell go off the Caruthersville Bridge."

One point must be mentioned before anyone concludes that two reckless people were going to endanger the lives of the search team that might be going in the water to look for a body. The FBI knew in advance that this was a publicity stunt. In fact, the FBI could have eliminated the necessity for a considerable amount of effort if they had simply agreed to announce that AJ's lifeless body had been found next to a bottle of sleeping pills. That was too simple for the FBI.

As Joseph Apted explained, "Look, we can't help every show business act that wants to pull off a hoax—and that's exactly what this is, a show business hoax. The Bureau has a soft spot in its heart for AJ after she blew away The Diaz Brothers, but we can't just announce she is dead. But we can certainly pretend to do a search, make sure no one gets hurt looking for the body, announce that she's dead, and make it seem legitimate. No problem."

We had met in his office, about a week before the main event. "I guess that makes sense. I just didn't want AJ to come to her senses later and ask why we didn't do it the simple way."

"Your girlfriend is still into making plans all the time?"

"All the time. Plan A, Plan B, and so on."

Joe Apted got up and closed the door to his office. "Look, you know, from time to time we have to make people disappear. Witness protection stuff where we want someone to think that the person who has become a federal witness is dead. I know that Amos Bunden has you on our consultant list. Tell you what. If you pull this off really well, maybe in the future we'll hire you to help out with some disappearing acts. We really aren't that good with show business type stuff. You could become one of our go to guys. Just call me when you come back across the bridge, and tell me everything is ok. Best of luck."

"Hey, if this is an audition, can I be like an honorary agent for the day? Can I have a badge so I can say 'Federal Agent' if something goes wrong?"

"Don't push your luck. You're on your own. And anyway, what can go wrong?"

At five o'clock, AJ kissed Amy Elizabeth goodbye. We left Nashville and headed west. AJ brought Layla for luck. She said we needed a guardian angel. We maintained contact by cell phone while we drove. We were either on the verge of one of the greatest hoaxes in the history of the American entertainment industry, or on the cusp of an absurd failure.

We ate dinner at Gaudo's in Jackson, and had no wine. We wanted to be at our best for what we had to do. We drank a toast to each other with glasses of water."

"To the future."

"To the future."

We were wearing our good luck outfits. I was wearing the same shirt and slacks that I had worn the night we met. AJ was wearing the blue denim shirt, black skirt, black tights, and knee high, high heeled black boots that she had been wearing that night. It was a symmetrical end to the first phase of our relationship. We had been together for ten months.

"You're being very quiet tonight, Jonah. Something on your mind?"

"Thinking about what we have to do tonight. Thinking about what a fantastic ten months it's been. Thinking about where we go from here."

"It has been fantastic. Plan B is insane, I know that, but it's a one-time deal." She moved her hand parallel to the table. "Smooth sailing. It should just go on and on like this. Our life should be one long first date."

"We have to talk about that . . . after the bridge."

She looked as if she had been shot. "That's horrible. How can you do this?"

"Do what?"

"You said we have to talk. When a guy says 'We have to talk,' it means he's breaking up with you. How can you break up with me? You can't break up with me! We're almost perfect together. Just because I dragged you on this crazy stunt, you are going to break up with me?" She was yelling and crying and pounding the table, all at the same time. She knocked over a glass of water. People at nearby tables were trying to catch a peek at what was going on.

"Of course I'm not breaking up with you. You're just excited about pulling off the hoax. Settle down. This is not the time to talk. We'll talk after the bridge. Sorry I mentioned it."

"You're not breaking up with me? Will you promise you're not breaking up with me?"

"I'm absolutely not breaking up with you, AJ. We just need to talk. Why would I break up with you? Why would you even think I was breaking up with you?"

"Because of Amy Elizabeth!" She invoked the name of her sister as if she was summoning a mystical power.

"What does she have to do with it?"

AJ replaced the ice cubes in her water glass before answering. "When we started dating, after she got over how fast things were going, Amy Elizabeth told me I was going to end up being your 'transitional woman.' She said that you were going to get back in the dating life with me, see what you really want in a relationship, and then move on to the major relationship of your life and leave me behind. Sometimes she's an idiot, but sometimes she gets things so exactly right that it scares me. She does have some really good insights—at times. If we're not breaking up, what are we going to be talking about?"

"After the bridge. I'm sorry I mentioned it. Lo siento. This is not the time."

"Lo siento. I guess we're both a little high strung right now. After the bridge."

After dinner we checked into a hotel. I thought that we might just mirror our first night together at the Brandenburg's and not make love, but AJ had far too much nervous energy and only one way to express it. Shortly after we were in the room, she started stripping off her clothes. I followed suit and we began kissing. We were still standing when I moved my mouth down to her breast and found an erect nipple. I reached between her legs and her thighs parted. She was wetter than I expected. I began to rhythmically and gently stroke her clit. Her pelvis responded to the rhythm of my hand. I heard her start breathing heavily. From the time we started she had said nothing. Suddenly, and surprisingly, I felt an unmistakable shuddering. She pulled me close, and her thighs clamped on my hand. The shuddering continued for a few seconds, then faded away.

It had all happened so quickly that we were standing in the middle of the room. She suggested that we lie down. She spread her legs and I think she expected me to enter her immediately, but I was in no hurry. I wanted to taste her. I buried my tongue between her legs, and her hips began rocking very slowly. She was delicious. I slipped a finger and then another inside her. In a soft voice she offered encouragement, telling me not to stop. Why would I? I loved giving her pleasure. After several minutes, in a voice that was half panting, half speaking, she muttered "Yes, yes, yes, YES!!!" and exploded again, her hips bouncing off the bed. Her eyes were closed tightly. Her hands clutched her breasts. I continued licking her until she pushed my face away. "Give me a few seconds."

I started to move up the bed. But she gently put her hand on my face. "Not-just-yet. Wait a little, and do it some more . . . please." I obliged. The next fire wave was a long time in coming. After it left, I moved up the bed and lay beside her. I stroked her face while she regained her composure. Finally, she smiled, and said "Three's enough. It's your turn."

She moved down the bed and took me in her mouth, all the while looking right up at me. It was heavenly. She kept bringing me almost to the brink of ecstasy, then slowed down, and then started up again. Finally, when I thought I couldn't take any more, I told her I wanted to be inside her. She climbed on and began moving very slowly.

I looked up at her and thought to myself that no matter how long I lived, nothing would ever equal the exquisite experience of AJ Golden riding me. She looked amazing. It felt amazing. I whispered, "I feel sorry for you."

"What are you talking about?"

"Because you will never know how wonderful it feels to be inside you. Or how amazing it is to look up at you and see you like that. You are the most beautiful, sexy woman in the world."

She laughed and tossed her head back, flipping her long hair and arching her body slightly away from me. As she did, I slid my thumb between her legs and against her clit. She continued to move on my penis and to rock against my thumb. With my other hand I gently squeezed one of her breasts. She mumbled something. I didn't catch what it was until the second time she said it. "Fire wave's coming." Her pace quickened and she let out a series of guttural groans. More than her movements, her excitement lifted me over the edge, and as I finished pouring myself into her, she collapsed on top of me.

She lay so still, that I thought she had fallen asleep. I knew she hadn't slept much the previous two nights. The room was silent. I began to kiss her. "That was very nice, Jonah . . . Is the alarm set?"

"For eleven thirty."

"I love you. Good night!" She kissed me on the forehead, rolled off, then turned onto her left side, with her back towards me. We cuddled like spoons. I lay behind her, my right hand holding her right breast, her hand on top of mine.

I whispered in her ear, "Talk about doing it like there was no tomorrow. What got into you?"

"You did." She giggled in response to her own joke. "Shhh. Talk later. I wanna try to sleep. Big night ahead."

Chapter Thirty-Three

At eleven thirty, the alarm went off, we got up, got dressed, and started the hour and twenty minute drive to the Caruthersville Bridge. We didn't check out of the room, figuring that after the bridge we might not want to drive all the way back to Nashville. We were driving to what I expected to be the one and only major theatrical performance of my life. I alternated between feeling elated and feeling like I was driving to a funeral.

As we drove, AJ and I were in contact by cell phone. I had her on speaker. As we got nearer to the bridge, AJ nervously began to remind herself of the plan by muttering the same words over and over, in sing-song fashion. "We follow the car out of the lot. I pass the car, driving really fast. They see me. Jonah passes the other car. He rides behind me. We both get way ahead. I stop my car. Jonah parks in front of me. I come out on the driver's side, naked. The trunk is open, but held by the twine. I open the trunk. I grab Mary Nell. Mary Nell goes into the water. I get in the trunk. I'm done. Jonah does his thing on the bridge. Mission accomplished . . . We follow the car out of the lot. I pass the car, driving really fast. They see me. Jonah passes the other car. He rides behind me. We both get way ahead. I stop my car. Jonah parks in front of me. I come out on the driver's side, naked. The trunk is open, but held by the twine. I open the trunk. I grab Mary Nell. Mary Nell goes into the water. I get in the trunk. I'm done. Jonah does his thing on the bridge. Mission accomplished . . . We follow the car out of the lot."

As planned, we pulled in and parked both cars at the last rest stop before the Caruthersville Bridge. AJ kissed me and went to the ladies room to get undressed for her role. I assembled Mary Nell, getting the broom handle screwed into the appropriate socket. The broom handle would hang out of the trunk and the trunk wouldn't close, but that was no problem. I secured the trunk with twine. AJ would be able to break the twine, open the trunk and easily remove Mary Nell.

The parking lot was nearly empty. As soon as AJ was back from the ladies room, we would start walking around the rest stop looking for the right car to be the trail car. I suspected we would look a bit suspicious, but it couldn't be helped. We needed a reliable witness to report the suicide. We wanted a car with Missouri plates and some indication that the driver would be credible when he or she told his tale. Missouri plates were a sign that the driver was headed over the bridge and not turning off on the Great River Road exit. If the car that we chose to be the trail car turned off, we'd have to go back to the rest stop and start over. A little league baseball decal or a soccer decal in the back window would be a sign that we had someone who would probably be believed when he or she told the story. A motorcycle club decal or a Grateful Dead sticker was a sign that the car was not what we wanted.

I wasn't going to be the one who reported AJ Golden's suicide. If I was the witness, people would investigate me and notice that I had a redheaded girlfriend with an uncanny resemblance to AJ Golden. We needed someone else to witness the tragedy and report it. AJ was going to fake her death; I was going to be there, and then, like magic, I was going to vanish into thin air as I drove the Camry away from the scene. That was the plan, and it seemed perfect.

I saw AJ wearing a blonde wig, coming out of the rest stop restroom looking as beautiful as ever. Her good luck clothes and her underwear were in a paper bag that she tossed in the backseat of the Toyota. She was wearing a beach robe; she was naked underneath. She put Layla on a leash and quickly walked her dog over to my car. For a brief while, Layla would be my dog.

The suicide note and a cheap set of clothing were already on the passenger seat of the Miata. The note read "Amy Elizabeth. I can't go on. Sorry. Lo siento. Love, AJ" Amy Elizabeth could confirm that the handwriting was authentic.

It was getting cool. I hoped it didn't take too long to find the right car, but before I had even started to look for a trail car, AJ announced, "I got the car. I got our witness. That Volvo over there." AJ pointed to a car parked in front of the rest room. "It has a Missouri Judiciary License Plate. Better than little league. Older man, about sixty, younger woman, his daughter."

"What if it's his girlfriend? They won't stop if it's an older man with a woman he's not supposed to be with."

"It's his daughter. I met her in the rest room. That's her coming out now. I gave her my T181 pendant. Never wear it any more anyway. Told her I didn't want it. People who commit suicide give stuff away. A finishing touch just for show. It'll have my fingerprints and likely some DNA on it." AJ gave me a quick kiss and a hug. "No time to walk Layla. Do that on the other side of the bridge." She kissed me again. "You think this is crazy. You thought it was crazy the whole time, but you're doing it for me anyway. I love you. Always remember this. AJ Golden loved you. Now! Go!"

The car containing the judge and his daughter was just starting up. AJ removed the beach robe as she got in her car, tossed it on the ground, and, stark naked, started up the Miata. I got in and started the Toyota.

I had been relatively calm. I had run more complicated plays on special teams at Vanderbilt. This was just another play and I had it down pat. But something

AJ had just said jarred my senses. As I drove from the lot I realized what it was. She had told me to remember that AJ Golden loved me. Past tense. AJ Golden loved me. PAST TENSE! Oh-my-god. AJ was going to go off the bridge. All that worrying that Amibeth would screw things up and giggle at the eulogy. AJ had found a way to solve that problem. AJ was going to make certain that Amibeth wouldn't be giggling. No wonder she had made love like there was no tomorrow. There was no tomorrow.

It couldn't be. I was just nervous about pulling off such a fantastic hoax. No way and no reason for AJ to go off the bridge. What did she mean? Why did she say, "AJ Golden LOVED me"? I decided to concentrate on my driving and not think about it.

We were almost to the bridge. AJ pulled in front of the Volvo; she was driving almost seventy miles per hour. A very light rain was falling, but the road wasn't slick. Visibility was down because of the rain; exactly what we needed. Everything was fine except for one thing. I was worried that AJ might be planning to go over the railing and off the bridge. "Remember this. AJ Golden loved you." What did she mean by that?

AJ and I were about three hundred yards ahead of the Volvo and past the midway point of the bridge. At the speed we were driving we had fifteen seconds for AJ to get out of the car, toss Mary Nell in the water and get into the trunk before the Volvo caught up to us. We had time to spare. AJ stopped the car. I pulled in front of her. As I got out of the car I checked to see that Layla was safe inside the Toyota. Layla was barking. A gentle rain was falling. Out of the corner of my eye I had seen a naked figure emerge from the Miata. I had seen something go over the railing, but when I had checked to be sure Layla was safe I had lost sight of what was happening. I hadn't seen AJ go into the trunk. I went to the railing. All I could see was the blackness of the river below.

I knew my role. I went to the railing and started screaming "Are you ok? Are you ok?" I didn't expect an answer. I just wanted whoever emerged from the Volvo to believe that he had seen a woman go over the railing.

The Volvo pulled up behind the Miata and stopped. A distinguished looking man with grey hair emerged. Everything was going according to plan—unless AJ was in the water.

It was time for me to give the best acting performance of my life. "Did you see that? Did you see that? The girl went in the water. Oh-my-god, the girl went in the water." It didn't take much acting ability to sound panicked. She might very well have gone in the water.

The man spoke with the somber and serious tone I would have expected of a judge. "If she did, she's dead. It's a hundred plus feet to the water. I know this bridge. God, that's horrible. Why were you driving so fast?"

I shook my head as if I was going to be sick. I might very well be sick, but I remembered my lines. "At the rest stop. Cute girl. I smiled at her. I'm married. I wasn't trying to pick her up or anything. I just smiled and she said, 'Don't bother flirting with me; I'm going to jump off the bridge. Don't waste your time. I'll be dead in fifteen minutes.' I thought she was joking. But when she took off and passed you I went after her. I thought maybe I could stop her. Grab her. But I couldn't. She went over the railing RIGHT IN FRONT OF ME. Oh-my-God." I took out my cell phone. "Damn. Battery's dead." Of course it wasn't. I didn't want the call traced to me. "Do you have a phone, sir?" To myself I said "Be polite, Jonah Slammer. This is going fine."

He took his cell phone from his pocket. "You know I wasn't sure what I saw. I saw a naked girl get out of the car and then something went over the railing. It looked a little different. Must have been the rain and the headlights. My goodness. Her poor parents. How old did she seem? I couldn't tell." A warm rain was continuing to fall. A couple of cars passed by as we were talking.

"Twenty-one, twenty-two. I don't know. She was pretty. Very pretty."

He dialed 911. "This is Judge Joseph Ancell. I'm westbound on the Caruthersville Bridge. A young woman has just taken her life by jumping off the bridge. I saw the whole thing. Yes I'll wait here. This is Judge Joseph Ancell, A-N-C-E-L-L., from Sikeston, Missouri. Thank you. Yes, I'll stay here and wait for the police."

A slim attractive woman, probably in her late twenties, was walking towards the two of us. She was wearing jeans and a long sleeved Vanderbilt Medical School Sweatshirt. She looked sleepy. "Dad, are you ok? What happened? I was asleep. Did we have an accident? Why are we stopped on the bridge?"

Judge Ancell hugged his daughter. "No. I'm ok. We're ok. A young woman, a little younger than you, just jumped off the bridge and killed herself. I love you so much Kristi. Thank God you're ok."

"Of course I'm ok . . . Why wouldn't I be? . . . Who is this man? . . . Oh-my-God. It was the blonde girl wasn't it. The one who gave me this pendant. I wondered why she gave it away."

"This young man tried to save her, but he wasn't in time. I didn't catch your name."

My code name was Jonah Slammer. Remember to slam the trunk. But there was no way I was going to give a name that could be checked and found to be phony. No business like show business. Time for my performance. "Good to meet you, Your Honor, Sir. Good to meet you, Miss Ancell?" I looked at the sweatshirt. "Doctor Ancell?"

"Doctor Ancell." She smiled when I called her by the correct title.

"Good to meet you. I'm . . . screwed that's who I am." I put my face in my hands. I sat down on the wet highway and took the opportunity to look under the judge's car, under the Miata, and under the Toyota. I knew AJ had been reluctant to go in the trunk. I wanted to be sure she wasn't hiding under one of the cars. She wasn't. I held my stomach and pretended to retch. "I'm screwed. All for stopping and trying to save her."

The judge and his daughter looked puzzled.

Showtime. I got up from my knees. "Ten months ago I had my license taken away for blowing .081 on a breathalyzer. My wife said that was the last straw. She was going to leave me. We have a two year old girl and I love both of them more than anything in the world. I haven't had a drop to drink in ten months. See. Here's my AA chip. Three hundred days sober." I was crying. I showed him a chip I had bought on e-Bay just for this occasion. "I've been working two jobs to pay off our debts. One's at an all-night gas station across the river in Missouri. The cops are going to come. When they find out I have no license, I'm going to go to jail. They'll take the car. My wife will leave me and take our little girl. Oh, God. All for trying to do a good deed and stop to try and save a crazy girl who wanted to kill herself." I spun in a half circle and stamped my foot. Then I stood up straight and shrugged my shoulders. "Oh well, sometimes things aren't fair. I deserved to lose my license ten months ago. It was my fault. Kind of ironic that I do everything right for ten months and it's all going to fall apart." I paused for a moment to let the judge think about my predicament. "Hey, you saw everything. You saw her go in the water. You can tell them. You don't need me." If it had been a little league dad or a soccer mom I would have given away a twenty dollar bill at that point. Bribing a judge did not seem like a smart move. "I am so screwed." I waited for the judge to say something.

"Sorry, son. You had the best view. You have to stay and tell them what you saw."

And that was it. It was over. Two hundred miles each way for nothing. It would be a terrible trip going back. Well, we had done our best. The police would come. They would get our statements. Eventually, they would check my car. They would probably open the trunk, and find a naked woman, who, by that time, would be a hysterical, claustrophobic naked woman. I might even be arrested for kidnapping her until things settled down and she gave a coherent statement. At least I hoped they would find a naked woman in my trunk. I still wasn't certain if AJ was dead in the water or alive in the trunk.

The judge wanted me to stay and it was all going to be for nothing. The hoax was going to be exposed. I would get a fine for illegally stopping on a bridge. It was a misdemeanor, so I wouldn't lose my investigator license. There was no time for a Plan C. The Amibeth tour was scheduled. It was going to fall flat, and so was Amibeth. Damn. A little league coach would have been better. AJ had picked a judge. He was going to say he saw a woman go in the water, but he was a judge. The proper legal thing to do was make me stay. And then, my guardian angel came to my rescue. Dr. Kristi Ancell.

"Daddy. Don't be a hard-ass. There's no reason to mess up this young man's life when he's trying to turn things around. We can wait for the police and tell them what you saw. You said you saw it." She looked and me and mouthed the words, "My dad's really a sweetheart."

The judge thought it over for a brief moment. "Please get in the car, Kristi. You're right. Just get in the car, sweetheart. It's drizzling."

"In a minute." Instead of walking to their Volvo, she went to the Miata and looked inside. "Dad. There's a pile of clothes in here with a note on top. Oh-my-God. It's a note to her sister, Amy Elizabeth. She signed it 'AJ.' Dad, it was AJ Golden, the girl who saved her sister and shot those two horrible men last summer. It was in the news all the time. Remember?" She looked at the license plate on the car and at the pendant "T181. It's her. It was her."

The judge looked at me and nodded, saying nothing. I ran toward my car, looked over my shoulder, yelled "Thank you, your honor. I swear I will never drink and drive. Thank you, thank you, thank you." I slammed the trunk closed, got in the car, and drove off the Caruthersville Bridge.

The rain was letting up. We had done it. I looked at Layla and gave a fist pump. AJ had to be in the trunk, but everything was quiet behind me. Maybe the trunk was soundproof.

I took the first exit on the Missouri side of the bridge and drove to the gas station that we had scouted the week before. I pulled up to the all night store, got out of the car, and went around to the trunk and opened it.

The trunk was empty. From inside the car I could hear Layla barking. The trunk was empty. I shut the trunk and looked to the sky. "Please, God. When I open the trunk, please have AJ be in the trunk." I opened the trunk. It was still empty. SHE WASN'T IN THE TRUNK.

Chapter Thirty-Four

SHE WASN'T IN THE TRUNK! I slammed the trunk shut, banged my forehead and then my fist on the trunk. I screamed "NO!!!!!"

AJ Golden wasn't in the trunk. She hadn't been under one of the cars. I had to face it. AJ Golden, the woman I had loved as much as I loved life itself had gone in the water. AJ was . . . AJ was . . . I couldn't say it, but I knew it. I could think of no other possibility. AJ was gone. I wasn't going to go all Romeo and Juliet about it, but life as I knew it was over.

And then I totally lost it. I started mumbling to myself and talking to Layla. AJ had asked me to walk her dog. Absent mindedly I grabbed hold of Layla's leash and walked her to the grass at the edge of the gas station. The fluorescent light was eerie, partly from my tears. I wondered how it compared to the light on the front porch of the house on Woodland Hills Lane where the picture had been taken. By all rights, AJ should have died that night. I counted the days. The attack was June 6. This was April 10. Ten months and four days. She had lived an extra ten months and four days. It wasn't anywhere near enough.

I was talking to myself and Layla. "Why? Why? Why? What didn't I see? Layla, don't people who are going to kill themselves give things away? She didn't give me anything." Layla was barking. "Oh-my-God, Layla. She gave me you, her precious doggie." I bent down to AJ's shih-tzu, the dog that was now my shih-tzu. "Layla, mommy's gone, I guess." I could barely think it, let alone get myself to say it. "Layla, you are now my dog, and I am going to be the best doggie daddy you can ever imagine. I will get you toys, and I will walk you, and when I have to go anywhere I will either take you with me or get a sitter for you. I will never put you in a kennel because AJ knew you didn't like that. You are my dog." I reached down and rubbed the side of her face. Layla bit my finger. "That's ok Layla. I know you're scared. I'm scared too. Your mommy's gone. This is the worst day of my life." My hand wasn't bleeding. Layla hadn't broken the skin. She rolled over so I could rub her tummy. "Good dog, Layla."

Layla and I walked back to the car and I put Layla in the passenger seat. "It's going to be a long ride home Layla. She didn't seem depressed. Did she seem depressed? You were in the car with her Layla?" Layla curled up and started to go to sleep on the passenger seat. I secured her seat belt through her doggie harness.

"Layla, she seemed happy. She said she could see being with me for the rest of her life. Guess it doesn't mean much when the rest of your life is measured in hours. She said that AJ Golden loved me. But why did she do it? Why? Why? Why? There is no why. There is no why. Maybe she was . . . Maybe she was so happy about everything coming together that she thought that she could fly. Maybe that's it. Maybe that's why she went over the railing. Maybe she thought that she could fly. Oh, God. I will never understand this. I guess there are some things you can't explain. Maybe she thought that she could fly."

That idea, crazy as it seems was better than facing the facts. I loved AJ and it wasn't enough for her. I thought of what she had said "Remember AJ Golden loved you." Past tense. The woman whom I thought would be the love of my life was gone.

What is a reasonable response when the worst thing imaginable actually happens? I suppose that I could have pulled myself together and commiserated with friends and family. In most cities that would be the most reasonable option. But Nashville isn't most places. No, I didn't start frequenting the honky tonks, drinking too much, and telling my sad tale of woe. At the time, that was my second choice; it was my Plan B so to speak. I picked a much better Music City option. Anyone who paid attention to my incoherent ramblings as I spoke to Layla after looking into the abyss that was the empty trunk of my brother's 1999 Toyota, knows what I did because the phrase "She thought that she could fly" represents the key lyrics to the song that I co-wrote that night with Skylar Jones and her friend Elana Grey.

The tribute song to AJ Golden, the Country Music Association song of the year for 2005, was "(She Thought She Could) Fly." It was first recorded by Fireball featuring Elana Grey, and later was recorded by Skylar Jones as the lead track of her Grammy and CMA award-winning album *No Cause for Shame*. The video of "Fly," by Skylar Jones, was Video of the Year for both the CMA's and the American Music Awards. I take neither credit nor blame for the overwrought video with angels playing harps and welcoming a young blonde woman into Heaven. I had nothing to do with the video.

Before the song "(She Thought She Could) Fly," Skylar Jones was a rising star with great potential. After the song and the album, Skylar Jones was a superstar, big enough that she could have become "Skylar"—one name, if that had been her desire. Still, everyone in Nashville and the rest of the world knows who you meant when you say Skylar, just as everyone knows who you mean when you say Reba, or Dolly, or Shania, or Barack, or Rush, or Oprah, or Amibeth.

The fact that we won the Country Music Association award for Song of the Year has a lot to do with the competition. This is Nashville. We were up against a drinking song, a cheating song, a song about how he drinks because she's cheating, and another song about how she's cheating because he's always out drinking. We cornered the market on serious songs that year. If I had to guess, we probably won with just a little more than thirty percent of the votes, but a win is a win and Elana, Skylar, and I get to keep the trophies.

Skylar did the music for the verse, all I contributed was the words and music for chorus. Elana Grey had the idea for the haunting bass coda of ten notes that ends the song: ACGBC AGCBC. Those notes, of course, represent the initials of Andrea Candy Golden Butler Cain and create a very haunting melody.

It is not a happy song, but remember, Milton's plan was that before Amibeth spoke and did whatever it was that she was going to do, there would be music—an uptempo country band. People would go away feeling that they had gotten their money's worth, even if Amibeth bombed out. Fireball was the group of studio musicians hired to open for Amibeth. When AJ and I left for the Caruthersville Bridge, Fireball had no lead vocalist. Milton heard Elana Grey perform the song the day it was written in Skylar Jones' apartment and Elana Grey became the lead singer of Fireball. Speaking with some admitted personal bias, Elana Grey was not just part of Fireball, Elana Grey was Fireball. Skylar Jones was not a consideration for the first Amibeth tour; Skylar Jones would have upstaged Amibeth.

In 2007, Skylar Jones and Amibeth did tour together. On the No Cause for Shame tour, they alternated with respect to who was the opening act. They performed at Shea Stadium, Wrigley Field, the Los Angeles Coliseum, The Coliseum in Nashville, the Superdome, and Safeco Field in Seattle. Twenty-four cities in twenty-four days. Over six hundred thousand people at an average of forty-two dollars a ticket. It was a combination of the music of Skylar Jones and whatever it is that Amibeth does in the live appearances. The genre cannot be defined. Amibeth Live was a pinch of reminiscence, a dash of philosophical stand-up comedy, and a taste of the questions that had been asked on the radio show—the kind of questions that make up those "Best of Amibeth" hours on the radio when Amibeth takes a vacation.

For the original tour, the one that opened right shortly after AJ and I travelled to West Tennessee, "(She Thought She Could) Fly" was the perfect bridge between the happy music of Fireball and the appearance of Amibeth, standing in front of the sixteen foot poster digitally derived from the photograph that Adele Federoff had taken. Elana Grey was, for several years, a one-hit wonder. She returned to school where she is frequently asked if she's the woman who wrote and recorded "Fly." It is a question she doesn't mind.

If it seems absurd that the events involving a twenty-two year old woman on the Caruthersville Bridge inspired the country music song of the year in 2005, you haven't lived in Music City—and you don't remember the 1967 hit by Bobbie Gentry, "The Ode to Billie Joe." Billie Joe McAllister jumped off the Tallahatchee Bridge, the song sold five million units, and Bobbie Gentry got a career that lasted a decade and included several wins at The Grammies. Things like that happen in the music business.

The song, however, was not the most unusual story to emerge from the events on the Caruthersville Bridge. One year later, in April 2006, a hoax began to circulate on the internet that AJ Golden had survived her fall from the bridge and somehow reached the jungles of Brazil where she had finally succumbed to her injuries. Allegedly, a primitive tribal group had formed a cult, worshipping AJ. The motto of the cult was "AJ morreu por nossos pecados," which is Portuguese for "AJ died for our sins." The cult was rumored to be carving tiny model bridges out of ojliagiba, a rare wood from the Amazon rainforest and wearing the miniature wooden bridges around their necks in the same fashion as Christians wear crosses. It is said that the internet message was read over three hundred million times, though I am not sure how many different individuals that represents. The Amazonian jungle area in which the cult was described as "the fourth most dominant religion" was said to be 268,826 square miles. That specific area is the exact size of the state of Texas, which should have been a clue that the story was a hoax. The other hint that the story was a confabulation is that there is no such thing as ojliagiba wood. Ojliagiba is Abigail Jo spelled backwards. As I banged my head against the steering wheel of my brother's Toyota, saying "Maybe she thought that she could fly" and listening to Layla bark, I had no idea that any of this would happen.

Amy Elizabeth would become Amibeth. The eulogy would be perfect. I knew exactly what the eulogy would be. I had seen her practice it. Half the time she broke down and giggled. Well, there would be no giggling now.

Chapter Thirty-Five

I sat in the car, too numb to move, and visualized the eulogy that Amibeth would deliver.

"I'm Amy Beth Golden. Abby Jo Golden, AJ, was my sister, and at times she could be a real bitch." The woman who had named herself Amy Beth at her second press conference in June, would look up at the mourners. She would smile, and shake her head. "AJ was always after me to do more and be more, but she did it out of love. In our family, where real love was a rare commodity, her love made all the difference in the world to me. And I loved her with all my heart and soul."

"No matter what problems we had growing up, AJ never took crap from anybody. One day when we were walking home from school, an older boy began tossing stones at us. No reason. Just something little boys do. One the stones hit me in the head and blood started running down my forehead. I thought that these things happen and I just sat there in the road, bleeding. But AJ chased him down—that girl could run. She gave him two black eyes. She was the younger sister, but she was always the protector."

"Ten months ago, bound and gagged, at a point where any normal person would have given up, my wonderful sister broke free and got to my stepfather's guns. You know the rest of the story. She saved my life." Amy Beth stopped to dry her tears. "Sorry. It's still hard to talk about that. What people don't know about that night is that after she killed the first monster, the one who chased her upstairs, she started screaming at the top of her lungs so that the animal that was downstairs on top of me would figure that things were ok, so that he wouldn't kill me and then go looking for her. She had the presence of mind to do that so she could come back and get him too. She was amazing at making plans."

"People have been asking why AJ took her life." There would be a long pause. "Why would a woman so full of life choose to end it? Things happen in this world, and sometimes there is no WHY. AJ could handle growing up under—shall we say—difficult circumstances. In the hospital after . . . after what happened at our home, she couldn't deal with people pointing at her because of the shooting. Yes, it happened. Yes, she shot two monsters. But that wasn't who she was and I think that she was afraid that for the rest of her life people wouldn't let her get beyond that. I have no idea why AJ took her life, and I suppose I never will." I kept imagining the eulogy in my mind. She would move a handkerchief to her teary eyes.

"But before going to that beautiful bridge over the Mississippi River, instead of taking care of herself, she spent much of the last ten months of her life helping me get my life together after my ordeal. And though I am not fixed, thanks to AJ, I am getting there. Thank you, AJ."

"And before we all start feeling sorry for AJ and for what happened on the Caruthersville Bridge, thirty-six miles from our childhood home in Kenton, there is more to say about those last ten months of her life. While AJ was devoting herself to me, and to my recovery, she fell in love. I am so happy that my sister spent much of the last months of her life with that man. The day she met him, she called me on the phone and told me that she had met the man that she might spend the-rest-of-her-life-with." Amy Beth would run the last six words together and stop to cry and stare at the podium. This was the part where she often broke down and giggled. I knew that at the memorial service she would just stop, stare at the podium, and then continue. "Sorry. Give me a moment please."

"She was going to spend the rest of her life with him, and she did. We were sisters and at times we had a second language. I'm not very good at whistling, but this is for you AJ." And she would whistle the phrase that AJ had whistled the morning after we met, "Ta-da-Ta-da . . . Ta-da'-da . . . ta-da-da-da." I had no idea what it meant. "Deep down inside, the girl that America saw as an avenging angel, a girl who had slain two serial killers was a romantic young woman in love. I loved her. I will always love her."

And then while the cameras would pan the audience looking for a grieving young man, the sixteen foot tall poster would drop from behind the podium. It would be the first look that the world would get of the picture taken by Adele Federoff, with the name Amibeth running from the lower left to the upper right corner. Amibeth. No Y. As if spontaneously, a group of college students hired by Milton Brandenburg would begin chanting "AJ lives. AJ lives. AJ lives." It would be too much to bear. I suspected that would be the point where I would turn off the television.

I thought about the last parts of the eulogy. Amy Elizabeth would give a thumbs up sign. The chanting would stop and Amy Elizabeth would continue. "AJ lives. Her spirit cannot be defeated. The spirit of all women, no matter how bleak their circumstances, cannot be defeated. AJ, I know you don't believe that Heaven is a real place. I know that you believe that we get one chance right here on earth and that Heaven is just how people remember us. But if there is a Heaven, AJ, and if you are looking down laughing at your silly older sister, I want you to know that I am not going to waste any of my chance. I will spend the rest of my life trying to make you proud of me. You wanted more out of me and you will see it."

"I don't understand why the world is like it is. But whatever I do, whenever I do it, I will be doing it as Amibeth, like on the banner behind me. Because Amibeth, without a Y—there is no WHY—isn't just a new name for me. It's a name for the fighting spirit that marked the life of my sister. I will never forget you, AJ, and I pray that the world never forgets you. You were a very special woman, and in spirit, you are still alive." Amibeth would take a deep breath and the audience would try to regain its collective composure.

"After I was raped, people tried to comfort me. Some people asked how I was feeling. Some people crudely, but meaning well, asked me what it was like. I told them it was like having my insides ripped open. It was degrading. It was humiliating. But this pain is far worse. And I am so angry at you AJ for doing this that I could KILL YOU . . . But of course, I can't do that. Instead I will simply love your memory and spend my life honoring it."

"May the Lord bless your memory, Abigail Josephine Golden. May the Lord keep you near Him. May the Lord shine his countenance upon you, and grant peace unto you, Abby Jo. Amen."

It would be a beautiful eulogy, and it would be the start of Amibeth. I wondered where I would go to watch the eulogy. I ended up watching the eulogy on the tenth floor of my building with Skylar Jones and Elana Grey. A lot would happen between the Missouri side of the Caruthersville Bridge and Wednesday morning.

We had gone to the Caruthersville Bridge to create interest in Amibeth, to have people watch the eulogy and remember what had happened to the Golden sisters in the summer of 2004. The eulogy was fine, but here's the irony. Before the eulogy, only 11,000 seats had sold for the entire tour, and 5,000 of those tickets were for the opening night in Knoxville. Even after the eulogy, only 6200 people showed up to see Amibeth on opening night. The eulogy didn't have the effect we had hoped, but the song, "(She Thought She Could) Fly," by Fireball featuring Elana Grey, made Amibeth.

On opening night, Fireball featuring Elana Grey and The Amibeth Experience received rave reviews. The Knoxville News Sentinel called it "The best ten dollar ticket in the history of Knoxville entertainment." The reviewer said "Last night Amibeth—that's Amy Elizabeth Golden's new name—told the world she wants to be a star on the radio. Listening to her last night this reviewer has no doubt that she will be a success. She is funny, insightful, a little bawdy at times, but, incredibly enough, she was very entertaining. The first time a joke fell flat she looked at the crowd, said 'Hey. Give me a break. Remember, I got raped.' And from that moment on, the audience was hers. The opening act, Fireball featuring Elana Grey brought down the house with their song "(She Thought She Could) Fly." Initially, I thought I would be writing a review on how Fireball stole the show. Then Amibeth came on stage, the poster came down from the rafters, and the show was hers. Amibeth appears next at Northwestern University in Evanston, Illinois where her sister, the late AJ Golden attended class for three years. If you missed it last night, drive to Evanston, or wait for the finale back in Nashville in less than two weeks. Tickets are available now. They won't be available for long. Two acts for less than the price of one. Don't miss it."

The empty seats in Knoxville were the only empty seats on the entire tour. Well, not quite the only empty seats. For each appearance, there was always one ticket left at the will-call window for Abigail Josephine Golden. That symbolic ticket was never claimed. The tour played to standing room only audiences.

For a little over five years, from April 2005 to June 2010, most of America lived with the notion that AJ had died at the Caruthersville Bridge; some people thought she had died in Brazil. Much of America saw Amibeth deliver her eulogy for AJ, either on live TV or on the news reports. Most people became accustomed to hearing Amibeth find the subject of AJ to be so painful, apparently, that she refused to discuss her younger sister. All questions about Amibeth were deflected into questions about Andrea. "My sister, you asked me about my sister. My sister Andrea was raped by my father, and wherever she is today, I believe in my heart that Andrea has somehow put that trauma behind her and moved on to a successful life . . . Oh, you meant my other sister. Sorry, I don't talk about that."

Amibeth couldn't talk about her sister AJ because Amibeth had an incredible reputation for honesty, and for her to discuss the late AJ Golden would have been less than honest. Fans of Amibeth spent five years mourning the death of AJ, wearing those T181 pendants, carrying those jeweled T181 designer purses, and showing up at the yearly Amibeth No Cause For Shame fundraisers with blond hair or blond wigs. The No Cause for Shame fundraisers had dozens of blondes wearing blood red colored T-shirts, and scanty short skirts—mimicking AJ's appearance in the iconic photo—and commemorating AJ's rescue of the woman who had become Amibeth.

But, the truth is this, AJ did not go off the bridge into the Mississippi River. The chanting girls were correct all along. AJ is alive.

AJ Golden did not die at the Caruthersville Bridge. AJ got what she wanted. She no longer had to worry about people coming up to her and asking "Aren't you the woman who shot The Diaz Brothers?" AJ Golden got anonymity. She had a name, of course, the name she used to attend Vanderbilt, the name that Milton Brandenburg had placed on her records the same day that he used his power as a member of the University Board of Trust to get Amy Elizabeth Golden admitted to the graduate school.

Until the day of the No Cause for Shame Fundraiser in 2010, the world thought that AJ Golden went off the Caruthersville Bridge. I spent several minutes thinking she had gone off the bridge. They were the worst minutes of my life. I was not faking when I was rambling to Layla, saying "She thought that she could fly." There was no reason for AJ to jump off the bridge, but things don't always happen for a reason. Sometimes there is no why.

When Amibeth gave the eulogy for AJ, she was under the impression that AJ was dead. AJ had decided to go with Plan Y, "Don't tell Amibeth what happened on the bridge until after the eulogy." It was cruel, but even Amibeth was later willing to admit it was necessary. Amibeth knew that she could never have made it through the eulogy without giggling if she had known that AJ was alive. Amibeth forgave AJ for not telling her what had happened on the bridge just as she forgave her for not setting the burglar alarm the night that the Diaz Brothers broke into the Congressman's home.

For some people, the nine most beautiful words that they might ever hear from the woman they love are "I love you, I love you, I love you."

For me, the nine most beautiful words were the words I heard from the back of the car while I was sitting at the Missouri end of the Caruthersville Bridge, lamenting my situation to Layla.

"Idiot! If I'm in the water, where's Mary Nell?"

"AJ?"

Chapter Thirty-Six

"AJ, is that you?"

"Of course it's me. Who else could it be? What do you think? Do you think I'm the ghost of AJ? They already did that movie. Patrick Swayze and Demi Moore. This is me. Ghosts don't bite." She took my hand, pulled it towards her and bit me. Hard. Well, harder than Layla had bit me.

"Ow! OK. You're AJ. And you're not a ghost. Come on up to the front seat."

She exited the back of the car, climbed in the front seat and closed the door. I had unhooked Layla and she jumped in AJ's lap. "My smart boyfriend is an idiot. Why in the world would I kill myself when you and I have what we have together and when I finally have what I have been trying to get for ten months?"

"Launching Amibeth?"

"That too, but now I don't have to worry about being AJ Golden any more. I'm not the girl who shot those two men—ever again. In the eyes of the world, she just went over the railing. I'm the same person I was before, I'm still in love with you, but I don't have to get upset about the AJ Bang Bang jokes. It's not me any more. You just can't imagine what it was like being on the front page of USA Today, everyone talking about me. I knew I couldn't have a life."

"I can imagine it. And it's the reason I have never teased you about wanting to be 'Red,' or that other name. I know you did this for Amibeth. I just hope it works out for you. Giving up your name is sort of a big deal."

"Yes and no. I'm the same person and we have each other. That's what really counts."

I looked at her and realized that this was the woman I was going to spend the rest of my life with—hopefully. I had gone from desperation to elation. We kissed. "AJ, when I thought you went off the bridge . . ." My mouth was dry. I couldn't talk. "AJ, when I thought you went off the bridge, the worst thing for me, next to the fact that you were gone, well that was the worst thing, that was almost everything, but the other thing was that I realized how rarely I say 'I love you.' I tell you that you're beautiful, and fantastic, and hot. I love you, AJ."

She put her hands on my face. "Jonah, you have been showing me that you love me for ten months, and I'm ok with the fact that you don't say it much. And YOU KNOW ME! How could you even THINK I went off the bridge. What were you thinking?"

"You weren't there in the trunk. I panicked. You had said 'Remember AJ Golden loved you.' Past tense! What happened? Where were you?"

"I just meant that I wouldn't be AJ any more." She looked at the confused expression on my face and then it hit her. "Oh-my-God, I never told you what was going to happen. I thought you knew. But it's Barry's car. You didn't know!"

"Know what?"

"Amibeth had a Toyota just like this. I assumed you knew. Oh, I am so sorry. Lo siento. You are not an idiot. It's my fault. I am so sorry." She kissed me and began crying.

"What happened? Where were you?"

"Back seat. On the floor. You know I hate small spaces, right?"

"You made that perfectly clear. We hired that animation guy to see if there were other options."

"Well, the back seat in a '99 Toyota flips down. When we were at the rest stop looking for a car with Missouri plates, I released the latches, and when I got in the trunk. I pushed the back seat down, crawled into the back part of the car, and flipped the seat back up. I figured you knew what I was going to do. I know. Assume nothing. I am so sorry. My poor Jonah. I am so sorry. I scared you to death. I didn't mean to."

I was creating a mental image of what had happened. She got in the trunk; she pushed the back seat down. She rolled into the car, flipped the back seat back up, making the trunk a closed space again, but without her in it. And I had been an idiot. Mary Nell wasn't in the trunk. Mary Nell had gone over the railing into the water. But I had looked in the back of the car. "Wait, you weren't sitting in the back seat."

"No. Of course not. I scrunched down low, by the floor, behind the driver's seat so no one could see me while I put on my clothes. At the rest stop, I shut the dome light so no one could see into the car. And after I changed clothes, I fell fast asleep."

"Asleep? You fell asleep? After all that excitement?"

"I fell asleep. I haven't slept in two nights. I didn't sleep this afternoon, I didn't really sleep well at the hotel after we got friendly. I fell asleep in the back of the car. I am so sorry. My poor baby. I am so sorry, Jonah. I wouldn't have done that to you in a million years. I thought you knew what I was going to do. I am sorry."

"I forgive you. I'm just glad you're alive. I'm a little numb right now." Was this the time to have our little talk after the bridge? Probably not. "It's ok. It's kind of funny I guess. You . . . sort of killed the mood. This was supposed to

206 | Richard Stein

be a time to celebrate. How much did you hear?" Maybe she had missed my hysterical ramblings.

"Not that all much."

"Good."

"She thought that she could fly. She thought that she could fly. She thought that she could fly. Why? Why? Why? There is no why. There is no why. There is no why. She thought that she could fly. She thought that she could fly. She thought that she could fly. I missed all that." She was laughing.

"All right."

"Jonah. Your hysteria was sweet. Don't be embarrassed. I thought it was a sign that you were in touch with your emotions. That's wonderful in a man, even if you were completely hysterical." She was laughing so hard she was almost crying.

"Thanks. And men don't get hysterical; they get agitated. Hysterical comes from 'hysteros' the Greek word for uterus. As a trivia buff I know that. And boys don't got no uteruses."

"You were hysterical. And what kind of grammar is that? Boys don't got no uteruses?"

"Oh, it's something I said when I was two years old. Mom was pregnant with Barry. I was a little chubby back then, and to tease me, my mother said 'Jonah, you are getting fat, or are you going to have a baby too?' Well, I'd been reading my dad's medical books, so I said 'Silly mommy. Boys can't have babies. They don't got no uteruses.' It's been a family joke for years. I guess it isn't all that funny."

"Two years old. You were reading your dad's medical books?"

"I was a precocious kid. That's why my mom thinks I'm such an underachiever, being an investigator. My dad's ok with what I do, but my mom has a hard time accepting it. Anyway, I'm at peace with it. It's her problem."

"You are not an underachiever. My boyfriend is not an underachiever! You are a fine investigator, and you just pulled off one of the greatest hoaxes in the history of show business. You are an undercover star. Just can't tell anyone." AJ was giggling.

"You think so?"

"Absolutely." Our adrenaline levels were falling toward normal. "You have to see the humor in this. This is funny. You have this great story. You like to tell stories. But other than the people who already know that I'm AJ, and knew what we were going to do, you can't tell anyone."

"You got that right, AJ. I can't tell anyone. And I won't tell anyone. I know how to keep a secret."

Simultaneously, we started singing the old Dana Twins song.

> I can keep a secret. I can keep a secret. I can keep a secret you
> know that I can. You say I'm a sweet boy. You call me your boy
> toy. But maybe baby maybe I'm a dangerous man.

AJ stopped laughing long enough to tell me again that I was not an underachiever.

"Thank you. Actually, considering that you are my girlfriend, I consider myself an overachiever."

We sat quietly for a few moments, holding hands. I got out of the car, then went in back and hooked up Layla's safety harness for the drive home. I went to the passenger side of the car. "Come on out. Please. We can't continue this discussion in the car. We have to talk. Why are you laughing?" The woman who was worried about Amibeth giggling at the eulogy was almost breaking up with laughter over a situation that wasn't the least bit funny.

Under her breath AJ was repeating, "She thought she could fly. She thought she could fly. She thought she could fly. It's too funny. Sorry. While you were hooking up Layla, I was thinking of that story you told me our first morning together. The story about the warehouse shooting when you were going down the hall and the perp had Debbie Lafferty as a hostage and you fired the gun and killed a woman, and the bad guy wasn't a guy. The bad guy was a woman and the woman you killed wasn't Debbie Lafferty, it was the perp. I must have heard you tell that story to people a dozen times, and every time you tell the story the person listening thinks you shot Debbie Lafferty. I'm laughing because I can see you telling this big story with misdirection. AJ's supposed to be faking a suicide, I thought she was dead, she wasn't in the trunk, no she is alive—except that you can't tell anyone. It would mess up the hoax. You can't tell anyone. I just think it's funny." She got out of the car. I was missing the humor, but if AJ was laughing I could be composed too.

We stood in the fluorescent light of an all-night service stop at the Missouri end of the Caruthersville Bridge. It wasn't the most romantic place, but after seeing the empty trunk of my brother's car, anyplace we were together was the right place. "AJ, I was going to make this little joke, a joke, about how I didn't to be your boyfriend anymore—and then give the punch line that I wanted to be your fiancée, but I won't make the joke."

She put her hand over her mouth before I continued.

"All I will say is this. AJ Golden, these ten months have been the most fabulous months of my life. You are the most interesting woman, the most interesting person, I have ever met. You brighten up my life. Even if you bring craziness to it, with stuff like Plan B, my world is so much better with you in it, that I want you in it forever. I want you to be the mother of my children someday. I want to grow old with you. You are a fabulous human being. I cannot imagine life without you. Well, actually I can imagine life without you. That's what I was doing here after I opened the trunk and you weren't there. That seemed pretty dismal. AJ Golden, I love you. Will you marry me?"

She looked at me very seriously, and then she said, "No!"

Chapter Thirty-Seven

"No?" It was the second worst moment of the morning and it wasn't even 3 AM. This was not going to be a good day.

"Well, first of all, you are supposed to have a ring when you do this. You are not supposed to ask a woman to marry you just because you are upset about thinking you lost her. Marriage is serious business. I am going to get married once and stay married for the rest of my life, but I am not going to get engaged on the spur of the moment and without a ring." She kissed me on my forehead. "But I do love you."

I took the box with the ring out of my pocket and got down on one knee. In my panic over thinking I had lost AJ forever I had forgotten about giving her the ring. "This was not on the spur of the moment. This was planned. This ring was my grandmother's ring. She and my grandfather were together sixty-two years before he died. I thought it would be good luck for us. I have thought this over like this was the most important decision I would ever make in my life because it is. You are the most important thing in my life. I love you. AJ Golden, will you marry me?"

"It's fantastic!" She put the ring on her finger. "Let's see. In sixty-two years, you'll be eighty-seven and I'll be eighty-four. Well, I'm greedy. I want even more of you than that. But that would be ok. But NO! AJ can't marry you." She kissed me and hugged me tight. "It's a beautiful ring." She was crying, and I was confused.

I stood up. "You said 'No, you can't marry me,' but you're putting on the ring. Are we engaged or not?"

She was running the conversation over again in her head. "Oh-my-God. That was my little joke. You just told me that your little joke was going to be that you didn't want to be my boyfriend any more, you wanted to be my fiancée. Well, I was thinking that you might ask me to marry you after the bridge, and that if you said 'AJ will you marry me?' that I would say 'No. I'm not AJ any more, you have to ask me by my new name.' I-forgot-that-part. Of course I will marry you. Ask me by my new name."

I got back down on one knee. I took her hand—she was already wearing the ring—"Elfleda Anastasia Whatever-your-last-name-is, will you marry me?" I broke up laughing at the name.

"YES! Elfleda Anastasia will marry you. That's not the name I've been using, but it's close enough. Of course I will marry you!"

Three years later at the wedding of Skylar Jones and her long-time boyfriend Rickey Stone, I would meet Skylar's father, the banker from Bozeman, Montana, Jonathan Grey. I asked him why he gave his daughter that beautiful, weird name, Elfleda Anastasia. He told me that he loved Chaucer, hence the Elfleda, and that he was a student of the Russian Revolution, therefore the Anastasia. He assumed that when his daughter grew up, even if she didn't enter show business, she would change her name to something that she liked. Jonathan Grey felt that people should be allowed to reinvent themselves when they became adults. Personally, I am very happy being Jonah Aaron, but that is not the point.

I asked Jonathan Grey what he would have done if his daughter had chosen to stick with Elfleda Anastasia. He smiled at me and said, "Well, it would have been her decision, but I would have suggested that she do exactly what your wife did when she assumed the name after Skylar discarded it. I would have suggested she combine the names and shorten them, and make Elfleda Anastasia into something simpler, like Elana."

Elana Grey and I got back in the car and started driving back from Missouri toward the Caruthersville Bridge to return to Nashville.

"Jonah, it might be a long engagement. Everyone teased us about rushing things at first, but we have to wait until Amibeth can be my Maid of Honor before we get married. If she gets as famous as she keeps saying she will be, the tabloids will be following her around and there's no way she could slip off and be my Maid of Honor without the whole 'AJ is dead' thing falling apart."

We had no idea what we were launching. The song hadn't been written at that point, and Fireball was still Fireball, not Fireball featuring Elana Grey. Once Fireball featuring Elana Grey became the opening act of the Amibeth tour, no one gave it a second thought a year later when Amibeth was Elana Grey's Maid of Honor.

"AJ. I mean Elana, whatever happens with Amibeth, happens. We did our part. Now she has to do hers. We'll cross that bridge when we come to it."

We both started laughing; then Elana started whistling, "Ta-da-Ta-da . . . Ta-da'-da . . . ta-da-da-da . . ." She paused for a moment. "I guess it's time I tell you what the song is."

"That would be nice, seeing how I'm going to marry you."

"I knew that all along." She started singing, but instead of the small voice she had used at Jerry's the night we had met, she put her heart into it and belted out the words, "Today I met . . . The boy I'm . . . gonna marry/He's all I've wanted . . . all my life . . . and even more."

"That's what the song is?"

"Yeah. I mean I wasn't ready to get married right then and there. I'm not a fool. I mean I knew you for like fifteen hours at the time. But you knew what I was all about, and you liked me for it. The sex was great. You made me laugh. We were able to talk about all kinds of stuff. I thought we had a lot of potential."

It was one of the sweetest moments of my life, and the day was only going to get better. "You got that right. And you know, sweetie, your voice is really good when you put yourself into it."

"I hope so, because I'm working on a plan. Don't worry. No bridges. No car trunks. It has to do with a song. I'm going to work on it on the way back to Nashville."

END PART ONE

PART TWO

Chapter Thirty-Eight

Five years later, Elana and I were still living in the ninth floor condo that we had begun to share the week we met. The living room looked the same—except for our CMA awards on the mantle, and a plaque commemorating Elana's triple platinum record on the wall behind the sofa. The desk that I purchased for her the week that she and I started dating had been joined by a bookcase for her infrequently used medical books, a small filing cabinet, and an autographed No Cause for Shame poster. The poster was a collector's item as it had been signed by both Amibeth and her sister, the presumed-to-be-late Abby Jo Golden. Fifty of the posters had been available on opening night of The Amibeth Experience Tour in Knoxville. We had Number 2 of 50. Milton Brandenburg had Number 1. Amibeth's penthouse, the living room of which had a twenty-two foot high ceiling, displayed the sixteen foot tall poster that had appeared behind her during her eulogy for AJ and throughout The Amibeth Experience Tour.

The guest bedroom where Amy Elizabeth had stayed before she became Amibeth still had a dresser, a bed, my autographed poster of The Dana Twins, and now contained a one hundred and twenty gallon saltwater fish tank. Milton had gotten me hooked on his hobby. Saltwater tanks are tough on hardwood, however, and the guest bedroom now had a tile floor. The beauty of saltwater fish is hard to match with non-living art and my mother, one of Nashville's most respected interior designers, had even managed to encourage some of her more adventurous clients to include a saltwater tank in their décor. The fish were not our only pets. Layla, our shih-tzu, was eight years old and going strong. I used to make fun of couples who slept with their dog in their bed; we had become one of them. We did not however go to the extreme of giving her only bottled water to drink.

Several new upscale restaurants had opened in The Gulch. One of the finest Mexican restaurants in the city, El Diablo, was located on the ground floor of our building. They served a drink called the Rodrigo Diaz, which included a double shot of tequila and was "guaranteed to make you lose your head." As far as the world was concerned, AJ Golden was dead. However, with Amibeth's fame and the yearly No Cause for Shame fundraisers, replete with women dressed up as AJ, AJ's role in the events on Woodland Hills Lane remained in the minds of the American public.

Amibeth had succeeded beyond our wildest dreams. That is not to say that there had not been difficult moments. The worst of these occurred when her strident take on the Duke Lacrosse scandal in 2006 almost derailed her career as it had barely started. In that incident, a stripper falsely accused three student-athletes of raping her at an off-campus party. Fortunately for Amibeth, she was rescued by one of her listeners. Britney from Baltimore called the Amibeth show and pointed out that the allegations of rape didn't pass what Britney called "the smell test." She reminded Amibeth—and the radio audience—about the second press conference on the steps of the Miller home after the events on Woodland Hills Lane. In that press conference, Amy Elizabeth had stated that while one should listen to all claims of sexual abuse, they were not all necessarily true. Amibeth abandoned her rush to judgment, and, doing something almost unheard of in talk radio, openly admitted that she had been wrong. The Durham County prosecutor eventually was disbarred for his conduct in the case. Amibeth "moved on to something else," and that something else was success.

While her radio show would continue, Amibeth was moving to television. She would be doing a twice weekly commentary on the major network morning show called *Wake up World!* Out the window of our condo we could see a twelve foot high billboard proclaiming "Coming to Channel 6, June 14, AMIBETH!!" In smaller letters, near her left ear, were the words, *Wake up World!* Amibeth's segment of the morning show would be produced in Nashville, which was unsuccessfully trying to establish itself as a "Third Coast," a television production center to rival New York and Los Angeles. Despite the city's aspirations, most of the filming in town involved production of music videos. Although Nashville did turn out a couple of series that ran on cable television, we were not in the league of New York or Los Angeles. Because of tax breaks offered by the Canadian government, we couldn't even hold the proverbial candle to Vancouver, British Columbia.

Amibeth's main residence was the eleventh floor penthouse atop our building. She also had homes in Tahoe and on Mercer Island near Seattle. The latter residence was obtained during her tempestuous relationship with Brett Phillips. They missed each other when they were apart, but they couldn't stand to be with each other for protracted periods of time. One advantage of being on the radio was that Amibeth could travel between her homes and still manage to be on the air. As if Brett's work as a consultant to the government's program on counter-cyber-terrorism wasn't enough of a problem, Amibeth's new commitment to television was certain to put an additional stress on that relationship.

Since my marriage to Elana went as well as any relationship between two young professionals could go, Amibeth, the self-proclaimed Advice Queen of Talk

Radio, repeatedly asked her younger sister for guidance on how to repair her oft-fractured relationship with Brett. Elana's answer was always the same. "Just quit being a self-centered diva who believes that the whole world revolves around her, get rid of the foul temper that goes with that attitude, and you'll be fine."

"In other words, I should listen to my own advice and do a better job listening to Brett. But if I quit being a bitch and got rid of my temper, I couldn't be Amibeth. I'd be ordinary again. I'd be Amy Elizabeth, AND I DON'T WANT THAT TO HAPPEN! But I do wish things could go as smoothly for Brett and me as they seem to go for you and Jonah."

Amibeth was correct that things generally went smoothly for Elana and me. In romantic comedies, the scene of the first kiss, or the first scattering of clothes on the way to the bedroom, or the marriage proposal, or the wedding, is the end of the story. Elana and I realized that those scenes are only the beginning. Marriages require work. By the spring of 2010, we had managed to live together, love together, work on the relationship together, and occasionally function as a team of investigators.

Except for a moment of panic on the Caruthersville Bridge and what Elana called a "minor misunderstanding" when Skylar Jones and I planned a surprise 25th birthday party for my wife, our relationship was indeed smooth. Of course, Elana uses the term "minor misunderstanding" to walking into her surprise 25th Birthday Party with a loaded gun in her purse as she contemplated shooting both her husband and her best friend, Skylar Jones, whom she suspected of having an affair. I will never again plan a surprise party for Elana.

While Elana and Amibeth were closer than ever, since the suicide hoax at the Caruthersville Bridge, Elana had had no contact with either her mother or her stepfather. James Miller, now divorced from Mary Nell, had become a United States Senator. In 2008, Senator Miller had been on the short list for vice-president until John McCain made a decision that led to one of the rare purely political comments on the generally apolitical Amibeth Radio Hour.

"Explain this to me, anybody. You're John McCain. You're running for president. The best thing you have going for you is that you have considerable experience and the other guy doesn't. So what do you do? You nominate a woman who is the Governor of Alaska as the vice-president. You're old. You put one heartbeat away from the presidency a woman whose competence on international issues is that she can see Russia. Hello, John McCain. I have Google maps on my computer. I can see Russia too. I was vice-president of the Senior Class at Colby College. I manage a multi-million dollar business and a large charity. Does that make me fit to be President? Actually, if it weren't for the fact that I'm just twenty-six years old, it probably would. Hello, John McCain. Nominate me. I'll lie about my age; women can do that. The Republican rank and file love your present choice. Yippee. The election isn't about the rank and file. Independents determine elections. You just gave away an election. If Future-President Obama wants to come on the show, I'll be glad to have him. I'll have that loser John McCain, too, if he wants to show up. This election is over."

Amibeth made the comment when McCain was actually ahead in the polls with his post-convention bump. Obama appeared on The Amibeth Radio Hour. John McCain politely declined the invitation. For two months, Amibeth hammered at McCain's choice of a running mate. "I may be for women, but I am for COMPETENT women. How can you trust a man whose first important decision as nominee is to pick THAT WOMAN as his running mate?" Controversy drives ratings, and Amibeth's ratings climbed. She appeared on Saturday Night Live playing herself and interviewing Tina Fey playing the vice-presidential nominee. On election night, some pollsters expressed the opinion that after the economy, the three things that defeated the McCain candidacy were Tina Fey, Amibeth, and McCain's choice of running mate.

It has been reported that when Senator McCain asked Senator Miller to tone his step-daughter down, Senator Miller told him that, "No one tones down Amibeth except her agent, Milton Brandenburg. Give the girl a break. She was raped and she lost her sister." Senator Miller had no idea that AJ was alive, and Milton Brandenburg wasn't going to tone down Amibeth. Milton was a Democrat and loved every moment of it.

The fact that Elana Grey was AJ Golden was known to a limited few. Besides Elana and me, that group included my parents, my brother Barry, Amibeth, Milton and Mona Brandenburg, Brian and his wife Melanie, Brett Phillips, Skylar Jones, Skylar's husband Rickey Stone, Andrea Candy Golden Butler Cain, and Joseph Apted of the FBI. Senator James Miller and three hundred million Americans were out of the loop. I would say that the fact that AJ Golden was alive was guarded like a state secret, but considering the revelations of diplomatic policy that have appeared on Wikileaks, the truth about AJ Golden was guarded much more reliably than a state secret.

The people I had worried about as being the weak links in the chain of secrecy were Skylar Jones and Rickey Stone, but their lips were sealed. Skylar and Rickey knew the truth because Rickey was there when Elana and I returned from the Caruthersville Bridge the morning that we faked AJ's death, the morning that we wrote "(She Thought She Could) Fly" in Skylar's condo. Rickey was hung over at the time and slept through his opportunity to co-write the song of the year, "Fly." He was so upset over missing what he regarded as his "one big chance" that he went into AA, and had been sober for five years, leading to his marriage to Skylar. A sober Rickey Stone also proved to be both a humorous and a very successful man.

Rickey heard the story of my experience on the bridge and had the idea for the cable TV series, *Jonah Slammer, Dangerous Man*, of which he is the star. Jonah Slammer, as played by Rickey Stone, is a depressed Nashville police detective/country music singer who solves crimes and catches criminals not only because he is a good detective, but because he is willing to take absurd chances such as leaping from three story buildings—always landing on the criminal—and walking into gunfire—which always misses him. Jonah Slammer is not heroic as much as he is a suicidal fool with a death wish. His girlfriend Jodie Black, a character played by Skylar Jones, disappeared and presumably died in the pilot episode. Rickey visits the cemetery in every episode to talk to her headstone. Though a hologram of Jodie is seen, Jodie doesn't answer, and it's as near to therapy as Jonah Slammer ever gets. While that suggests that the show is somber, it is a comedy of the absurd, with weekly musical appearances by Rickey Stone's band, Two in the Morning, playing the obvious role of Jonah Slammer's band, ironically named Oh Happy Day.

Rickey missed out on the CMA award for writing "(She Thought She Could) Fly," but had received an Emmy nomination for best actor in a comedy series. He also received a nomination for Country Music Song of the Year in 2007, as co-writer of the theme from *Jonah Slammer, Dangerous Man*, a ditty entitled "I Forget to Remember to Forget." That song was co-written by the Nashville songwriting quartet of Rickey Stone, Skylar Jones, Elana Grey, and Jonah Aaron. For the fourth and final season of the show, that theme song was replaced by the old Dana Twins hit, "Dangerous Man." Rickey didn't mind having his song dropped from the show. He had a starring role in the movie based on the life—and possible death—of the Dana Twins, a film being shot under great secrecy about twenty miles outside of Nashville. Changing the theme song to "Dangerous Man" was a great way to promote the movie.

Among my many ties to *Jonah Slammer, Dangerous Man*, I supervise security on the set of the show, which is taped in Nashville. The job pays well, and I have gotten to meet a number of A-list guest stars in the process. That has made Aaron and Associates a nationally known investigative agency. As Elana jokes, "AJ launched so many careers by jumping off the Caruthersville Bridge and killing herself, that I'm glad she lived to see it." Obviously, so am I.

That Elana's oldest sister Andrea, a woman whom we called Andrea Candy Golden Butler Cain (ACGBC) knew my wife's secret might seem surprising. Andrea had foresworn all interactions with her two younger sisters because she did not want her husband to find out about her past. However, Elana felt that ACGBC had been through so many traumas in her life that she shouldn't have to experience the loss of a sister. Stating that it was a "medical emergency," Elana had managed to get through to her sister at CMI, Chicago Medical Institute, just as the news of AJ's death was reaching the general public. ACGBC's response was somewhat disturbing. "You didn't have to call. As far as I was concerned you perished in a fire years ago." Elana could not determine whether or not ACGBC was joking in the few seconds that she stayed on the line before hanging up.

Elana had mixed feelings about being unmasked as AJ Golden. While she didn't mind that I sometimes called her AJ when we were alone, she was perfectly comfortable being Elana Grey, former singer and songwriter, now screenwriter, and sometime medical student. Medical school is a four year program. Five years later, Elana had completed less than three years of the curriculum. She had spent almost as much time on leaves of absence as she had in class. The young woman who had created some very imaginative plans while in her early twenties had diverted her creative energy to writing the screenplay for a movie—*The Dana Twins: The True Story*—and designing some very complex plots for the fourth highest rated scripted show on cable TV, *Jonah Slammer, Dangerous Man*. By the end of the third season of the show, Elana had become the lead script writer.

Elana even got to appear before the cameras in the final episode of season three. There was concern that the show might not be renewed, and Elana got to appear as "The Woman in White," a singer who appeared on stage with Jonah Slammer. In the final scene in the episode, Jonah Slammer was prepared to stand up to a killer riding a six hundred and fifty pound Harley moving towards him at fifty miles an hour. "The Woman in White" intentionally let her shih-tzu get loose. Jonah Slammer was suicidal but he couldn't let a little dog get hurt. He picked up the dog and carried it to safety. The killer on the motorcycle swerved after him, lost control of his bike, and crashed into an oncoming truck. Such was the world of Jonah Slammer. Despite the fact that Amibeth's Caruthersville Bridge Clothing developed a line of Woman in White attire, Elana felt no obligation to reprise her role.

At times, Elana considered disclosing that her apparent suicide had been a hoax and that she was living as Elana Grey. One potential time for what she and Amibeth referred to as "The Great Revelation", would occur on Saturday June 12, 2010—two days before the premiere of Amibeth's television show. Every year at the annual No Cause for Shame banquet, held at the Hyatt Regency Hotel in downtown Chicago, Amibeth gave an award to a woman whose achievements had advanced the cause of women in general and the beliefs of the No Cause for Shame Foundation. The proposed speech that Amibeth would deliver would say, "For a distinguished career which has included killing the Diaz Brothers making the whole thing possible, pretending to jump off the Caruthersville Bridge, thus launching my tour and radio career, not to mention her own career as a singer, songwriter, and script writer, and for making progress toward becoming a doctor, the award goes to my sister Abby Jo Golden, publicly known as Elana Grey." Needless to say, that announcement would fuel the ratings for the premiere of Amibeth's television show.

While the two women loved the idea, as Amibeth's manager, Milton Brandenburg held veto power over major career moves. Revealing that the suicide of AJ Golden had been a hoax would—according to Milton Brandenburg—be a short term boon for the ratings, but a long term ratings and career disaster. He regarded Amibeth as both a psychologist and a performer. A serious psychologist couldn't be associated with using a phony suicide to spark her career. As far as show business was concerned, Milton felt that "anything goes." However, despite Amibeth's mega-million dollar 2007 tour with Skylar Jones, he saw Amibeth as being far more than show business. If Elana wanted to reveal that she was AJ Golden, it would have to be done in a way that did not reflect adversely on Amibeth. Had we not investigated a suspicious death as a favor for Joe Apted of the FBI, the fact that Elana Grey was AJ Golden might have remained a secret forever.

Chapter Thirty-Nine

On Saturday morning May 22, three weeks before the No Cause for Shame Fundraiser, and a week before we were planning to take a short cruise to the Greek Isles, we received a phone call from Joe Apted, who was still the Director of the Chicago office of the FBI. After what Joe jokingly referred to as our "audition at the Caruthersville Bridge," Elana and I had consulted for the FBI on several occasions, assisting them in making protected witnesses disappear. Elana worked out the broad outline of the plans; I supervised the details.

We put Joe on the speaker phone. "Are you guys retired as investigators, now that you have so many irons in the fire?"

"I still carry a business card that says Jonah Aaron, Private Investigator. What can I do for you?"

"I have a case for the two of you. It's something very different from what I have called about before. As a personal favor, I need you to look into a suspicious death for me. The Nashville Police Department ruled it a suicide. A Special Agent from the Memphis office looked into it, and he thought it was suicide. Under the circumstances, I don't want to irritate the Memphis FBI office by assigning an agent from Chicago to an official investigation, and I don't want to piss people off by burying this in the consulting budget. Something bothers me about the case, and I'd appreciate it if you would look into it for me as a personal favor. It'll be just a few of days of work."

I suspected that this might be a colossal waste of time, but, in my line of work, staying on the good side of a federal agency is always a wise move. Considering what the FBI paid consultants, passing on the stipend seemed a minimal sacrifice. "OK, Joe. What's the story?"

"A year ago, in March 2009, the FBI in Chicago received a phone call from an agitated woman claiming that several people on a research drug study had been murdered. She didn't know how it was done. She didn't know who did it. She didn't know why it was done. However, since she was a research nurse on a drug study with 'too many deaths,' we decided to take a look. We talked to the doctors who ran the study and we interviewed the nurse who had called us. We found nothing."

"Not surprising. People in drug studies die all the time. What kind of drug?"

"Cancer drug."

"Well that speaks for itself. Cancer patients die even if they aren't on a study."

"Exactly, Jonah, but we looked at it thoroughly. A year went by, and we were going to permanently close the case file. We checked to see if anything had popped up in the interim. We learned that a research report based on the study had been published in the Journal of Cancer Medicine."

"That's a big time medical journal. My dad reads it."

Elana nodded her agreement.

"So, the FBI had some medical consultants read the manuscript. It's easy to summarize. The study had been done at ten major medical centers. At each institution, half the patients got Treatment A and half the patients got Treatment B. At nine of the centers, the results were similar with Treatment A and Treatment B. But, at Chicago Medical Institute, Treatment A had a huge excess of deaths. During the first month after receiving treatment at CMI, seven of twenty patients getting Treatment A died and only one of twenty patients getting Treatment B died. At the other nine medical centers the death rate averaged out to one patient out of twenty patients in each treatment group. There were indeed six extra deaths associated with Treatment A at CMI. The manuscript in the medical journal was concerned with the overall results, and the overall results were that Treatment A did worse."

"No kidding."

"But, if you kicked out the data from CMI, Treatment A and Treatment B were identical with respect to the number of early deaths. When the manuscript was published in the medical journal there was an editorial comment from the statisticians. They said there was only a one in six hundred thousand possibility that nine of the treatment sites would have results like that, and one treatment site would come out so differently. One in six hundred thousand is the kind of odds you have for taking a coin and getting heads nineteen times in a row. Our nurse informant may have been on to something. There might have been a series of murders after all. That got us interested again to say the least."

"I should think so. What did you find that time?"

"We really took a close look at the seven deaths on Treatment A at CMI. All but one of them occurred while the patients were in the hospital, not after they were discharged, and all occurred between one in the morning and five in the morning. The study required the patients to be in the hospital for twenty-one days. We checked to see if there was a doctor or a nurse or a pharmacist or anyone at all who was in the hospital at all the times when someone died. We couldn't identify anyone on-call at all those times. The patients who died on the study all had autopsies. Nothing suspicious was found. The patients had cancer of course, they had to have cancer to get on the study, but the cancer wasn't progressive except in one patient."

Elana interrupted, "Of course, like you said, Joe, one patient in twenty would be expected to die even if there was nothing hokey going on. That's what happened at all the other institutions and in the Treatment B group at CMI."

"Exactly. We figured that the death from progressive cancer was the expected death, the one in twenty phenomena, just like you said. We looked at the other six deaths really carefully. No heart attacks. No strokes. No blood clots to the lungs. Their hearts just stopped. The coroner said they had a fatal cardiac arrhythmia, cause unknown. That's just saying that they died because their heart stopped and they became dead."

"What about poison?"

"That's what we thought. But we didn't find anything. Given your help with the Muffin Mancuso case, years ago, I should mention that we even checked for thallium—though it wouldn't cause arrhythmias like this—and we checked for arsenic, and every poison known to us. Nothing. No poison. And it gets even more confusing."

"How could it get more confusing? It's totally confusing. And where do we come in?"

"Hang on. I'll get there. The study was blinded. That means that no one at CMI knew who was getting which treatment, Treatment A or Treatment B. I won't bore you with the details now about how the study was blinded; I'll send you the information instead. Basically the doctors and statisticians we had look at the case couldn't determine how anyone at CMI could figure out which treatment group an individual patient was assigned to. That data was only on a computer at Bauer Labs, the company that ran the study. That way, Bauer could break the code when the patient completed treatment in order to analyze the results. We found nothing to implicate Bauer. In fact, since Treatment A, the treatment group that had the extra deaths, was Bauer's experimental drug, 886-JHG, Bauer Labs was the last group in the world that would have screwed up the study that way. If there were extra deaths in Group B, we would have suspected Bauer as being involved. Extra deaths in Treatment B would make the Bauer drug look good and Bauer might make a ton of money. But the extra deaths occurred in the patients getting Treatment A, Bauer's experimental drug. We felt that Bauer had nothing to do with it. We looked at Bauer anyway. We had our computer security people check their computers. They found no evidence that Bauer's system had been hacked. The last we heard, Bauer was giving lie detector tests to their employees. So far, nothing has turned up. So, we have an additional problem. How do you kill six people in one treatment group on a clinical trial when you can't figure out who is in Group A and Group B? If we ever figure out that one, we'll most likely solve the case, but we couldn't do it, and neither could our experts in clinical trial design."

"What does your nurse say now?"

"That's the problem, Jonah, and that's where you and Elana come in. The nurse can't say anything. She's dead. After we blew her off in February of 2009, our nurse informant called back in June 2009. At that time, she said that she was worried that her husband might have been involved, that he was the only person that she knew who was smart enough to do whatever it was that had been done. Of course, she had no idea what it was that had been done. Her husband was a consultant on the study. We had already talked to him and a number of other people after her first call, and we felt he had no involvement in the deaths. In any case, either because of her suspicions or for unrelated matters, she had left him and filed for a divorce. She also left CMI. In June, 2009, she went to work at the University of Chicago. Eight months later, toward the end of February, 2010, she moved to Nashville and began to work at Vanderbilt. She was living out in Bellevue, Tennessee. I guess that's a suburb southwest of town."

"Right. It was the area that really got hit by the flood."

"I'm getting to that. The flood plays a role in all this. She called the FBI for the last time a little less than a month ago, towards the end of April. She said that she had information that would support the idea that patients had been murdered. But then she started talking about seeing a ghost, someone whom everyone knew was dead. She said she saw a ghost in Chicago and again in Nashville. I can't explain what she saw in Chicago, but she was a nurse, she worked at Vanderbilt, and Elana is a medical student. Maybe she saw Elana and thought she recognized AJ Golden. Elana, have you been in Chicago lately?"

"Not for five and a half years."

"Hmnn. There goes my theory about the ghost. Anyway, she also said she was sorry that she had implicated her husband because now she was certain that he had nothing to do with it. She said she would only talk to us in person. She didn't trust the phone lines."

"Paranoid." Then again, paranoids can have enemies. "So what happened. Did you send someone to talk to her?"

"We sent a Special Agent from Memphis, a man named Howard Neill. We would have called you to go see her, but you were starting your vacation. Then, Nashville had the flood. It rained, and it rained, and it rained some more."

That was an understatement. The weekend we went on vacation, the first and second of May, Nashville got fifteen inches of rain. Tens of thousands of people had their homes badly damaged. For several months, the Grand Old Opry had to relocate back to the old Ryman Auditorium. The Schermerhorn Symphony Center was shut down for eight months. For a few days, many roads were impassable; people were marooned. Power was out. Phones were out. Ten people drowned in what people called the thousand year flood. If Opryland Hotel hadn't had the good sense to evacuate, the death toll could have been in the hundreds. Brian and Melanie Brandenburg got four feet of water in their living room. We had offered them our guest bedroom, but since they had a baby, they had moved into Milton and Mona Brandenburg's five bedroom home while their place was undergoing repairs.

Joe Apted continued his story. "The part of Bellevue where our nurse lived is called Harpeth Commons. Even up here in Chicago I saw the pictures on TV of that soccer field with the concession stand totally submerged. That's where Harpeth Commons is. The road to her subdivision, Coley Davis Road, was closed from Saturday at 5 PM until 11 PM on Monday night, May 3. The power was out until a little before midnight Monday night. Hey, did you guys get any water?"

"On the ninth floor of a high rise? We don't get water unless the glaciers melt. But thanks for asking." We had been giving that reply for weeks. Since we had been on vacation, and had been unable to participate in the start of the recovery, we had donated a considerable amount of money to the relief effort.

"Glad you're ok. Anyway, Agent Neill couldn't get to Harpeth Commons. He got as far as the corner of Highway 70 and Coley Davis Road, a mile and a half away, and had to check into a motel. He telephoned the nurse twice to tell her he was on the way, but then her cell went dead. Without power, she couldn't recharge the battery. Power was out as well as the roads being out. He kept checking on the roads, but they were impassable for a couple of days. Monday night he gave up and went to sleep around 10 PM. He woke up a little after midnight, and found out that the road had been opened around eleven. He drove to her place right away. He got there as the paramedics were leaving with her body a little after twelve fifteen. She had died of a gunshot wound to the lower chest, right below the breastbone. The autopsy showed that the bullet tore up her aorta, the main blood vessel leading from the heart, and she died in seconds. The coroner ruled it a suicide, but, considering that she died just before she was scheduled to talk to the FBI, I'm not convinced that the coroner is correct."

"No kidding."

"Anyway, that's why I spent so much time talking about the deaths on that study. This just isn't a case of determining if it was a suicide or murder. This may tie into six murders and might be part of a cover up. I wanted you to know what you might be getting into. As I said, the nurse's death was ruled a suicide. The homicide detective who investigated the case, a man named Marty Hogan, felt that it might be murder. Obviously, I'm talking to you about it, so I have my suspicions. You guys would be a fresh set of eyes. If you take the case, I'll FAX you everything I have. Something about this case really bothers me."

"Something! How about a number of things?" I looked at Elana. She nodded. "We'll do it. Elana doesn't go back to med school for another month, and she enjoys being an investigator. We'll do it together. I'll need Elana to sort out the medical angle for me. I'll call you in a few days, let you know what we found out."

"Glad you're taking it on. Like I said, the contact with Nashville Metro Homicide is Marty Hogan. I hear they call him 'The Wizard,' though I don't know why."

"I know Marty. Good man. Heck of a football player in the day. What's the name of the victim? When I call Marty to set up an appointment I'll need him to pull the file in advance of talking to me."

"He'll be expecting your call, Jonah. I spoke to Marty Hogan a few days ago. He had no interest in going behind the backs of his bosses and investigating the death after it was ruled a suicide, but he was glad to hear someone was still looking into it. He said he knew you. Anyhow, you'll love the name of this nurse. Kind of a stripper name if you ask me, but nobody asked me. Down in Nashville she went by Andrea Cain, but when she first contacted the FBI she was using the name Candy. Candy Cain, but C-A-I-N, not C-A-N-E."

I was at a loss of words. Joe Apted had no idea that Candy Cain was Elana's sister. This was the first that we were hearing that she had been in Nashville, let alone that she was dead.

"Jonah, did you get that?"

"Yeah, I got it." I looked at Elana, covered the phone and whispered, "Are you ok?"

"I'm fine." If she was about to cry, she was successfully holding back the tears.

"Joe. I tell you what. Send us what you have, and we'll get on it. I got the name. One of us or both of us will see Marty today if we can get an appointment. It's Saturday. I don't know if he's working. And Joe, I have one last question . . ."

Before I could even start to ask my question, I heard him chuckle at the other end of the line. "No Jonah. You don't get badges, and you don't get to raise them and say 'Federal Agent' if the going gets rough."

I guess I had worn that one out, but that wasn't my question. "Actually, I just wanted to know if you were planning to be at the fundraiser. We haven't seen you in a while."

Joe was one of the four thousand people who annually paid $250 for a ticket at the No Cause for Shame Fundraiser. Except for a trivial amount that went for administrative costs, every penny raised by No Cause for Shame went to charities dealing with abused women and children.

"I'll see you there, Jonah, Elana. Absolutely. And no offense Jonah, you and your wife do excellent work, but if we ever reach the point that the FBI issues you a badge so you can hold it up and say 'Federal Agent', the country will be in one hell of a mess."

"It's no longer my ambition."

"I'll send you the entire case file. I have your FAX number. By the way, while The Bureau won't be paying you, Bauer Labs has a reward for anyone who can figure out what happened and get their drug back on track. I have no idea what the reward is. As a Federal Agent I'm not eligible for a reward, so I never looked into it. Frankly, I doubt you'll solve that part of the case. No one's come up with anything. But considering what we pay consultants, you might actually come out ahead by being off the books. If you signed on as a consultant for this one, you'd be ineligible for any reward from Bauer."

Considering that this was now a family matter, I had no problem taking the case for free. "Yeah, that's fine. We'll give it a couple of days. No problem."

"Thanks a lot! Call me if you find anything. Good luck."

Andrea Candy Golden Butler Cain. We had crossed paths again. I hung up the phone and put my arm around Elana's shoulder. "Are you sure you're ok?"

"I'm fine. She was my sister, but she wasn't really a part of my life. After she left home, I spent twelve years thinking that she was dead. Since you found her, I've had a few years when I thought she might be happy. Now she's at rest. It's not the most wonderful ending, but I can handle it. You know what bothers me most though?"

"That she's dead?"

"No! That she was down here in Nashville and didn't call us. She knew we were here. When we met her in Chicago that one time, you gave her a business card. She could have looked up your number on the Internet. She could have gotten in touch with Amibeth. She was here for over two months from what Joe said. We were here until the end of April. We left for that hiking tour of the Grand Canyon and Bryce Canyon on May first. She could have called us. When she cut off contact with Amibeth and me she said it was to keep her husband from finding out about her past. But she had left him, and she still didn't call us!"

"I think she may have had some trust issues."

"No kidding."

I hugged her again. "Are you really ok?"

"Jonah, I really am ok. As a medical student I've had patients die. Trust me. I've lost patients that I was a lot closer to than I was to my sister. I was ok then and I'm ok now."

I kissed her cheek. "All right then. Let's just do our job." The FAX machine was starting to print out the material from the FBI. The first page said 'Page 1 of 632.' "If you want me to stay, I'm glad to stay here as long as you want. Otherwise, I'll go talk to Marty and you can start going through that file and see if Joe overlooked anything. Check that the journal article he talked about is there."

"Works for me."

I called my brother Barry and told him I would be working on a special project for a few days. Instead of joining the Brandenburg Entertainment business, as I had once expected, Barry had joined me, Karen Bing, and Elana, as part of Aaron Investigations. Over time, Barry was taking on a greater and greater share of the work and was doing an excellent job.

Amibeth was in Seattle with Brett Phillips. It was only a little after eight o'clock there, and her phone went to voice-mail. We would break the news to her later. I called Nashville Homicide. Marty Hogan asked me to come on over.

Elana was collecting the papers as they came off the FAX machine. "Jonah, I was just thinking. Joe Apted thought that I might be the ghost that my sister saw."

"So?"

"Well, Andrea knew I was alive. She knew I was living as Elana Grey. If she somehow saw me at Vanderbilt, she wouldn't consider me a ghost."

"You're right. She wouldn't."

In addition to the possible murder of six patients on a drug study and the unexplained death of Candy Cain, we needed to find a ghost. I kissed Elana goodbye and walked out the door whistling "We're Off To See The Wizard" from *The Wizard of Oz*.

Chapter Forty

The Homicide Division of the Nashville Police Department is located in Police Headquarters, across the street from City Hall, downtown, on James Robertson Parkway. Police Headquarters is a functional rectangular red brick building with small windows and no architectural charm. When the building was completed, the construction crew took the leftover bricks and built Marty Hogan using the same rectangular architectural plan—or at least that's the legend in the Nashville Police Department. Marty is six feet five inches tall, weighs two hundred and sixty five pounds, has almost no body fat, and played tight end at the University of Tennessee. He was a fifth year senior when I was a freshman at Vanderbilt, and I had the misfortune of trying to block him on the opening kickoff of our game against UT. It was my last play of the season. My ears didn't stop ringing for four days.

I went on to have an undistinguished career on special teams at Vanderbilt. Marty was offered a free agent tryout by the NFL's Carolina Panthers and eventually joined the police department. Marty always greets me in the same manner, "Hey, Jonah, is your head still attached?" Marty is charming in his own way.

"Hope so. How's The Wizard?"

"Good as can be for having to catch up on paperwork on a Saturday. I was hoping you would decorate the place by bringing Elana, but I'm glad to help you out. Even my boss is glad to have you on the case." Nearly everyone in town had forgotten about the shooting at the East Nashville Warehouse, but the police remembered. That was helpful at times, and this was one of them.

"I was thinking about bringing Elana until the FBI starting faxing us several hundred pages of interview summaries. She's wading through that while I get to see The Wizard." Marty's nickname had nothing to do with his aptitude as a detective. As the prototypic crew-cut police officer, Marty is the technical advisor to *Jonah Slammer, Dangerous Man* and has a recurring role as well. Marty plays The Wizard, the police officer who instructs Jonah Slammer in proper, safe, and reasonable police procedure, only to have Jonah Slammer do the opposite. It is a comedy-drama after all.

Marty invited me to sit with him in Homicide Interrogation Room Number One. He placed a brown file about an inch thick between us. "After we talk you can look at this as long as you want, or copy it all. Obviously, it can't leave the building."

"If you say so."

"Look, ordinarily when a Private Investigator comes by to look at a case, implying that the Nashville Police may have done a shitty job, I am offended—even when the investigator is a friend of mine and a friend of the department." I started to raise an objection but Marty waved his hand to stop me. "Not offended this time, Jonah. This wasn't our finest moment. This case happened around the time of the flood. You know that, but you probably have no idea how it affected the case. What do you know?"

"Candy Cain. Harpeth Commons. Right around midnight, May 4. Dead. Gunshot wound to the lower chest. Ruled a suicide."

"All true. Frankly, I believe that except for the flood it might have been ruled a murder—at least there would have been more consideration given to ruling it a murder. But that's just my opinion, and it doesn't count for much. Just like it doesn't count that the FBI was coming to meet with her and she died before they could get together. Don't look surprised that I know that. They didn't tell us why they wanted to interview her, only that she was a witness not a suspect. Anyway, it's been ruled a suicide and the police investigation is over. It's all yours." He pushed the file in my direction.

"What are the details?"

Marty put on his glasses and started leafing through the report to refresh his memory. "As you know, the Great Nashville Flood of 2010 was May 1 and May 2. Coley Davis Road, the only road in and out of Harpeth Commons—and all the adjoining complexes—was underwater and impassable from Saturday at 5 P.M. until Monday night at 10 when the Harpeth River went back below flood stage. The power and landline phones went out at Harpeth Commons, where Candy Cain lived, just before midnight on Saturday night. It was hot and humid and people were scared. About five miles away, we had to start using rowboats to rescue people off porches and later off of rooftops. If I may say so myself, we did a great job with that stuff."

"So I heard. Police and Fire Department did a fabulous job. Was it that bad at Harpeth Commons?"

"Not at all. Relatively speaking, but only relatively, they were lucky. Like most of Nashville, the area is hilly. At the worst, some people got three or four feet of water in their living rooms. Candy Cain's townhouse, and the two townhouses on either side of her, stayed dry. Candy Cain got water up to her top step; no more than that."

"Lucky."

"Lucky, if you consider ending up dead to be lucky. Anyway, while the roads and the power and the phones were out, people in Harpeth Commons actually did pretty well. Without power, freezers were defrosting, so people on the high ground took their grills and had barbeques. If you went out there shortly after the flood you would have been impressed with how people banded together. The folks without damage have been helping the people with water damage remove drywall and stuff like that. It's great the way Nashville has pulled together."

"Community pride. Elana and I have been away, but we gave a donation to the Rebuild Nashville Foundation. But can we get to the story? Or are you just trying to get out of doing paper work by giving me a recent history lesson?"

"Caught me there. I'll get to the point. Our victim, or as the coroner says, our suicide, Candy Cain spent Sunday and Monday with the three other people who lived in the adjoining townhouses, Greg Cole, the young man who lives at 3829 Harpeth Commons Drive and Tim and Amanda Walker, the couple who live at 3833 Harpeth Commons Drive. Both the Walkers and Mr. Cole described Candy Cain as being quiet, a good neighbor, and not having much of a social life. The four of them spent most of the day Sunday and Monday playing board games—Scrabble and Trivial Pursuit—and talking about baseball. Sounds like your kind of people."

"Exactly."

"Around 11:50 Monday night, the power came back on—for a while. Everyone in the complex gave a great big cheer; people went back into their own homes. Candy Cain got on her computer, sent an e-mail and got a reply."

"Anything that might be connected to her death?"

"No way. It had to do with a fantasy baseball league that she and Greg Cole were in. He told us that he got her in the league at the end of spring training as a way of flirting with her, but it hadn't led to anything between them. After the e-mail, I'm not sure what she did. Greg Cole, on the other hand, went to his townhouse, also got on the computer for a minute, then noticed that he had a puddle in the kitchen from his freezer defrosting. He decided to throw out all of the meat and other perishables that had been in his freezer. He put it all in a trash bag and walked to the dumpster about a hundred and fifty yards away, walking past Candy Cain's place and the Walker's place in the process. Just before midnight, he was walking back and saw a figure in black on the front porch of Candy Cain's place. He thought he saw light from inside like she was letting someone in. He was pretty far away. I've been out there at night and the way the place is lit, and with the distance, it's hard to say what he could see. Exactly at midnight . . ."

"You're being very precise with the times aren't you?"

"You'll see how in a second. Exactly at midnight, the power in Harpeth Commons went back out. It was a power glitch, nothing sinister, nothing related to the shooting. We checked with Nashville Electric. When the power first came back on at 11:50, too many people put on their air-conditioners. There was a brief blackout that lasted ten minutes, midnight to 12:10. Greg Cole had just made it back inside his townhouse when the lights went out. Seconds later, he heard a gunshot next door. He knew it was a gunshot because he served as a medic in Iraq and—to quote him—'I know a gunshot when I hear it.'"

"The lights went out—then bang!"

"You got it. He ran over the short distance to Candy Cain's townhouse and banged on the door to see if Candy was ok. The Walkers came out of their townhouse at about the same time and saw him running towards Candy Cain's townhouse. Basically, that establishes that no one went out the front door after the shooting. If they did, they would have bumped into Greg Cole or the Walkers. While the Walkers stayed in front, Greg Cole went in back. He had a flashlight with him and he found that the back patio door was locked and the bar to keep it from sliding open was in the track. No one had left Candy Cain's townhouse out the back door either. Unfortunately, he couldn't see into the townhouse."

"Wait a minute. No went out the front or the back. I have to assume they found no one with the body. So, why are you convinced it wasn't a suicide?"

"Not convinced. Just suspicious. There was a third way out of the townhouse. An upstairs window. That's where I think our killer may have gone, but I'll get to that. Anyway, Greg Cole went back in front where people were gathering and banging on the front door. The call went in to 911 at 12:03. There was no easy way to break in. The front door is solid and the glass patio door has metal inserts. After several minutes they called the management company and asked someone to come by with a key. Around 12:15 Jenna Hooper, from the management company, arrived. She lives at the complex but she was asleep. She let Greg Cole in. He was afraid of what he would find, but he had been a medic, so he advised the others to wait outside. He was in there for a couple of minutes until the paramedics arrived at 12:19."

"Is that long? Not the four minutes he was alone with the body, the time it took the paramedics to arrive?"

"Maybe, but give people a break. Because of the flood, everyone had been working quadruple shifts. At midnight a lot of the emergency crews went home. In fact, so many people had been helping out that the crew that arrived was a Tennessee Bureau of Investigation emergency crew. The TBI crew had been working all weekend, and from what I have heard, thank God for them. They really carried their share of the load. By the time the paramedics arrived, Candy was dead. The autopsy said that the bullet just about severed her aorta. She wouldn't have had a chance even if they arrived immediately. They didn't even bother with CPR. They put her in a body bag and took her to the morgue in North Nashville."

I was still waiting to hear why Marty thought it was murder. Everything I had heard so far pointed to suicide.

"As the paramedics arrived, Officer David Johns, from the Nashville Police Department arrived home. He lives in Harpeth Commons, a block away from the shooting. He is a patrol officer. He saw the ambulance in front of Candy Cain's place and came over to see what was going on. The paramedics were leaving. He and Greg Cole walked through the townhouse. Greg checked downstairs. The body had been in the main hallway. You can basically see the kitchen and the living room from there. No one was downstairs. And yes, Greg Cole checked the closets, the pantry and the bathroom. No one was upstairs, either. Officer Johns not only checked all the rooms, he checked the attic. It was empty. However, the bedroom window upstairs was wide open. It's in the back of the house. With the heat and humidity almost everyone had opened windows for ventilation. It doesn't mean that someone went out the window, but it is possible that someone did exactly that while Greg Cole and the Walkers were at the front door."

"Wait a minute. If someone went out a second story window, that would be a ten foot, twelve drop. Good way to break a leg and limit the getaway. Was there evidence of a rope?"

"We looked at the window sill and the wall of the upstairs bedroom. There were no marks. There was no rope, but you wouldn't need one. If you hung from the window sill, your feet would only be about seven feet off the ground. Second, you're forgetting about the flood. Fifteen inches of rain made the ground so muddy that no one would break anything in a jump. They'd land in soft mud. They'd get messy, but they would be able to get up and walk away, or run away. And before you ask, there was so much of a mess in back from Greg Cole going in back of the townhouse and people walking their dogs, that the crime scene investigators couldn't identify any suspicious footprints. The point is that Greg Cole said he thought he saw someone going in Candy Cain's townhouse just before midnight and there was a way to get out."

"That's it? Did anyone see someone come out the window?"

"No. Remember the power was out from midnight until 12:10. The bedroom window is in the back of the house. The back of 3831 Harpeth Commons Drive, Candy Cain's place, is also the back of 3728 Harpeth Commons Drive, one street over. There are no fences. It's just an open area where people walk their dogs. Watch your step if you go out there. In any case, we interviewed everyone who backs up on the open area—the whole odd numbered side of the 3800 block and the even numbered side of the 3700 block of Harpeth Commons Drive. No one saw anything, but it would have been hard to see anything. It doesn't mean that no one went out that window."

The Wizard liked the idea that this was a murder and not a suicide, but nothing he said had me convinced. "What did the forensics show?"

Chapter Forty-One

Marty had the details committed to memory. "First of all, there was no note. But a third of suicides don't leave a note, so obviously that doesn't rule out suicide. The gun was registered to our victim, Candy Cain. She had purchased it two weeks earlier. The only fingerprints on the gun matched the victim, and the gunpowder tests were positive."

"That certainly suggests that she shot herself."

"I know. Just telling it like it is. Trying to show you why the coroner made a rational ruling even though I think he's wrong. If there was an intruder and a struggle, the intruder could have turned the victim's gun on her."

"Were there any signs of a struggle?"

"One lamp was overturned." He showed me a picture of the hallway of Candy Cain's townhouse. The outline of a corpse and the bloodstains were clearly seen. "Remember, the power was out, and she might have bumped into a lamp before she shot herself. At least that's what the coroner said. As for using a gun, that always makes me think of murder when a woman does that because women prefer pills but . . ."

"Fifteen percent of female suicides use guns. Still it seems kind of hard to turn a gun completely around. I mean think about it." As expected for an interrogation room, the table was bare except for the chart. I looked around for something to hold. I decided on my wallet. "Let's pretend this is a gun and I have it pointed at you, the intruder. If you grab it and turn it around at me . . ."

Marty grabbed the wallet and twisted it toward me.

"See, you can barely get it pointed to my left side. To get it pointed to the middle of my abdomen or the middle of my chest you'd have to rip my arm out of joint or break my wrist. I assume the victim's shoulder wasn't dislocated and her wrist wasn't broken."

"Hmmn. No, the only injury was the gunshot. But an intruder could have grabbed the gun and taken control of it. As for the gun, we have the additional history from the ex-husband that when she was in her mid-twenties she tried to kill herself by taking a ton of pills. We checked out that story and it's true. So, since she had taken pills and failed, it makes sense that she would try a more reliable means. A gunshot right below the breastbone is pretty reliable. And, of course, the history of a prior suicide attempt always raises the probability that a suspicious death is suicide."

"I thought you felt it was murder."

"Just trying to be objective, Jonah. The evidence goes both ways."

I thought over what Marty was saying. Except for the absence of a reason, it was not unreasonable to think that Andrea Cain had used a gun to kill herself. "Why did they move the body? She was dead. Why not leave it in place for the crime scene team? Isn't that standard procedure?"

"You're right. But everyone was exhausted after the weekend of the flood. Detective Johns sealed the scene. Like I said before, the paramedics were from Tennessee Bureau of Investigation. They were heading back to their Headquarters, and TBI Headquarters is right across the street from the morgue."

"Out there on R. S. Gass Boulevard."

"Right."

"Hey do you know who R. S. Gass was?"

"No. Enlighten me."

"He was a famous tuberculosis expert in the nineteen thirties."

"And what does that have to do with our case?"

"Nothing. You know me. You know I like to play bar trivia. I just love stuff like that, especially when the case doesn't make any sense."

"Can we get back to the case? By taking the body away for autopsy, the team from the TBI didn't have to stick around and wait for a crime scene team. If they left the body for the Crime Scene team, someone else would have to come back to take the body to the morgue. They had their ID. They knew it was Candy Cain. Greg Cole identified her. Everyone was overworked. The flood led to a lot of things happening that wouldn't otherwise happen. In this case, the body was taken to the morgue before the crime scene people took a look at it. But frankly, I don't see how that matters."

I thought about that. Ordinarily the paramedics would take a living victim to a hospital or leave a corpse for the criminalists to identify and to assess the wounds at the crime scene. Under the circumstances of the flood, what happened made perfect sense. "What else is there in the file?"

"Well, we looked into our victim's life. We talked to her friends. No enemies. No drugs. No gambling. Not in a serious relationship. No one close to her except the ex-husband, and he's in Chicago, and trust me we looked at him, probably a lot more than we should have. Everyone says she was a dedicated nurse. I talked to nurses on the cancer unit at Vanderbilt. Nobody had a bad word to say about her. None of them accepted the fact that she had killed herself. They all said there was no reason."

"Sometimes people kill themselves for no apparent reason."

"Agreed. Sometimes the reason isn't apparent, but there is a reason, and I can't find one. No one could. We interviewed her ex-husband up in Chicago, but the divorce was final and the papers were signed the last week in April. No sense killing someone after writing them a check for half a million dollars."

I gave a low whistle at the amount of money. "Unless you're angry about giving her money."

"Which is what we thought. But his alibi held up. He's a big hockey fan. He used to play college hockey himself. So did his girlfriend by the way. Good looking woman, younger than he is. Anyway, the night of May 3rd they were at the Stanley Cup Playoff game in Chicago. The Blackhawks were playing the Vancouver Canucks. His girlfriend was his alibi, but we also interviewed people in the adjacent seats. Dr. Cain and Dr. Devin were at the game all night. He seems to have gotten on with his life. There's no way he could have done it. Of course, he could have hired someone, but we looked at his financials, and there's no money unaccounted for. We ruled him out; you're welcome to try and rule him back in."

"That's it?"

"Basically, yes. We had no evidence for murder, some forensic evidence for suicide, but no reason for suicide. Once we ruled out our one suspect we had nothing other than a "figure in black" who may not have been there. Either it was going to be ruled a suicide and the case would be closed, or it would be ruled a murder and it would likely go unsolved forever."

"So they ruled it a suicide just to keep the statistics good?"

"Not at all. The last thing we needed in the middle of all the flood damage was for people to think that there was a killer running around in the shadows. We were afraid people might start shooting their neighbors. There were a lot of people working late hours removing debris, carting stuff away—still are a lot of people doing that late at night. Tennessee Bureau of Investigation had the case. There was pressure to rule it a suicide, and since it was her gun, her prints on the weapon, and no one was actually seen leaving the townhouse, that's what happened. It was ruled a suicide."

From what I had heard, it probably was. I didn't know why Andrea Candy Golden Butler Cain had taken her life, but at this point I had a woman who had seen a conspiracy when there may not have been one, and who had seen a ghost when there are no ghosts. All I had to suggest that she had been murdered was a neighbor who had seen a figure in black that might have been a shadow, and no solid theory about where that person went. I would have to talk to Greg Cole, but there was a more immediate issue. "What happened to the money? You said that she got half a million dollars in the settlement. Where does that go?"

"A charity, a legitimate one, No Cause for Shame. And we looked. Ninety six cents of every dollar that is collected goes to organizations that help victims of abuse. After we had closed the case, it made me wonder about the husband again. I mean, the woman worked with cancer patients and instead of giving the money to some cancer charity in her will, she gave the money to victims of abuse. It made me wonder if her husband beat her—or something. Of course, even if he did, that wouldn't make him a murderer."

For me, there was an obvious reason why Candy Cain had picked that charity, but I had no reason to tell Marty Hogan that Candy Cain was Amibeth's sister and that the money was going to Amibeth's charity. "But you must have something to make you think it was a murder."

"My gut. I'm The Wizard. Sometimes when the evidence isn't exact you have to make a guess. I don't see this woman being as natural as can be for two days during the flood, and then going inside her townhouse and killing herself. If she was thinking about killing herself, why not do it when the water was rising? Why go inside, send an e-mail that means nothing, just part of a game, and then kill yourself? It makes no sense to me? I believe that Greg Cole saw someone in black, and I believe someone went out the window. And why would she shoot herself just as the power went out and why halfway down the hallway from the front door to the living room. The coroner said she was standing up when she allegedly shot herself. Why not sit down in a chair or lie down in bed and be comfortable in your final moments?"

"Good questions." I pretended I had a gun in my hand. I pointed it at myself and found that I closed my eyes before pretending to pull the trigger. "I don't know. But when I went through the motions just now, I closed my eyes. Maybe she didn't even know that the lights went off."

"Didn't think of that. But that doesn't rule out murder. The way I figure, someone was there, Andrea Cain had them at gunpoint, the lights went out, and the other person took the opportunity to grab the gun and kill her." His pager went off and he checked the number. "It's my agent. Good luck. Remember, nothing leaves here. Copy whatever you want." He handed me the file and started to leave the room.

"Your agent?"

"Yeah. I've been waiting to hear if they're going to use me on that show that they're trying to spin off from *Jonah Slammer*. Bethany something or other."

"Hope you get it. And it's *Bethany Fibonacci*, like the mathematical sequence."

Marty stopped at the door. "What the hell are you talking about? Mathematical sequence?"

"A Fibonacci sequence is a set of numbers where each number is the sum of the previous two numbers. It has all sorts of biological applications. I was a math major, remember?"

Marty shook his head in exasperation. "After I take this call, I'm going to get back to work. Hey, are you going to be on the new show?"

"Probably not." In addition to running security for *Jonah Slammer, Dangerous Man*, I also play the recurring role of Aaron, Jonah Slammer's trusted roadie and confidant. Basically, I just nod, and say an occasional, "If you say so." I took the job that put me in front of the cameras on *Jonah Slammer* because the music scenes involving Rickey Stone and Two in the Morning were filmed at a real night club that has a bar and a bartender. The network and the production company wanted a guarantee that someone would be on the premises at all times to make certain that Rickey didn't fall off the wagon. As head of security, I assigned myself to that task and I succeeded at keeping Rickey Stone sober.

For an hour and a half I went over the file page by tedious page. Everything confirmed exactly what Marty had told me. Andrea Cain was described as a quiet person and a wonderful nurse. The timeline was exactly as Marty Hogan had described it. Both Greg Cole and Officer David Johns confirmed that they had checked the townhouse room by room, closet by closet, and that no one was hiding there. The autopsy report was unremarkable except for a gunshot wound just as Joe and Marty had mentioned. The forensics were exactly as The Wizard had said. The more I looked, the more it seemed like a suicide. Then, as I came to the end of the file, I found a copy of an e-mail.

TRADE CONFIRMATION NASHVILLE FANTASY BASEBALL KEEPER LEAGUE AUTOMATIC COMPUTER GENERATED MESSAGE

Adam Taylor (*adamtaylor121270@gmail.com*)
Sent: Monday May 3, 23:58
To: Andrea Cain
Confirmation of trade between The White Squirrels (Andrea Cain) and The Dark Side (Greg Cole)

WTSQ trade PUJOLS STL UT 45, HART MIL OF 33, DUNN WAS 1B 33
DARK trade WEEKS MIL UT 8, BRUCE CIN OF 10, VOTTO CIN 1B 14

Trade posted by WTSQ Monday May 3, 23:53
Trade posted by DARK Monday May 3, 23:54

Serial killers didn't bother me. Ghosts and shadows didn't bother me. Rising flood waters scared me a little. Fantasy baseball gave me the creeps. I looked at the transaction and tried to decipher the code. The trade was between Andrea Candy Cain and Greg Cole. The Wizard had told me that Greg Cole had invited her into a league as a way to make conversation.

The fantasy baseball trade was likely the key to the case. It wasn't just a simple trade. Six years earlier, when I had gone looking for Andrea Golden, I had tracked her down via a message she had left in a visitor's book at Graceland. Now she was speaking to me again, from beyond the grave, and the message was loud and clear. It said, "I didn't kill myself."

I copied the notice of the fantasy baseball trade and I copied the autopsy report. Marty's gut was right. He had the evidence but he didn't know what he was looking at. I did. I'd have Barry explain it to Elana when I got back to our condo. If Elana was going to work on the case she had to understand why I felt that the evidence said that her sister had been murdered. With respect to my fantasy baseball addiction, as of May 15, 2010 I had been sober exactly eleven years, seven months, and eight days. I wasn't taking any chances. Barry would explain it to Elana.

As I was leaving the building, I ran into Marty again. *Bethany Fibonacci* had received a go-ahead from the network for thirteen episodes and Marty had been asked to appear in all of them.

When I reached my car, I looked at my license tag. My view of Andrea Golden having killed the father who raped her repeatedly is very simple. "Good for her." Knowing that T 181, was actually Tl 81, the symbol for thallium and its atomic number, the Tennessee license tag on my Lexus had been T181 for several years. I barely knew the woman and I found myself experiencing a personal loss. Elana and Amibeth's sister had led a difficult life and, from the sound of it, had experienced a difficult death. The symmetry was less than pleasing.

Chapter Forty-Two

An hour later, Barry, Elana, and I were in our living room, and Barry was trying to explain the mathematical intricacies of fantasy baseball to Elana. Finally, he gave up and tried a simple analogy. "Suppose you have a case where someone was shot and you can't decide if he committed suicide or was murdered."

That was something Elana could follow. "OK. Finally, I know what you're saying."

"Then, you find out that the person had an expensive bottle of scotch he always talked about drinking when the right time came around. However, when he was shot, he was drinking cheap scotch and the rare bottle was sitting there unopened."

Elana thought it over for a moment. "It would be murder! He would have drunk the expensive scotch if he was going to kill himself. He wouldn't get another chance. Hey, that was a plot point on *Veronica Mars*."

"You were expecting Shakespeare?" Barry continued. "Anyway, now assume that seven minutes before the fatal shot was fired, the person who died went online and bought a ticket for a Keith Urban concert or a Taylor Swift concert or a Skylar Jones concert or even an Elana Grey concert that was three months or a year in the future. What would you think?"

"Again, it would be murder, not a suicide! If you're making plans for the future, you aren't likely to kill yourself seven minutes later."

"Exactly. That's what's going on here." Barry took a long pause before continuing. "This league your sister was playing in is a league where fantasy player contracts carry over from year to year. The owners of the fantasy teams, Greg Cole and Andrea Cain, can have one of two strategies. They can play to win this year, or they can play to win next year. The month of May is a little early to give up on this year, but the trade that Andrea made is a trade that gives up present value to get her fantasy team in shape to win next year. It's really a pretty good trade for both teams, but what matters to the case is that just before midnight she was making a trade that looks to the future. Greg Cole was focusing on this year, and

Andrea Cain was playing for next season. At 11:53 she was doing the equivalent of buying a ticket to next year's concert."

"Then why didn't you say so? Why did you go into all that complicated stuff about auction budgets, and salary inflation in keeper leagues, and how one side of the trade involves more talent but also more salary?"

"Because . . . Because . . ." Barry was stammering in his excitement. "Because fantasy baseball is such a neat game, and I was trying to explain the whole thing. But you're right. All you need to know is that your sister Andrea was playing for the future seven minutes before she was shot to death!"

"Thank you, Barry." Alcoholics stay out of bars. I limit my exposure to fantasy baseball. I summarized the situation for the three of us. "There were no other e-mails. She got no phone calls on her land line or her cell. The police checked. At 11:53 on Monday night May 3, 2010 she was planning for next year—the 2011 fantasy baseball season. At midnight she was shot dead. Unless Andrea underwent an amazing spontaneous change of heart in those seven minutes, she was murdered. That figure in black that Greg Cole said he saw on the front porch may actually have killed Andrea Cain. Of course we have no idea why she was killed or if it had anything to do with what she said happened in Chicago, if there really were murders in Chicago. Maybe it has something to do with the time Andrea spent here in Nashville. Most murders happen for fairly mundane reasons. Maybe she had a boyfriend, or a girlfriend, and that person got jealous about not being able to contact her because of the flood. Who knows? But it certainly looks like Andrea did not shoot herself!"

Elana still looked a little puzzled. "I understand that, but the one thing I don't understand is Greg Cole. Does this mean he had something to do with it?"

"No. Marty said Greg is sort of a nerdy guy. Greg told Marty that he got Andrea into the fantasy baseball league at the start of the baseball season as a way of flirting with her. The trade isn't sinister or anything."

Suddenly, Elana started to cry and shook her head. "Sorry. It's starting to get to me. It almost doesn't matter that she was my sister. I see this poor woman, scared, opening the door, probably holding a gun because she's scared, and the gun gets turned toward her and BANG! End of everything! Dead! But it is my sister, and I know what she went through in her life. I grew up in that house. We shared a bedroom. And it's just so horrible that her life ended that way."

I got up from the sofa and held her in my arms.

Barry started to leave. "Look, I'll leave you guys alone. Sorry about your loss, Elana."

We walked Barry to the door, and said our goodbyes.

I put my hand under her chin and lifted it up a little. "Do you feel like talking about it, sweetie?"

Elana looked down at the floor. "Not much to say. Even if we figure out who killed her, even if we can figure out what happened in Chicago, my sister's dead.

Bringing someone to justice might make me feel better, but she's still dead. It's just that . . ." she stopped, tears filled her eyes, and she paused before continuing, "it's just that I always thought that the three of us—me, Amibeth, and Andrea—would get back together. I always hoped that someday she wouldn't want to keep her past a secret from her husband, or, more likely, the marriage would end. Not all marriages last forever."

I kissed her on the forehead. "Ours will."

"I know. I love you."

"I love you, too, Elana."

She had stopped crying. She looked at the stack of papers from the FBI. "That can wait a while. We have two choices." She took a deep breath and exhaled. "We can write a country song about Andrea Candy Golden Butler Cain, just like we wrote a song when AJ sort-of died, or we can make love and see if it makes me feel better."

"Do you feel a song coming on?"

"Not this time! How about we give up with the song and go with door number two." She pointed to the bedroom and then shrieked as I picked her up and carried her to bed. In the six years I had known her, she hadn't gained a pound.

After a couple of jolts of endorphins and a lot of cuddling had Elana feeling better, we decided that she would continue attacking the pile of information from the FBI while I drove to Harpeth Commons. I had given up my sporty Lexus SC 430 and now drove a Lexus sedan. It was almost a straight shot from our condo to Harpeth Commons, during which Broadway changed names several times, but I took the highway that looped around the city and saved a few minutes. On the way, I listened to Amibeth on the radio. Milton's No Cause for Shame network was honoring Amibeth's upcoming move to television with weekend marathons of the best of Amibeth. Ironically, while Amibeth was a diva in her personal life, on the radio, there was never any doubt as to who was the most important person on the air. It was always the caller.

"Hi, Amibeth. I'm Susie from San Antonio. I'm your biggest fan."

"OK, Susie, but how can I help you become a fan of yourself?"

Amibeth borrowed from the blogs of her boyfriend, Brett Phillips, mixed in a large dose of common sense, added a small dash of the knowledge from her Master's Degree in Counseling, topped it all with some humor and had the recipe for success on the radio. Her philosophy was simple. Communication is the key to all relationships. It's not sex, money, or in-laws that are the problems; it's the inability to communicate about those issues. *Listen to the other person!* Relationships are partnerships; if you always put the other person first, don't complain when you end up last. If you have children you have to be responsible for them—*always!* Out of those simple thoughts, a little bit of humor, a number of phone calls, and an occasional rant, Amibeth fashioned an entertaining hour. One of her classic rants on having children was on the air as I drove into Harpeth Commons.

Right to Lifers say that pregnant women who want to terminate a pregnancy should have to examine an ultrasound before they have an abortion. Pro Choice groups go ballistic over that. It's not for me to dictate strategy to anyone in the abortion controversy, but if you believe in choice what's wrong with an informed choice. Of course, it would be just as rational to demand that anyone seeking obstetric care and planning to take a pregnancy to term should be required to watch some educational material on the financial and emotional cost of raising a child, including some information on what having a baby does to a relationship.

Let's face it, as with so many things, we get it backwards. We demand that sixteen year olds get a Driver's License before they can drive a car, but any eleven year old who can spread her legs can get pregnant and be a mommy with no training at all. Babies are precious and we just let anyone have one. Too bad hormones have side effects. It would make a lot of sense to put every ten year old girl on contraceptive injections and not let her come off until she passed some sort of parenting test.

Of course hormones do have side effects, so I'm not seriously advocating that. Please don't go jumping on my case for that idea. I'm just saying that if we had safe hormones, such a program would be more intelligent than the ridiculous system we have now.

I got off the highway at exit 196, made a left onto Highway 70S, and then a right onto Coley Davis Road. I passed a number of apartment complexes and a nursing home before turning into Harpeth Commons. I parked in front of Andrea Cain's townhouse, took Layla from the car, and began to walk around the complex. Across the street from what had been my sister-in-law's residence, four homes showed signs of flood damage and were in various stages of repair. It was warm and it was Saturday, but construction crews were at work.

There was nothing to be learned from the front side of the townhouses in the daylight. Elana and I would come back at night and check the visibility from the point where Greg Cole claimed to have seen the figure in black on Andrea Cain's front porch. Layla gave me an excuse to be walking in the grassy area behind the homes. A large man walking a small dog is not seen as threatening.

The Wizard was right on one account. People used the area to walk their dogs and were not compulsive about picking up after them. But he was wrong on another matter. Going out the second story window and landing in soft mud was impossible. Each townhome had a twelve foot by twelve foot concrete patio adjacent to the back wall. Marty said that there was no evidence that anyone had used a rope ladder. Anyone jumping from the second story window would probably have broken an ankle. Marty had missed that when he had visited the property after the flood.

In all likelihood, when Marty toured the crime scene, the patios had been covered with a layer of dirt. Marty wears expensive shoes. He had gone in back, stepped on some dog poop, or had started to sink in the mud, and had given only a cursory look to the back of the townhouses. He hadn't realized that there were concrete patios.

The more I thought about it, the more I realized that there wasn't any reason for anyone to go out the second floor window. Even if someone went upstairs to look for something, no one came into Andrea Cain's townhouse for almost fifteen minutes after the gunshot. Lights were out for some of the time and it would have made more sense for a killer to come back downstairs and use the rear door.

If no one went out the upstairs window, either Andrea Cain had shot herself after all, or the killer had stayed in the townhouse until after Greg Cole and Officer Johns had checked the property. But where in the townhouse could someone have hid? Why would anyone take the risk of staying? I needed to talk to Greg Cole and to Officer Johns and I wanted to take a look inside 3831 Harpeth Commons Road.

Chapter Forty-Three

"Can we help you?" Small dog or not, the Walkers had come outside to check me out. Layla greeted them with a growl. She hadn't mastered the idea that her role was to make me look non-threatening.

"Hope so. I'm Jonah Aaron, and this is Layla. I'm an investigator hired to look into the shooting that happened here last month."

I shook hands with the Walkers as they exchanged nervous glances. Mr. Walker, a slightly overweight man in his mid-twenties spoke for the two of them. "I thought the police said it was a suicide. Was that wrong?" A murder next door was not a comforting thought, and crime was never good for property values.

"Not sure. I've just started looking into it." I asked the question I knew would be a certain conversation starter in Nashville for months. "How bad was the flooding here?"

Amanda Walker was very pregnant and looked very uncomfortable as she rested her hands on her swollen belly. Her description of the flooding matched what I had been told by Marty Hogan. The Walker's side of the street didn't get any damage. "We were worried that water would come in the back, but the water all ran to the side of the building. We got about a quarter inch of mud on the patio, but the first rain washed it clean."

"Anything you recall about the night of the shooting?"

Amanda Walker's response was consistent with what she had told the police. After the gunshot, the Walkers and Greg Cole had arrived at Andrea's front door almost simultaneously. According to the Walkers, Greg Cole had checked in back, and had been unable to get in. Then he had returned to the front door and called 911 and the rental agent. While they were waiting, Greg Cole had told them about the figure in black that he had seen on Andrea's front porch. "He was scared something had happened to her, but we couldn't get in and he couldn't figure out what to do. We just waited."

"Is anyone living in Andrea Cain's place now?"

"They moved out her personal belongings, clothing and stuff, but her furniture is still there. I spoke to the rental agent last week. Andrea's attorney made some sort of deal with the management firm to keep it furnished and show it that way in order to improve the chances that someone would pick up the sublet."

That made sense. I thanked the Walkers for their time, walked back in front of the row of townhouses and knocked on the door of Greg Cole's townhouse. No one answered. I left a note on the door, asking him to call me. Before I could walk down the front steps, Amanda Walker came out the front door of her townhome. "He's probably not home. I think he has a new girlfriend. He's never around on weekends any more, but he'll be back on Sunday night. I always see his car in its spot on Sunday night. He goes to work early on Mondays. If you run into him here, have him show you his collection. Even I think it's neat and I'm not even into that stuff."

"Collection of what?"

"Star Wars stuff. Greg is one of those guys who makes his own costumes and appears in parades. I ran into him at the public library a few months ago. Darth Vader and Luke Skywalker were there in costume, encouraging kids to read. Darth Vader knew my name and said hello to me. He removed his helmet, and it was Greg. If I see him, I'll tell him you were looking for him."

"Thanks. I left him a note. Please tell him I'm not trying to make trouble. Maybe that will encourage him to call. By the way, did you sense there was anything going on between Greg Cole and Andrea Cain?"

"Like what?"

"I don't know. Single guy. Attractive woman. Two days together on the porch. I just wondered if there was something happening."

"You think Greg's a suspect?" She laughed at the idea.

"Just trying to figure out what happened."

"No way. First of all, he's just a sweet nerdy guy. He couldn't hurt anyone. Plus, he liked her, and she liked him, but there was nothing going on. I've been around enough couples that I can tell if something's happening. They would have been a nice couple, but he was shy and she was still getting over her divorce. The ink was barely dry. She wasn't going to ask him out. There was nothing going on. Certainly nothing that would make him do anything to her. Plus, there was no time for him to get out of her town house after the shot, and then be starting back towards her place when my husband and I came out our front door. And he was truly scared when we were on the porch. I thought he was going to smash out a window, but he decided not to."

"Thanks." I headed over to Officer David Johns' townhome. It was easy to find. The patrol car parked in front was a dead giveaway. Officer Johns had been in the Nashville Police Department for almost twenty years. I estimated his age at late-forties, maybe early-fifties. He was in surprisingly good shape for a man his age. He didn't have the rock solid physique of Marty Hogan, but he hadn't developed the pot belly typical of so many veteran police officers.

Officer Johns was less pleased to have a private investigator on the case than was Marty Hogan, but he was willing to give me a few minutes of his time. "I came in to that nurse's place and that guy was so nervous I thought he was going to pee in his pants. I mean, he had been a medic in Iraq, but I guess it's different when someone you've been with all day is shot in their own home. He kept saying 'Why would someone kill her? What did she ever do to anyone?' Over and over, he kept saying that."

"He was sure she hadn't shot herself?"

"He was certain. He started telling me about the figure he had seen on the porch. It sounded spooky. A figure in black. But he was totally convinced, and he convinced me. He told me to be real careful going upstairs and to be sure to check the attic. We had a Nashville cop shot and killed fourteen years ago doing an attic search for a fugitive. He didn't have to warn me about that."

"I remember. I was in high school back then. So, you took the upstairs and he took the downstairs."

"Yeah. I took the real job, and took the risk. That's what they pay me for. I checked the upstairs bedroom, the bedroom closet, the upstairs office, the office closet, and the two upstairs bathrooms, as well as the attic. The attic was empty; there was nowhere to hide up there. Let me tell you, if the power hadn't been back on, I might have just waited for Nashville Homicide to do the work. I'd have let them search the premises. But I was there, and people had been on duty since Saturday. There was no one upstairs, or downstairs for that matter."

"Are you sure?"

"Well unless Greg Cole was blind, there was no one. Look, all these two bedroom townhouses throughout the complex have the same floor plan as mine. Come on in, I'll show you. Could you just hold the dog in your arms. I have a cat."

"Thanks for the warning."

On the first floor, a narrow carpeted hallway ran from the front door to the patio door in back. Andrea Cain's body had been found in the hallway about halfway back to the patio door. Suicide isn't always logical, but looking at the floor plan, it was a totally unreasonable choice of a place to end one's life. The bedroom or the living room would have made more sense. I could see why Marty Hogan had been suspicious that Andrea Cain had been murdered.

As one entered the townhouse, a staircase, just to left, led upstairs. All the downstairs rooms, the dining room, kitchen, and living room, were to the right of the hallway. There was a coat closet and a small powder room on the left side of the hallway. From the point where Andrea Cain had been shot, one could see the entire living room and the kitchen. One would have passed the dining room on the way to the body. The only places that had to be checked were the coat closet, the powder room, and a walk-in storage pantry in the kitchen.

"When I got back downstairs, Greg told me that he had checked the closets and the pantry. He had even checked under the sofa. There really wasn't enough space there to hide. Nada. He was a little less nervous by then. That's when the paramedics arrived and he identified the body for them, and that was it. I put up some crime scene tape that I had in the car. I couldn't put up an official seal or anything. Homicide did that in the morning. But, unless the kid was blind there was no one downstairs."

"What about the bedroom window. Marty Hogan told me there was a window open."

"I noted that. We figured that the killer might have gone out that way, but even if the killer hung by their hands, it would have been a seven foot drop to the patio. There wasn't enough dirt to cushion a fall. I don't see it happening that way."

At 11:53 Andrea Cain had been looking forward to the future; at midnight it appeared she had permanently changed her mind. "Unless the killer was very lucky in jumping out that window, you're almost certainly right. Thanks for the tour."

Based on the fantasy baseball trade, Andrea Cain hadn't killed herself, but there hadn't been a killer present and she was dead. What other scenarios were possible? I considered that Greg Cole, in a state of panic, had skipped one of the closets or the pantry. Nothing else came to mind.

I had arrived thinking that Andrea Cain had been murdered. Now, I wasn't sure. I tried Greg Cole's door one more time before I left and got no answer. That just about summarized the entire situation. No answer.

I turned on the radio and listened to Amibeth as I drove home. Amibeth was responding to a woman who had called in hoping that the Queen of Talk Radio could tell her how to save her marriage.

"Honey, the reason you're not getting the answers you want is that you're asking the wrong questions. You're asking me how to save your marriage. Relationships involve two people. From everything you told me, he isn't interested in saving the marriage. He has moved on. It's sad, but it's true. The question isn't about saving the marriage, the question is how to get you to land on your feet and figure out what to do with the rest of your life."

"That's what my therapist said. I thought you could come up with something."

"Sorry, sweetie. I try to come up with the best answers I can, but you have to ask the right questions. You have to ask the right questions."

The call ended, and Amibeth went on to comment that when you are getting nowhere solving a problem, always consider whether or not you are asking the right questions. It was pure Brett Phillips philosophy of problem solving. The trouble was that I was asking the right question and I was getting nowhere. My question was the obvious one. Did Andrea Cain kill herself or was Andrea Cain murdered? I needed more information. I needed to talk to Greg Cole.

Chapter Forty-Four

Elana's afternoon reviewing the cancer study had been no more productive than my afternoon at Harpeth Commons. "I downloaded that journal article that Joe Apted quoted. The results were exactly like he said. Except for one of the treatment groups at CMI, five percent of patients died during the first two months on the study. At CMI, there were seven deaths in twenty patients with Treatment A; that's thirty-five percent. I can't say that's impossible without someone doing something to help it along, but it sure looks that way."

"Got it, so far."

"A copy of the research protocol was included in the material that the FBI sent us, and now I know how the study was designed, but, as best as I can tell, there was no way to figure out which patients were getting which treatment, which means I can't see how anyone could mess up the study by killing some of the patients in one group."

"Why don't you just explain it to me. But do me a favor first."

"Sure. What?"

"Put on some clothes. It's hard for me to pay attention to what you're saying." Elana was wearing a short negligee that covered little more than was covered in the No Cause for Shame poster.

"Sorry. Wasn't thinking." She left and returned a minute later wearing a white t-shirt and a pair of jeans. She looked just as hot as before but the appearance was less distracting. "Is this better?"

"Not better, but at least I can concentrate on what you're saying. Tell me what you found out. Go slowly. Pretend I don't know very much medicine."

"Jonah, I don't have to pretend. You don't know very much medicine."

"Yes I do! I've helped you review for exams all through medical school. Try me."

Elana sighed. "OK. I will. This is a study of patients with advanced lung cancer. Patients in Group A got standard chemotherapy plus the experimental drug, JHG-886. Patients in Group B got standard chemotherapy plus a placebo. So, if you know medicine, my dear husband, the first question is this. What's the standard chemotherapy treatment of lung cancer?" She sounded certain that I had no idea.

"Carboplatin and paclitaxel."

"How did you know that? How did you remember that?"

"The research protocol is sitting here on the coffee table. I'm reading upside down. Right in the first paragraph it says, 'carboplatin and paclitaxel.'"

She stared at me for a few seconds, started to laugh, then began to laugh harder. She picked up the protocol and playfully hit me with it. "Thank you for making me laugh. That's the first time I've laughed since we found out about my sister." She laughed again. "OK. Let me go over what I have."

"By the way, that's not the only reason I knew. My father was one of the investigators on the study in the mid-1990's that established carboplatin and paclitaxel as a standard therapy. There was fascinating dinner table conversation at my house when I was growing up. We talked about sports and cancer medicine. Not much talk about decorating. I think my mother would have been a much happier person if she had a daughter as well as two sons." My mother had major complications when my younger brother, Barry, was born and was unable to have a third child. "I think that's why she loves you so much. You're the daughter she never had."

"Well I'm glad she considers me her daughter, since I have chosen her to be the real mother that I never had." Elana had not spoken to Mary Nell since the day she had left Highland Heights and driven down I-65 to Nashville in June of 2004. We had planned and paid for our own wedding; Mary Nell had not been invited.

"You better watch that. You start referring to my mother as your mother and we'll have to move to West Virginia or Kentucky. Tennessee doesn't allow stuff like that; we're more civilized."

It wasn't funny but Elana was laughing again. "You're my lover and my best friend. What's wrong with you being my sort of brother? OK, I'll get serious."

"That would be nice."

"As I was saying, there were two treatment groups. Group A was chemotherapy plus the study drug, Group B was the same chemotherapy plus a placebo. The study was randomized. That means that once the patient agreed to participate in the study, a central computer back at Bauer Labs, the company providing the drug, determined if the patient would be in group A or group B. The study was done in a double blind fashion. Neither the doctors nor the patients knew which treatment each patient was getting. That prevents any bias in evaluating symptoms or measuring the tumor response. In fact, not even the pharmacist who brought the drug up to the in-patient unit knew what the patients were receiving."

"Wait! How did they manage that? How did they get the right medicine to the right patient without knowing if they were in Group A or Group B?"

"Really neat how they did that. There were two hundred and twenty patients on the study. This group of drugs was initially developed at CMI, so CMI got the study going first, and they got to enter forty patients. The other nine institutions each entered twenty patients. Each patient had a code number. CMI was institution number one, so for every patient treated there, the first two digits were 01. The patients there were 01-01, 01-02, 01-03, 01-04 and so on up to 01-40. Johns Hopkins was institution number 2, so the patients there were . . ."

"02-01, 02-02, 02-03, 02-04, and so on. I got it."

"OK. Glad you're with me. Each patient got chemotherapy. We already talked about that. Since it was the same chemotherapy for patients in both treatment groups, the chemotherapy didn't have to be done in a blinded fashion. Everyone on the study got carboplatin and paclitaxel. As I said before, the Treatment Group A got the drug, JHG-886, and the Treatment Group B got a placebo. The drug or the placebo was given as a continuous intravenous infusion, one IV bottle every twelve hours, for twenty-one days. The patients had to be in the hospital for that part of the study. If you were at CMI, for example, when you went on study, the pharmacy got forty-two bottles for you. If you were patient number one at CMI those bottles would be 01-01-01, 01-01-02, 01-01-03, 01-01-04, 01-01-05, and so on, all the way to 01-01-42; forty-two bottles to be given over twenty-one days. They always started in the morning, when they had more staff to monitor for problems. The odd numbered bottles were hung in the morning at 8 AM. The even numbered bottles were hung in the evening at 8 PM. If you were supposed to get 886-JHG, then the drug company sent forty-two bottles containing 886-JHG. If you were supposed to get the placebo, then the drug company sent forty-two identical appearing bottles containing a placebo. The bottles all arrived at CMI with either the drug or the placebo already inside. When the patient went on the study, no one at CMI knew what was in the bottles. They just knew from the labels what bottles to hang on each patient and when to hang it. The only place where it was recorded what the patients were getting was in a central computer back at Bauer Labs. Like I said before, that's the company that made the drug."

"So Bauer knew. They could have messed up the study. If more patients in the placebo group died, then their drug, which was part of Treatment A would look good. The drug would get approved by the FDA, and they would make millions—possibly billions."

"Right, Jonah, but the extra deaths were in Treatment Group A, the patients who were getting Bauer's experimental drug, 886-JHG. Someone at Bauer had access to the code, but if Bauer killed off patients in Group A, they hurt themselves in the process. The FBI even considered that someone might have done this to manipulate the stock. The stock dropped from 72 to 65 when the study failed, but the Securities and Exchange Commission didn't find anyone who was selling large quantities of the stock expecting it to fall."

"So who benefitted from the study being a disaster?"

"That's the thing. Apparently no one benefitted. Basically, there was no simple way to know who was getting which drug, and even if someone did know, there was no obvious motive to sabotage the study. Other than that, everything is crystal clear."

"And your sister, Andrea, told the FBI that she knew that people were murdered and she had some knowledge about what happened. If she did, she's a lot smarter than we are. Then again, she had been working on the project full time. Maybe she saw something we're not seeing. Or maybe she was wrong. Is that basically it?"

"No, there's more about how they kept people from determining who was getting which treatment. In a blinded study, like this one, there is often some way to figure out who is getting which treatment based on side effects. The doctors like to know if the patient is getting a new drug. The patients like to know as well. They try to game the system."

"Shocking!" I was being facetious. "But how?"

"Well, if half the patients get a drug and half get a placebo, and the drug causes a rash, for example, it doesn't matter how well you blind the study by coding all the bottles. All anyone would have to do is see who develops a rash, and he or she would know who is getting the study drug. But 886-JHG doesn't cause a rash. However, it does do something interesting. It can affect something called the QT interval."

"Now I feel like I don't know any medicine. I have no idea what you are talking about."

"Ha. Ha. Told you."

I stared back in silence.

"Sorry. Lo siento. Anyway, I'll make this as simple as I can, but we can't skip it because if people were killed, this may be how it was done, but I don't see how."

"Go ahead."

"OK. You know what an electrocardiogram is?"

"An electrical recording of the heart. All those squiggly things that move up and down."

"Except we don't call them squigglies. They have letters of the alphabet assigned to them. The time interval from where the heartbeat starts until the heart repolarizes, that means it gets electrically back to where it started, is called the QT interval. The QT interval is usually around four tenths of a second."

"Cutie? As in my wife, the love of my life, is a cutie?"

"Flattery will get you everywhere, but no. Q-T. Letters of the alphabet. Q and T. Got it?

"Got it."

"Well the study drug, 886-JHG, increases the QT interval. It usually goes from 0.4 seconds to 0.45 seconds. That may not sound like much, but it matters because if the QT interval gets all the way up to around half a second, the chance of having a fatal cardiac arrhythmia increases. So, if you could look at the cardiogram and look at the QT interval you could tell if the patient was getting the drug, 886-JHG, or if the patient was getting the placebo."

"But it can't be that simple or the FBI's experts would have solved the problem of how someone figured out who was getting the experimental drug and who wasn't. I may not know medicine but I can figure out the investigative side of it. So what's the catch?"

Elana nodded. "Here's the catch. For all the patients on the study, all the patients in both treatment groups, cardiograms were taken every morning. But all of the cardiograms at all of the institutions were submitted electronically to a central monitoring station in South Dakota where the cardiograms were read by a computer. The doctors and nurses who were treating the patients didn't get to see the cardiograms or get to know the QT intervals. No one did."

"South Dakota?"

"Yes. Black Hills Monitoring got the cardiograms. If the patient was having a heart attack or a life threatening problem, then, according to the research protocol, and only then, would Black Hills Monitoring send the doctors taking care of the patient a copy of the cardiogram. An elevation of the QT interval to a critical level on the morning cardiogram would generate a message too. But that didn't happen during this clinical trial. No one at CMI ever got any information regarding the cardiograms or regarding the QT intervals. When the FBI investigated the deaths, they went to South Dakota and had doctors take another look at the cardiograms. There were no critical problems that should have led to a notification. So, apparently, that wasn't it."

"Could that computer in South Dakota get hacked? Seems like if you had the cardiogram information you'd know the QT intervals and you'd be in business if your business was killing people who were getting the experimental drug. Even if the QT numbers weren't in the danger zone, if you hacked the system and got the QT numbers, that information would let you figure out who was getting the drug, wouldn't it?"

"That would work. Except that if you hack a computer system you always leave a computer signature that it's been hacked. The FBI had their best security experts check it out. There was no unauthorized access to the system. And, by the way, the FBI looked at who was doing the interpretation in the Black Hills in the first place. It's all automatic. There is no one there. The electrocardiogram is sent in electronically and a report is generated. Only if there was a major problem is a human being involved. In any case, the patients had cardiograms taken every morning and no life-threatening problems were detected. The morning electrocardiograms never showed a dangerously high QT interval. Why are you smiling, Jonah?"

"Because if we hadn't been on vacation at the beginning of May, this would have dropped in our laps before we had all these answers from the FBI. We'd be figuring we had it solved, then we'd wait a few days and we'd find out we were nowhere, and start all over. This is frustrating but at least we're ruling things out. What's next, cutie?"

Cutie smiled. "That's it basically. To summarize what we have, the drug comes in coded bottles. No one at CMI or any of the other hospitals could break the code. The only other way someone might have figured out who was getting the drug and who wasn't getting the drug was to check the electrocardiograms, but no one could do that. Like the experts hired by the FBI, I can't see a way that anyone could figure out who was getting what. I'm stuck. Any ideas?"

"Not a one. It sounds impossible."

"That's what I thought. I'm only a med student, but real doctors didn't do any better. There's no way to figure out who got the drug and who got placebo. And there's no way to kill patients in one group without knowing which group they were in."

I was shaking my head; I was lost.

"The patients who died, died of cardiac arrhythmias. Tests for poisons were negative. They checked the bottles of the drug. They considered that maybe the drug was stored the wrong way or shipped the wrong way and the drug decomposed or something. Frankly, they were shooting in the dark at that point. The bottles that were supposed to contain 886-JHG contained exactly what they were supposed to contain, 886-JHG."

"Wait a minute. What did they check? The bottles were all infused, weren't they? They should have been empty."

"Right, but the empty bottles were saved so they could be returned to Bauer Labs and you know how a bottle is never completely empty. They did micro analysis on what was left in the bottles. Plus, when the patients died before completing twenty-one days, they had a lot of full bottles that never got given to the patient. Nothing was wrong with the bottles. No poisons. So, the question is this: Why did the patients develop cardiac arrhythmias? No answer to that either."

"Could the drug do that on its own?"

"Sure. The drug increases the QT interval and that creates a risk of a fatal irregularity of the heartbeat. But if the drug did that on its own, it would do it at every institution, not just in Treatment Group A at CMI. And why at night, after the morning cardiogram was ok. So, we had patients getting an electrocardiogram every day. No major problems were seen. Then, for no apparent reason, in Group A, only Group A, and only at CMI, six patients had their hearts stop in the middle of the night."

"I think it's time to take a break."

"Dinner and go listen to music?"

"Dinner and go back to Harpeth Commons. I want to see what that place looks like at night. I want to check the lighting around the time when Greg Cole said he saw 'a figure in black' on the front porch of your sister's townhouse."

"Right. And speaking of my sister, I spoke to Amibeth on the phone while you were out at Harpeth Commons. Interesting reaction. She wanted us to find whoever did it. She just assumed that Andrea didn't kill herself. Then she started thinking out loud about whether she could use the story now that Andrea was dead. She says the story has everything—incest, our dad's murder, Muffin Mancuso, the serial killer, and, now, a possible conspiracy in a drug study. She says there's no reason to keep quiet any more. Great story, huh?"

"Whatever. Not for me to judge. You killed yourself—so to speak—to advance her career. How can we criticize her for taking your other sister's death and using that in some way."

Elana tilted her head back and forth as she thought it over. "Good point. Where do you want to go for dinner?"

Chapter Forty-Five

We ate Mexican food at El Diablo with Rickey Stone and Skylar Jones. As always, the restaurant was crowded and noisy. In keeping with the devil motif, the tables all had fiery red tablecloths, and the waitresses wore peasant blouses with red skirts and red bandanas. With the homemade guacamole made fresh at the table, not in the kitchen, we got a whiff of avocado and lime juice as soon as we approached our seats. We politely declined the offer of a pitcher of beer as we sat down. Skylar was eight months pregnant with their first child. It was going to be a little girl. With Rickey in AA, neither was drinking alcohol. With Elana hoping to get pregnant neither was she.

Once Brian and Melanie Brandenburg had their baby, spontaneous get-togethers were almost impossible. Brian was finishing his first year of fellowship in rheumatology. Melanie was completing the first year of her training in endocrinology. Occasionally, we joined the Doctors Brandenburg and went to The Sports Bar to play bar trivia. We even joined them at Jerry's karaoke bar, from time to time. Brian and I had improved our vocal impression of the Dana Twins, though we didn't even attempt to master their choreography. Nonetheless, with Skylar and Rickey living one floor above us, and with the four of us connected to the *Jonah Slammer* show, Skylar and Rickey were the friends we saw most frequently.

We had eaten at El Diablo so many times that Elana referred to the place as our downstairs dining room. As with most restaurants, the size of entrée portion was enough for two people. We ordered the guacamole appetizer to share, and a round of iced teas. Elana and I split an order of camarones escondidos, grilled chicken stuffed with shrimp, while Skylar and Rickey split a large order of fajitas. Tennessee was trying to lead the nation in obesity, and sharing entrees was our effort to buck the trend. The slow service gave us time to talk about our upcoming trip to Greece and Skylar's upcoming vacation from show business.

"I really am not going to miss it. Singing is fun. Touring sucks. I'm almost thirty. Rickey and I don't need the money. I am going to play mommy for at least a year. And with *Jonah Slammer* over, Rickey will be around too." Though all the episodes hadn't been broadcast, they had all been taped, and the sets had been struck. "I still say that when that final episode airs in three weeks, you are going to be sorry that you didn't take the part. It's going to be controversial as anything. It's a career maker! You know you wrote it for yourself before you chickened out."

The scene that Skylar was talking about was a lesbian sex scene that featured The Woman in White. The character wouldn't actually be nude. She would be covered in paint just as AJ was covered in blood in the famous No Cause for Shame poster. Lee Graham, whose major claim to fame had been a role on *Gossip Girl*, was Season Four's Woman in White. She had already parlayed her expected notoriety into a starring role in Milton Brandenburg's film *The Dana Twins: The True Story*.

"Yeah, it would have been a career maker, but what career? I'm a writer, not an actress. You know I only took that part in Season Three because we thought the show might get cancelled and it was likely my only chance to be in front of the camera. And that part was barely a speaking part. Plus, as Jonah says, if I did that nude scene in the Season Four finale, it would be on the internet FOREVER! And, someday—maybe—I am going to be a doctor. Can you imagine having a patient come in and start talking to you about seeing you near naked on a re-run, or on You Tube."

Skylar chuckled. "Oh, yeah. Doctors are supposed to be respectable. No, wait. I forgot who we were talking about. It's my friend, Gun Girl . . . But even if I didn't have the role of Jodie Black, and even if I wasn't pregnant, I wouldn't have had the guts to take that role either. Not living in Nashville. You did the right thing. This town is too conservative. And," she tapped her belly, "I wouldn't want my daughter to see it."

As the sun began to set, Rickey and Skylar said their good nights at El Diablo and headed back upstairs. Elana and I reluctantly went back to work on the case of Andrea Cain and drove out to Harpeth Commons. It took twenty-five minutes to get to Greg Cole's townhouse. We parked in front of Andrea Cain's place and checked to see if Greg Cole was home. He wasn't, and the note I had left for him was still on his door.

Just as Greg Cole had done on the night of May 3rd, we walked to the dumpster and began walking back to the car checking to see how visible someone would be if they were standing on one of the front porches. Each townhouse had a porch light. If the light was on, the front porch was clearly visible; if the light was off, the porch was mostly in shadow, illuminated only by the adjacent neighbors' porch lights and by the moon. A perfect half moon was out.

"What do you think?" We had stopped about a third of the way back to Andrea Cain's townhome.

Elana looked around. "What was the moon like on May 3?"

"Three quarter moon . . . I checked before we went to dinner."

"Hmmn. If the porch light is off, you can't see the porch clearly, but it looks like it would be hard to hallucinate a figure in black."

"Just what I was thinking. If Greg Cole says he saw a figure in black while he was walking back from the dumpster, then he probably did. And if he did, where did that person go? I mean, the only option is out the second floor window, but you'd have to be lucky not to break a leg. Frankly, I think it would be almost impossible. Or you could hide in the closet or pantry, and not get found because Greg Cole didn't look." I shook my head. Nothing was hanging together. It was like trying to reason through a time travel paradox. Elana and I got in the car. "I think we've done enough for day one."

"Except we've accomplished nothing."

I nodded. "We got started. Tomorrow we'll go to the hospital and talk to the nurse who knew Andrea Candy Golden Butler Cain the best, and see if we can figure out a motive for someone to kill her other than that drug study." As always, I was singing Andrea Candy Golden Butler Cain as the notes ACGBC, the notes to the song "(She Thought She Could) Fly."

"Yeah. Except that it seems wrong, somehow, to keep singing her name like that, now that she's dead."

"ACGBC?" I spoke the letters this time without singing them.

"ACGBC! Andrea! That's who she was." Elana rested her head in the palms of her hands. "It's just so sad."

I took her hand and kissed it. "So sad."

"Love you, Jonah. You are the one constant in my somewhat crazy life."

"Love you back, Elana."

It was still very sad, but it also wasn't that late. I asked Elana if she wanted to check out the second show at The Bluebird Café.

"Sure. But it's Saturday. We don't have reservations. We'll never get in."

"You're Elana Grey, former singing star, former songwriter, senior screenwriter on the hottest show taped in Nashville. We can get in."

But we couldn't. Instead we went to Bistro 360 for a late dessert and laughed about it all the way home.

Chapter Forty-Six

After a quick breakfast, Elana and I drove to Vanderbilt Hospital to see Linda Martinson, the Head Nurse on the eleventh floor medical unit. Most of the patients there were hospitalized for treatment of leukemia or other cancers. The police reports clearly identified Mrs. Martinson as Andrea Cain's closest friend at Vanderbilt. Elana had called on Saturday to set up an appointment. I doubted that we would learn anything new, but in a case as confusing as this one was, it made sense to get information from the primary sources.

It was Sunday morning, a little before noon, when we arrived. The medical team was just completing rounds. My father had always complained that in his day the residents worked too much, routinely being in the hospital over one hundred hours a week. Now residents could not be required to be present more than sixty hours a week. Shifts were shorter. My father was not one to complain, but he was concerned that the house staff no longer had a sense of attachment to their patients. Patients were passed along from shift to shift and didn't "belong" to any one resident. The old rules had been changed to protect patients from being cared for by exhausted doctors. The new rules created the risk that incomplete information was transmitted at the more frequent shift changes. I would wait until Elana was a resident, if she ever got that far in her medical career, to form my own opinion about the work load and the schedule. For purely selfish reasons, I liked the idea of having my wife home and awake once in a while.

Linda Martinson met with us in the family conference room near the nurse's station. It was a small room with a formica table that seated six. It was where doctors conferred with families when bedside discussions seemed inappropriate. The room had been home to many discussions of death, but I doubted that it had been the site for discussions of suicide and murder.

Mrs. Martinson looked about forty years old. She was tall and thin, with curly brown hair that extended a little below her shoulders. She wore a wedding ring, but no other jewelry. Despite the fact that Elana was a medical student, she had never met Mrs. Martinson. Elana wouldn't get to rotate on medical subspecialties like the cancer unit until her fourth year.

"Thanks for meeting with us, Mrs. Martinson. I'm Jonah Aaron. This is my wife, Elana Grey. She's a medical student working on the case with me."

"Like I said on the phone, I'd like to help you out, but I have no idea what I can do to help."

"What we are trying to do is get a better understanding of Andrea Cain as a person. We're trying to figure out what she was like. Trying to see why she might have hurt herself, or why someone else would want to hurt her. So far, the investigation isn't making much sense."

"The whole thing doesn't make any sense. She was tired at times, but never really depressed. She was energized by the patients. Patients are afraid when they come in here for chemotherapy or for pain management. Andrea was great at telling people the truth but telling it in a way that was comforting. Sometimes the best treatment is to stop therapy and focus on comfort. I think that at times Andrea was frustrated taking care of patients whom she felt would be better off in hospice, getting comfort care."

I couldn't see that as leading to anything, but before I could move the conversation along, Elana asked "Did she ever get in trouble arguing with doctors about the treatments that the patients were getting?"

"No. That was never a problem. She knew how to ask questions without offending the doctors. If she thought one of her patients was being over-treated, she would just ask the doctor to educate her about the disease that the patient had. Sometimes she learned something and reassessed the situation. Sometimes, it was the doctor who decided to reconsider what he had been planning. Andrea was not a troublemaker. Everyone knew she had the patient's best interests at heart. Patients liked her. The doctors liked her. We all liked her."

This was interesting, but I was looking for a motive for murder, not a character reference. "Was there anyone who didn't like her?"

"Not that I knew of. I mean when she started here at the end of February she was in the midst of a divorce. Ironically, I think that it was difficult because she was still in love with him, even though she was the one who left him. I asked her once if she thought about going back and trying to work it out. She told me she felt terrible for hurting him by leaving him, and she said that he had moved on. She said she didn't want to hurt him again by disrupting his life. She said it was all her fault for not being able to talk about things and that if she was ever in a relationship again she would do what Amibeth said and 'Communicate, communicate, communicate.' God, did she ever love Amibeth. She was always talking about what Amibeth had said the day before. She couldn't listen to the show because she worked the 7 AM to 3 PM shift, but it's available on the Internet. She told me that from the time Amibeth went on the air, she had never missed a single show. I know all those women call in and tell Amibeth that they are her biggest fan. Well, Andrea Cain really was one of Amibeth's biggest fans."

So, despite maintaining a distance from her sister, Andrea had followed Amibeth's career. In a way, that was sweet. "You said that she talked about what she would do if she was ever 'in a relationship.' As far as you know, was she seeing anyone?"

"No. She told me that she was going to simplify her life for a while. That was her phrase. 'Simplify her life' unless something very interesting came along. She wasn't dating anyone. There was a man in her complex that was her friend, Glenn or Greg or Gary something. I don't remember, but she said he was probably too shy to ask her out, and she was happy with that. She said she wasn't ready to start dating anyone, that she had plenty of time."

"When was that?"

"Just a few days before she died. I think Andrea intimidated most men. She didn't dress provocatively or anything, but she had an amazing figure even if she didn't show it off. She just seemed very sensual. I think men could tell that she would be a lot to handle. Most nurses up here are right out of nursing school, in their twenties. She was a little older—more mature. I think she was in her mid-thirties."

Elana spoke before I could calculate Andrea's age. "She would have been thirty-six in July."

I asked the standard questions that I knew the police had asked. "Do you know if she had any problems with alcohol or gambling? Any hints that she was using drugs?"

Linda Martinson laughed as I started the series of questions. "Andrea? You've got to be kidding. No. She led a very dull life. Her hobbies were reading mysteries, watching television, and playing some statistical baseball game that she had just gotten into. I can't tell you about that. I don't know much about baseball. I've been here fourteen years. I've worked with a lot of nurses. I've seen nurses get upset and depressed over their work. I've had nurses that I've told to take some time off. Andrea Cain wasn't one of them. She was a survivor. She could handle whatever life gave her. She confided in me that a long time ago she had taken pills when she was really depressed. She said she couldn't believe how crazy she had been back then. I know what the police said, but Andrea Cain did not kill herself. Please do what you can do to find out who killed her."

I gave her my card and asked her to call if she thought of anything else. We made our way back to the large bank of elevators that would return us to the lobby.

"You know, my father always says that doctors shouldn't take care of their own families, that they can't be objective. This is just as bad. It's almost impossible to investigate the case when I feel so bad for you because it's your sister. I think we should give it just a couple more days and, unless we start making progress, give up."

Elana squeezed my hand as we got in the elevator. "We'll probably be done in a couple more days anyway."

"Probably. Maybe sooner than that. We have one loose end, Greg Cole. If we don't hear from him today, I'll try and track him down."

"And in the meantime?"

In the meantime, we spent a leisurely afternoon visiting my parents. "We're sorry for your loss, Elana. There's not much else we can say. Did they have a memorial service?"

"The nurses organized a small memorial service for her in the hospital chapel the Friday after she died. She was buried in Chicago two days later with just a graveside service. Only four people showed up at the graveside: her best friend in Chicago, Gail Riley, Andrea's ex-husband, Eric Cain, her ex-husband's new girlfriend, Kerry Devin, and her next door neighbor here in Bellevue, Greg Cole. Even though it had been ruled a suicide by then, the FBI was interested in who showed up at the graveside service. They listed the names in the reports they sent us."

While I was contemplating why Greg Cole had flown up to Chicago for the graveside service, my father began muttering, "Gail Riley and Eric Cain. Those are two names out of my past."

"You know them, dad?"

"Yes. Gail Riley is a major figure in Cancer Medicine. She's been chief of the cancer program at CMI for over a decade now. She has scores of publications. She and Eric Cain were interns the same year at CMI back when I was still there in the mid 1980's. You could tell even then that Gail Riley was going to be a star. She had taken time to get both an M.D. and Ph.D. at Harvard. Also she is one of the most attractive women that I ever met." He paused to reflect on that for a moment. "Eric Cain was on the cancer service with me the following year when he was a resident. Fine doctor, but just a little—different. Aside from once being married to Andrea, how does he fit into your case?"

We told my father about the clinical study at CMI. Like the experts hired by the FBI, my father had no insights as to how someone could have broken the code and figured out which patients were getting the experimental drug and which ones were getting placebo. "The police ruled him out, right?"

"That's right. He was at a hockey game. Air-tight alibi. Not only did he have ticket stubs, his girlfriend was with him, and the people sitting in the same section remembered him being there for the entire game. An empty seat at a Stanley Cup game would have been noticed, especially since he was a season ticket holder and everyone in that section knew him. He was known for screaming his lungs out when the Blackhawks scored a goal."

My father chuckled. "Sounds like him. If I remember correctly, Jonah, he was a big hockey fan. I think he played college hockey, too. Since he's a cardiologist, I haven't kept up with him. The only time I've seen Eric Cain in the last twenty years was at a meeting of DIME."

I was not familiar with the organization. "DIME?"

Elana answered before my dad had a chance to reply. "DIME. Doctors for Intelligent Medical Expenditures. We've talked about this, Jonah. As a nation we spend eight thousand dollars per person each year on health care, nearly three trillion dollars. That's 17% of the gross domestic product, more than any other nation in the world, and we rank near fortieth in health care statistics like life expectancy because we have such an unregulated and irrational system of what we do."

My dad's expression showed his frustration with the situation. "That's right, honey. DIME is a symbol for the fact that we could probably deliver just as effective health care if we only spent ten cents of every dollar on health care instead of seventeen cents. We'll never get back to that point. The only thing we can hope to do is keep it from increasing. But no one knows how. Technology makes things more expensive and there are no simple solutions."

There certainly were no simple solutions to our case. Unless Greg Cole could give us some answers, I suspected that we would never have an idea about what had happened at CMI or at the townhouse at Harpeth Commons.

Chapter Forty-Seven

A little before eight on Sunday evening, Greg Cole phoned and asked if we could meet him at his townhouse at nine. At half past eight we headed out to Harpeth Commons. We brought a portable computer loaded with accident analysis software and a twenty-five foot ruler. One of the insurance companies that used our services on occasion has an accident simulation system. One can plug in a scenario and the software can calculate the probability of various injuries being sustained. I was curious if anyone could have jumped out of the second story window onto concrete and walked away, limped away, or even crawled away, and I wanted to use exact measurements.

"Why are you bringing your gun, Jonah?"

"Because the case doesn't make sense to me, and I don't have any idea what we are walking into."

"Do you really think he had something to do with my sister's death?"

"No, but better safe than dead."

"You realize you're going to scare the heck out him with that gun."

"I'm wearing a light jacket. He won't even know I have a gun."

"It's eighty-four degrees out. He's going to wonder why you're wearing a jacket."

"Hopefully, his place will be air-conditioned. Look, the whole thing has us going in circles. From what Marty Hogan told me, Greg Cole saw someone go in to Andrea's townhome. The fantasy baseball message says she didn't kill herself. If someone killed her and didn't go out the window, then that person was in the townhouse when Greg Cole looked around. He may have seen that person when he checked the closets and the walk-in pantry. Nothing happened. Why not? Did he know the killer? Was Greg Cole somehow part of a plan to kill your sister? I know that makes no sense, but I'm just not getting this whole thing. I don't know what I'm walking into; I just want to be sure that we're both walking out."

"I agree. It makes sense to take a gun."

"Then why are you asking about my taking a gun?"

"Just so I feel better about bringing MY gun. But I have it in my purse. He won't notice that." As a part-time employee of a detective agency, Elana had a carry permit.

I laughed. "Just don't shoot anyone unless you have to."

"Don't worry, honey. I will not embarrass the agency."

For the second time in two nights, Elana and I drove out to Harpeth Commons. We parked in the empty space in front of what had been Andrea Cain's home and walked towards Greg Cole's townhouse. As we got out of the car and walked to the front door, Elana tapped me on the shoulder, "Now, there's something you don't see every day."

"What are you talking about?" I didn't see anything out of the ordinary.

"On the ground. Those lawn gnomes."

"So. He has tacky taste and has lawn gnomes. What's the big deal?"

"No, Jonah. They're not regular lawn gnomes; they're Jawas, from the original Star Wars movie."

I looked them over. "Oh yeah. From Tatooine. They're the scavenger species."

Elana looked at me like I was the one from another planet. "How did you remember that? I thought I was cool for recognizing them as Jawas."

"Trivia expert. My brain is full of useless stuff. You know that."

"Let's hope Greg Cole can fill our brains with useful stuff."

"No kidding."

We knocked on the door of Greg Cole's townhome, and a tall balding man welcomed us in. Greg Cole stood at least six feet five inches tall, but must have weighed no more than one hundred and seventy pounds. I guesstimated his age at forty. I introduced myself and introduced my wife as Elana Grey.

"Sorry to take a day to get back to you. I was visiting my girlfriend. She lives out of town. Come on in and look around. People either love it or hate it. I hope you like it."

The gnomes were only the vaguest hint of what was inside. Greg Cole's townhouse wasn't so much a home as a museum honoring a galaxy far, far away. The dining room had a standard table with a set of chairs. However, on the far wall there was a print showing the wasteland of Tatooine along with its two suns. A large breakfront in the corner of the room held a sculpture of Padme Amidala. The walls of the living room were covered with light-sabers, but not the cheap plastic ones that can be purchased at a drug store. These were expensive metal lightsabers with autographs of the actors etched in the metal. The wall over the sofa contained a print of Bespin's Cloud City. I thought Elana was compulsive about keeping our condo clean, but this place was absolutely spotless.

"There's more upstairs if you two want to see it."

Elana turned to me. "We'd love to take the tour, wouldn't we, honey?"

"Absolutely. I've never seen anything like this."

Greg Cole became animated in response to the encouragement "You ain't seen nothing yet."

We walked up the stairs to the second floor. The walls of the stairway were covered with autographed posters from each of the Star Wars movies, as well as posters from Star Wars conventions and from the animated Star Wars series. We walked past the master bedroom at the top of the stairs. "Nothing in there worth seeing. Right this way to the office."

We walked past the washer and dryer into a room that had to be seen to be believed. Two large mannequins and three display cases dominated the room. One mannequin wore the costume of the Dark Lord of the Sith, Darth Vader. The other mannequin wore the costume of Boba Fett, the Mandalorian bounty hunter. Only a desk with a computer made me certain that we were still within the confines of our own galaxy. The display cases contained rare Star Wars collectibles, mostly action figures from the original Star Wars series, all in the original packaging.

Elena was fascinated by the quality of the costumes. "Where did you get these? Are they originals from the movie?"

"No. I'm part of an international costuming club. We make our own costumes."

I was very impressed with the quality of the work. When I was a senior at Vanderbilt I had met a grad student in Computer Sciences who was into that sort of stuff. "Hey, you're part of the 501st Legion, right?"

He smiled at my mention of the name. "Uh, huh. You got it."

Elana tapped me on the shoulder and whispered in my ear. "Aren't you embarrassed about bringing a gun here?"

"Yeah, but he is on the Dark Side." Despite that fact, he seemed as harmless as R2-D2.

Greg Cole interrupted our conversation. "You haven't seen the neatest thing." He removed the helmet from his Darth Vader mannequin and placed it on his head. "Jonah, I am your father." The voice came out sounding like that of James Earl Jones, the actor who portrayed Darth Vader in the movies.

"You're too young to be my father, Greg."

Greg Cole tried again. "Jonah, I am your brother!" He took off the helmet and laughed. "Isn't technology wonderful? I'm into computers. I work for . . . well, it doesn't matter who I work for. Anyway, I modified some spyware voice disguise technology to make this happen. I am too young to be your father. I'm thirty-three. Glad to get a chance to show it to you."

Elana was admiring the detailed work on the costumes. "Do you have any collectibles that aren't tied to Star Wars?"

"Yeah, I have one fantastic non-Star Wars Collectible, but I don't usually show it to anyone. I'm afraid people will think it's in poor taste, but I . . . Wait a minute, it just hit me. Elana Grey! You wrote the song about AJ going off the bridge. Well, then you can't be too critical."

I looked at Elana. I had no idea why our writing the song was relevant, but I wanted to find out. We entered the master bedroom. Not since 2005 when we had been in the Lake Shore Drive condo that Andrea Cain shared with her husband Eric, with its three walls of Night Shadow memorabilia, had I seen anything like this. The walls were covered with posters of Skylar Jones.

For a moment, Elana was speechless. I asked the question. "Is this what you wanted to show us?"

"No. No! I'm just a big fan of Skylar Jones. I've seen her in concert like twelve times. Now that I have a girlfriend I'm going to take all the posters down. In fact if you hadn't left me your business card, and I hadn't called you, that was my plan for tonight. Anyway, that's not what I brought you here to see." He walked to the closet and opened the door revealing a large safe. Considering the Star Wars treasures openly on display, I couldn't imagine what was so valuable that it was kept under lock and key.

As he unlocked the safe, Elana finally made a comment. "You know, speaking as a woman, I think it's a good idea to take down the Skylar Jones posters, otherwise you may never get laid."

"Yeah. Probably right. The one time my girlfriend was here, we never made it upstairs. We ended up in the living room."

Greg Cole had returned from the safe with his prize possession. I realized why our writing the song about AJ Golden's suicide was relevant. "My God. It's a Shotgun Sister Triumphant Statue."

Elana moved towards it and for a moment I was afraid that she was going to try and destroy it. Despite all the AJ memorabilia sold at the No Cause for Shame Fundraisers, Elana had emphatically requested that Amibeth not sell Shotgun Sister, an unauthorized statue based on the events that occurred on Woodland Hills Lane. Elana's response was totally unexpected. "It's fabulous. It's lifelike. It looks just like m . . . her." She whispered in my ear, "And the tits are just like mine were before I went on the pill." She continued admiring the statue. "You know I've seen these before. I didn't remember that they were so lifelike. My God, there's a miniature skull in the ceiling! I don't remember that either. I love it. Why is this so valuable?"

Greg Cole smiled from ear to ear. "Look at the box. It's not 'Shotgun Sister Triumphant'. They made three thousand of those cheapies when AJ refused to sign a contract. Those are common. This is "AJ Golden Triumphant." It's the prototype for the ones they couldn't make when AJ Golden didn't sign on the dotted line. This is number one of one. It's the holy grail of AJ Golden collectibles. I mean us Star Wars folks talk about Jedi warriors in a galaxy far away, and I'm a fan of Skylar Jones, but once upon a time there was this fabulous heroic woman, and she's gone. Her sister Amibeth talks about bouncing back from horrible things that happen, but AJ was a victorious woman. That's why the women wear the clothing and the blonde wigs at the No Cause for Shame Fundraisers. I know that the two of you memorialized AJ in a song, so I think you understand where I'm coming from."

Elana continued to admire the statue. "How much is it worth?"

"It's one of a kind, and I'm not selling it. I suppose if Amibeth herself wanted to buy it, and auction it off at her fundraiser, I'd sell it to her for—let's say fifty thousand dollars, but that's not going to happen." He paused for a moment. "It is truly priceless . . . But you didn't come to see this. You came to talk about my neighbor, Andrea. Let me put it away and we can go back downstairs."

As he re-entered the closet, Elana whispered in my ear again. "I want it. We have to buy it."

We started down the stairs. "Little pricey, but I suppose we could build a display case for it and keep it in the living room. Maybe we could ask my mom how to display it together with the CMA awards for the song. We'll think about it. Are you really interested? That headless body in the front hall is kind of gruesome."

"Yes!!! I know. But I want to have it. It's real. The Shotgun Sister Triumphant ones don't look like me . . ., I mean like AJ, and in Shotgun Sister Triumphant the body is in the wrong place. I want it."

"We'll talk about it."

"I'm being silly aren't I?"

"Uh-huh." Then again no one ever made a lifelike action figure of me playing on special teams for Vanderbilt football.

Chapter Forty-Eight

We entered the living room and Elana and I sat on the sofa.

Greg sat in the large chair that backed up against the door to the patio. "Can I get you guys something to drink?" He picked up a stack of coasters from the corner of the table before we replied.

"No thank you."

"No thank you." I was almost embarrassed to refuse, but he was a Dark Lord. More importantly he was still a suspect.

"OK." He neatly stacked the coasters, and placed them back precisely where they had been. "What do you want to know?"

Elana allowed me take the lead. "Mainly about that night. The shooting. What do you remember?"

He stared at his shoes before answering. Obviously, the topic made him uncomfortable. "Still makes me sad to think about it. We'd spent the day with the Walkers out on the front steps. The worst of the flood was over. The water was going down. People across the street were starting to rip out wallboard and move things out into the street. We were a little embarrassed about escaping with so little damage on our side of the street. We went over and helped out until it became dark. Then we came back here and talked baseball. Did either of you ever play fantasy baseball?"

"I used to. I'm in recovery."

"Hey, I get that. It's an addictive game. Anyway, Andrea moved in to the complex in late February, just as Spring Training was starting. She saw me sitting on the porch reading a baseball magazine and checking some computer printouts one day in March and asked what I was doing. She said she needed to develop some new interests. She liked baseball, so I got her into the league. I'll admit it; I was mainly looking for an excuse to talk to her. She was so attractive, and I really didn't know what to say to her." He swallowed hard and paused. "I explained the game to her, but you played before, Jonah. She made the classic beginner's mistake. She only knew who the superstars were. She overbid on them, and except for those players, she ended up having a roster of nobodies. When she realized she was going to be fighting to stay out of last place, she asked me what to do. My main concern was that she not give up and quit the league. If she did that, then I wouldn't have anything to say to her."

"Makes sense."

"But after the flood, when we were all out on the porch, it was clear that she had figured the game out to some degree, and she realized she had to get some underpriced talent. So we negotiated the trade. What I liked best about the trade was that it meant she was aiming at next year. It meant I'd have something to talk to her about this year and next. I never was very good with women. Those two days that I spent on the porch with her, and helping out across the street on those flooded homes, that was one of the best times I had ever had talking to a woman. She made me feel important, like I mattered to her. I almost had the nerve to ask her out."

This was all consistent with what we had heard previously. "Of course, I didn't ask her out. When the power went back on, I just went back to my place, cleaned up what little bit of a mess there was, and took some spoiled food to the dumpster. That's when I saw the figure on her porch. If it hadn't been dressed in black I would have figured it was the FBI guy she was waiting for."

"She told you about meeting the FBI?"

"Yeah. She told me she had information about something very important. We didn't talk much about it. I didn't want to pry. Hey, do you know what she was talking about? I never found out. I was kind of curious."

"We're working on it?"

"Good luck. I mean, I'm sure she would have wanted someone to figure it out. I know she was proud of herself for figuring out that something was wrong with the study. She said it was the most important thing she ever did except for protecting her sisters from her father."

"She said that?" As far as I knew, ACGBC's basic story was that her family had died in a fire.

"She confided in me that her father had molested her, and that she had made certain that he never bothered her two younger sisters. She said that she had worked on some important drug studies in the past, but that the most important thing she ever did was to protect her sisters. She was proud of them. Never gave me any details about them, but she was really happy that what she had done helped both of them turn out ok."

I looked at Elana and smiled. My wife had turned out a lot better than ok. "Hmmn. So what else do you remember about what happened that night?"

"Well, I saw the figure on the porch and I saw Andrea let him or her in. I couldn't tell much. Black top. Black pants. Black cap. At least that's what I think I saw. I couldn't tell if it was a man or a woman. Not real tall. Maybe five feet five, five feet six. Hard to say. I was at ground level and they were on the front porch. Until I heard the gunshot, I just figured it was a friend. The funny thing was I don't think she ever had a friend visit her the whole time she was here. Anyway, I was looking at my watch, because it was going to be International Star Wars Day in a few seconds . . ."

"Wait. International Star Wars Day? You lost me again."

"Sorry. Monday, the day the water started going back down was May Third. At midnight it would be May Fourth. That's International Star Wars Day. You know, 'May the Fourth Be with You.'" He chuckled as he said the phrase.

I had never heard that before, and I started to laugh. "Like May the Force Be with You."

"Exactly! It's an in joke in Star Wars Fandom. May Fourth is officially known as International Star Wars Day. Anyhow, just a few seconds past midnight, the lights went out, and BANG I heard a shot. I headed on over, but I couldn't get in. The front door was locked; the back patio door was locked. I went back in front and we called 911 and then we called Jenna Hooper from the management firm. I thought about breaking down the door or a window. For a while afterwards, I thought maybe I should have, but when I read the autopsy report, I realized it wouldn't have mattered. She was dead instantly."

"You read the autopsy report?"

"Sorry. I meant I asked the police about what the autopsy report said. I wanted to know if I screwed up by not trying to come to her rescue. They said it didn't matter. That she was dead in a few seconds after the shot. Anyway, we all waited outside—me, and the Walkers, and a couple of other neighbors. Then Jenna Hooper came and let me in. I was afraid of what we would find, but I was a medic in Iraq so I figured I was the best one to go in. I had the others wait outside. There she was. I will never forget what I saw when I came in that townhouse. Body on the floor. Wearing a robe. As long as I live . . ." His voice trailed off. "Never forget it. Anyhow, she was dead. I was going to pound on her chest, but I could tell it was pointless. And that's where I was, sort of in shock myself when the paramedics came, and Officer Johns. He wanted to search the place himself, but I felt so useless, that I told him I'd check downstairs—the closets and the pantry—and that he should check upstairs. I remember warning him to be careful in the attic. There was nobody there. The killer must have gone out the upstairs window. At least that's what the Homicide Detective told me. I was so angry when I heard they ruled it a suicide that I was going to go down there and tell them to reopen the case, but then I realized that it didn't matter. She was dead. Nothing was going to change that."

"You seem sure she didn't kill herself."

"Yeah. Lots of reasons. First, she had no reason to. Secondly she told me about overdosing ten years ago. She joked about it. She called it underdosing. She told me that when she had taken the pills that time, her husband found her. Of course, he wasn't her husband then. But she said she realized how horrible it was for him to have found her. She said there were a lot of reasons not to kill herself, among them that she didn't want to die, but she said she would never put anyone through that—finding her body. I can't believe that she killed herself. I mean, we weren't that close, but after saying that she wouldn't put someone through the experience of finding her, I just can't believe that she would shoot herself next door to me, when I might be the one to do just that."

"When did she say that? That she wouldn't put someone through that."

"Sorry. I don't remember. I guess we were talking about death. She had been considering going to work for The Hospice. She was tired of taking care of chemotherapy patients who she felt might be better off getting comfort care. I guess that's how the topic came up, but I don't remember when."

We were going back and forth again. First, it looked like a suicide. Then, Marty Hogan thought it was murder. Then, the coroner ruled it a suicide. The fantasy baseball trade said it was murder, not suicide. There was nowhere for a killer to go; so there was no killer; it had to be suicide. Now, we were being told that she said she'd never kill herself; it had to be murder. Back and forth and back and forth. As always, when I was frustrated my mind drifted to trivia. Ping pong, also known as table tennis, is a sport invented in England in the 1880's. I'd never had that question come up in a trivia game, but questions about the origin of tennis come up frequently. The French invented tennis, while the British invented lawn tennis.

I was so lost in thought that Elana took over the questioning. "We heard that you went up to Chicago for the burial. We were a little surprised. From what we heard, it didn't seem that the two of you were that close."

"Not as close as I might have liked to be. It just seemed like the right thing to do. I couldn't do anything for her that night. At least I could be there when they put her in the ground. We had talked about funerals, that time we talked about dying. She said that no matter when she died, she wanted a closed casket so people would remember her the way she was when she was alive. I figured I could go and make sure it happened that way. It wasn't as bad as I thought it would be. Eric and Kerry, that's her ex-husband, Dr. Cain, and his friend, Dr. Devin, were there. Dr. Gail Riley was there, too. Nice people."

Some of his answers didn't add up, but I had nothing left to ask. "Do you mind if we go outside and measure the drop from that second story window. Everyone keeps saying she didn't kill herself, and neither you nor Officer Johns found the killer in the house. I guess we better reconsider that someone went out the window. I figured someone would have broken an ankle landing on the patio, but maybe not. You said the figure in black was about five feet six inches tall?"

"That's my best guess. I could be off a little, either way."

I had brought a 25 foot retractable ruler. The buildings were all identical. Greg Cole volunteered to go up to his bedroom and drop the measuring tape out the window. We walked around to the back. It was a beautiful night for Nashville in June. The temperature had fallen into the upper seventies and there was little humidity.

The sill was thirteen feet above the ground. Someone five feet six inches tall going out the window and hanging from the window frame with their arms extended, would have about a six and a half foot fall to the concrete.

Elana finished taking the measurement. "So you think someone went out the window after all, Jonah?"

"I have no idea. I'm totally confused. There are parts of his story I'm not buying."

"What's not to buy?"

"I'll tell you when we're alone."

Greg Cole had walked around to the back of the townhouse. "You guys got everything you need?"

"We got exactly what we came for. Thanks for your time. Sorry to put you through it all again."

"That's ok. I hope I helped you."

Elana and I walked back toward our car. "OK, Jonah, what am I missing?"

"Maybe, nothing." I kissed her on the forehead. "You are a wonderful wife, and you're good at being an investigator, but you're about as good at investigating as I am at medicine. You believe what people tell you. It doesn't always work."

"Huh?"

"Your sister was married to Bradley Butler and didn't talk about her past during the entire time they were together. When she did, he left her. She was married to Eric Cain for eight years, and as far as we know, never talked about her past. When we met her in Chicago she was adamant about having nothing to do with you and Amy Elizabeth for fear that Eric Cain would realize that she was the oldest Golden sister, the one who had been sexually abused by her father. Now we find out that Greg Cole knows that she was molested by your father. Instead of telling the story that her family died in a fire, she told him that she had two sisters and that she was very proud of them. When did she tell him all that? He told us he never even asked her out. He never had the nerve."

She thought it over. "Hmmn. Either she totally turned over a new leaf, or maybe they were closer than we thought."

"That's not what I asked. When did she tell him? When?"

Elana considered the question before speaking. "Well, Mrs. Martinson said she wasn't seeing anyone, and that was a few days before she died. That isn't exactly first date material. I'm confused too. Maybe she told him because she knew they were never going to have a relationship."

"That's one possibility."

"Or maybe being marooned in Bellevue due to a flood breeds intimacy, and she decided to share."

"With the Walkers there the whole time, or for most of it?"

"I guess . . . What are you driving at, Jonah?"

"I'm not really sure. Some things just aren't adding up." I had an idea, but I didn't want to raise Elana's hopes. "C'mon let's try that software. If someone fell six and a half feet onto concrete covered with a little dirt, let's find out the chance that they would break an ankle."

We got in the car and turned on the laptop. Elana plugged in the information and gave the result. "Seventy-nine percent."

"Only seventy-nine percent. God, someone could have walked away." I was more confused than ever.

"Not quite. That's seventy-nine percent for breaking one ankle; it's twenty-one percent for breaking both ankles. It looks unlikely that anyone went out the window." She took a deep breath. "Despite everything, I guess my sister killed herself after all."

I put my arm around her shoulder and silently, we sat in the parking lot trying to figure out what to do next. There was no obvious next move. "You know there's another possibility that we really haven't considered." I paused to think it over. "No. It doesn't fit all the information, but . . ."

"But what?"

Before I could answer, the quiet of the night was shattered by a loud noise. I turned to Elana. "WHAT THE HELL WAS THAT?"

Chapter Forty-Nine

The second noise was easy to identify. It was gunfire—from behind the townhouses.

Elana and I got out of the car. We advanced slowly toward the townhouses. Our guns were drawn but pointed towards the ground. All over the complex, lights were coming on. As we reached the sidewalk in front of Greg Cole's town house, a large figure, dressed in black, emerged from behind the row of townhouses. He was trying to run while rubbing his eyes at the same time. When he reached the area where the ground sloped gently down toward the sidewalk, he lost his footing and tumbled down the hill, rolling to a stop at my feet. He was screaming, "The son of a bitch blinded me!"

From behind the townhouses, Greg Cole emerged carrying a light-saber in his right hand, and a pistol in his left hand. He was sprinting. The light-saber was aimed squarely at the head of the figure in black. "Blinded you? You're lucky I didn't have a real gun."

The best I could manage as I holstered my guns was to ask, "What the hell happened?"

Greg Cole was catching his breath, "I thought you guys left."

"We were just sitting in the car talking for a minute. What happened?"

"Tell you in a second. Can you get him to shut up?" The man was still shouting about being blinded.

I put my hands on the shoulders of the figure in black. "Hey, my wife's a medical student. If you get quiet, she'll take a look at you."

The figure in black went silent and Elana began to examine him. With no equipment I doubted she could do much of an exam.

"A little after you left, I heard some tapping on the glass of the door to the patio. I went to the door and found this idiot pointing a gun at me and telling me to let him in. I told him I needed to use a key to unlock it—which isn't true by the way. I reached up and grabbed this light saber from the wall. Anyway, you saw how I modified that Darth Vader helmet."

"Hard to forget."

"Well, I modified this thing too. It has a military strength laser. He laughed when I pointed it at him. Not laughing now is he?"

I looked at the figure in black. Elana was checking him out. He wasn't laughing, but he wasn't screaming. He also wasn't seeing the fingers that Elana was holding in front of his eyes. He kept asking "How many what?"

I turned back to Greg Cole. "What did he want?"

David Johns, the Nashville Police officer, had made his way over to the scene. "What happened? I heard gunshots."

Greg Cole was proud to reply. "This guy pulled a gun on me trying to get me to open the back door by my patio. I fired in self-defense with the light-saber. It's a perfectly legal weapon. If it were a pistol, he'd be dead. Of course if it were a pistol he probably wouldn't have laughed when I pointed it at him. He never saw it coming."

I wondered if the figure in black was ever going to see anything coming ever again. I didn't know much about lasers, but I suspected that both of his retinas might have been fried.

Elana joined the conversation. "Can't tell how bad the damage is without an ophthalmoscope, but right now he's totally blind. What's going on?"

Greg Cole looked at the figure in black, sitting on the grass a few feet from us. "He wanted to know where someone was. Buffy or Muffy. I'm not sure what he was saying. The patio door was closed and I couldn't hear exactly. I had no idea what he was talking about. But I saw the gun. He said he'd kill me if I didn't tell him what happened to whatever her name was. I couldn't think of anything else to do. Am I in trouble?"

I shrugged my shoulders and the police officer answered the question with a question. "Who fired the gun?"

"He did. This is his gun. He dropped it when he put his hands up to his eyes."

David Johns looked at the man in black and then back at Greg Cole. "Then the way I see it, Greg, you were within your rights as a homeowner. Self defense. You can't fire a gun in the city limits. That charge against him will stick for sure. There's no law about firing a light-saber." David Johns chuckled at the absurdity of the situation. "Way to go Darth Vader. I'll call it in and stay here until the radio car comes. They can take him to the hospital and then on to jail."

The figure in black said nothing except that he wanted a lawyer. Elana and I walked back toward the townhouse with Greg Cole. I suddenly realized why the death of Candy Cain didn't make any sense as either a suicide or a murder. "Look, uh, Greg, it's not for me to tell you what to do, but considering this probably has something to do with the shooting that happened here on International Star Wars day, isn't there someone else you might want to check on? I mean, if they're trying to get information out of you, someone else might be in danger."

A look of concern crossed his face. "Could you guys stick around for a minute?" He pulled his cell phone from his pocket and speed dialed a number.

He smiled when he heard a voice answer at the other end of the line. "Honey, are you ok?" We listened as he explained about the figure in black, the guns, and the light-saber. The two of them argued back and forth for about half a minute. Finally, after convincing her to lock the door and not let anyone in, I heard Greg Cole say, "Look, honey, we have to trust someone and I have a gut feeling we can trust these two. Their names are Jonah Aaron and Elana Grey. They're investigators, but they're also the songwriters who wrote the song about AJ Golden."

"She says she'll talk to you." He handed me the phone without telling me who was on the other end of the line. He didn't have to.

Elana had no idea what was going on, and was even more confused when I took the phone and said,"Hello, Andrea. This is Jonah Aaron. It's nice to hear your voice."

Chapter Fifty

Andrea Cain, as in her previous interaction with the FBI, did not want to discuss anything of import over the phone. Her paranoia struck me as reasonable. We agreed that Greg would lead us to her, and that the four of us would then go to someplace safer—the condo on the ninth floor of a building with a doorman. I thought of calling Joe Apted, but it was near midnight in Chicago and I couldn't think of anything he could accomplish before morning. Also, I wanted to get a better handle on the facts before I spoke to him.

Elana talked to Andrea on the phone while Greg Cole packed up enough clothes for several days. Then Greg, Elana, and I got in the Lexus and headed to an apartment complex in Holladay, Tennessee, about seventy miles west of Bellevue, where Andrea Cain had been staying.

I always check to see if I'm being followed, and a black SUV leaving Harpeth Commons after midnight, as we pulled away from Greg Cole's townhouse seemed more than coincidental. I chose to consider our options while we drove.

Elana was elated that her sister was alive and had just finished calling Amibeth and sharing the news. "How did you figure it out, Jonah?"

"I didn't have it completely figured out. But, it didn't make sense that she committed suicide, and if the figure in black killed her, there was no good explanation for where that person went. Plus, he knew too much about Andrea."

From the back Greg Cole, who seemed half asleep mumbled, "Why don't you tell me what you figured out. I'll tell you if you've got it right or wrong."

That sounded fair to me. "OK. Andrea saw someone on the front porch who frightened her. She figured that with the flood and all, calling 911 wouldn't get a response, so she got her gun, opened the door, and invited the person in black into her townhouse—at gunpoint. They were walking from the front hall toward the living room when the power went out. The figure in black took that opportunity to grab for the gun and Andrea shot her and killed her."

"Her?" Elana hadn't figured out that the first figure in black was female.

"Sure, it was a woman. It had to be in order for the paramedics to buy it when Greg intentionally mis-identified the body as being Andrea. That explains

278

how the person was shot in the middle of the chest. It's almost impossible to turn a gun around a hundred and eighty degrees toward the person who is holding it without breaking their wrist. The figure in black died almost instantly, and that left Andrea in the dark, literally, trying to figure out what to do next."

Greg Cole said nothing but Elana interrupted. "But why not just call the police at that point. They might not come for an intruder but now that there was a dead intruder the police would have to come."

I tapped Elana on the shoulder to get her attention and mouthed the words, "We're being followed," before I responded to her comment. "Right. The police would come for a dead intruder, but for some reason she didn't call. Maybe she didn't trust the police. Maybe she was afraid she'd be in trouble because of the shooting. Greg, help us out here."

"Andrea knew she wouldn't be in trouble. The person she shot had killed several people. Andrea just didn't trust the police. She decided she had to get away. It worked pretty well, until tonight."

I continued to work through my scenario of what had happened. "OK. So there was Andrea with a dead body at her feet and she decided to put some of her own clothes on the body of the woman in black. As I remember from the police report, it was just a robe. The plan was to get the body identified as being her. Obviously, the two of you worked that out when you went around to the back of the townhouse."

"She was afraid that someone else might come after her, a guy named Hamilton. So I told her to wipe down the gun, and put it in the hands of the woman in black. Once she did that, the fingerprints on the gun would match the fingerprints of the dead body, and I could identify it as being her and throw Hamilton off the trail for a while. Plus, the tests on the woman in black would be positive for gunpowder since her hands were on the gun when Andrea pulled the trigger. It would look consistent with her being the one holding the gun."

"That's pretty good. That was quick thinking. Where'd you get that idea?"

"CSI. I watch a lot of TV. Until Andrea and I started dating I didn't get out much. Anyway, Andrea said that she had been fingerprinted once. We figured that in a day or so they would run fingerprints of the corpse and find out it wasn't Andrea. But because the flood disrupted everything, they never got around to running the prints. I told them it was Andrea and they just assumed it was Andrea."

CSI shows had changed the world of criminal law. Juries were demanding forensic evidence to establish guilt, and criminals were taking precautions to avoid leaving forensic evidence behind. On television, the CSI's always found the guilty party. In real life, the demand for a DNA match meant that the guilty often went free. In this case, Greg had learned enough from watching television to design a plan good enough to confuse the medical examiner and the police.

I continued my guesstimate of what had happened. "So Andrea hid in the closet or the pantry."

"Pantry. Andrea's very claustrophobic. Hey, why are you two laughing. That's not funny."

I should have figured out that Andrea would have picked the large pantry rather than the small closet "Sorry. One of us up here is very claustrophobic, too. We had an extremely bad experience one time related to that. We're not laughing at Andrea. We're laughing at ourselves."

"Good. Andrea's a wonderful woman. She's a little quirky, but there's nothing wrong with that."

"Nothing wrong with that. So she stayed hidden while you searched downstairs and David Johns searched upstairs. You knew she was hiding in the pantry but you told Officer Johns that the place was empty. Then, sometime in the middle of the night, she snuck out."

"You got it. I figured she'd take off and that I'd never see her again. I mean, when I came to the back door right after the shots were fired, we just talked a little while and she begged me to help her out by telling the cops that the dead body was her. But around three in the morning she rang my doorbell and we've been together since. I've been working at my job, but I'm out there every night. When no one figured out that the body wasn't her, we figured maybe that was good. Maybe, whoever had come looking for her would figure she was dead. That's why I went up for the funeral. To make sure no one opened the casket."

Elana was following the tale. "OK. Then tonight someone who worked with the woman in black, and who hadn't figured it all out, came looking for information and you got him with the light saber."

"There's only one little problem that I can't figure out, Greg. The autopsy describes a thirty-five year old woman who had breast implants. Did they send a clone of Andrea Cain, or did something happen to the report."

There was no reply from the back of the car. Finally Greg Cole said, "Something happened to the report."

I considered the possibilities. There was really just one option. "Hacked the system! The police told me you were a computer guy. You got into the system and edited the report between the time it was typed up and the time it got sent to the Nashville Police. Way to go, Greg." If I hadn't been driving I would have given him a high five.

"Are you kidding? They have one of the most secure systems in the world. No one could hack into that system."

I didn't want to argue, but any system and any computer that connects to the Internet can be hacked. "Are you saying someone did it from the inside?"

"Not naming names, but you might assume that us Star War folks include a lot of computer geeks."

Before the man in black arrived on the scene, I had been thinking that Greg Cole knew too many intimate details of Andrea Cain's life. I had started to consider that he had learned them AFTER the shooting, not before. Without Greg Cole's explanation, the autopsy report had me confused. Now, it all fell into place.

About three miles short of Holladay, I announced that we would be pulling off at the rest stop near milepost 130. Greg Cole spoke from the back seat. "Why are we doing that? We'll almost be at Andrea's by then."

"We've been followed. A black SUV has been behind us since we left Harpeth Commons. It's time to deal with whoever is in that car."

"Then why are we pulling off at a rest stop. Wouldn't we be safer going on to Andrea's?"

"I don't want to lead him all the way there. If something goes wrong, this is safer for Andrea."

"The guy I blinded had a gun, and if this is his partner, he's going to be angry! Are you sure you know what you are doing?"

Elana answered for us. "Being angry makes you stupid. He's interested in you and he's interested in where we're going. We know what we're doing. Been there. Done that. Got the T-shirt." As if to emphasize her point, Elana stretched, pulling her T-shirt taut against her breasts. "And we have two guns and a light saber. Only one of him."

I pulled the car off the highway and eased it to a stop in front of the rest room. As if she needed a pit stop, Elana exited via the passenger door and ran inside. Over her shoulder she yelled "May the force be with you."

A little luck wouldn't hurt, either.

Chapter Fifty-One

The SUV parked a few spaces past us, on the driver's side. A tall man wearing a black shirt, a light black jacket, and black slacks got out of the SUV, walked to my side of the Lexus and tapped on the window. Through the glass I could hear him yelling, "One of your tail-lights is out." I rolled down the window, and he continued. "I was riding behind you. Wanted to let you know. There's usually a cop out here running a speed trap. Just want to save you a ticket. You ought to come out and take a look."

My hands were folded in front of me. My gun was in my right hand, hidden by my left elbow. It was aimed at his abdomen. "Thanks. I'll take my chances. Soon as my wife gets back from the rest room, we're out of here."

He had expected me to get out of the car. He reached inside of his coat and started to pull a gun.

I opened the door quickly knocking him to the ground. I exited the car with my gun aimed at his chest. "Take your gun from the holster, thumb and index finger on the grip, and put it on the ground. Now!"

"Or else what? You'll shoot me?"

"No. I'll borrow the laser gun from my friend and put your eyes out."

From behind his car I heard Elana yell, "Car is empty."

"Put your damn gun on the ground and stand up, slowly."

Having no alternative, he followed instructions.

"Now, why did you follow us from Bellevue almost halfway to Memphis?" I liked letting him think we were headed to Memphis.

"I can't tell you. I'm authorized by a government agency to find out what happened at Mr. Cole's townhouse the night of May 3rd. Beyond that, I can't say anything."

"Which agency?" Except for the fact that the man in black had taken a shot at Greg Cole's townhouse, it was a plausible story.

"I'm not authorized to tell you."

"Do you have a badge?"

Softly, he muttered, "No."

"So, basically, you're just a guy who tried to pull a gun on me at a rest stop." Time to bluff. I raised the gun and pointed it at his nose. "Give me a reason not to shoot you."

His eyes widened. "Call my boss. It's on speed dial. Number one." He stood up, and with his left hand, he offered me his cell phone.

When I reached for it, he threw a right hand punch at my head. Throwing a punch at someone holding a gun on you is never a smart move. In order for the move to work it requires a very quick punch, the element of surprise, and the fact that the person holding the gun is unwilling to use it. He was lacking on all three accounts. I ducked, and pushed him to the ground. I restrained myself and didn't shoot him in the foot. My failure to shoot him had convinced him that I was unwilling to fire my weapon. So much for restraint. He came back at me.

I lowered the gun and with full force I punched him in the left eye. I heard a crunching sound as the punch landed. He dropped to the ground, moaning.

"You can still drive away from this. For the last time, what is this about?"

"We needed to find out what happened to the woman we sent to the townhouse."

"Whom are you working for?" I realize that most investigators would have said "Who are you working for?" but there was no reason to use poor grammar.

"I'm not talking."

But maybe his cell phone was. I speed dialed number one. A male voice answered. "Hamilton here."

"Hamilton, did you send two guys to a townhouse in Bellevue, Tennessee tonight?"

"Who is this?"

"The guy who has a gun aimed at one of the men you sent out to Harpeth Commons tonight."

"What do you want?"

"Information. What is this all about? Six people died on a drug study. Someone killed Andrea Cain because she knew about it." There was no reason to share the fact that Andrea Cain was not dead. "What is this all about?"

He answered in a soft monotone. "I'm not telling you anything."

"Your man here said he was with the government."

"If he misrepresented himself, that's his problem."

Except for my Lexus and the SUV, the rest stop was completely empty. "Your man was very brave." I pulled the trigger and ended the call. I'd let Hamilton worry about whether or not his man was dead.

I had fired into the ground and the man in the black shirt was alive. The problem was what to do with him. I doubted that he would tell us anything useful. I took the SIM card out of his cell phone, and placed the phone behind the rear wheel of my Lexus. If there was a GPS feature, once I backed up, it wasn't going to be of any use to anyone.

"Sweetie, get me the handcuffs from the glove compartment." I stood over the man in black. "Turn over so I can cuff you." He offered no resistance. I removed his wallet to check his I.D. The wallet contained forty-two dollars but no identification. I left the cash and placed the wallet back in his pants. I opened the trunk, took out some duct tape, and used it to cover his mouth and to bind his legs together. Greg Cole and I lifted him and placed him in the back of his SUV.

I considered leaving the man at the rest stop and calling the highway patrol, but it would be over ninety degrees by noon. If the police didn't take our call seriously, he would bake to death in the back of his SUV.

I called Joe Apted and told him what had happened. Then, Elana and Greg drove in the Lexus, and I followed them in the SUV. We reached Andrea's apartment in Holladay a little after two AM. I checked that our captive was secure in back of the SUV and took a call from Joe Apted before going upstairs to Andrea's apartment.

The apartment was much smaller than Andrea's townhouse in Bellevue. It consisted of a living room, a tiny dining area, a small kitchen, a bedroom, and bathroom. The furniture had obviously been purchased from a second hand shop. The apartment was spartan, but had fulfilled its purpose. It had kept Andrea Cain safe for nearly three weeks.

At first, I couldn't tell if Andrea was happy to see Elana and me. She was too busy embracing Greg Cole. Greg was just happy that we had found her unharmed. In his phone call, before we had started out from Bellevue, he had told her about the man in black arriving at his townhouse. He was now telling her about our experience at the rest stop. Eventually, she made her way over to Elana. "Come on. Give me a hug! It seems you're kind of stuck with me."

Greg had started to nap on the sofa. Elana hugged her sister then pointed to Greg and mouthed the words, "Does he know?"

Andrea laughed. "My God. Someone is carrying a bigger secret than I am. That's a change." She shook her head. "No. Just because I'm sharing more about myself these days doesn't mean I'm betraying confidences, Ms. Grey. By the way, congratulations on getting married, and on your CMA award, and on anything else you might have done. I am so proud of you and happy for you." Tears rolled down ACGBC's face as they hugged again. "All I did since you saw me last was get divorced, get myself killed, and get a new boyfriend. In that order." She laughed at the absurdity of the last statement. "Not much to catch up on—except those killings in Chicago. How did you two get involved."

Elana explained that the FBI had invited us to take an unofficial look at the situation. "The FBI thought that if you had been murdered, and hadn't committed suicide, then it was more likely something really had gone on at CMI."

"Damn right something happened at CMI, but it was someone in the government that killed those people. It had to be. Do you think I can trust the FBI?"

I spoke before Elana could answer. "Why do you say it was the government?"

Andrea looked at me, then at Greg Cole, and back at me. "If I tell you why I think it was the government that was involved in those deaths at CMI, you're going to think I'm crazy. Just have the FBI dig up the body that's buried as Andrea Cain. Once they do that, they'll know what I'm talking about. I just hope the FBI isn't behind all this. If they are, we're all going to be in deep shit. I guess it's time to trust someone. May as well trust you and the FBI."

That was a relief. I hadn't been sure that I would be able to sell her on Joe Apted's plan. "Well, I'm glad to hear that, because I've spoken to Joe Apted of the FBI. In addition to bringing him up to date, I wanted to get his advice on what to do with the man in the back of the SUV. We have instructions to wait here for an agent from Memphis before heading back to Nashville. Special Agent Howard Neill is on his way. He should be here in about an hour and a half."

I expected Andrea to be upset that it was Howard Neill that was coming. Instead she laughed and said. "Hope it goes better than the last time he came to meet me. That time I was dead when he showed up." She smiled. "Look, if you can't have a sense of humor and joke about yourself, what's the point of being alive?"

Chapter Fifty-Two

I wanted to learn as much as I could about what happened at CMI before Agent Neill arrived. "Andrea, what Elana and I want to know is how you figured out what was going on with the study. We've been looking at that study inside out and upside down and we can't figure out how the code got broken. And the FBI is at a loss too."

"I don't know either. I never told the FBI that I had figured it out. I just told them that I knew something had happened. The woman in black. She was working at the pharmacy at CMI. That's why—well that's one of the reasons I left CMI."

Elana was trying to put the facts together. "Who was she?"

"You're gonna say I'm crazy if I tell you, but I'm not." Andrea thought it over. "I'll just wait until they exhume the body and you'll find out then. The woman who came to my house that night came there to kill me. That's why I had my gun when I opened the door. And that's why I'm alive today!"

We took turns looking out the window until a black sedan pulled into the parking lot and Special Agent Neill arrived. He was the prototypic FBI agent—six feet tall, dark, and square shouldered. We kept the door on the latch until we had seen his badge, then let him in to the apartment.

He took turns shaking hands with each of us. When he came to Andrea he told her, "You have no idea how glad I am to see you." Andrea smiled somewhat flirtatiously and Agent Neill continued. "Both for your sake and for mine. I got a reprimand for letting you get killed when I was supposed to meet with you in Nashville the weekend of the flood. They're going to have to tear that up since you're alive." He turned to me. "Where's your prisoner?"

I looked out the window and pointed to the black SUV parked in the lot, two cars over from his.

"All right. That's good. We can move him to my car later, and I doubt anyone will see. Don't care if they do. If anyone asks questions, I'll just show my badge. I talked to Joe Apted. I just have one question. Mr. Aaron, are you sure that the man you spoke to when you called on the cell phone was named 'Hamilton'?"

"Absolutely!"

Agent Neill took a seat in the living room and we all followed his lead. "Hamilton! Well, maybe this is starting to make sense. Here's the situation. The man who came to your townhouse tonight, Mr. Cole, the man you surprised with your laser weapon, isn't talking to the police. However, his fingerprints were on file. He's a former police officer from Hutchison, Kansas. Three years ago he led a heroic hostage rescue at a branch of the Bank of America. After that, for practical purposes, he fell off the face of the earth. If I have to bet, we'll find a similar story when we identify the man you have in the back of the SUV. The key is Hamilton."

Elana spoke first. "Who is he?"

"The official FBI position on Hamilton is that he is a lunatic asshole. He used to be with the CIA, but they terminated him. The only reason the FBI knows about him is that after 9/11 all federal agencies shared material. A lot of stuff we thought was bullshit turned out to be true. Did any of you ever hear of Operation Ted Bundy?"

Amibeth had told me about that on our trip back from visiting Margaret Romanov. I had told her it was an urban legend.

Agent Neill continued. "Almost twenty years ago, Hamilton had the absurd idea that instead of executing serial killers, the CIA should use them as hired assassins. His reasoning was that if they got caught and killed, no big loss, and if they were successful—it would be wonderful. Fortunately, he never got anywhere with that one. No one in their right mind would turn over a serial killer to the CIA. Operation Ted Bundy went nowhere, so Hamilton went a hundred and eighty degrees in the other direction and decided to recruit civilians or law enforcement types who had performed heroic acts. He assembled a small squad of agents under his personal direction."

I interrupted. "Holy shit. I think I met the guy. A little over six feet tall? Green eyes? Large birthmark on his right cheek? The guy came to meet with me and offer me a job after I was involved in a shooting in an East Nashville warehouse."

"That's Hamilton, Mr. Aaron. Why did you turn him down? Just curious."

I almost had accepted the offer. My girlfriend had dumped me. I had once considered working for the FBI. "Because by charter, the CIA is not supposed to conduct operations within the United States, and foreign languages are one of the many things at which I'm no good. When he told me it was ok to be working in the United States, I told him to take a hike. I told him that going to prison was something I didn't think I would do very well either."

"You may be right on that one, Mr. Aaron. In any case, the FBI has no idea why Hamilton and his crew got involved with a drug study at CMI. Of course, right now Joe Apted and I are the only two people in The Bureau who know that Hamilton is involved with this mess. Once we have our analysts on it, we'll figure out the motive, hopefully."

From the time Agent Neill was halfway through his story, Andrea had started smiling. "Then I'm not crazy after all."

"Excuse me, Ms. Cain. No one in the Bureau thinks you're crazy. We did doubt your story at first, but when the statisticians said that there was a one in six hundred thousand chance that things would come out the way they did, we started believing you. The fact that we didn't accept the conclusion that you committed suicide indicates just how seriously we took you. You're a very smart woman who uncovered a dangerous plot. If it hadn't been for you, Hamilton and his friends would have gotten away with it. No one thinks you're crazy."

Andrea was shaking her head and pursing her lips. "No! Not because of that! Because of whom I saw. The woman in black. Now I understand!" Andrea looked as determined as she sounded.

Agent Neill interrupted. "Well, I'm sure it's some sort of obscure hero who got taken in by Hamilton's story of saving the world by unconventional means."

"NO! Operation Ted Bundy wasn't an urban legend. It was real too. The woman I shot to death at my townhouse, the woman I saw around the pharmacy at CMI, was Muffin Mancuso. You're going to find out when you exhume the body, so I may as well tell you now. She was a serial killer. Amos Bunden called her The Unforgiving." She turned to Elana and me. "I would have told you before Agent Neill arrived, but you would have said I was out of my mind. Hamilton must have found her, faked her death, and signed her up."

I began to consider how the FBI could have messed up the forensics of the case.

Elana spoke before I could say anything. "Andrea, Muffin Mancuso couldn't have been recruited by Hamilton and the CIA. She died in a car crash."

Andrea threw her hands up in the air, "I knew you'd never believe me. It was Muffin Mancuso! When she got to my townhouse that night she told me to put my gun away, that I should know she wouldn't hurt me. I know Muffin Mancuso. I told you that I had slept with her back when I was living in Memphis. She was lying about not hurting me. She came to kill me. She had a loaded gun in her purse. I found it after I shot her. I have it now. If I hadn't fired my gun when she grabbed it, she would have killed me. It all makes sense now. I thought the government was involved, and I was sort of right."

Getting the prison system to release a serial killer into the custody of the CIA hadn't worked out for The Agency. It seemed that we weren't the only ones who had solved the case of The Unforgiving. Hamilton had apparently done the same thing. For our efforts, we had a working relationship with the FBI. For Hamilton's efforts, he had gotten the services of a serial killer. It was the technical details of faking the death that had me momentarily perplexed, and I had a question for Greg Cole. "Greg, you saw the original autopsy report. What color were the eyes of the woman in black?"

"Damnedest thing. I thought it was a typo at first. It said one eye was green and one eye was brown. But then it said she had been wearing a brown contact lens to make them look the same, so I guess it had to be accurate." He was squeezing Andrea's hand to offer moral support to her seemingly outrageous claim.

There couldn't be that many women who, like Muffin Mancuso, had eyes of different colors. Despite the forensic evidence that had come to light in 2004, it seemed that Muffin Mancuso had been alive until that night at Andrea Cain's townhouse. Agent Neill was back on the phone.

Elana looked at her sister and looked at me. "Jonah, she's wrong isn't she? Muffin Mancuso died in a car crash. They had DNA and dental evidence. Right?"

I thought it over. We were in the business of faking deaths, but we hardly held a monopoly on the practice. "No. They didn't have perfect DNA evidence. That's why Amos Bunden had argued to exhume the body. Remember? The FBI had DNA that had been obtained from one of the crime scenes. The DNA from Muffin Mancuso's parents showed that The Unforgiving was their daughter. Since they had no other children, Muffin Mancuso was The Unforgiving. That part was proven."

Elana interrupted. "So what's the problem?"

"The Mancuso's didn't want their daughter's remains disturbed. The FBI relied on dental x-rays to make the identification of her body. What they had were dental x-rays from the corpse, and dental x-rays provided by Muffin Mancuso's dentist in Memphis. They matched. The x-rays that the dentist provided could have been switched to create a phony identification. That's why Amos Bunden wanted the body exhumed. If Andrea's right, and I believe her, those dental x-rays were definitely switched. Hamilton likely had dental x-rays on a corpse, got that body into Muffin Mancuso's car, and got the dental x-rays from that corpse into the chart that was in the office of Muffin Mancuso's dentist."

Agent Neill was off the phone. "In addition to exhuming the body in Andrea Cain's grave in Chicago, my boss in Memphis is going to get a court order to exhume whoever is buried in Muffin Mancuso's grave. I was listening to you while I was on the phone. I had heard from Mr. Apted that you're an expert on faking deaths, Mr. Aaron. Did you come up with that idea about changing the dental x-rays just now? That was pretty good."

"It's not even my original idea. Sue Grafton, the mystery writer, used it in one of her early novels back in the eighties. I think it was *B is for Burglar*, or maybe it was *C is for Corpse*. In that story someone broke into a dentist's office, and dental x-rays were switched leading the police to misidentify a burned corpse. Nowadays, if a dentist has his x-rays on a digital system, all you have to do is hack his system and getting a misidentification is really easy."

I was about to deny having carried out that type of plan when Agent Neill interrupted. "Assuming you're right, it's just another bit of evidence tying Hamilton to this whole thing. In terms of that study at CMI, we don't know why and we don't know how, but at least we know who, and that's a good start."

We walked down the stairs to our cars. It was still dark. Agent Neill, Greg Cole, and I moved the man in black from the back of the SUV to the trunk of

Agent Neill's car. I gave Agent Neill the SIM card from the cell phone so he could try and reach Hamilton again.

Agent Neill headed back to Memphis with his prize. As I loaded Andrea's bags in the trunk of my car, ACGBC broke into laughter at the sight of my license plate. "T181. My God. That's hysterical. How long have you had that license plate, Jonah."

"Five years, ever since I figured out it was supposed to be TL 81."

"What was supposed to be TL 81?" Greg Cole had no idea what we were talking about.

I turned to Elana and Andrea. "We really ought to tell him the story. This isn't fair."

Andrea looked at Greg. "He knows about the thallium and about Daddy. He just doesn't know about the pendants and who my sisters are."

And so, on the ride back to Nashville, we told Greg the story of the Caruthersville Bridge and how Andrea's sisters were AJ and Amy Elizabeth Golden.

"So, I've been with AJ all night and didn't know it. That's kind of neat. No wonder you figured out that Andrea was alive. You guys are professionals at faking a death. We're amateurs, but we did pretty well, didn't we?"

"You did very well. Your only mistake was that when you were talking to me about Andrea, you told me things that I was certain she hadn't shared with anyone before the shooting. That meant that you had contact with her after the shot was fired, and that meant she was still alive. Of course, it still makes no sense. Why on earth would someone, especially a former CIA agent, kill several people in order to sabotage an experimental drug study? What's the point? And we still don't know how they broke the code."

Everyone else slept or tried to sleep in the car while I drove back to Nashville. Despite the fact that I am a little paranoid and don't accept food or drink from suspects, I am not one to believe in government conspiracies. I believe that men walked on the moon; it was not faked at a Hollywood studio. I do not believe in a government cover-up related to the Kennedy assassination. I do not believe that aliens landed at Roswell—but I might be wrong on that one.

Now, we had evidence of a plot by a CIA agent, presumably a former CIA agent, to sabotage a drug study. I knew what the phrase "rogue agent" meant. It meant an agent whose actions would be disavowed by the CIA. At this point, I really didn't care what the FBI did with the information. CMI and Bauer Laboratories had to be told that the study had been compromised, but beyond that, I didn't care if the FBI covered up the story of the murders or not. One rogue agent, Muffin Mancuso, was dead. Another rogue agent was blind. A third rogue agent was in FBI custody, though I wasn't sure what the charges would be. For all I knew, they might conclude that the actions at CMI represented a terrorist conspiracy to disrupt health care and ship him off to Guantanamo.

Our investigation into the death of ACGBC and the deaths at CMI had been reduced to two questions. How was it done? Why was it done? One of Amibeth's mantras was that sometimes there is no why, that things just happen, but there had to be a reason why the 886-JHG study had been sabotaged.

Andrea no longer had her marriage to Eric Cain to protect, and there was no reason that the three Golden sisters couldn't have a relationship. Our work appeared to be done. The FBI had the resources to investigate the murders at CMI; we certainly didn't. All in all, it had been a very good two days of work. I had no idea how profitable it was going to turn out to be.

Chapter Fifty-Three

A little after noon, I was getting out of bed, when I heard the sounds of a woman in the throes of sexual ecstasy. I assumed Andrea and Greg were enjoying themselves in the guest bedroom. I put on a robe, went to the living room to tease Elana about how noisy her sister was, and found my wife and Andrea drinking coffee and giggling like schoolgirls. Andrea looked up at me. "Sorry if I woke you. It's your wife's fault."

"It is not my fault! I just asked her a simple question and she went all *When Harry Met Sally* on me."

I thought back to what I had been hearing. Considering the answer, I wondered what Elana's question had been.

"Your wife and I were talking about my years in Memphis and she wanted to know if I got off when I was with clients. I told her sometimes yes and usually no, but that I had a pretty good repertoire of fake orgasms to let the guy think he was making my night. That was level 4 of 5."

I chuckled. "Very impressive. I'm sure any man hearing that up close and personal would think he was a super stud."

"That's the general idea. And hopefully super stud would tip well or call back and ask for me again." She returned to her coffee as if we were having a casual conversation. I guess we were.

I poured myself a cup of coffee and walked over to join them. "Does level 5 of 5 make the neighbors bang on the walls?"

"No!" She rubbed her eyes before continuing. I doubted anyone had had much sleep. I noticed that even so, she had already washed her hair and gotten made up as if for a night out. "It's actually quieter, but it involves a lot of grabbing and scratching and rolling my eyes back in my head. Because it leaves scratches, I could only do it if I knew for sure that the guy didn't have a woman at home. And there was always a risk that he'd call 911 if he thought I was dead. I had that happen once. Let me tell you, I had my clothes back on and I was out of there in seconds." She gave a little laugh and shook her head. "I used to advise the other girls to stick to level 4." Andrea pointed to Elana. "By the way, considering what she saw in her bedroom when she was a little girl, your wife seems to have grown up with a surprisingly healthy attitude toward sex. But you obviously know that after all these years."

"It didn't take me years to figure that one out."

"I suppose not." Andrea got up from the table. "Well, I'm going to leave you two alone. I'm going to go back in the bedroom, call my attorney and tell him I'm not dead. See if I have to sign anything. Then I'm going to call Eric and then call Gail Riley. They cared enough to come to my funeral. They deserve to know I'm alive. And I have to call Vanderbilt and see about getting my job back. We're supposed to stay here until we hear from the FBI, right?"

I confirmed that that was the general plan. I wasn't expecting trouble, but I wanted to stay in the safest place I knew. She gave me a hug as she passed.

As she hugged me, Elana yelled at her, "Remember what I said about my husband!"

An exasperated look crossed Andrea's face. "It was a dream. It was a fucking dream. And it was your dream!" She stopped in mid-thought. "Oh, you're kidding me, again. Right?"

"Of course I'm kidding."

As she reached the bedroom door, Andrea looked over her shoulder at me. "You do realize that you married a lunatic, don't you?"

I had had similar thoughts about my wife from the time we had planned the fake suicide at the Caruthersville Bridge, but I would never refer to her as a lunatic—at least not to her face. "I prefer to think of it as being married to a beautiful, brilliant, hot woman with a great imagination. She makes life interesting."

"Whatever! I'm glad you appreciate her. It's good to see her happy." Andrea returned to the guest bedroom. Even though it was mid-day, Andrea was wearing high heels, a pink v-neck blouse, and tight black slacks.

Elana was wearing no makeup and had an Amibeth Tour 2005 baseball cap on her head. She was barefoot, wearing jeans, and had on a T-shirt with a picture of a dog that resembled Layla and read 'I don't give a shih-tzu.' I kissed her on the cheek and started to look over her shoulder at her computer screen. "Good morning, beautiful. Don't you feel a little underdressed around your sister?"

"She's a trip, but she is who she is. Actually, it's kind of sad the way she got dressed up this morning. For the last few weeks she was so scared that someone would come looking for her, that she hadn't worn anything that she couldn't run in. She's been living in jeans and sneakers and carrying a purse with a gun in it. Just take it as a sign that she feels safe with us." Elana took a sip of coffee and focused on the computer screen.

Unexpectedly, Andrea stuck her head out of the door from the bedroom. "You tell him that I helped you. Just because he's yours doesn't mean he has to think I'm a dumb blond. I am a nurse." She was giggling as she closed the door.

I gestured toward the papers that Elana had scattered in front of her on the coffee table. "What's this? And what is she talking about? Helped you with what?"

"Oh, we figured out how the 886-JHG study was sabotaged, and now I'm trying to figure out why."

I thought back to the events of the previous night. As best as I could remember, when we went to sleep we were still confused as to how someone had managed to kill patients receiving 886-JHG at CMI. "Who figured that out—and when?"

"She and I figured it out this morning, but you share in the credit because if you hadn't been screwing my sister, I never could have done it."

"I wasn't . . ."

"Of course you weren't! It was my dream. Don't you remember my poking you in the ribs and waking you up and telling you that I forgave you for boinking Andrea because it helped me figure it out?"

I didn't remember. "Care to explain?"

"Simple. First, we were both real old and living in a retirement home."

"How old?"

"Old! I don't know, Jonah. Don't ask questions like that. It was a dream. We were old, like eighty or something. Can I tell my story?"

I nodded.

"Anyway, I walked into the room that you and I shared—in the retirement home—and there you were, doing it with Andrea. And I got furious!"

"I can imagine."

"Yeah, but not for why you are thinking. See in my dream, we were in our eighties and you had problems getting it up for me, but with my sister, you were doing just fine."

I had learned from experience that when Elana had a weird dream, the best course was to go with the flow. Usually her dreams were quickly forgotten. Occasionally her dreams led to a plot twist on *Jonah Slammer, Dangerous Man.* "No wonder you were in a bad mood in the dream. You weren't getting any."

"No, that wasn't the problem! Since you couldn't get it up, you were giving me tons of oral, so I was happy as a lark. It was an ego sort of thing. I couldn't get you hard, but my sister with the big plastic tits could. It hurt my feelings. So I started yelling at you, and you explained that you had taken Viagra. Are you following me?"

"Yes, I'm following you, but how does this relate to what happened at CMI?"

"I'm getting to that part. You told me you were taking Viagra, and I said to you, 'Jonah, honey, you know you're not supposed to do that because you take those nitrate pills because of your bad heart.' See, even though you were fooling around with my sister I was looking out for you, because I love you so much. Wasn't I sweet? And actually I felt relieved because it was the medicine not Andrea, that got you hard. Of course, thinking about it now, I suppose I should have been angry because you didn't take Viagra for me, and you took it for her, but since it was a dream, you can't blame me for not being totally logical. Right?"

I began to suspect that there was no dream, and that Elana had solved the problem while awake, and then made up the story to humbly explain away her brilliance. I was also totally confused as to how this related to CMI. "Go ahead."

"Well, that's when it came to me. And it's all thanks to you banging my sister." She gave me a kiss. "And this morning I told her that if she tried doing it for real, she would go over the ninth floor railing, and she helped me figure out what was done."

"I still don't get it. How does that solve anything?'

"You don't get it?"

I tried figuring out what there was to get. "No!"

"It's simple. You know all those commercials, where someone is talking about being ready when the time is right. Those commercials tell you that if you're taking nitrates for heart disease, you shouldn't take any of those other erectile dysfunction drugs. I never really paid that much attention. I just know that if you take Viagra and nitrates you can get a dangerous drop in blood pressure."

"I'm still lost. This is fascinating, but I need a clue. What does your story have to do with anything?"

"Everything! The point is if you gave nitrates to everyone in the world, it would only hurt the patients taking an erectile dysfunction drug."

I got it. "And there might be a way to give everybody on the 886-JHG study something, and only the patients getting the experimental drug would have problems. You wouldn't have to know what drug each patient was getting in order to mess up the study. You wouldn't have to break the code. That's what you're saying, right?"

"Exactly! Isn't that neat?"

It was a lot better than neat. It was a viable solution to what had been an unsolvable problem. We had been asking the wrong question. We had been trying to figure out how the code had been broken. The correct question was how one could have sabotaged the study without breaking the code, and Elana had found the answer. "Yeah, it is neat. So what drug would do that for 886-JHG? I'm not a doctor, but since you said you figured it out—or the two of you figured it out, there must be some drug that could be used to do that."

"The three of us figured it out. Remember, without you, there was no solution." She laughed. "Andrea and I aren't sure exactly which drug was used, but that's the principle of the thing. Since 886-JHG prolongs the QT interval. All you would have to do is give EVERYONE in the study something to prolong the QT interval. In the patients who weren't getting 886-JHG, the QT interval would start out normal, and if it went up a little bit, nothing would happen. In the patients getting 886-JHG, the QT interval would already be up, but still not dangerously up. If it went higher in response to whatever was done to them, those patients could have fatal irregular heartbeats. You could kill people without even knowing who was getting which drug. You probably wouldn't kill all of them, but you'd kill some of them and . . ."

"And that's exactly what happened at CMI. Six people out of twenty died that way."

"I called Joe Apted. He's having the lab test for drugs that affect the QT interval."

"They didn't do that before?"

"No! They tested for poisons! These drugs aren't poisons. They're just regular drugs that should be avoided in patients with an increased QT interval. Andrea showed me the page in the research protocol that listed all the drugs you aren't supposed to give to patients taking 886-JHG. I had seen the list, but it didn't register at the time. Of course, no one else figured it out. But when the FBI finds one of those drugs in the bottles," she snapped her fingers, "the three of us will have solved the problem of how they did it. They're gonna find something!"

"Hey, do you have the paper Joe faxed us with the number to call at Bauer Labs? There's a reward for getting their drug study going again."

Elana found the page and handed it to me. We had no idea why Hamilton had been involved with sabotaging the study but we could leave that to the FBI. I called Clinical Studies at Bauer Labs, and was put on hold.

Chapter Fifty-Four

Still on hold.

"Elana, can I ask you something?"

"Sure, sweetie. What?"

"Are you ok about last night?"

"What about it?"

"Going around the rest stop with a gun drawn. I was just wanted to know if you were ok with that."

"Of course I'm ok with it. If I wasn't ok with it, I wouldn't have done it. I brought my gun to Greg Cole's on my own. It was my decision. I'm fine. But thanks for asking." She got up and kissed me on the cheek.

"Just checking that you're not taking risks that make you uncomfortable."

"Minimal risks. I'm adventurous, not reckless. But I hear you. When I get pregnant, I'm going to quit working in the field with a gun." Elana had been off the pill for a month and a half.

"Just wanted to be sure you were at peace with it. You ran away from being AJ Golden."

She gave me a half smile. "Yeah. But I was only twenty-one back then, and shooting those two men was the only public thing I had ever done. Now, I've been a singer-songwriter, a wife, and a medical student. Plus, I've worked on *Jonah Slammer* and the movie about the Dana Twins. It's different now. It wouldn't matter to me if everyone knew that Elana Grey used to be AJ Golden."

"Really?"

"Yeah. It would be ok. In fact, right now my medical school friends who know that I work with you and carry a gun think I'm out of my mind. First of all, because they think it's risky and second, because they think I wouldn't have any idea what to do with a gun if I had to use it. If they knew that I was once AJ Golden, it would let them see me for who I am. And killing two people is no big deal anymore. I suspect that at least a half dozen of my classmates have killed people just by making mistakes taking care of patients."

"That's not a reassuring thought."

"Anyway, I wouldn't mind if it came out that I was AJ Golden. Not gonna happen. But no problem if it does."

"Interesting. When you started admiring that AJ Triumphant statue last night, I started wondering where your head was at."

"Neat choice of words. Where my head was at." She laughed. "And don't buy the statue for me as a surprise. It really wouldn't go with the décor. But I did like it . . . Anyway, I've had almost six years free of that part of my past, and I really think that I needed that freedom to get where I am today. The trouble is that there's no way to put it all back together. I can't just become AJ Golden, the girl who shot two serial killers. I would become AJ Golden, the woman who killed two serial killers and then faked her death and hid from her true identity to spark her sister's career. Milton says that would be horrible for Amibeth, so there's no point in doing that. All in all, I'd say it worked out well. We have each other. We have this place, good friends, a great life style, and, as of this morning, I even have Andrea back in my life."

"True enough. But if you could somehow be known for being AJ Golden, without the downside of having been responsible for a hoax, would you go for it?"

"In a heartbeat. But it can't happen. If people knew I was AJ Golden, they would know about the hoax."

"Maybe not. I think I have AJ Golden's ticket back to the land of the living without any negative consequences for Amibeth." I slid a piece of paper in her direction. It was a handwritten draft of a press release I had written while I was lying in bed.

Her eyes lit up as she read it. "That's incredible. I thought I was good at making plans and dreaming up scenarios. Do you think you can get the FBI to go along with this?"

"I don't know, but the FBI is going to owe us. I figured that since we were working for free, they might do us a favor."

"Do you have the rest of a plan? As long as there are no bridges and no surprise birthday parties, you actually are just as good at plans as I am."

"Had to bring up the surprise birthday party, didn't you?"

"Always."

I was on protracted hold. Elana returned to looking over the data. At least we could laugh about some of our worst moments. To me, Elana looked much hotter in jeans and a T-shirt than Andrea did all dolled up and I had minimal interest in the 886-JHG study now that Andrea was alive and we had essentially proven how patients had been murdered. "Hey, you want to go back to bed and get friendly? It seems like you already did a full day's work. They're not picking up. I can call back later."

"We'll get friendly tonight, sweetie! I'm looking at this data. Now I'm trying to figure out what it means, and trying to figure out a motive."

"Fine. I'll hang on."

I stayed on the phone and in another minute or two, Jillian Trent, the Director of Clinical Research at Bauer Labs, picked up. For weeks, she had heard from doctors all over the country that cracking the code regarding who had and who hadn't received 886-JHG was impossible. The theory was that the study had been sabotaged as an inside job.

Bauer Labs had gone so far as to give lie detector tests to every employee in the Clinical Research program. Since it was a condition of continued employment, no one at Bauer had refused to take a lie detector test. The tests had uncovered nothing, and had left morale at absolute zero.

Bauer Labs had tried to organize a repeat study, but without an explanation of what had happened at CMI, doctors weren't interested in putting patients on a clinical trial involving a drug that appeared not to work. Jillian Trent was ecstatic to hear Elana's theory.

After fifteen minutes, I hung up the phone. "That was very interesting. You won't believe what I just found out."

Elana looked up from the papers she had been poring over. "What?"

"Bauer Labs and the FBI labs both have fluid taken from the bottles that were used in the 886-JHG study. Bauer is going start an analysis immediately. If they come up with a drug that would be especially dangerous in patients with an elevated QT interval, we are in line for a substantial reward."

"Yeah. How much?" Elana was back to looking at the papers trying to make sense out of the data.

"I don't want to get your hopes up, but it's a lot. What exactly are you looking at cutie?"

She didn't even crack a smile at my pun. "Trying to figure out what happens now that the results from CMI are excluded from that multi university study. Those extra deaths at CMI made 886-JHG look worthless. But early deaths aren't the whole story. Another issue is how the drug affects the overall survival of the patients. I have all this data that was available on the internet." She pointed at a computer printout. "If you exclude the data from CMI, which seems not only reasonable, but necessary now that we think we know what happened, the average survival is nine months in the group getting chemotherapy plus 886-JHG and seven months in the group just getting the chemotherapy. Remember, these were all patients with advanced lung cancer so that's not out of line with what would be expected."

"So what you're saying is that the drug actually works. It's not a cure for cancer, but it adds two months to survival."

"Right. And if the study gets repeated, or if the FDA decides looks at what happened overall and kicks out the information from CMI, the drug will probably get FDA approval. There's a lot of money involved. Money is a reasonable motive for murder, but I don't see how. It seems backwards. I can just about imagine a drug company killing people in the control group to make their drug look good. But who would kill people getting the drug to make a drug look bad?"

We had reached another dead end. It was time to get back to basic investigative principles. Follow the money. "If it is about money, how much money are we talking about?"

"I'm not sure. 886-JHG never had a price tag on it. It was an experimental drug, so for purposes of the study, they had to give it away for free."

We had no way to determine what the drug would sell for or how much potential income Bauer Labs had lost. But I had a way to estimate it. "Bauer stock is publicly traded. Its net profits are public information. If we look up the company's net profits, look up the percentage drop in Bauer stock when it was announced that the drug didn't work, multiply the net profits by the percent drop in the stock, we will have an estimate of what the profits on 886-JHG were expected to be."

With Bauer earning profits of approximately $30 billion a year, and the stock having fallen about ten percent when the results of the 886-JHG study were announced, it looked like the drug was projected to generate about $3 billion a year in profits if it got approved. Billion with a B. Unfortunately, I had no idea who could have made money by—for lack of a better word—killing the drug.

We checked that those astronomical numbers were consistent with the market for drugs. Profit margins are high in the pharmaceutical industry. To make three billion dollars in profits, the drug company would have to sell ten billion dollars worth of drug. There are approximately 200,000 new cases of lung cancer in the United States each year. Most of them die. If all 200,000 of them got 886-JHG at some point in their disease, that would work out to fifty thousand dollars per patient in order to generate ten billion in sales. The first time we got that result, we thought we had made a mathematical error, but we hadn't. We called my father who informed us that some anti-cancer drugs cost over a hundred thousand dollars per treatment. 886-JHG was a relative bargain.

Unfortunately, that got us nowhere. For half an hour we kicked around ideas. The best we could speculate was that someone had tried to extort money from Bauer by threatening to mess up their study. Bauer felt the study was tamper proof and had refused to pay. Somebody, perhaps Hamilton, went through with the threat. There were two basic problems. The FBI hadn't told us of a threat to Bauer Labs, and there was no reason for Hamilton to do it. We decided to give up for a while.

"Hey you didn't answer my question before. You talked to someone at Bauer. How much are they going to pay us as a reward?"

"You're sure that there are drugs that elevate the QT interval?"

"Lots of them. We're gonna be right. What's the bonus?"

In a simple monotone designed to hide my enthusiasm, I announced, "Twelve million dollars. Bauer was trying to organize a repeat study and were getting nowhere. They needed four hundred patients to do the study, and they estimated it would cost them thirty thousand dollars for each patient to get the job done. So they made the reward equal to the twelve million dollars that a repeat study would cost."

"That's a lot of money!"

"Yeah. But since we estimated that the drug would make them three billion dollars—a year, that's about four tenths of a percent of what they're going to make each year if the drug gets approved."

"Four tenths of a percent?" She did the math in her head. "Then, it's not a lot of money. In fact we're being ripped off . . . No, I'm joking . . . But, that's too much . . . I have no idea what to do with that. It could change us."

"Change us how? What's going to be different? You'll buy lingerie at La Perla instead of the Hustler Hollywood store. How is it going to change us?"

"Quit kidding. You know I buy my lingerie from La Perla anyway. That's not the point."

"And the point is what? It's only money. We already have a lot of money. Nothing will change." I walked over and gave her a hug. "But if you think it's too much, look at the bright side then. First of all, we don't have it yet. No one has proven that your theory about a drug affecting patients with an increased QT interval is right. Secondly, after we give Andrea her share, it will only be eight million. After taxes, our share will be nearer to five million."

Elana started to laugh. "That's still a lot of money. Anyway, I'm not sure we can take it."

"I told you. It won't change anything. What? Are you really worried that if we had more money it would affect how we feel about each other?"

"No! It's only money! It would take a lot more than money to affect how we feel about each other." She paused for a moment. "OK. I've gotten used to the idea. I'm fine if we get it; I'm fine if we don't. And like I said, we may not be able to take it."

I had no idea what Elana was thinking. "Why not?"

"Because medical students and residents and faculty are prohibited from taking so much as a ball point pen from a drug company. Considering that the medical school probably gets a hundred million dollars in grants from drug companies, it's hypocritical. But those are the rules. Personally, I think it's bullshit on the part of the medical school, but it probably applies. Easy come; easy go." Elana snapped her fingers for emphasis.

"Then it's a good thing you're on a leave of absence until July 1, and technically not a med student. Right now you're an employee of Aaron and Associates. We don't have a policy of not working for drug companies. It's our money." I demonstrated that I knew how to snap my fingers just as well as she did.

"What about the fact that Andrea worked for CMI?" Elana had gone from not wanting the money to being sure we could get the money in less than a minute.

"Not a problem. I told Ms. Trent that you were working with someone who had been at CMI and she said that was ok. All that mattered was that we weren't federal employees. I mentioned our unofficial unpaid relationship to the FBI; she said that wasn't a problem."

"So we're eligible to get the money?"

"Looks that way."

"Hey. I know what we can do now."

I leered at her.

"No, not that. We'll do that tonight. Last night was Sunday. We recorded *Jonah Slammer* while we were out."

We had seen the episode get taped at the studio in north Nashville, but it was always fun to see the finished product. "Good idea. I'll see if Andrea and Greg want to join us."

Before I reached the door of the guest bedroom, we both heard the same kind of noises that had heard from the kitchen earlier in the morning.

"Or not."

Chapter Fifty-Five

Early Monday evening, Amibeth returned to Nashville from Seattle. After a tearful reunion with Andrea, she announced that we were not spending a beautiful evening inside the condo. Having take-out on the deck was not an option either. Despite Joe Apted's recommendation to stay in a safe place, we were going out to dinner to celebrate the reunion of the Golden sisters.

Usually Amibeth prefers the tonier places in Nashville but the Sundown Grille also has a larger outdoor serving area and that's where we would eat. At least that's what the Queen of Talk Radio initially told her loyal subjects. To my shock, when I said I was in a mood to both celebrate and drink, and therefore would rather go somewhere in walking distance, she agreed to go to Watermark—across the street.

While the others were finishing getting dressed, I found Amibeth alone in the living room. "What's the occasion? You were too reasonable. I thought you'd just call up a limo when I said I wanted to go somewhere in walking distance."

"A limo is too fancy, Jonah Aaron. I don't want to call attention to myself. Plus, I need to develop my ability to compromise."

This was beyond reasonable. "Is television doing this to you?"

"Not television." Her tone was downcast.

"Did you and Brett break up? You're trying to be human, or at least life-sized, instead of bigger than life." I put my hand on top of her head. "Life-sized."

She sighed and gave me a brief hug. "I knew you were a good detective. Am I that transparent?"

"Not really, but the change is noticeable. I'm sorry. I always figured you two would work everything out. I haven't heard from Brett in a while. What's going on?"

"Janie Barnes."

"Who is Janie Barnes? Never heard of her."

"She's a twenty-five year old computer whiz who invented some software thingy that was the big hit of the Vegas computer show last year. I saw her on TV. She's a sweet nerd. She thinks Brett is sophisticated and cool. He says he is finished with his high maintenance woman. Forever!"

"I'm sorry to hear that. I really am."

"No. It's good actually. Having Brett around brought out the worst in me in some ways. He amplified my flair for the dramatic. I got too much of a kick pushing his buttons at times. I need to do what my sister did. Find someone reliable and stable, but capable of putting up with her occasional craziness. You don't have anyone to fix me up with, do you?"

"Not really." Silently, I counted off my closest friends on my fingers. My brother Barry had been dating an actress for a couple of years. Brian and Melanie Brandenburg had just had a baby. Rickey Stone and Skylar Jones were expecting a child. "Not many unpaired friends in our social circle."

"What about friends with that TV show, *Jonah Slammer*?"

"You think acting types are likely to be reliable and stable?"

"Good point."

"Look, I'm really sorry about you and Brett. Thanks for sharing. Did you tell Elana?"

"Not yet. I didn't want to put a downer on things. She's all excited about having Andrea back in our lives and about this medical thing you're working on." Amibeth managed a weak smile. "For a second there, Jonah Aaron, you were sounding like me on the radio with that 'Thanks for sharing' comment."

"I have rarely missed a show. Not in the whole five years. I always wanted to listen and hear what I had helped create. Plus, how many times can you listen to sports talk radio and hear that the Titans need to get a first rate wide receiver, or that Vince Young can't lead the team."

Elana had entered the room. "Talking football with my sister, sweetie."

I looked at Amibeth for a cue. She shook her head. "Sort of."

"Men are so predictable. But I love you anyway." Elana kissed me on the cheek. The whole group had assembled. It was time to go to dinner.

When I had phoned Joe Apted after leaving the rest stop outside Holladay, he had asked me to watch over Greg and Andrea and keep them in a safe place. However, since I wasn't technically working as a consultant, I felt no obligation to obey FBI suggestions. Amibeth had decided we were going out, and we were going out.

While Monday May 24 was a very good day for Elana, Andrea, and me, it was an extremely bad day for Jeffrey Hamilton. The FBI identified the body in Andrea Cain's grave as being his reclamation project, Muffin Mancuso. Having learned little from the man that Greg Cole had blinded and from the man I had restrained at the rest stop, the FBI used the SIM card I had obtained to call Jeffrey Hamilton and inform him that his only two living associates were in custody and that Muffin Mancuso was dead. They compounded the bad news by telling him that he was about to be indicted on six counts of murder related to the deaths at CMI and requested that he surrender to the FBI. They didn't expect that he would comply.

At that point, Jeffrey Hamilton drove toward the Canadian border. Before he left the ranch house in La Grange, Illinois, where he had been living for the last two years, he called Bauer Labs to claim his reward for solving the mystery of the deaths on the 886-JHG study. To do so, he had to profess knowledge of what had occurred at CMI. The need to make that confession was the reason that he had not attempted to claim the reward previously. Unfortunately for Jeffrey Hamilton, he had reached Jillian Trent forty-one minutes after I had spoken to her.

Jeffrey Hamilton was detained by Customs' Agents in Port Huron, Michigan, as he tried to leave the country. In a lawsuit entitled *Hamilton v. Bauer Laboratories, Elana Grey, Jonah Aaron, Andrea Cain, and the Federal Bureau of Investigation*, Hamilton claimed that Elana and I were employees of the FBI, and not eligible for any reward money, and that the twelve million dollars should therefore go to him. At the time we were served with papers, in late May, I was upset at the thought of having to give up the reward, but was intrigued by the idea that Elana would end up telling a judge or a jury about her dream. I thought that hearing Elana's testimony might be worth giving back some of the money—but not all of it.

In a motion for summary judgment—legalese for asking the court to throw Hamilton's entire case in the trash can—Elana and I were able to affirm that we were doing a favor for Joe Apted and that at no time had I claimed to be working for the FBI. Furthermore, while the FBI had told me to keep Andrea and Greg in my condo and out of harm's way, we very publicly went to dinner at Watermark on Monday night. Clearly I was not protecting anybody for the FBI. The court ruled that Elana and I were not acting on behalf of the FBI and therefore we were entitled to the reward.

The dismissal of his lawsuit was a disaster for Jeffrey Hamilton. He had planned to use the reward money to finance his defense in the criminal case which he knew was forthcoming. The forty-one minutes between our two phone calls cost him not only the reward, but also a considerable amount of time.

Had Elana taken me up on my initial offer to go back to the bedroom, and had I hung up the phone before talking to Jillian Trent, Jeffrey Hamilton would not only be a rich man, he might be a free man. Good lawyers are expensive, but they can do wonders in complex criminal cases. When Elana declined my invitation for some afternoon delight, I had stayed on the line waiting for someone to pick up the phone. Hamilton ended up with a federal public defender whose only success in the case was in getting the death penalty off the table.

Whether Elana and I made love early Monday afternoon or late Monday afternoon was of no consequence to our relationship. For Jeffrey Hamilton, it was like a butterfly flapping its wings in Hawaii and a typhoon hitting the Federal Penitentiary in Marion, Illinois, where he now resides, having accepted a plea bargain of thirty years to life.

It would be Tuesday afternoon before we heard from Joe Apted. Joe informed us that the even numbered bottles from CMI, the bottles that were scheduled to be administered on the night shift, had been found to contain both cisapride and furosemide. Cisapride, a drug used to promote gastric emptying, had been taken off the market in the United States because of its tendency to increase the QT interval. Furosemide is a safe and powerful diuretic that causes the body to lose potassium. A low level of potassium makes it more likely that an increased QT interval will produce a fatal cardiac arrhythmia. Bauer Laboratories concluded that Elana, Andrea, and I had "provided substantial information leading to the re-evaluation of research studies regarding the effectiveness of 886-JHG in treating lung cancer."

In legal terms that meant that we were entitled to the reward. Joe thanked us for helping to solve the murders at CMI. I faxed him the proposed press release that Elana and I had put together, and, after calling Elana and me "lunatics," he agreed to release a modified version of the statement to the press on Saturday June 12th. Considering our ability to use various forms of media to influence public perception, that was all that we needed.

Chapter Fifty-Six

Tuesday night, we dined outdoors at the Sundown Grille. During dinner, Amibeth gave a toast to Andrea. "I started working on this great eulogy for Andrea on Saturday afternoon, but it seems my brother-in-law and his wife messed it up by finding her alive. I'll settle for that. So, I'm saving those remarks for my fundraiser. So, at this time, all I'm going to say to this year's winner of the No Cause for Shame Award is this: Welcome back, Andrea. I love you."

Amibeth continued. "As for my other sister," she looked around the restaurant and realized that people might hear what she was saying, "No Cause for Shame Awards are like Nobel Prizes. You can't get them posthumously. So just let me say, that if AJ were alive, I'd give her an award, too."

The dinner conversation was basically light hearted. We talked about Amibeth's new television show, and the people with whom she would be working. We discussed the fact that instead of responding to callers, she would be conducting interviews and presenting features. Amibeth had told her sisters about the end of her relationship with Brett, and the women were joking about potential new beaus. We talked about the fact that *Jonah Slammer* was ending and that Elana was returning to medical school and would not be writing for *Bethany Fibonacci*. Despite prodding from Amibeth, Elana and I would not reveal anything about what would happen in the series finale of Jonah Slammer and would not discuss how Bethany Fibonacci tied into the series. Those were the two issues of greatest interest to the fans. We are, after all, very good at keeping secrets.

The discussion didn't turn to the study of 886-JHG until Amibeth had paid for the check and we had returned, in two taxis, to the condo. Amibeth had heard all of the details of our investigation, and realized that she might have a major news story on her hands. She wanted to understand one thing—motive.

We were seated on the deck, overlooking the lights of the city, and Amibeth was doing her best impression of an investigative reporter. "So, Elana, what's your best guess as to why this happened? Why did Hamilton and Muffin Mancuso—and whoever else they were working with—do this?"

Elana presented her hypothesis that having failed to extort money from Bauer Laboratories, Hamilton and company had gone ahead with a plot to sabotage the study. Unfortunately, Joe Apted had checked with Bauer Labs, and they denied that had happened.

Amibeth wasn't buying the theory. "Bauer has no reason to lie at this point. It must be something else. Jonah Aaron, you're the investigator. Why do people commit crimes—in general, I mean?"

"Same reason they do lots of things." I thought about cases I had worked and rattled off some common motives. "Money, love, power, revenge, jealousy."

Amibeth thought for a moment. "What about the money? Who comes out ahead money-wise when the drug study failed?"

Elana interjected. "No one. Or at least no one was selling the stock short to make a profit when Bauer's stock dropped. The FBI looked at that."

Amibeth got up walked to the railing and looked over the city. I didn't know if she was admiring the view, or thinking about the sabotaged drug study. "Elana, what's the average age of patients with lung cancer? Approximately."

My favorite medical student responded, "I don't know. Probably sixty-five or so."

Amibeth continued looking at the city. "Well then, I'll tell you who made money when the drug failed. The Federal Government made money. That's who."

I had not known Amibeth to be a government conspiracy theorist. "How do you figure that, Amibeth?"

"It's like this. If the drug raises healthcare costs, private insurers raise premiums. They come out the same in the long run. But, assuming Elana is right . . ."

Elana had looked it up on her smart phone. "Sixty-six years."

"Thanks, Elana." Amibeth continued. "Roughly half the patients with lung cancer are old enough to be on Medicare. A new expensive drug, approved by the FDA, means more costs to the government. You said the drug would cost ten billion a year. If the average age is sixty-six about half of that is paid by Medicare. That's five billion dollars a year. That's fifty billion dollars over the next decade. If 886-JHG proved to be successful, fifty billion dollars would get spent over the next ten years, just so some people could spend a couple more months dying of cancer."

I had listened to Amibeth for years on the radio and usually had a good idea of what was coming. This was different territory, and I was seeing a new side of my sister-in-law. Her theory might be totally wrong, but she had a provocative analysis. It was my turn to talk. "Amibeth. Maybe I'm just drinking the Kool-Aid here, but as crazy as that sounds, it makes sense. If you were an ex-CIA guy, like Hamilton, trying to get back in the good graces of the government, or—to be more paranoid—if you were the CIA trying to make sure that the government didn't go belly up, keeping fifty billion dollars from being spent would seem like a good idea. And obviously, in the long run, there's a lot more money involved. This could be a pilot project. If they got away with sabotaging 886-JHG, who knows what they would go after next?"

We all started talking at once and finally stopped to listen to the student doctor in our midst. "Do you really think we have reached the point in this country that our total inability to control health care costs has led the government to start sabotaging research? That's insane." She paused for a moment. "Except that it might be true. There's got to be something else the government could do."

Amibeth shook her head. "Maybe not. I suppose you could create more stringent requirements about what the government would pay for—but the new health care law says that you can't establish a threshold of benefit per dollar. It's against the law for example to say that you have to gain a year of life for every one hundred thousand dollars spent. You can't establish a ratio."

That was news to me. "What? Why not?"

Amibeth knew her stuff. "Well, you remember when the Democrats wanted to limit health care costs by giving people the option of discussing, just discussing, whether or not they wanted aggressive end of life care. Basically one in every four dollars spent by Medicare is in the last year of life. Well, she whose name shall never pass my lips, the one who ran for vice president, said that Death Panels were being created. Political analysts called that statement of hers the biggest political lie of 2009, but the Democrats got scared and they put it in the bill that you can't create a threshold demanding a specific amount of improved survival for a certain amount of money spent. And trying to control the prices of drugs is unlikely. The pharmaceutical companies would oppose it. The Republicans would call it socialism, and say 'Leave it to the Market.'"

Greg Cole joined the conversation. "But the market doesn't apply because people don't pay for anything. It's paid by insurance so people don't realize that they have a stake."

"I have to do a feature on this on my new show. There was a government conspiracy, or a conspiracy involving a former government agent—maybe a present government agent—so that a drug wouldn't get approved, just to save the government money. It makes more sense than any other idea."

For the first time since we had gone out on the patio, Andrea started to speak. "And I thought it was about me. Me and Muffin."

Amibeth turned to her sister. "What are you talking about?"

Andrea sat quietly and said nothing.

Amibeth walked over to her sister. "We're family here. What are you talking about?"

Andrea stared at the deck for a few moments, then lifted her head and started to unburden herself. "It's like this. Muffin Mancuso and Hamilton had been lovers for years. Muffin had gone to pharmacy school under an alias to create her cover. We met again, by accident, at CMI and it was electric. And I could really talk to her, not like with Eric where I had to be careful not to say anything that would give him an insight into my past. I told you when you came to visit me at our place on Lake Shore Drive that she was the first person I truly loved."

I noticed that Greg Cole was holding her hand. Evidently he had heard this during their three weeks together.

"She had dumped me back in Memphis because I was young. Well, I wasn't young anymore. She had done some horrible things. I knew that. But that was in the past. I fell in love with her all over again. I had never cheated on Eric with another man, but I kind of felt that she didn't count because she was a woman and because I knew her before I knew Eric. Anyway, Hamilton found out. Muffin told me that Hamilton had told her that if she didn't stop seeing me, he would mess up the one thing that mattered to me—my work. When people started dying, I thought it was Hamilton trying to intimidate me. That's why I never told the FBI the full story."

I could almost see the logic. "But Andrea, if Hamilton was going to kill someone to get Muffin Mancuso back, why wouldn't he just kill you?"

"That's exactly what I finally concluded. That's why I broke it off with Muffin, called the FBI, and left CMI. I didn't tell the FBI about Muffin for two reasons. One, they would think I was crazy, if I claimed that she was still alive. And two—I was in love with her."

Relative to killing people to control health care costs, Andrea's motivation in not telling the FBI the entire story from the beginning was perfectly understandable. "How did Hamilton get in to tamper with the drugs? Or do you think it was Muffin who tampered with the bottles?"

"I don't know. I like to think Muffin had nothing to do with it. Hamilton and Muffin were living together even though she and I were involved. She had an access card to the pharmacy. All he would need is a fake ID to get in the building at night. He had been with the CIA. I'm sure he could have done that."

I was certain that he could. "What tipped you off? Why did you finally call the FBI?"

"The 886-JHG study got started at CMI since the JHG series of drugs was developed there. We got to enter patients into the study before the other centers entered patients. Once other centers entered patients, I saw that the death rate was five percent everywhere else, and much higher at CMI. I realized that Hamilton might actually have been doing something to mess up the study. I called the FBI. By then we had completed entering forty patients. We were done. I figured that if Hamilton was really responsible, the FBI would find something. But they didn't. I didn't want to point any fingers at Muffin. I loved her, and I was hoping she had nothing to do with this." Andrea was unsuccessfully trying to hold back her tears.

I doubted that Muffin Mancuso was an innocent bystander, but that hardly mattered at this point.

Amibeth asked, "What happened after that?"

"I wanted to get away from everything. I changed jobs, got an apartment on the south side, and went to work at the University of Chicago. Muffin came to me. We lived together for a while, and it was wonderful, but then I became afraid that Hamilton might start killing patients there, too. I was scared for the patients and scared for myself. If patients died unexpectedly at the University of Chicago, I would be a common thread, and people might think I did it. So, I left for Tennessee. I came to Nashville because you and Elana were here, but I was too embarrassed to call you. I broke it off with Muffin, but that tipped her over the edge. She started stalking me; she called me at work several times. She said that I had really hurt her and that bad things happened to people who hurt her or the people she cared for. I loved her, but I knew about her past, so I bought a gun. I called the FBI, told them that I had seen someone who was supposed to be dead, and that I needed to talk to them. This time I was going to tell them about Muffin. And when she came to my townhouse that night, I had the gun. I loved her, do you understand. I loved her." She was crying. "But the lights went out and she grabbed my gun, and I knew she would kill me if she got the gun so I pulled the trigger. And I was telling the truth when I told you that she had brought a gun to my townhouse. She came there to kill me!"

I wasn't sure if she was crying for herself or for Muffin Mancuso. It didn't matter. Greg Cole and Amibeth were hugging her. Amibeth turned to me. "Jonah Aaron, I know you're not a lawyer, but as an investigator you have to know what the law requires. Did she do anything legally wrong?"

I gave my best professional opinion. "She didn't lie to the FBI. She suspected a crime. She notified the FBI. She didn't tell them everything she suspected, but she didn't know for sure that Hamilton or Muffin had actually killed the six people. I suspect that the FBI will welcome Andrea as a material witness. But like you say on your radio show, for a professional opinion, consult a professional who can evaluate all of the facts of the situation. She needs to talk to an attorney." Which is exactly what she would do.

Andrea had stopped crying. In a little girl voice, totally not in keeping with her physical appearance, she asked, "Amibeth, do I still get my award at your fundraiser?"

Amibeth hugged her. "Of course you do."

Andrea turned to me, "Do you think we'll get the reward from Bauer Labs?"

"As far as I know, government employees were the only exclusion. I don't think you'll have a problem with your share of the reward."

This was the first that Amibeth had heard of the reward. "Just what are we talking about here? What reward money?"

Elana and I explained to Amibeth about the reward for getting 886-JHG back on track for evaluation. The money might be beyond Andrea's comprehension, but for Amibeth it was an amount she could take in stride. It was less than her five year television contract. "Jonah Aaron, you do realize what this means don't you?"

I saw her smiling, but I didn't know where this was going. "What?"

"If that reward goes through, the next time we go out to eat, you can pick up the check, and every other check after that."

"That's fair enough."

Chapter Fifty-Seven

While Amibeth turned her attention to the motivation behind Hamilton's sabotage of the study at CMI, Elana and I focused on the revelation that AJ Golden was alive and well. I would like to say that we ventured down that road in the interests of Elana's mental health and that we wanted to eliminate the duplicity that had come to characterize our existence. However, that was merely collateral benefit. Revealing that Elana Grey—singer, songwriter, screenwriter and sometime medical student—was AJ Golden had but one purpose. It was a promotional event for the movie about the Dana Twins, no more and no less.

To accomplish this without having a negative reflection on Amibeth, I requested that the FBI issue a statement that AJ had been in witness protection for the past five years. Considering that we had helped solve six murders at CMI as well as given final resolution to the case of The Unforgiving, I didn't find my request that unreasonable. Joe Apted responded that he appreciated our efforts but that the only thing from which my wife needed protection was her own sense of misadventure. Evidently, embellishing the truth as a favor to private citizens is not in the repertoire of the FBI.

However, at our request, on the Saturday afternoon of the 2010 No Cause for Shame fundraiser, the Chicago office of the FBI did issue the following terse, accurate, and incomplete press release. "Abigail Josephine (AJ) Golden, the younger sister of Amy Elizabeth Golden (Amibeth), is alive. Her whereabouts have been known to the FBI since the time of her apparent suicide at the Caruthersville Bridge. In the interim, Ms. Golden has rendered occasional service to the FBI, for which the Bureau is grateful. While Ms. Golden may make a personal statement at some future time, the FBI will have no further comment on this matter." That statement was not everything we had hoped for, but it turned out to be perfectly adequate for our purposes.

Over the years, Amibeth, Elana, and I had become adept at manipulating public opinion, and the FBI statement was not how most people learned that AJ Golden was among the living. Shortly after the FBI press release, Amibeth tweeted this message to her four point six million followers: "My sister AJ is alive

& may be at tonite's event. Important reasons not to have shared before. Sorry for that. Tell your friends." People told their friends who in turn told their friends who in turn shared the news.

Two hours later, a blogger with several hundred thousand regular readers informed the world that on May 16, 2010 in Jaurez, Mexico, a man by the name of Tomaz Diaz had been killed in the crossfire of a gun battle between Mexican police and members of a drug cartel. That fact is true and has been confirmed by independent sources. Diaz is a common name. There was no evidence that the Tomaz Diaz in question was related to The Roofers. There was no evidence of any revenge plot against AJ. However, in light of the announcement that AJ Golden was alive, the blogger speculated that Tomaz Diaz was the brother of The Roofers and that AJ Golden had been in witness protection until danger had passed. While the FBI never said that AJ had been a protected witness, if you ask people anywhere in America outside of Nashville why AJ Golden vanished from the public eye for several years, the answer that you are most likely to receive is that she was in witness protection. In Music City, most people now believe that the suicide hoax was a publicity stunt for the song, "(She Thought She Could) Fly." It is considered "an awesome way to promote a record". Very few people hold to the radical notion that AJ faked a jump from the Caruthersville Bridge in order to promote her sister's career. AJ is happy. Amibeth is happy. Milton is satisfied.

Among the people who became convinced that AJ was in witness protection, and hence under contract to a federal agency, and thereby unable to receive the reward from Bauer Laboratories, was Jeffrey Hamilton. A sworn affidavit from the FBI stating explicitly that AJ Golden was never in witness protection ended Hamilton's pursuit of that legal theory. Those court documents are sealed and have no impact on people's interpretation of the events in question.

Jeffrey Hamilton's plea bargain required that he confess to his crime in open court. He did not have to inform the court as to the motive behind the six deaths at CMI. While the FBI has never stated that Jeffrey Hamilton killed six people in order to save the government billions of dollars, no more logical explanation has been forthcoming.

While the FBI has been silent with respect to Jeffrey Hamilton's motivation, Amibeth has discussed the deaths at CMI on the radio, on television, and in a hearing room of the United States Senate. She believes that the sabotage of the 886-JHG study underscores our total failure to limit health care expenses and is a warning to America about the draconian solutions that will become necessary if we cannot find rational approaches to limiting expenditures on health care. It may seem absurd that people were murdered in an attempt to keep an expensive drug from getting to market. However, when one is a reporter whose former stepfather is a United States Senator, one not only gets an audience, one's comments carry a modicum of credibility.

Whether the recent Senate hearings will lead to more intelligent efforts to limit the cost of health care is in doubt. 886-JHG adds a couple of months to the lives of people with lung cancer. Unfortunately, diverting government money to pay for 886-JHG leads to many undesired consequences. The Congressional Budget Committee looked at the number of policemen and firemen who would not be employed if 886-JHG went on the market. Drugs save lives, but policemen and firemen save lives too. Based solely on the reduced number of law enforcement and firefighting personnel, it was projected that the approval of 886-JHG would cost the nation fourteen months of life for every month added to the lives of cancer patients.

Nonetheless, 886-JHG won unanimous FDA approval since, as one member of the FDA panel stated, "How can you deny lung cancer patients a chance at a few extra months?" It is no wonder we spend more money on health care than any other nation in the world and rank near fortieth in life expectancy. If we continue to muddle along our present path, the country may eventually decide that Jeffrey Hamilton was a misguided hero who was ahead of his time.

On a much happier note, the No Cause for Shame Fundraiser was, as reported on the society pages of the Chicago newspapers, a fabulous gala event. The Vice-President of The United States and his wife attended, as did six members of Congress. One of them, a United States Senator with presidential ambitions, was Amibeth's escort for the evening. They have only been dating for a couple of weeks, but the young woman who couldn't find a suitable role to play while enrolled at Colby College could end up playing the role of first lady.

It is always fun, if somewhat deafening, to walk into a room the size of a football field, containing several thousand people, as the band is blasting out "(She Thought She Could) Fly." ACGBC—Boom Ba-Boom, ACGBC—Boom Ba-Boom! Having never missed a No Cause for Shame fundraiser, I avoided the temptation to turn to my wife and remark, "Hey, they're playing our song," I no longer have to suppress a laugh when the AyJayers break into their chant of "AJ lives, AJ lives, AJ lives."

I feel sorry for the blonde women who came to the Grand Ballroom of the Hyatt Regency Hotel dressed in blood red T-shirts and short skirts, wearing T181 jewelry, or ojliagiba pendants. All evening long, they had to fend off interviews as the press searched for "the real AJ." Knowing that people might be scanning the crowd for her, Elana and I planned ahead. In previous years, Elana had donned a blond wig, as well as the rest of the AyJayer uniform, and blended in with the other AJ look-alikes. For the 2010 Fundraiser, my redheaded wife, whose legal name is now Abby Jo Golden-Aaron, wore a lovely teal strapless evening gown. Elana Grey is now relegated to being her professional name.

The event raised almost three million dollars for the No Cause for Shame foundation, including a donation of five hundred thousand dollars that Amibeth announced had been given by "Mr. and Mrs. J. D. Aaron." That would ordinarily have earned us a seat at the head table, but at the behest of the FBI, my wife and I were seated with Eric Cain, his girlfriend Kerry Devin, Gail Riley, and her husband Larry. Joe Apted had suggested that seating arrangement as he hoped that alcohol would loosen tongues and that, as trained investigators, we might determine if any of the doctors at CMI had assisted Jeffrey Hamilton.

Elana and I weren't drinking, and when Elana volunteered the fact that she couldn't, because she was pregnant, Gail Riley responded with the following comment. "Larry and I thought we wouldn't have children. Then, when my biological clock was running down, we changed our minds. Our boys are twelve and thirteen, and I've learned one thing. There is absolutely nothing in the world as wonderful . . ." she paused long enough to have everyone hanging on her words, "as going back to work on Monday morning." Elana promised that someday she would steal that line and use it on television or in a movie.

Eric Cain and Kerry Devin made up for the wine we didn't drink as they were celebrating the fact that three days earlier the Chicago Blackhawks had won their first Stanley Cup in forty nine years. At a function where ninety percent of the men were wearing tuxedos or dark suits, Eric Cain and his date were wearing Chicago Blackhawks jerseys.

Dr. Gail Riley and her husband were dressed more appropriately for the occasion. Dr. Riley, who was as attractive as my father had stated, turned out to be a country music fan and was thrilled to be seated with Elana Grey. She even went to the lobby and purchased a copy of Elana's old CD single, "(She Thought She Could) Fly," so that my wife could autograph it. Dr. Riley and her husband were not fans of *Jonah Slammer, Dangerous Man*. Then again, the demographic for that show tends to skew a little younger.

As Greg Cole had mentioned, Dr. Kerry Devin looked to be in her early thirties. She couldn't stop talking to Elana about *Jonah Slammer, Dangerous Man*. If my wife hadn't gotten Kerry talking about hockey, she would have spent the evening as the captive audience of a devoted fan while I listened to Eric Cain talk about his favorite subject—Eric Cain. Considering that he wrote an autobiography when he was twenty-eight years old, that shouldn't have been a surprise. What did surprise me was that I truly enjoyed listening to him tell his stories.

The only information that I obtained relevant to the case was that both Eric Cain and Gail Riley were excited that 886-JHG had been approved by the FDA. They were happy to discuss their role in the planned studies involving the next drug in the series, 887-JHG. During the course of the discussion Eric Cain kept commenting that he or Gail or Kerry should have been able to figure out how 886-JHG had been sabotaged. He stated that even though the problem had been solved by some lucky son of bitch—his words, not mine—he had no idea how a killer had broken an unbreakable code. The FBI had not released details of what had happened, and Eric Cain and his colleagues had no idea about the drug interaction theory that Elana had dreamed up. I left the Hyatt Regency Hotel that night convinced that Jeffrey Hamilton had not received assistance from the doctors affiliated with the 886-JHG study.

The high point of the evening was when Amibeth gave the Woman of the Year award to her older sister. Six years after the attack on Woodland Hills Lane, a ten foot tall No Cause for Shame poster provided the background as a teary Amibeth struggled through the following words, "I grew up in a terrible home situation. At the age of twenty-two I was raped. I survived because of the heroic actions of my younger sister, AJ. However, another reason I survived was that the horror of my childhood was mitigated by my older sister who protected me from my pedophile father. What she did is her story to tell. I will not pre-empt her. She did what she felt she had to do, and then she left home. Her own father convinced her that her only value was as a sex object and as a teenager she worked as an escort. She moved beyond that. She put herself through nursing school. She worked as a caregiver. Recently, she made a major contribution to society by uncovering an effort to sabotage a drug study. Until now, she has desired to protect her privacy, but this year she is willing to step forward and receive her due. This year's Woman of the Year Award from the No Cause for Shame Foundation goes to a woman whose life illustrates that there is no cause for shame in being a victim. Her life story shows that one can rise above the worst things that happen to you. The award goes to my older sister, Andrea Golden Cain."

I don't know if there was a dry eye in the house. I couldn't see. I do know that Andrea got a standing ovation, though, admittedly, many of the men in the audience were merely saluting the plastic surgery. Andrea's white dress revealed a substantial amount of cleavage. When the applause died down Andrea addressed the crowd.

"I never spoke in public before, so I'll keep it brief. I want to thank my sister, not only for giving me this award, but for having her foundation to help people who have been victims of abuse. As you know, I am one of them. I learned to keep secrets. I'm not saying that all secrets should be revealed, but I'm revealing one of mine. A number of you are wearing pendants or purses that say T181. But the original pendant doesn't say T181. It says TL 81. TL is the symbol for thallium, and 81 is its atomic number. It's a poison. I learned that in the seventh grade, two years after my daddy started messing up my life." A wide smile crossed her face. "You know, there has to be a special place in hell for people like my father, and I am not sorry that I sent him there. It was the only way I could keep my sisters safe."

Some people in the crowd gasped as Andrea continued. "Tonight is a celebration. And this organization has a lot to celebrate. I am so proud of the work my sister does. But we can't lose sight of the problems that make this organization necessary. And this organization, tragically, is very necessary. Thank you all, very much."

The applause started, and the crowd gave Andrea a second standing ovation. Amibeth informed me later that her website has sold several thousand TL 81 pendants since the event. The response to Andrea's comments made it clear that no prosecutor will ever indict Andrea for her use of thallium. As for her association with the crimes of The Unforgiving, the FBI didn't have much of a case and agreed to take no action in exchange for her testimony against Jeffrey Hamilton, testimony she was more than willing to provide.

As for AJ, the Queen of Talk Radio's major statement about her younger sister was in a forum far less dignified than the United States Senate, and far less elegant than the No Cause for Shame fundraiser. It was on the series finale of the Jonah Slammer show. The final episodes had been taped before our adventure involving 886-JHG. However, one scene, made to appear as if it had been taped at the actual No Cause for Shame event, was added in post-production.

In that scene, Amibeth delivered the following lines before giving her younger sister the award as Woman of the Year. "For killing the Diaz Brothers, making the whole thing possible, for disappearing after last being seen at the Caruthersville Bridge, thereby launching her career as a singer/songwriter, and accidentally helping launch my first tour, and for her career as a script writer, the award goes to a woman who has spent five years in witness protection, my sister Abby Jo Golden, known to the world as Elana Grey."

It took people a while to realize that Amibeth wasn't kidding about Elana Grey being her younger sister, AJ. Once people realized that Elana Grey and AJ Golden were one and the same, the press hounded her for interviews. When asked what we had been up to recently, my wife replied, "Oh, just the usual stuff for a young married couple. We've been having lots of sex, trying to get pregnant. It worked. We finished writing for our old TV show, *Jonah Slammer, Dangerous Man.* I've been doing re-writes on our script for the movie about the Dana Twins. We solved a major crime that involved six murders, making us millions of dollars in reward money, and possibly destroying the economy of the United States in the process. Just the usual stuff for a young married couple."

The reporter laughed, and asked what we really had been up to. AJ wasn't joking. It had been an interesting month. As for the pregnancy, our daughter Ariel is due around Valentine's Day 2011. The movie about The Dana Twins will open in the summer if all goes well.

My wife is a remarkable woman, and not because she has been a successful singer/songwriter and screenwriter, or because she may be a physician someday. What is remarkable about my wife is that despite coming from a dysfunctional family, she is an optimistic woman with a sense of adventure, a wicked sense of humor, and the ability to give and receive love. As they would say in the movies, she had me at "lo siento." Despite the absence of a positive role model when she was growing up, I have no doubt that she will be a wonderful mother.

When I saw AJ softly singing a ballad at Jerry's the night I met her, I missed the fact that when she gave it her all, she would succeed as Elana Grey, the lead singer of Fireball. I had no idea that she could write either a song or a script. How well do any of us know the people with whom we fall in love at the time we fall in love with them?

I never imagined that I could help engineer anything like the events at the Caruthersville Bridge, or have a role in writing a CMA award winning song, or in the development of a television show. Maybe AJ saw something in me that I didn't see. Maybe it wasn't even there in the beginning. Maybe it all required having her and her imaginative mind in my life for it to blossom. Sometimes things just happen and there is no rational explanation. Amibeth uses the phrase "Sometimes there is no why" to tell people that they are not responsible for the horrible things that have happened to them. I think that the phrase may also relate to the undeserved good luck that I have had.

AJ says that she never could have done it without my support, but I am not so sure. Once AJ survived The Diaz Brothers, I think she was going to accomplish whatever she wanted to accomplish in life. However, I am thrilled that she wants to believe that I am partly responsible. I am not sure how much I have stabilized her life, but I realized from the beginning that the time I would share with her would be the best time of my life. So far, it has been.

I was never concerned about making large sums of money, and while I have been extremely lucky in that regard, there is truly only one fortune that I have gained in my life—the love of AJ Golden. As long as I continue to appreciate that fact, there will be, in the words of Amibeth, No Cause for Shame.

THE END

Edwards Brothers Malloy
Thorofare, NJ USA
April 29, 2013